BLOODY NOVEMBER

Guilio Dattero

PublishAmerica
Baltimore

© 2006 by Guilio Dattero.

All rights reserved. No part of this book may be reproduced, stored in a retrieval system or transmitted in any form or by any means without the prior written permission of the publishers, except by a reviewer who may quote brief passages in a review to be printed in a newspaper, magazine or journal.

First printing

All characters appearing in this work are fictitious. Any resemblance to real persons, living or dead, is purely coincidental.

ISBN: 1-4241-4738-7
PUBLISHED BY PUBLISHAMERICA, LLLP
www.publishamerica.com
Baltimore

Printed in the United States of America

This book is dedicated to Reidsville's finest:
Past, Present and Future

Acknowledgements

For their support:

    My wife Cathy Dattero and my mother Marilyn Dattero
    My grandmother Clara Dixon, whose life still inspires me

Proofreading:

    Diana Reid Haig (and her relentless No. 2 pencil)

Technical Advisors:

    Chief of Police Edd Hunt, Reidsville Police
    Lt. Tom Saunders, Reidsville Police
    Sgt. John Pulliam, Reidsville Police
    Sgt. Brian Oakley, Reidsville Police
    Det. Tim Altizer, Reidsville Police

    Det. Y.T. Sansour, Guilford County Sheriff's Office

    Special Agent Rick Cullop, North Carolina S.B.I.
    Special Agent Jerry Webster, North Carolina S.B.I., Ret.

    Tony Grogan, Assistant District Attorney

    Kevin Smith, Esquire

    Susan Fitzgibbon

    Tilda Balsley

Deborah Butler and Rhonda Wheeler

Dr. Hugh Fraser
Dr. Stanley Harrison, Jr.
Dr. Cecil Burkhart

Photography:

Tim Talley

PROLOGUE

"Yeah, it looks good, Keith," Ferrell replied, as he inspected the broad area of green and white block tile. The floor had a nice shine to it and showed no sign of the heavy traffic from the busy weekend. Ferrell directed Hall to a spot that he'd missed, and he glided the buffer over to it.

Outside, they moved with stealth, sprinting through the woods like leopards slicing through the jungle. They moved as one, with discipline that reflected rigorous hours of training. They stopped at the tree line, close enough to view the side of the building yet still remain concealed...thirteen minutes.

Ferrell and Hall chatted briefly about the busy evening. Hall, a lanky seventeen-year-old, was one of the store's more dependable employees. Ferrell had given him extra hours, because he was a good worker and needed the money. Hall was a quiet kid, something of a loner, but Ferrell liked him.

Ferrell went back to the stockroom and cut down the lights in the front of the store. Then he went to the back doors, checked, then re-checked them to make sure they were locked. He was aware of several grocery store break-ins recently in town, including his own. The store manager had made the staff aware of other break-ins to Harris Teeters in Greensboro, High Point, and Reidsville so Ferrell was careful to use all security measures every time he closed the store.

He stopped by Hall's work area and spoke with him once more. "You know the alarm code, right? If you set it off, the Police Department's gonna charge us. Be sure to cut the lights down back here when you're finished."

Hall shouted over the buffer noise, "Yes sir!" He was anxious to finish and get to what was left of Saturday night. He recited the security code, and Ferrell gave him the okay sign and waved good-bye.

Emerging from the woods, they darted up to the south side of the building. The lead man peered around the corner to the front doors, then looked back at the other two. He whispered into his mike, and they raced to join him at the corner. They dashed to the front sidewalk and positioned themselves behind a drink machine and advertisement displays.

The green van had been circling the area when the driver looked in his rear view mirror and noticed a police car approaching him at the intersection. The driver of the van turned right and the police car soon caught up with him. The officer activated his blue lights and, when he did, the driver of the van reached under the seat for a .38 revolver and hid it under his right thigh. He exchanged a glance with the passenger and pulled the van over to the curb. As he did, the police car sped around him and drove away. The passenger radioed a warning to the crew...nine minutes.

Ferrell returned to his office, picked up the moneybag to make the bank deposit, locked the office, and headed to the front door. He looked at the side parking lot and saw his car parked alone in the middle of the lot.

Ferrell walked out and re-locked the door. As he turned to head down the sidewalk, a large black shadowy object swept in front of him. As he felt the blow to his face, his legs buckled under him. The next thing he knew, he was lying on his back pinned against a couple of newspaper racks. His body felt limp; his face was pounding. He shook his head trying to regain his senses. He felt warm liquid trickling down from his forehead, and the cold, hard end of something pressed against his cheek. In a moment, he was alert enough to know that he was in trouble. He adjusted his vision and looked up at the most evil eyes he had ever seen. But the eyes were all that he could see, against a backdrop of black November sky.

CHAPTER ONE

Tuesday had been busier than usual. Clark hoped things would have slacked up a little after the hectic weekend, but no luck. He glanced at the stack of police reports then reluctantly picked up the next one. It sounded like a couple thousand he'd read before: Ex-boyfriend breaks into apartment of ex-girlfriend, steals belongings, ransacks the place. *How utterly original.* He tossed the report on the desk and considered trashing all of them.

The pile of papers reflected a sameness that he found difficult to handle. Difficult like a dull headache, and he was getting one of those too. Each report represented a different case, a different victim, but tonight they all ran together in a maddening collage. Burglary this. Larceny that. Every story different, yet the same. After he read several more, the narratives began to overlap, and facts commingled as if victims and suspects leapt like dancing demons from one report to the next. To the next.

Reading reports and assigning them to his staff was one of the more tedious parts of Lt. Clark Dixon's job. Like listening to your worst college professor deliver an endless anthropology lecture in monotone. No voice inflection—no relief in sight. And then there was always the issue of too many cases to assign to the five detectives in the unit. It was part of the job description that they worked incredibly hard for modest pay. Clark was proud of his men.

As he read the next report, the phone rang, and caller I.D. showed it was a call from his house. "Hey, sweetheart," he answered. It was his daughter Alex, second oldest of the four kids.

"Are you gonna work all night?" she asked.

"I'll be home soon. Everything okay?"

"Yeah, Dad. I thought you'd be here by now. You don't want to raise a latchkey kid, do you?"

"Latchkey kid? Alex, you're twenty."

"So? Twenty-year-olds can get in trouble without adult supervision."

Clark laughed. "Not the twenty-year-olds who enjoy driving privileges. How did your classes go today?" Alex attended the local community college.

"All right. I finally got my mid-term back in calculus."
"How'd you do?"
"Made an 'A'."
"Oh, how disappointing. We'll have to work on that, won't we?"
"Ha, ha! Funny."
"Proud of you."
"Hurry up. I've got supper ready."
"All right, already. See you in fifteen minutes."
"Bye."

It was nice to come home to Alex. She was the only thing standing between him and an empty house. After he finished the last report, he leaned back in his chair, took a deep breath, and stretched. He surveyed his office and noticed it was a mess. Banker boxes of old, unsolved cases stacked in the corner. Files on the windowsill. Stained coffee mugs on the file cabinet.

His eyes wandered over to the credenza by the door. He scanned the photographs and plaques, things that he rarely took time to notice. They were snapshots of milestones from a career that, to him, spelled mediocrity. He gazed at his rookie school class photo. There he stood on the second row, the idealistic, enthusiastic rookie. Next, the promotional picture taken when he made sergeant; he was shaking hands with then-Chief Richard Broward. *Great guy, hated to see him retire.* Then he glanced over to the picture of his promotion to lieutenant, posing with current Chief Mike Brinks. *Full-time careerist and part-time asshole.* Next on the credenza sat his Officer of the Year plaque, dated 1997. Everything looked dusty and faded.

Then to the picture of his ex. His ex. Looking at it still hurt like it was yesterday. It had been nine months since the divorce, but for some absurd reason, he couldn't trash that photograph. *Maybe I'll get rid of it tomorrow.* Officers close to him would stop by to chat, and occasionally they would notice the picture, but they knew better than to talk about it.

The phone rang, but it didn't register with him until the second ring. He stared at the receiver a long moment, considered not answering, but gave in. "Lt. Dixon, may I help you?"

"Lieutenant, this is Wilkens. Pulling overtime, huh?"

"Just trying to get a jump on the reports for tomorrow. I wouldn't want you guys to come in unchallenged and bored. Where are you?"

"Downstairs putting up some evidence. Capt. Simmons just stopped by and asked if I could help him tonight with the community watch meeting at the civic center. He needs help setting up and wants me to pitch in on the

Q&A. He thinks we're going to take some hits on the crime increase in the area." Wilkens had a sympathetic quality in his voice.

"Sure," Clark replied, "but avoid any comments about the City Council's debate over cutting police positions. Since that hit the papers last week, it's been a hot button issue. There're a couple of troublemakers in that community watch group that are notorious for booby trapping us on stuff like that."

Wilkens acknowledged and hung up. Clark had a lot of confidence in him. Bradley Wilkens was dependable and, most importantly, had enough smarts to shut up when he was supposed to. Clark returned to the reports when his pager buzzed with the number to dispatch.

"Stuartsboro Police, this is Stevens."

"Hey, Brenda, this is Lieutenant. I just got your page."

"Hey, Lieutenant. What are you doing up there working so late?"

"So much work, so little time," Clark said in a melodramatic tone.

Brenda laughed. "I hear ya."

"You know, if a certain telecommunicator I know wouldn't answer the phone every single time it rings, then we wouldn't be drowning in this sea of crime reports. All this is really your fault."

"Oh, don't make me the bad girl. I have to answer the phone. It's my job. Ain't that the way it works? I answer phone, then I send police officer on call. Police officer completes report and routes to detective. Detective investigates."

"Okay, okay, you got me. But only on a technicality. What's up?"

"Lieutenant Johnson wants you to give him a call at the E.R."

"What do they have?"

"They're taking a report of a sexual assault that happened on Fleetwood Street."

"When did it happen?"

"Some time earlier today. That's all I know."

"Thanks, Brenda. I'll call him on his cell. Oh, and Brenda?"

"Yes, sir?"

"Take it easy answering that phone, will ya? You're killing us."

Brenda giggled. "If I didn't know better, I'd think you're trying to get me fired."

"See ya." Clark then called Lt. Edd Johnson.

"Johnson."

"Hey, it's Clark."

"Workin' late, huh?"

"Yeah."

"Just wanted to fill you in on a sexual assault since you're still there."

"How bad is it?"

"I think it's legit, but I don't think the victim's being completely honest about all the details. It happened on Fleetwood Street this morning. The victim is Regina Murray, twenty-one. She spent the night with a girlfriend. They had a party, a lot of guests, and most of them spent the night too. She said one of the guys raped her early this morning, but it was dark and she couldn't make him out that well."

"Any struggle? Anybody hear anything?"

"We're getting to that now."

"Any suspects?" Clark asked.

"Yeah. A guy named Stanley Lowe. You know his brother, don't you? Donnie."

"Donnie Lowe?" Clark paused to think. "Donnie Lowe...yeah. Hadn't heard his name in a while. Come to think of it, he got out of prison in the last few months, or so I've heard."

"What a shame it wasn't Donnie. That way we could use his D.O.C. sample to match up to the sample we recovered."

"If Stanley is your man, then Donnie's sample will still help us."

"How?"

"They're brothers. Assuming they have the same parents, we can take Donnie's prison sample and if Stanley is the perp, the DNA profiles will be strikingly similar. Just curious though. Why did she take so long to report it?"

"Ah, she's changed her story a couple of times. But it could be that she's still traumatized. We called Help, Inc. and they've got a counselor en route. Who's on call?"

"Esposito."

"Didn't I hear Wilkens on the radio a few minutes ago?"

"He's helping at a watch meeting tonight; Esposito's your man."

"I'll get Brenda to give him a call."

"See you in the morning."

"Right."

Clark hung up and glanced back over at the photograph of Samantha. In some ways, it was the only photograph on the credenza. The only one that offered free hurt for the taking. The only one that he tried to overlook and never could. He felt scarred, he imagined, like some of the victims in the reports that he just read.

He locked up his office, and headed for the elevator. As he rode down, he sang a line of "Please Release Me", one of his favorite songs. He liked the echo in the elevator and singing usually gave him a lift. He chuckled to himself, because he knew he couldn't carry a tune, but that never stopped him.... *"Please release me, our love has gone, We've tried and cried for far too long, Release me, Sam, I must move on...."* He stopped singing just as the elevator doors opened. Good timing.

Brenda waved and buzzed him through the front door. The November night bathed his face with a chilly breeze and refreshed him. Clark crossed the street, then turned around. It was a ritual for him—to glance back at the PD to the large illuminated clock with the Roman numerals at the top of the building's façade. He liked that clock. It seemed to cast a watchful eye over downtown. This was the original clock dating back to the construction of the building in 1933. The clock had been salvaged, then restored when the building was renovated several years ago. He saw it as a symbol of strength and continuity. He looked up at it and smiled.

* * *

About an hour later, Det. Wilkens finished his presentation, and the attendees gave him polite applause. This watch group was one of the more active chapters, but the cooler weather had kept some people from attending. Like most of the thirty-some watch groups in Stuartsboro, senior citizens dominated this one.

Most of the people headed to the exit, but a few stayed to put away chairs, sweep, and clean up the refreshments. Capt. Simmons, pleased with the program and the turnout, walked over and shook Wilkens' hand. "They loved you, Brad."

"Of course," Wilkens joked, holding his arms out to the side. "What's there not to love, Captain?"

Simmons chuckled. "Any time they give input like that, it's a sign that you've made a connection. Say, I couldn't interest you in a spot in Community Policing, could I?"

"Thanks, Captain. But I'm enjoying my work in CID right now. Besides, Lt. Dixon would kill you and me. 'Treason' I think he'd call it." Wilkens was African-American, in his mid-thirties, tall, a little heavy, but handsome, and he was impressive in presentations. He was professional, but he could be soft and cuddly like a teddy bear when he needed to be. "I really enjoyed their interest level. You can feed off that, can't you?"

Before Simmons could reply, Mrs. Ruby Walker, a faithful watch member, walked briskly over to them and interrupted the conversation.

"Thank you, Officer Wilson. This was a very nice program tonight. Come back to see us, won't you?"

Wilkens glossed over the incorrect name, and offered a smile. "Thank you, ma'am. It was a pleasure to speak with you folks. I thought we had a good group here tonight." He presented the petite, grey-haired woman with his business card and told her to call him any time he could help her. It was an automatic reflex for him, the card thing. Like he received some sort of commission for each one he handed out. She beamed at the card like it was some kind of trophy that no other attendee won this evening.

Wilkens, always the observant one, instantly noticed Walker's features, her perky gait, and large glasses with thick lenses that dominated her appearance. As she walked away, he grinned, thinking that it would be too easy to draw a caricature of her.

Simmons whispered to Wilkens that he was lucky to get away from her with such an abbreviated conversation. "She's a sweet old lady, ya know, but she can flat out dominate a meeting if you let her. Long-winded, and then some."

Wilkens nodded. He and Simmons loaded their equipment in the SPD van, and returned inside to make sure nothing was left behind. Simmons heard a garbled noise, turned, and saw his police radio on the counter by the stage. He walked over, grabbed it, and said, "Leave that behind and Chief Brinks would demote me to sergeant before you could say, 'Jack Sprat'."

* * *

Just after midnight, Ruby Walker walked over to her living room window, which faced the back of The Meadows apartment complex. As she turned off the lamp, she heard a noise in the parking lot. A medium-sized U-Haul truck, with no headlights burning, was slowly backing into a space several doors down from her unit. It struck her as very odd. Normally, she didn't see that kind of vehicle in the complex. And certainly not at this late hour.

She cut off the overhead light, and then pulled the curtain back a little farther to study the scene. She raised the window and listened, but heard nothing, so she quietly opened the front door and peered through the crack. A hooded man got out of the passenger's side and another man, who she assumed was the driver, met him at his door. The two men looked around, and then spoke in a low volume; all she heard were muffled sounds. As the shorter man smoked a cigarette, the other one looked around again, then reached inside the truck, and came out with a long metal object about the length of an umbrella. It looked shiny under the streetlight. She tried to re-focus as the two men talked briefly again, and walked with haste out of view toward her building.

Ruby stood there a moment and tried to frame what she had just seen. She prided herself on knowing all the goings-on in her building, and this was an unusual event. *This will take some looking into.* Maybe, just maybe, this would be her chance for center stage at next month's watch meeting.

If she only knew.

CHAPTER TWO

As Clark pulled into the driveway, his headlights hit the "For Sale" sign in the front yard. The house had been on the market since the divorce, and it seemed as though the sign had become a permanent fixture of the property. He had received several offers, but nothing serious. It was a buyers' market in the area, and houses were slow to sell.

The house was a two-story colonial, with off-white siding and Williamsburg blue shutters. The yard was beautifully landscaped with crepe myrtles lining the winding driveway. Red and pink azaleas grew in clusters in natural areas, and Chinese maples and a few dogwoods added pleasant accents at strategic points around the front yard.

Clark enjoyed yard work and it showed in the overall appearance of the property. From March to October, this was his sanctuary, a satisfying diversion from the pressures of police work. Here, unlike at the office, he answered to no one, not to any of the 15,000 residents of Stuartsboro, not to the mayor, nor to his chief. Nobody. Cops desire control, and here he could control all the outcomes, call all the shots. Here, unpredictable crime trends, inadequate budgets, and pushy citizens gave way to tangible things that were measurable—an end in themselves—and, yes, successful. His yard was his release.

Clark approached the back door and noticed that the siding under the light was beginning to show wear. The last time he painted the house, seven years ago, he had done it all by brush and it looked great. He recalled that life was great then, too. All four of the kids were still at home, and he and Samantha were still having some good times. Since the divorce, though, the house seemed to gradually lose its appeal, fading like the most recent coat of paint. He was still proud of it, but he knew he had to sell, to divide the assets, move on. Deep down in his heart, he wished a buyer would never show up.

Alex had placed his dinner on the counter, ready to reheat. Cold dinners had become one of Clark's infamous signatures over the years. As the microwave chirped, she walked into the kitchen.

"Hey," she said, greeting him with a kiss on the cheek. "I was hoping you'd get home on time. This is a new recipe I'm trying out. You know how I love surprising you with my experiments in the kitchen." She smiled optimistically.

"Long day, sorry. If I'd known about this, I would've dropped what I was doing, and run lights and siren home." He tasted the stew and it was a little hot. "So you had a good day?"

"Not bad," she replied. "Organic chemistry is a little easier now. I made a ninety-one on a pop quiz today. I don't know if it's the new lab assistant or if the study group helps, or what, but things seem to be clicking better."

"Good deal," he said approvingly. "This assistant. Wouldn't be of the tall, dark, and handsome variety, would he?" Part joke, part fatherly inquiry.

"No, Dad. She's short, fair, and cerebral. Not quite my type."

He chuckled, added a little pepper to the stew, then took a bite of a hot roll. He was enjoying the meal and the company. As he glanced at Alex, he noticed what a beautiful young woman she'd become. She had long, soft brown hair, her mother's luminous blue eyes, and a creamy, unblemished complexion—the picture of wholesome beauty. Of the four kids, she was the most driven, an overachiever.

"That's great news about your class," Clark remarked. "You really have to pass that for your pre-pharmacy program, don't you?"

"Oh, yeah. Organic has converted a lot of pharmacy majors into very good teachers. Survival of the fittest, you know. You have to sink everything you've got into making the grade. Sort of like with you and your job."

Clark smiled, and made a conscious decision not to counter her remark. It had been a long, tough lesson that he learned over one career and one failed marriage, but he had finally learned it: Don't engage in defensive arguments about your work at home…you'll never win. He continued to devour his meal. He was hungrier than he had realized.

The phone rang; Alex hopped up and sprinted to the den to catch it. Instinctively, Clark's parental radar kicked in as he eavesdropped from the kitchen table. With years of experience, he was good at deciphering who the caller was and why they were calling. He did this by closely monitoring his kids' volume and voice inflection, amount of pause and, most importantly, the number of giggles. After a few minutes of listening, he formulated his guess: "Let's see, I'd say Rebecca or Jenny, and it's about some new guy at school."

Alex returned to the room, carrying a stack of books. "Finished?" she asked.

"Just about. The stew is great, sweetheart."
"Recipe compliments of *Thirty-Minute Meals*."
"Rachael Ray?"
"My idol."
"I have enough left over to take to work tomorrow. Was that Rebecca?"
"Yeah. How'd you know?" she asked, dropping her books with a thump on the table.
"Oh, just a guess," he replied, with a modest grin. He made a mental note to chalk up another one for Dad. He didn't ask her what the conversation was about. He knew better.

After supper, Clark went into the den and started a fire. It was getting cooler in mid-November, and this would be a nice finish to a long day.

As he reclined and enjoyed the warmth, he made a call to check on Brianna and Ian, who lived with their mother in Rallingview. He did the best he could to keep in touch with them daily. They moved there a little over a year ago, just before the divorce, and continued to go to Stuartsboro Senior High. Brianna was a senior and it would have been devastating for her not to graduate from SSH. It was a ten-mile commute, but Samantha worked at a social services office about a mile from the school.

After two rings, Ian answered. "Hello." His voice was crackling, changing.

"Collect call from the Green Bay Packers. Do you accept charges?"
"Hey, Dad. What's up?"
"Whatcha doin'?"
"Homework."
"Did you see the Packers game Sunday?"
"You know I did. Wouldn't have missed it for nothing. Favre was awesome. That put 'em up by two games over the Vikings, didn't it?"
"Three. But they need the lead since their next four or five games are on the road." They chatted a few more minutes about sports and school, and JV football at SSH, where Ian was equipment manager. Typical guy talk. Talk that Clark missed a lot. Ian was his right-hand man, since Clark's oldest, Michael, was away at Carolina. Ian was fifteen, at such a challenging stage in his life, and it burned in Clark's gut that he couldn't be there every day for him. Clark's parents divorced when he was a teen and he vowed not to do that to his children. But he learned the hard way that sometimes promises couldn't be kept. "Is Brianna there?"

"Naw. I guess she's working."

Clark heard a voice in the background as Ian spoke, and knew it was Sam.
"Mom wants to speak to you," Ian said. "Hold on."
Clark braced himself.
"Hello, Clark," Samantha said in a strained voice.
"Hey."
"Don't mean to ruin the party, but he's got homework and it is past ten. Can you call back tomorrow? I'm really not trying to be unreasonable."

Bitch. "Sorry I missed Brianna," he said. He started to apologize for calling so late, the result of working late, again, but he realized not to go there. "Everything going well for you?"

"Yes, it is," she answered cooly. "The County is giving us three days off for Thanksgiving this year. Something to do with state inspectors coming in for an audit."

The conversation was short and strained. As usual. When he hung up, it hit him. Thanksgiving for the first time…alone…after twenty-six of those with her. He had thought about it recently, but now it really came home. Suddenly, without notice. The way bad news arrives at the door without warning. No ringing of the doorbell, no knock. Just barging right in. The way Clark had done for years in his work with "no knock search warrants". But now he was like the criminal, and the cops, named Bitterness and Loneliness, had found him. There was nowhere to hide.

CHAPTER THREE

Clark slept surprisingly well considering how the day had ended. He had left a window up overnight, so the room felt chilly when he got out of bed. The cool air had given him a neck ache, which he tried to work out as he stumbled to the bathroom. After a good shave, he stepped into a hot shower and enjoyed the water beating against his neck, hoping some additional time would compensate for any lost sleep. The pulsating water felt good against his back, and it revived him.

With the likelihood of court today, Clark selected a charcoal grey suit, and a maroon and grey striped necktie to go with a freshly pressed white shirt. He pulled polished black loafers with tassels from a shoe bag and slipped into them. Next, he strapped on his ankle holster, and slid his Sig-Sauer .380 semi-automatic in it.

Looking in the bathroom mirror, he adjusted his tie and took quick inspection. Looking professional was always a priority for him. At fifty-one, Clark still possessed an athletic body and a chiseled, well-defined face. He had always taken pride in his physique, and stuck to a strict exercise regimen. He knew the importance of a sharp appearance, something he learned in his early days when he wore a uniform. A command presence, good first impression.

He put on his size 44 coat, and went to check in on Alex. Careful not to wake her, he kissed her on the forehead, and she stirred a little. He went down to the kitchen, poured a cup of coffee, and headed to the station.

Clark arrived at the PD, collected the paperwork in the squad room, and headed for his office up on the second floor. A few more police reports had trickled in overnight, but not bad for mid-week. Clark tried to arrive at work every morning at 7:00 to chat with the night shift supervisor getting off duty.

He met Lt. Johnson near the elevator, looking beat, dragging a little after pulling his twelve hours. Johnson had that "third-shift look" about him. A little frayed around the edges, showing wear like an old pair of shoes. It was a look that veteran cops could spot a mile away.

"Morning, Lieutenant," Clark said. "How'd the rest of the night go after we talked?"

"Uh, not too bad. Not bad," he answered as he gathered mental notes from the shift. "We had a couple of wrecks and a pretty bad domestic over on Ellison Street. Ended up making an arrest there off a violation of a 50-B order. The guy's a Slade, I know you know him. Can't think of his first name. From the Slades on Neal Street. We got a .38 off him that came back stolen, plus he's a convicted felon, so he's a 'had lad'." He thought another moment. "Uh, we found another B&E at Saunder's Amoco at around 4:00." Johnson yawned and said, "Smash and grab."

"Oh, brother." Clark knew what was coming next.

"Yeah, you guessed it. Saunders came to the scene and wasn't very happy, even though we found the B&E. What's that, his third since July or August?"

"Third or fourth," Clark added. "Looks like the Chief may be having an unannounced visitor this morning. Did you do a K-9 track? You know that'll be the first question the Chief will have."

"Couldn't. John's out of town on training, and Sgt. Edwards, his back-up, is on vacation."

"Video tape?"

"Perp took it with 'em."

"Par for the course, next to nothing to go on. Lucky to get a tape, then luckier still to get a decent one where the perps can be I.D.'ed." Clark didn't bother to ask about fingerprints; those were nearly always a lost cause. Gloves were becoming the staple of most burglars, at least those with half a brain. Clark was irritated with how Hollywood had exaggerated the success of finding identifiable prints. Everybody always expected you to come away with them, and you looked incompetent if you didn't.

"Go get some sleep," Clark said, as he saw Johnson disappear around the corner. He admired Johnson, considered him trustworthy, and that was a quality that Clark didn't take for granted. Johnson was just ahead of Clark on the seniority list, and Clark hoped that Johnson would be the next patrol captain.

Clark read the reports and except for the Amoco case and two car break-ins, the rest of the overnight reports were inactivated. When he entered the conference room, Wilkens was already at work, conducting a telephone interview. Detectives Whitaker, Sloan, and Esposito slowly filed in behind Clark. Sgt. Cunningham was on vacation, so Clark was down to four worker bees this week. Vacation for one detective translated into that many more cases for the others; meanwhile, the cases just kept rolling in. Clark knew the reality was that his men barely had time to work existing leads on cases, let alone go out and develop them. It was one of those truisms in investigative work that detectives would talk about and police administrators would cringe when they heard.

"Morning, guys."

"Good morning, Lieutenant."

"Mornin'."

"Steve, how did everything go with your assault last night?" Clark asked.

"Pretty well," Esposito answered. "She gave a good statement, and I've got a decent lead or two to go on."

"Any more luck with the I.D. on the suspect?"

"Some. Turns out she resisted the guy. Said she scratched him up, arms and face mostly."

"Good for her. That's something, anyway. How's the Lowe guy looking?"

"I think he's looking good for it. Just need to locate him, hopefully find a couple of scratch marks, get a sample, and he's hammered."

The detectives began to read the reports as Clark poured a second cup of coffee and joined them. Morning conversation was usually subdued. The time was spent reading the reports, which were passed around the table until every detective read every report.

By the end of the meeting, Clark had his men off and running. He spent the remainder of the morning in his office answering e-mail and listening to voice-messages, and occasionally fighting the temptation to glance at the picture of Samantha.

* * *

Ruby Walker slept a little later than usual on Wednesday morning. She made coffee, and sat at the kitchen table, writing out some bills that were due. After that, she made a phone call to Margaret, a longtime friend, to catch up on news.

"Hello."

"Margaret, this is Ruby. Just calling to see if you're still alive. How're you feeling?"

"Well, hey Ruby. Sweet of you to call. I guess I'm doing pretty good. Doctor Edmonds changed one of my antibiotics, and I seem to be doing better."

They spoke a few more minutes, mostly about little aches and pains. They talked about grandkids and about good deals at Food Lion. Senior citizen discounts at Golden Corral. The weather. Anything and nothing. Conversation then shifted to a trip that Margaret had been planning for several weeks, to visit her sister in Burlington, but had to delay because of her surgery.

"When are you planning to go see her?" Ruby asked.

"I'm thinking about driving over there this weekend. If I do, would you be willing to feed my cats while I'm gone?"

Ruby replied that she'd gladly take care of things while Margaret was away. Ruby made it her business to help her friends any way she could—for the reciprocal leverage she gained. That was the kind of reputation she had in her circle, but her friends put up with her anyway. It was Ruby.

They said their good-byes, and Ruby went into the den to watch the news. She felt a burst of cold air, as she prepared to sit down near the door. She noticed that the window was open, and she reached to close it. As she did, it sparked her memory to last night and the mysterious scene in the parking lot. And just like that, a senior citizen with no real plan for the day, and no real agenda in which to sink, was energized and ready to roll. She quickly dressed, grabbed a container of brownies from atop the microwave, and headed to The Meadows office.

CHAPTER FOUR

The Meadows apartment complex was located on the southwest side of Stuartsboro, one of the nicer areas of town. The retirement village sat at the end of Farmington Estates, a quiet middle-class subdivision known for its plush, manicured yards and white rail fences. If peace and quiet started at the Estates, it was fast asleep by the time it reached The Meadows. It was that private.

The Meadows opened in 1984 with twenty-eight apartments. Four years later, another twenty units were added and, in 1995, the final phase was completed which consisted of a two-story handicap-accessible building with forty-eight apartments. Building Three, or simply Three as it was called, was tucked into the back corner of the property. A group of local investors purchased the land for expansion from First Baptist Church, located next to the complex. A large grove of soft white pines and hilly terrain provided The Meadows with such a natural barrier that even the church couldn't even be seen from the complex. The hourly ringing of the bells in the church tower was the only proof of its existence. The Meadows was a world unto itself.

Building three featured an elevator, and all the amenities of nicer apartment communities around the city. The bedroom and living room were larger than those in the first two phases. Residents on the second floor had a nice little terrace where they could sit and enjoy the evening view. All in all, life in Three gave you a little slice of status. That's where Ruby Walker lived.

The recreation building was in full swing when Ruby arrived. She stepped inside the office, brownies in hand, and saw the manager, Howard Simpson, seated at his desk on the telephone. He motioned her in and indicated a chair, as he continued his conversation.

"That's right," Simpson said, "one apartment is available in Building Two, and one will be available in Building One in about three weeks…Yes, fixed income and age sixty-five…Waiver of age with handicap."

As he continued his conversation, and scrawled on a note pad, Ruby inspected him. He was a portly man in his late fifties, with pale complexion, and thin streaks of greasy black hair plastered across his head. She thought he always looked a little dirty, and his shirts were never pressed. She was surprised that an apartment complex as nice as The Meadows would tolerate that kind of appearance. *Well, he does get repairs handled quickly.*

"That's right, I'm Howard Simpson. Uh-huh. You too, ma'am. Goodbye." He then turned his attention to Ruby. "How are you today, Mrs. Walker?"

"Just fine, Howard. Sounds like you're looking for another tenant. I didn't know that we had any vacancies right now." The line played right into the info she was looking for.

"Oh, yes. Ms. Fargis just moved into a nursing home, her arthritis got to be too much for her. And Mrs. Phillips is moving in with her son in Charlotte. I'll miss both of them. They're such sweet ladies. So friendly."

Ruby paused; Simpson's remarks seemed sincere. It almost made her feel a little guilty for judging him. Pre-occupied with conversation, she forgot the brownies in her lap. She reached over the desk and handed him the plastic container. Ruby was careful to use Tupperware instead of a paper plate. That way, it ensured her of a return trip to the office. "I made some brownies for you, Howard. I know how you like my brownies."

"Why thank you, Ruby." Excitedly, he took the brownies and placed them beside the telephone.

Moving on in conversation, she carefully pursued her inquiry. "Howard, I was wondering, are there any new residents in Three? I'm very active in the community watch group, as you know, and I want to make sure that we do our best to invite everyone. The turnout last night at the center was a little low." Ruby imagined that if the activity she saw with the U-Haul was connected to the village, then it most likely had to do with someone in Three. The building was set at the back of the property, a nice walk from the rest of the village.

"Let me see. The most recent move-in was, uh, probably in 3-17. You're in 3-14. Right, Ruby?"

"That's right, 3-14." To guide his thoughts, she added, "I'm on the back, right of the stairwell, second from the end." She knew that 3-17 was Naomi Morris, a dead end.

Simpson continued. "Mrs. Morris is 3-17. Upstairs, we got 3-39 on the back, Mr. Hampton; he's been with us about, say, a couple of months. And Marcellus in 44, since, uh, let me look." Howard flipped through the Rolodex, and stopped at a pink card. "Mr. Marcellus has been with us since June. The only other tenants to join us this year would be Mr. and Mrs. Davenport on the front in 9."

She noticed that most of the cards were white, but a few, like Marcellus', were colored pink. She had to ask. "What do the pink cards mean? I'm just curious."

Simpson managed a smile. He knew Ruby for exactly what she was. A one-woman grapevine, the nosiest biddy in The Meadows. But she looked adorable in those large framed glasses, and, after all, she could make a mean batch of brownies. "Why, yes, Ruby, aren't you the observant one." Then he explained to her that the pink cards represented those tenants who had some sort of handicap. Color-coding the cards made the government paperwork a little easier to do at the end of the month.

Ruby shifted the conversation to current events and happenings at The Meadows. It was filler conversation, though, and she was feeling a little disappointed with what she found—or failed to find. Who was to say that the activity last night was anything significant, anyway? Or that it had anything to do with the new residents? She sighed. "Thank you, Howard. I'll make it a point to contact them before next month's meeting."

Simpson jotted down the names and apartment numbers and handed the note to her.

"I hope you enjoy your brownies. Now, you call me when you're finished, and I'll stop by and pick it up," she said, pointing to the Tupperware.

"I don't mind bringing it to you. That's the least I can do."

"Oh, no. I insist on coming back. You just give me a call." She waved, smiled, and walked out.

Ruby noticed all the activity in the rec room and walked across the hallway to check it out. She spotted Selma Jones sitting on one of the large sofas, reading a magazine. Maybe a pay-off. Selma also lived in Three, up in 47.

Ruby and Selma caught up on news. When Ruby saw an opening, she pounced. "I hear you have a couple of new neighbors in 39 and 44."

Selma paused a moment, and slowly repeated the apartment numbers aloud. Then she said, "Yeah, that's right. 39 is Harry, I don't know his last name. He retired from Sherwin Williams. A truck driver. He has the loveliest twin granddaughters."

"What does he look like?"

"Well, he's about my age. He's a little on the short side, I'd say a little taller than you. He has the prettiest head of thick, white hair."

When Selma mentioned the hair, it struck a chord with Ruby. "Oh, I know who you're talking about now." Ruby had heard that he was something of a catch in the village. "Who lives in 44?"

Selma replied, "You know, Ruby, I don't know much about him. He's a black fella, about twenty-five, I'd say. Mostly stays to himself. Rarely goes out, drives one of those special vans. So sad though, he's paralyzed, since an accident several years ago. Drunk driver hit him. Isn't that a shame? In a wheelchair for the rest of his life. So sad."

Ruby, deep in thought, didn't comment. She wasn't too interested in Harry Hampton, but maybe she'd pay the Davenports a visit tomorrow. Marcellus was wheelchair bound, but that didn't really matter. She didn't trust anyone she didn't know, and know very well. Marcellus' apartment *was* on the back, where the truck parked. What were they doing there backing in with a U-Haul truck that late at night? And what was that odd-shaped thing that one of them pulled out of the truck? They looked like they were up to no good. Her curiosity was spiking a little.

She headed back to her apartment and the first thing she did was walk into the kitchen and over to the stove. She set the oven on preheat. Time to make some more brownies.

* * *

Greg Marcellus was sitting at the kitchen table eating a sandwich, when he heard a knock at the door. He rolled his wheelchair over to the door and peeked out the window. Then he unlatched the lock, opened the door, and looked up. "Yes?"

"Good afternoon, my name is Ruby Walker. I live downstairs in 14. I stopped by to say 'Welcome to The Meadows'."

Marcellus didn't reply.

"I made you some fresh brownies," she said, as she handed the plate to him through the opening in the door.

Caught a little off guard, he received the gift, and stammered, "Tha-Thank you, Mrs., uh...."

"Walker, Ruby Walker."

"Mrs. Walker, yes. Would you like to come in?"

Without answering, Ruby walked in and immediately made notes. She scanned the living room and noticed it was of the same layout as her own. The room was neat, but sparsely furnished. She noticed what looked like business papers spread out on the coffee table and the television on to CNN.

"Please have a seat, Mrs. Walker." Marcellus was polite.

She sat in a side chair next to the door, as he wheeled over near her. She examined him more closely as they talked for a few minutes. He was neat, spoke softly. They talked about life at The Meadows, mostly, and the conversation eventually shifted to his car accident. He shared with her how it happened, and she was impressed that he seemed to accept that he would never walk again. He offered her something to drink, but Ruby had seen enough. He seemed nice, something of a recluse. Clean, too. As Marcellus spoke, her thoughts shifted to the Davenports downstairs, and her next move.

As she prepared to get up, Ruby made her pitch to Marcellus to attend the next community watch meeting. "I guess you've found this to be a quiet neighborhood?"

"Real nice and quiet, ma'am."

"You didn't happen to see a U-Haul truck in the parking lot last night, did you?"

"A truck? Which parking lot?"

"The back one here." She nodded in the direction.

"No. Tell you the truth, I turn in early most nights. Why? What happened?" Now, she had his curiosity.

She explained to Marcellus what she had seen, the two men, the way they acted, and so forth. She mentioned the odd-shaped item they retrieved from the truck and how they seemed to whisper, while looking around. Then she remarked, "Oh, well. Probably nothing."

"Wish I could be of help to you. Sorry." Then he added, "Hope I can make it to the watch meeting next month."

He wheeled over to Ruby, thanked her again for the brownies, and she was gone. He closed the door and thought for a moment about his visitor and the welcome gift of brownies. She was a nice lady, but very snoopy. He liked the idea of attending next month's community watch meeting. It would be a chance for him to get out and meet some people. He whirled around in his wheelchair and, as he instinctively began to roll back across the room, he caught himself and grinned. Slowly, he rose from the wheelchair, walked over to the phone, and called a number.

CHAPTER FIVE

The temperature had dipped into the low 30s overnight, and a dusting of snow barely covered the ground. Clark was up early and, for a change, ate a decent breakfast as he read headlines in the local newspaper. When he took his first sip of hot coffee, he thought how good it tasted, and that the first sip was always the best. With the coffee, he enjoyed a piece of whole-wheat toast, bacon, and cooked apples.

In local news, he read that the Sheriff's Department made arrests in two armed robberies, a crime on the rise in the area; any arrest was something of a relief. The newspaper also covered the SPD's successful search warrant on Hairston Street, and he was glad for the coverage. Clark had been the media contact for the PD since making lieutenant ten years ago. He knew the PR value of the daily release of arrest reports, regardless of significance. Only about six grams of crack was seized, along with an illegal shotgun, but he knew to get the story out there, just the same.

Clark finished off the last bite of bacon and then went upstairs, shaved, showered, and got ready. He dressed in a pair of pleated tan slacks, with a crème dress shirt, and then selected a brown tie with small paisley designs of navy and maroon. After he slipped into a pair of cordovan wing tips, he put on soft brown muted plaid sports coat.

He went back to the kitchen for more coffee then headed out the door. As he pulled out of the driveway, he glanced at the house. The snow had collected on the front porch overhang, and settled on the blue shutters. He preferred warm weather, but snow slapped against the house was always a picturesque scene.

At the office, Clark read the police reports from the previous day, and made the assignments. Sgt. Cunningham, his assistant, was still on vacation, and Wilkens had the day off. Down to three men. Out of eleven reports, six were inactivated, which meant that five had to be worked: Two car B&E's, one shooting into occupied property, a forgery, and an embezzlement. Cases kept coming in as his detectives got farther behind.

Just as he read and assigned the last report, Patrol Captain Richard Blackburn walked in his office. Blackburn was on his final leg, four months to go to make his thirty years and pull his pin. He had served his entire career capably with the SPD. Like most of Clark's colleagues, Blackburn was a hometown boy, who came to the SPD fresh out of college. He was well known around town, especially by senior citizens who had cheered for his dad, a star baseball pitcher for the Stuartsboro Luckies back in the 1950s. Blackburn was about 6'03", physically fit, with dark grey intelligent eyes, and a trademark black mustache he always kept. He still had the look of a military recruiting poster.

"Lieutenant, top o' the morning to you," Blackburn said in a poor excuse of an imitation Irish accent.

"Morning, Richard. You're welcome in my office, long as you don't sit there harping on how many days you have left 'til retirement," Clark said, grinning. Blackburn's daily countdown to retirement had become a joke around the office.

They chatted for a few minutes, mostly about the morning reports. Blackburn told Clark about a call he had just received from the mother of a sexual assault victim. The mother had complained about how the Department handled the incident. It was the same assault that Lt. Johnson had briefed Clark on the previous morning.

Clark told Blackburn about the arrest of a local man named Slade in the case. "What was her complaint?" Clark inquired. "We made the arrest and seized a stolen handgun from a convicted felon. Not too shoddy for police work."

"Slow response time, mainly; I guess she wanted us there before the first punch was thrown. She also griped about the officers being rude," Blackburn answered. "Said the officers smarted off at the victim. Not what they said, but how they said it. We've heard that battle cry a million times, haven't we?"

"That's it? That's the complaint?" Clark asked, rolling his eyes.

"Not quite. There's more. The daughter's now saying the guy, Slade you say, sexually assaulted her. Only she didn't report it 'til late last night."

"Why was that?" Clark asked.

"You tell me." Blackburn handed him the supplemental report that told the story.

Clark read the narrative in a couple of minutes. "Says here no forensic evidence was present, and no visual signs of assault were observed. Where're the *CSI* guys when you really need them? I assume no outcry witnesses, according to the report. Not exactly a pristine case to present to the District Attorney."

"Yep, your typical 'he said/she said' case. No telling how many of these cross your desk in a year, huh?"

Clark didn't comment but he knew this case was one of the more difficult ones to prosecute. Whether it was a legitimate sexual assault or not, you could invest a lot of man-hours on the investigation and it would never reach the courts. Like so many cases. Too many cases. "The drill". Countless hours on the evidence and collection process, on interviews, polygraphs, and I.D. line-ups, only to have the felony reports trashed. Or witnesses develop a change of heart. Or businesses just decide to write off the loss. Etcetera, frigging etcetera. There were so many important cases, but far more diversions.

Clark thought for a moment. "Think I'll give the assault complaint to Sloan and Esposito. Send them out there today, see if they can shake up a little something. Do you know if Slade's still in jail?"

"As of 8:00 this morning, he was. It's a no-bond crime."

"Good. Maybe he'll stay there awhile. Lt. Johnson told me that Slade's a felon. So if my guys make him on the sexual assault, maybe we could pick up a capable, even if unwilling, informant," Clark said in a calculated tone. He learned over the course of his career that the old adage "A good informant is worth a hundred cops" was untrue. A good one was worth a hundred and twenty.

Blackburn handed Clark the callback note from the concerned mother, and headed for the door. "Can you give her a call?"

"Sure." Clark put the note on the "to do" pile which seemed to be growing by the minute.

He took another sip of coffee and sent a reply to an e-mail message from the Chief. Just as he was getting up to fax the reports to the local newspapers and radio stations, his phone rang. "Lt. Dixon."

"Clark, Greg. How's it going?" Special Agent Greg Williams, Greensboro office of the State Bureau of Investigation. Clark and Greg were old friends, dating back to high school days at Stuartsboro.

"Just when I thought my morning could get no worse," Clark joked.

"No way to speak to a fellow Stuartsboro Ram, is it? Let me speak to your supervisor, pal," Williams retorted.

They chatted a few minutes, then came their patented moment of reminiscing about the glory days. Talk of Ram state titles in basketball and football. Old classmates they've run into. Or arrested.

"Say, Clark, do you ever wish you could go back to '72? Do you ever think about it? Dream about it?"

"Every other day. But, what the hell. I'd make the same mistakes all over again and feel more stupid than I do now."

"Point taken." After a pause, Williams got on with business. "Just a reminder about the intel meeting at our office next week. Hope you can make it."

Clark looked at his desk calendar and saw where he had made a tickler note. "I've got it down. Should be no problem."

They chatted several more minutes, as most of the conversation keyed on the topic of violent robberies in the Piedmont area, which included Stuartsboro. Williams was the point man for the Bureau on the task force that was investigating the robberies and other violent crimes.

"We've had a string of violent robberies since summer," Williams said. "Very little to go on, but several look connected. Gangs of three, four guys, very aggressive, covered head to toe, well-organized. They've fired shots during the robberies just to intimidate. We think the same group has hit grocery and convenience stores, a super hardware store, and two banks around High Point. I'll e-mail you some intel on them."

"What kind of weapons?"

"In a couple, assault rifles and maybe Uzis."

"Uzis? You gotta be kidding."

"Wish I was. Funny thing, though, they're using revolvers instead of semis. Kind of a throw-back to our early days, huh?"

"No casings left behind."

"That's right. Nothing left but a bullet. Then you have to be lucky enough to recover one that's in good shape."

"Any bullets worth analyzing so far?"

"A couple. Most have been too deformed. Problem is the ballistics software in the lab is down this week, so we'll have to wait until next week or the week after to get any matches with the holidays coming. Say, uh, Clark, speaking of holidays…"

Clark knew what was coming.

"…are you back in the saddle, yet?"

"Getting there. Just no interest right now." Clark lied. Some interest, not much know-how. In a perfunctory manner, Clark asked Williams about his family, and then they talked shop a little more.

After he hung up, Clark sat there for a moment, synthesizing the last two conversations of the morning with a couple of his closest colleagues. The conversation with Blackburn only scratched the surface of the frustrating realities of police work. Questionable cases and integrity issues with victims. Perpetual streams of reports and calls for service. Working shorthanded. No money for overtime. Frivolous complaints against officers. Small, no-nothing property crime cases. Placating the heavy-hitters in the business community. Getting bogged down on the petty, little shitty stuff...*Cops were like rats on a tread wheel, running as fast as they could. But no matter how fast they ran, they ended up in the same place.*

Then Williams. Always the shining success story. One of the Bureau's brightest stars. Assistant SAC in the Piedmont District, and heir apparent to the throne of SAC in a year. Williams had done so well for himself. Made more money, still married, and his pockets were loaded with prestige... *"Say, Clark, do you ever wish you could go back to 1972? Do you ever think about it?" Every day lately, Greg, every day. If you're a shiny new Cadillac, then I'm a rental car with a busted transmission.*

He took one last sip of coffee that had become as cold as his view of his career.

* * *

The walls of the upper level conference room were lined with oak wainscoting that was salvaged from the old building; the wainscoting had been sanded down to the grain, re-stained, and moved to the large new room; it offered a handsome, rich look. The high ceilings and Palladian windows had been retained in the renovation, as well as ornate crown moldings, and other aesthetic features. The windows allowed brilliant afternoon sunlight into the room. The conference room represented a blend of the old and new, and in a sense, was a symbol of the meshing of old and new philosophies of policing in the Department.

Chief Brinks, at fifty-seven, had the suave, polished look of an IBM executive. He ran an organized, businesslike meeting with his supervisors. This particular meeting was impromptu and carried very little good news. The Department expense accounts were overspent and the message was loud and clear during the meeting: Slow down budgets to a trickle for the next few weeks. The City had run into its share of hard times with the closing or downsizing of textile and tobacco factories, problems that plagued most of western North Carolina. It forced police managers to do more with less. "Frozen positions" had become a feared phrase.

Brinks was promoted to Chief of Police a year before Clark made lieutenant, and had worked his way up from the Administrative Lieutenant spot. He was a lateral transfer from Burlington PD, and quickly gained notoriety as being the best shot in the Department—especially if the target was a fellow officer's back. Working administration afforded him the opportunity to work closely with former Chief Broward and develop management skills and the knowledge of inner workings of a police department. Some perceived him as a zealous ladder-climber, with aspirations of running for Sheriff after retirement. But regardless of what anyone thought of him, he ran a tight ship. Stuartsboro was viewed as the flagship agency in the area due, in part, to his leadership.

During the Chief's presentation, Clark drifted back to the conversations in his office, as he ran a mental PowerPoint of his biggest cases and achievements. He did have his share of collars when he was active in cases. He recalled a few of the bank robbery arrests he'd made in the mid-to-late nineties. Bank robberies usually drew significant media and community interest, and were satisfying to work. He remembered some violent shootings he had worked. Burglaries. Some decent drug cases during a short stint in narcotics. But now, things didn't seem to have any salt. Lately, he was just going through the motions. A small town guy, who wanted to make it count, settled instead on running a status quo course to the finish line of a so-so career. He snapped back to present, as he heard his name called.

"Lieutenant Dixon, are we boring you?" Brinks asked.

Clark realized all eyes were now on him. "Sorry Chief. Bad headache," Clark replied. A little of the truth.

"It's your turn," Brinks said.

Clark proceeded with his briefing from C.I.D., informing them about recent crimes and trends. He talked about the Slade arrest and subsequent complaint, and the news from Agent Williams about the increase in violent robberies in the area. He presented an update from the Narc Unit, at Capt. Blackburn's request, and the status of an upcoming drug roundup.

After Clark gave his presentation, Administrative Lieutenant Hoffman carefully covered aspects of the budget, and various training and certification issues. He was followed by Capt. Simmons, who discussed upcoming community policing events. And last, Capt. Blackburn spoke about patrol topics, briefing them on the K-9 report, enforcement activities, and the inadequate staffing level in his division. Clark wasn't listening, though. He gazed at Blackburn—with a large dose of envy. *Four months to retirement.* Clark wished he and Blackburn could magically exchange career spots simply by sliding their badges across the conference table to each other.

The meeting lasted well past six o'clock, and when it was over Clark needed some fresh air. As he walked out the front door of the Police Department, he was surprised by a snowfall. He looked up at a streetlight, watching the snowy mist radiate the glow of the light, even to a sparkle. He crossed the street to his police car, and looked back at the illuminated clock high atop the building. The clock had stopped at 4:35. He remembered hearing somewhere that snow was a symbol of death. He wondered if that were true.

* * *

Ruby Walker was in a hurry to get home to catch the weather report on the 6:30 news. The grocery store was jam-packed with people who, like her, were shopping early for Thanksgiving because of the threat of snow.

The bagboy loaded the trunk of her gray Buick with most of the groceries, but she placed a couple bags of eggs and piecrusts on the front seat beside her. On the way back to The Meadows, it began to snow, and she reminded herself to be careful between the car and the front door.

As she parked at the apartment, the snow stopped. She took deliberate steps to her door, unlocked it, and left it ajar. She turned on the porch light so she could see when she returned for the rest of the groceries. She walked back to the kitchen, placed the bags on the table, and reached for the light. As she did, a strong hand reached out and grabbed her hand, twisting it behind her back. Before she could scream, an arm reached around her from behind with such force that it knocked the breath out of her. She struggled, flailing her legs, kicking behind her, and trying to strike the attacker. She jerked her head back quickly, trying to hit the attacker with it, but the action only caused her to drop her glasses.

In a swift motion, a large plastic bag was shoved over her head, and wrapped tightly in a knot at the back of her neck. She kept trying to kick behind her, but all she struck was air. Almost instantly, she sucked the plastic into her mouth as she frantically gasped for breath, the slightest breath. She quickly began to suffocate. Within seconds, her face turned beet red, then purple. Her kicking slowed. Her eyes were bulging, vessels in her face rising. She shook her head from side to side, making low, muffled, gurgling noises.

There was a whimper and then there was silence. Slowly, her legs collapsed, and her body began its relax into death. As her heart took its last beat, she was dropped to the floor.

CHAPTER SIX

The morning sky over Stuartsboro was a thick depressing gray, a remnant of the night's snowfall that still lay scattered on the ground. Clark listened to the radio on the drive in to work and found the news to be as dismal as the weather. *Mornings like this hold your spirit captive, make you yearn for spring.* Three miles from work, along his route, there was an elevated view of the eastern sky, and from that point, he had seen some breathtaking sunrises. But not today.

Thursday had been a quiet day, so Clark only had a few police reports to read on Friday morning. The light snowfall last night seemed to keep criminal activity in check; bad weather usually brought that kind of positive result. Clark surmised that criminals, for the most part, were a lazy lot—snow, rain, and ice were a little too much for those in the market for an easy car B&E or a larceny.

After he read the last report, he realized that none had to be assigned, and no detective would get a new case today. A nice breather for his men, and it meant a good day of catch up on their cases. Things would seem a little less stressed around the office, if but for a day.

Clark was listening to his voice messages when he heard Detectives Sloan and Esposito talking in the hallway. He yelled for them, and they walked in and took a seat. He continued on the phone, jotting down notes and glancing occasionally at them, as they engaged in a whisper of a conversation. They seemed so compatible, almost to a humorous degree, yet different in a number of respects.

After the last message, he hung up the phone and greeted them. "Good morning, guys. How's everything?"

"Pretty good."

"Okay, Lieutenant. How 'bout yourself?"

"Not bad," Clark answered. "Looks like a quiet twenty-four yesterday, nothing assigned this morning. Guess that means you'll be all caught up by five o'clock," he said with a little smirk.

The guys chuckled. They knew there was no such thing.

"Jerry, you had court yesterday, right?"

Sloan nodded.

Clark looked at Esposito and asked, "What about you?"

"I'm on standby for superior court on a plea, but no district court."

"Good," Clark replied. Then he told them about the Slade arrest the other night, and the sexual assault complaint the victim lodged later through her mother. He spoke of the potential to flip Slade, due to the serious gun charge against him. "He's still in the county jail, or at least he was yesterday. It's not likely he's getting out any time soon, with the domestic and the felony weapon charges."

Esposito interjected, "Yeah, I heard a stolen gun at that."

Sloan followed with a devious smile. "Aggravating factor in sentencing. He's on a sinking ship."

Clark's turn. "That's the way I see it. I'd like for y'all to go out to the jail this morning and put the squeeze on him. See what you can find out. There's no evidence of a sexual assault, so basically it's his word against hers. If he's smart, he'll deny it. But if you can get him, at the least, to admit that he had consensual sex with her, we'll let the D.A. haggle through the details. It'll be that much more leverage against him that we may be able to use later."

"Leverage for what?" Sloan asked.

"Information." Clark told them about his conversation with Agent Greg Williams, and the intelligence on the violent robberies. "It just may be a matter of time before we get hit by one of these gangs. They're getting closer. Williams told me that revolvers seem to be the handgun of choice. No casings left behind. Nice and neat. They work with precision, tight." He paused a moment. "I'm sure it's a coincidence but the gun Slade was caught with was a .38 revolver, a little unusual for our area. Maybe Slade knows something or has heard something since he's been locked up."

Sloan and Esposito asked a couple of follow up questions about their assignment and they were on their way to the jail.

Clark took a little breather as he enjoyed a second cup of coffee with a breakfast bar. He grinned, thinking about their upcoming round with Slade at the jail. Clark was a little envious; he missed that kind of play, the meat and potatoes of police work: Shoe leather on the street, interrogation, knocking on doors, sniffing out informants.... Timeless qualities of solid police work. The same kind of effort and work that made a detective a good one in the 1950s still made for a good one today—lose the fedora and you couldn't tell the difference. People haven't changed, only the technology. Unfortunately, the desk job took all Clark's time, and then some. When he managed to get out in the field for an hour, two hours of paperwork awaited him in the office. The proverbial one step forward/two steps backward syndrome.

Then he thought about his men. Jerry Sloan was the junior detective in the unit, and something of a maverick. He possessed an outgoing personality and seemed to get along with everybody. He was twenty-eight, single, and loved the ladies. The quintessential young, enthusiastic southern detective, right down to the Skoal snuff. Sloan had a medium, slightly stocky build, with a close-cut crop of red hair. He was an avid hunter, in a region where hunting was the second largest religion, just behind the Baptists. He could be a little impulsive but he was becoming a relentless investigator, and he focused on making good arrests. He had the reputation on patrol of being 'enforcement heavy', and his work ethic earned him his detective shield quickly.

Clark shifted to Steve Esposito. A soft-spoken guy who made good chemistry with Sloan. Esposito, who was Hispanic, had a more subdued temperament and was the analytical sort. He was thirty-two, about six feet, and possessed a slender, athletic build. A devout Catholic and family man, he was married and had three small children. Esposito was a conscientious worker, almost to a fault, and Clark believed that Esposito felt like he had to be a notch better than his colleagues. He spoke fluent Spanish, a tremendous asset for the Department. Other agencies around the county called on him for translation services in interviews. Most police agencies, especially those in the South, were way behind the curve on employment of qualified Spanish speaking officers. Clark worried that a department would eventually steal Steve away. He was worth his weight in gold, all 175 pounds of him.

Clark was interrupted in thought when his secretary, Marilyn, called him on the speakerphone.

"Good morning, Lieutenant."

"Good morning, Marilyn. Did you make it in to work, okay?" he asked, in reference to the overnight snowfall.

"No problems at all. Lieutenant, George Perdue is here to see you; he says you know him. I know you're busy, but he says that it's very important. He seems upset about something. Do you have a moment?"

"I'm really behind this morning. The Chief wants to meet in a few minutes, and I still need to take care of a few things before the meeting. Can you see if you can help him?"

"Sure thing," she said and hung up. Marilyn was such a jewel. She had pulled Clark from so many fires in the years that she worked for him, and she was adept at intercepting and handling unannounced visitors.

Clark re-focused on his paperwork but a minute later Marilyn called back.

"Sorry Lieutenant, but Mr. Perdue said that he just has to speak with you. He said it's urgent. Something to do with a flag."

A flag? What was that all about? Clark had known Perdue for years, attending the same church. Perdue was retired, and retirees usually had lots of free time on their hands; that could spell disaster in a day already overflowing with commitments. Working in a small town, Clark learned over the years that he had to skillfully manage interaction with longtime acquaintances, friends, and friends of friends or he'd never get his work done. But if Marilyn couldn't intercede, there must be something to it.

Clark walked out to the lobby, greeted Perdue, and escorted him into the conference room where they took a seat. Clark quickly scanned his visitor and guessed that Perdue was in his late seventies. Perdue had deep lines in his face and dark eyes that looked tired. He knew that Perdue had been widowed for at least twenty years and lived alone. "It's good to see you, Mr. Perdue. Been a while. I guess our church is so large that you don't get to run into some people that often. What can I help you with today? Something about a flag?"

Perdue forced a smile and then proceeded to tell Clark about his predicament. "Someone has been removing the American flag from the front of my house. It's happened, I guess, four times in the last couple of months."

"What do you mean by 'removing'? Stealing?"

"No, no. They just take the flag out of the pole holder on the front porch and throw the flag on the ground," Perdue explained in a slow, deliberate pace.

"Somebody is removing it from the mount, and throwing it to the ground, but they aren't stealing or damaging it?"

"That's right."

A short pause as Clark tried to figure out a tactful way to get through this quickly. "You think maybe a strong gust of wind's blowing it out of the holder?" He paused to allow Perdue to ponder a moment. "Are you missing anything from around the house? Anything been damaged?"

Perdue explained that the wind couldn't have blown the flag from the holder due to the high angle at which the flag was inserted. To the latter questions he answered, "No, nothing seems to be missing or damaged. Just the flag thrown down."

Clark knew Perdue well enough to believe he was a rational, sensible man. "You're a war veteran, aren't you?"

"That's right, I am," he said slowly, proudly. "Korean war."

Clark had a busy morning ahead, probably looking at another ten-twelve hour day. Still, he couldn't help but feel something for Mr. Perdue. Clearly, this was a very low level incident—even meaningless to some, just not to Perdue. The flag was a sacred symbol to Perdue and the incidents were something that Clark imagined had already caused Perdue some degree of anguish.

"Tell ya what, Mr. Perdue, we'll place your residence on our seven-day special attention list. If it happens again, we'll see if we can check the flagpole for prints. How does that sound to you?"

Perdue seemed to ease up a bit, approving of the plan. They shook hands as Clark walked him to the door, offered him a parting note of assurance, and Perdue left.

Marilyn looked up from her typing. "You're a saint."

"Takes one to know one." Clark smiled, checked his watch, and walked back to his office. He went to his desk and made a note to call Perdue in a week to check on his situation. These follow-up calls, "compassion calls" as he called them, were something he enjoyed. He collected his note pad and hustled to Chief Brinks' office.

* * *

Margaret Rierson was getting a little impatient. Her luggage was packed, and she was ready to leave for Burlington, but Ruby Walker wasn't answering her phone. Margaret considered getting the young lady next door to take care of her cats.

She called Ruby's number one last time, but still no answer.

CHAPTER SEVEN

By mid-morning the County Courthouse was in full swing, with overflow parking in all three of its lots. Esposito and Sloan hunted for a spot to park, and after circling the building twice, they whirled into a space marked "Law Enforcement Only" near the jail entrance. As they walked to the door, Sloan reached inside his sports coat, pulled out a mug photo of Mario Slade, and handed it to Esposito. "Here ya go. Know him?"

Esposito studied the photo as if it were a piece of abstract art. After a moment, he lit up with a bit of an expression. "Yeah, yeah I think so. He hangs out on the north end of town, around Rob & Ray's Mart. I made his brother or maybe it was his cousin, Marcus, on a car B&E a few months ago." He took the photo and clipped it to the front of a dummy file he brought with him. The two inch thick file contained Slade's rap sheet and record; most of the file consisted of blank paper and forms he threw in, designed to make Slade think there was that much paper on him.

Sloan smiled when he glanced at the folder. He liked Esposito, watched his techniques and tricks, and tried to learn from him. "Tell ya the truth Steve, I had a couple of run-ins with Slade when I was on patrol. You may wanna lead on this one. What do ya say we play good cop-bad cop and I'll be bad? Think it'll work?"

Esposito laughed. He knew that cops had overused the ploy for years. Used it, and relied on it like a beat up old telephone book you couldn't part with. Nonetheless, when the strategy was well placed and the target was primed, it could still do the trick. "Let's just see how it goes," Esposito replied. "We may not even get to see him if he's been appointed an attorney."

Inside the dispatch lobby, a sea of people was engaged in activities. Deputies, police officers, and troopers were everywhere, shuffling around, chatting with attorneys and witnesses. Jailers and inmate trustees were scurrying about, preparing to deliver lunch upstairs to the inmates. The lobby was large and loud with noises reverberating off the hard walls and floors. With both district and superior court in progress, the place was a zoo.

Sloan wandered up to a bosomy jailer at the communications window and chatted with her. Esposito scanned the crowd and saw Sergeant Claybrook from the Sheriff's Department. He walked over to him, shook his hand, and said, "Read about your robbery arrests in the paper. What broke the cases for you?"

"Extraordinary detective work," Claybrook said jokingly, as Esposito laughed. "Crimestoppers' tip on one of them was the thing that jump-started the case. On the other one, we had a good video from the store camera, if you can believe that. We circulated the photo at the Greensboro intel meeting and one of the detectives from High Point made the I.D. You guys here for court?"

"We're looking at a Slade guy in lock-up. Patrol arrested him the other night on a domestic charge. They got a gun off him and he's a felon, so we're looking to get something out of this from him. Oh, by the way, you been hearing about any robberies with revolvers lately?"

"Revolvers, uh-uh. Why?"

Esposito then relayed the intel to Clayton. "Seems kind of odd to me that these gangs are using such high-powered rifles with revolvers, and not 9's or .45's. They're shooting up stores just to frighten people, gain control."

"Sounds like an experienced crew. Revolvers, huh? A little unusual, like you say. I'll keep an eye out, and check our reports for anything recent. See ya."

Esposito stepped over to collar Sloan, who was still hitting on the female jailer. "Ready to beam up?" Esposito asked. As they walked to the elevator, he looked at Sloan and smirked. "Down tiger. Just 'cause it's mating season for deer...."

"I just love a woman in uniform."

They secured their Glock .45's in the lock boxes in the hallway, and were sent up the elevator. A jail supervisor met them in the prison lobby and said, "Slade's on the way."

They stepped inside the small interrogation room, which also doubled as an inmate/attorney conference room. The room was barely large enough to accommodate a six-foot table and chairs. One broken chair was turned on its side in a corner. An ashtray, overrun with cigarette butts and ashes, sat in the middle of the table, and there was a rusty dented wastebasket beside the door. Esposito coughed slightly as he entered the room, overcome by a stifling plume of cigarette smoke. The haze of blue smoke lingered annoyingly and Esposito figured that lawyers and clients must have used the room continuously over the course of the morning.

Esposito looked at the conference table and noticed the surface was thoroughly marred in every spot where there was a chair—the wear and tear of banging, raking, sliding handcuffs. He scanned the room and believed that it smelled of something much worse than stale smoke. It reeked of the odor of whining degenerates, the kind who returned to this room, time after time, as if it were their den. The stench of criminals who were always pawing for a better deal, crying that the world wasn't good to them, wasn't fair. Always bilking counsel, squeezing the system for more. He wondered how many pitiful excuses and self-centered editorials had been cast over this table.

After Esposito and Sloan briefly discussed the interrogation strategy, a jailer escorted Mario Slade into the room. He was handcuffed and shackled, and the jailer sat him in a chair next to the head of the table. Instinctively, Esposito sat at the head, diagonal from Slade. This would give Esposito the ability to move in on him, if the opportunity presented itself.

Sloan sat across from Slade, and handed him a cigarette. Slade watched him warily, filtering his view of the detective with the kind of mistrust and fear that Slade had learned as a teen running the streets. Sloan lit his cigarette and Slade took a long satisfying draw. Slade had rolled up the sleeves on his orange jumpsuit to expose thick, buffed biceps. Sloan was impressed and saw Slade as the kind of guy who could do a set of one-armed curls with an eighty-pound dumbbell and then yawn. Slade was short, maybe 5'06", but he was muscular and well toned. He had that beefed-up prison yard look about him.

"What's up, Slade?" Sloan asked. "You ain't lookin' too smart in orange, my man."

"Fuck you, Sloan."

Sloan chuckled, obviously pleased with himself.

Esposito looked down at his file. *I guess good cop-bad cop is off and running. Here we go.* Then he tossed the thick file, with Slade's photo attached to the cover, on the table between the two of them. Slade glanced down at it nonchalantly, and then took another long draw on his cigarette.

Esposito began. "Mario, we're here to talk to you about Jaquinta Johnson. You made a mistake when you hit her the other night, but you made it a lot worse for yourself when you got caught with the gun." *There's the bait, now give him some line.*

Slade sat idly and continued to smoke, appearing to be unimpressed. He was a career con who had heard all the sales pitches. He stared with coal black eyes at Esposito, took another intense draw on his cigarette, and laid it in the ashtray.

Esposito watched as Slade placed his cuffed hands in temple formation in front of him. *Visual cue of self-importance and arrogance. This is starting to smell like a stalemate.* Esposito countered by glancing at his watch and reducing eye contact with Slade. He began to hammer Slade a little over the gun charge. After a couple more minutes of interrogation, Esposito broke the dialogue with him, altogether, and turned to Sloan for a minute to discuss an unrelated matter.

After a minute, Slade dropped his hands to the table, leaned slightly forward, and made an effort to re-engage.

Barrier removed, Esposito continued. "Jaquinta's upset, Mario. And you know her mama. She's pushing this thing hard, too. You messed up when you hit her." Esposito opened the file and read Slade's record to him. He highlighted the felonies and then discussed Slade's sentencing points, should he face another conviction.

Slade sat up, cleared his voice, and clanged his cuffs down on the table. "Look man, I ain't did nothin' to that ole bitch, and forget her old lady! I didn't hit her man, straight up. We was just chillin' the other night. Then she gets all crazy, and shit. Went and threw some keys at me, so I grabbed her," as he raised his hands and demonstrated.

Sloan chimed in. "You got a baby by her, Mario?"

"Yeah. A little girl." Slade resettled in the chair and took a few seconds to calm down. Then he reached for his cigarette.

Time to draw in the line a bit, and Esposito pursued. "Grabbin' her ain't all you did from what we hear. Just what part of her did you grab, anyway?"

Up to this point, Slade's eye contact with the officers was penetrating and straight ahead, focused like laser lights. Esposito watched Slade closely for a visual cue and, true to his suspicion, it happened. As Slade prepared to reply to Esposito's question, his eyes shifted up and to the right, as if he were examining a clock or picture on the wall over Esposito's shoulder. *Strong indicator of story construction. Here it comes.*

Then Slade answered, "Naw man, it won't nothin' like that. I didn't lay a hand on her, swear to God, man." He went on to explain the details of his relationship with her, and how they had hit some rocky times.

Esposito moved in closer, picking up the heat. "Look Mario, straight up with you now. What you did with her or to her ain't nothing compared to the time you're looking at with the gun charge." As he said that, he placed an emphatic finger down on Slade's photo, and Slade's eyes followed as if on a pre-chartered course.

"When the feds get through with you, Mario," Sloan interjected, "your little girl will be a big girl driving the car of Jaquinta's new man. You'll be a faded memory."

Slade looked coldly at Sloan, then back to Esposito.

"Worst thing you can do now is lie about having sex with her," Esposito said. "Own up to it, get it outta the way, and then focus on the big stuff." He had inched forward and was now close enough to reach out and kiss Slade.

Sloan kept up the pace. "Come on Mario. Nothin' wrong with sex that gets a little rough. What's wrong is to lie about it. It's a no-nothin' charge. Don't hang yourself on something stupid."

Slade slumped a little and paused. Sloan and Esposito exchanged a quick glance of optimism.

"Say I did get a piece," Slade said, "and she was givin' it 'til she got all crazy and shit."

"So tell us, if that's the way it happened," Esposito said. "We'll pass it on to the D.A. that you cooperated."

"What am I lookin' at?" Slade asked, now weighing his options.

Sloan replied, "Probably very little. The .38's your problem."

Esposito added, "With your record, you're looking at some hard time on the gun, Mario. You may be habitual felon status."

"What the hell is that?"

"Habitual felon. It means fifteen years, mandatory seven." Reeling the line in now.

After the detectives interrogated him a few more minutes, Slade admitted that he had sex with Jaquinta. He told them that she "got an attitude" in the middle of things, and that's when the trouble started.

"Tell ya what," Esposito offered in a controlled tone, "you tell us about the gun, where you got it, and we'll make a call for you. You ain't gotta tell us now, but we better hear from you by, say, next Wednesday. Fair enough?" Esposito knew from the record check that the gun was reported stolen three years ago, so proving Slade knew the gun was stolen was a reach, at best.

"You got a card?" Slade asked.

"One more thing," Esposito added, as he handed Slade his card. "Heard of any three- or four-man gangs around here using revolvers and assault rifles or Uzis on robberies?"

"Not me, man, forget that," Slade snapped.

"Ease up, Mario," Sloan said. "We got none of that on you. If you ain't in it, don't worry about it. But if you want to help yourself out, check around a little. We'll make it worth your while."

"White or black?" Slade asked, showing a little interest.

"Don't know for sure."

After the interrogation, the jailer returned and took Slade away. Esposito and Sloan rode the elevator down. They agreed that things went well, and felt like they took a good shot at Slade.

"Slade's connected," Esposito said. "I got money that says he'll dig up something if there's anything out there. By the way, you do bad cop really good. Excellent casting."

Sloan grinned, satisfied that he had pleased his mentor.

They walked out of the elevator and retrieved their service weapons from the lock boxes. After Esposito snapped his gun in its holster, he looked around for Sloan, but couldn't find him. Sloan had walked back over the window and was flirting again with the jailer. Esposito went over to Sloan, patted him on the back, and said, "Let's go, wild man."

CHAPTER EIGHT

Bette Dixon scraped the last spoonful of tuna salad from the bowl onto Clark's plate, against his raised hand and objection. She ordered him, "Eat this last bite. It wouldn't hurt you to put on a couple of pounds. When's the last time you ate a decent meal?"

"I'm doing fine; will you stop worrying so much," Clark said. "Alex is doing some cooking and she's becoming quite the chef." His reply fell on deaf ears. He knew before his reply that she wasn't going to be impressed. "Besides, I need to cut back a little at the table anyway. Eating a lot of salads, soups that kinda thing." Clark seemed to have this conversation frequently with his mother and he had drawn two conclusions over time: Mothers never stop worrying about their children, regardless of their age, and mothers always treat them like they're still twelve at the kitchen table.

"Eat all of your salad. I have a fresh coconut pie and it's good."

He took the last bite of tuna salad with a cracker. "Thanks, but I better travel light today. May try to get a workout later. This was really great, thanks."

They sat at the table for a few minutes, chatting about family and Thanksgiving plans.

She asked about all the kids and what they had been doing. "Have you heard from Michael lately?" Michael was twenty-three, Clark's oldest and he was away at the University of North Carolina.

"Spoke to him last weekend," Clark said after thinking for a moment. "He's finishing up with his student teaching block this semester. We swap e-mails two or three times a week. You know he graduates in the spring."

She smiled and nodded. "I'm proud of him, Clark, that he wants to be a teacher."

"Yeah, me too. He's done well in his assignment. One semester to go and he'll be out there with a real job in the work force. I'll feel like I got a raise with him out of school. 'Course, Brianna will be going to college next fall, but at least I won't have more than two in at a time. Things are pretty tight right now, but hopefully the house will sell soon."

Bette Dixon turned from the sink and studied her son carefully, as he got up from the table. "Clark, if you ever need to borrow some...."

He cut her off in mid-sentence. "I've told you a thousand times, I don't need your money. Everything's gonna work out fine." And as if he had to come up with some creative addendum to the dialogue to convince her of that, he added, "The realtor is showing the house tonight. Sounds promising, too." It seemed to Clark that every time he visited her lately, she corralled the course of conversation, steering it into a discussion about his finances and her willingness to give him some money. This was as tedious as it was predictable, but she meant well.

"Have you seen or spoken to Samantha lately?"

"I spoke to her the other night when I called to check on Ian and Brianna."

"How is she?"

"Seems to be doing well." He wondered where this was going.

"Is she seeing anyone, that you know of?"

Enter knife and twist. He still couldn't stomach the idea that Samantha was getting on with her life. But he knew it was just a matter of time before she would be seeing someone, assuming that she wasn't already. Yet in the back of his mind, he kept thinking that there might be a chance for some kind of reconciliation. Just some feeling that things would work out, fall back into place.

As he paused to assemble an answer for his mother, he was rescued when his pager buzzed. "Hold on a second," he said, and then read it. The number was to a cell phone; it was Sloan or Esposito. "Can I use your phone?"

She nodded, but he could tell by her expression that she was still anxiously poised for a response. Clark stepped outside with the phone and called the number.

"Starksy and Hutch," Sloan answered.

Clark chuckled. "Now that's a scary thought. I'd say you're more like Abbott and Costello. How'd everything go at the jail?"

"Uh, not too bad, Lieutenant," Sloan replied. "We had a good talk with Slade and think he was pretty straight up on stuff. He skirted on the sex thing with Johnson, but he finally came around on it...."

"Just how far around did he come?" Clark asked.

"He admitted that he had sex with her *and* he said it was consensual, at least to a point. Slade said she got an attitude in the middle of it, and then they started arguing. He said he grabbed her after she threw something at him, and it was off to the races after that."

"Good enough," Clark replied. "If she says something similar then it sounds like a wash by the time it lands on the D.A.'s desk: Boyfriend/girlfriend, she's got a baby by him, part-time lovers. Who's gonna do the felony report?"

Clark heard muffled noises, then Sloan came back on line. "Steve said he'll take it."

"How'd it go with the gun?" Clark asked.

Sloan handed the phone to Esposito. "Hey Lieutenant. Slade didn't give us nothing on the gun, at least not yet. We gave him a deadline of next week to call us. But I think we got his attention on the charge. We talked going federal with him and laid it on thick about his record. By the end of our little chat, he gave us one of those looks like he was gonna drum up some info."

"Do you think he's involved in any of these area robberies we talked about?"

"Nah, I really don't think so," Esposito replied. "He's small-time, sort of a loner. A street-level player with women problems. He doesn't have the discipline for something like that, at least that's my take on it."

Clark took a moment to absorb the response. "You think he knows anything about the robberies?"

"Hard to say. But if he does, or if he hears anything, I betcha he'll call us. He's got some time to nose around; when they do give him a bond, I expect it'll be pretty steep."

"Good job. Tell Sloan good work, too," Clark said. "Anything else?"

"Uh, yeah," Esposito hesitated. "I think that Sloan's in love and wants to be sent to jail." Sloan grinned and so did Clark.

Clark replied, "First of all, I'm afraid to ask about the jail thing. Secondly, he's always in love with something or somebody. See y'all at the office." He felt good about their findings. Esposito and Sloan were young detectives, but they had good instincts.

When Clark went back inside, his mother was clearing the table. He hoped that she had forgotten the last line of questioning right before the page.

"Everything all right?" she asked.

"Yeah. Just routine stuff."

She hated that kind of brush off from him, but she rarely challenged it. She loved his police business, and made it a point most every day to listen to her scanner. Occasionally, she would even call him at work when she heard sirens or a hot call on the scanner and her curiosity got the best of her. She was a retired nurse, and loved the exciting contrast of police work, watching court TV, or reading a good murder story.

"Come back Monday," she proposed, "and I'll fix barbequed chicken thighs."

She sure can play dirty. She knows all my weaknesses. Well, one of them for sure. A store-bought barbeque sauce called Pansie's Finest mixed with brown sugar and orange juice. "Sounds too good to turn down," he said. "You're on."

As he told her good-bye, his pager buzzed again. This time it was the communications office, but he waited until he got to his car and made the call on his cell phone.

Telecommunicator Clara Lewey answered. "Stuartsboro Police."

"Clara, this is Lieutenant. I just got your page."

"Hey, Lieutenant. Lt. Festerman just called me and wanted me to relay to you that there's a 10-67 call you may want to send a detective to."

10-67 meant DOA. Dead body. And every time Clark heard that ten code spoken or broadcast, his heart would drop, kind of the way he felt as a youth when he plummeted to the bottom on a roller coaster ride. He knew the potential on every 10-67 call. It could be a natural causes case that could be handled and cleared in a matter of a few minutes. Or it could turn out to be a suspicious death where the floodgates opened and his division would be submerged in the investigation for twenty-four or forty-eight hours. He equated the difference in the calls to a 100-yard dash and a twenty-six-mile marathon.

"Anything out of the ordinary on the call, or do you know?" Clark asked.

"Lieutenant really didn't say, other than the deceased was elderly. He just wanted to make you aware of the call, just in case you had somebody available to send to it."

Clark pondered his staffing level. "Can you check and see if Price is in? If he is, tell him I'd like for him to go and check it out." Clark asked her for the address of the call, thinking it would ring a bell, but it didn't. "Clara, would you radio me and let me know if Price is on the way?"

A minute later, Price was en route and Clark radioed to Lt. Festerman and told him that he was heading to the call, too. Clark had confidence in Det. Price Whitaker's abilities as a juvenile detective, but he lacked experience in adult investigations.

Ten minutes later, Clark arrived at the scene and Festerman met him on the walkway at the victim's apartment. Clark noticed three patrol cars, Whitaker's unmarked Ford, and an EMS truck at the scene. Several apartment residents were gathered on the sidewalk, talking and closely eyeing the activity.

"Thanks for sending Whitaker over," Festerman said. "Everything looks okay but I just wanted to get a second opinion."

"Second opinion? You make us sound like a couple of doctors," Clark said, smiling. "What do you got so far?"

"Elderly female, seventy-nine, eighty years old," Festerman said. "History of heart problems. Everything in order in the apartment. Looks okay. Her sister found her."

"What about her car? Valuables?"

"Didn't drive, no car. Everything looks secure in the apartment. Purse, other stuff laying around in plain view."

So far, so good. Slowly, he felt a heavy weight getting lighter on his back. On calls like this, it was like he was toting a forty-pound bag of sand. With every bit of good news, a little sand would pour in a steady flow through a hole at the bottom.

"Let's go take a look," Clark said.

Inside, a patrol officer was seated in the living room, completing the police report. Another officer was inspecting the residence, checking points of entry and searching for clues of anything suspicious.

Whitaker walked over to his lieutenant. "She's in the bedroom. Looks like she died in her sleep. Nothing disturbed, nothing out of place. Medical problems. Heart and high blood."

They walked slowly down the hallway to the bedroom, taking cursory inventory of a bathroom and spare bedroom along the way. When they entered the bedroom, they saw the deceased lying in the bed. Two EMS techs were taking notes, and filling out related paperwork.

One of the men looked up at Clark and said, "Hey Lieutenant. Looks like she died overnight in her sleep. Rigor's set in; lividity's obvious."

Clark chatted briefly with him. "What's your time of death?"

The tech looked at his watch, and did the math. "Looks like fourteen, sixteen hours maybe. That'd be my guess."

"Who was she?" Clark asked.

Whitaker referred to his notepad. "Yvonne Tucker, eighty, lived alone here. She worked for the City in the finance department years ago, I'm told. We've already called the medical examiner. He's approved release of the body. He called Tucker's doctor. He was satisfied with everything."

"Does the sister have any concerns?"

"No. She's good," Whitaker replied.

Clark thought things were looking satisfactory. "Price, take some good photos. Got your digital with you?"

"Yes, sir."

"Be sure to check with the neighbors, do the usual canvass. Confirm that the house was tight. And Price, stay as long as you need," Clark advised. He knew there was no substitute for a methodical, deliberate investigation in a case like this, and that always meant time.

"Sure thing. What about securing the apartment, Lieutenant? Check with the sister or the manager?"

"Manager."

Lt. Festerman finished a cell phone call, and then stepped over to Clark. "We just got a wreck call to go to so I need to clear one of my guys. Okay?"

"Yeah. I think everything's okay." Whenever Clark made that statement in a scenario like this, he never quite felt totally confident. All the sand never completely poured from the bag. From experience, he knew the naked feeling created by leaving these scenes and wondering if some precious piece of evidence was left behind or a key observation overlooked. Once you left, you could return, but it could cause some irreversible problems with evidence integrity. *You get burned on this once, and the scar from it follows you the rest of your career.*

After discussing a few more issues with Whitaker, Clark headed back to the office to wrap up for the day, and the week. He was looking forward to spending some time this weekend with Alex, Brianna, and Ian.

On the drive back, something was bothering him. He realized after a moment what it was. For some unexplainable reason, he couldn't help but feel a little sadness for this woman, Yvonne Tucker. Why? He didn't even know her. Maybe it was because she died alone. Maybe it was because it made him think of his own mother.

CHAPTER NINE

The parking lot of King's Inn Pizza in Rallingview was packed as Clark and Alex pulled in. Brianna and Ian lived a few blocks away and had arrived just ahead of them. They met at the entrance, and Brianna gave her dad a hug. As they all entered the restaurant, Clark reached over and patted Ian on the back.

King's Inn was an old favorite of the Dixons. Clark and Samantha had loved to bring the kids here because the food was always good and family night specials were offered. But best of all it was because the large dining room was usually noisy and drowned out the chatter and laughter created by four rambunctious kids. He noticed how the restaurant remained unchanged, keeping the same look for years: The juke box at the back of the room, the red and white checked tablecloths, the menu selection, even the blue cheese dressing. A reliable sameness. It brought back some good memories to Clark as they slid into the wooden booth and scanned the menus.

"Bri, have you heard from U.N.C.-Charlotte about your application?" Clark asked.

"No, not yet," she replied. "They talk like it'll be the first of the year before they send out acceptance letters. I should be hearing something from Guilford College before Christmas. They place a lot of emphasis on S.A.T. scores, and I did pretty good on the last test."

"Quit braggin'," Ian interjected.

Brianna ignored him. She knew that was the best way to aggravate her younger brother.

"Which school are you leaning toward if you get accepted by both?" Clark asked. As she thought about it, Clark noticed that she was looking a little more serious, a little more mature since he had seen her last. Perhaps it was the conversation about college, or maybe it was just the infrequent contact with her since the break-up. He also noticed subtle changes in her appearance. Brianna was now about the same height as Alex. Her brown hair, a shade darker than Alex's, was cut a little shorter. But like Alex, Brianna was trim and fit. She lettered in tennis and swimming, the latter her passion since her freshman year.

"I'm not sure," she answered. "Guilford has a better criminal justice program, but Charlotte is cheaper. Guilford offers courses in Spanish, and I like that. You've always said that Spanish would be a real asset for me, and boost my chances for a job at a higher level of police work."

"Like I've told you, get that four year degree, and with the Spanish background and your abilities, you can write your own ticket," he replied.

Clark was pleased with Brianna's goals. She had shown a career interest in law enforcement since her sophomore year. Clark felt that most cops either loved or hated the idea of their kids following in their footsteps; Clark fit the former category. He believed that Brianna would pursue a better route and find the work fulfilling, like he once did. He wondered if, somehow, he could find redemption in his work with Brianna finding success and satisfaction in her own.

The waitress, a cute petite blonde with a cheerleader's enthusiasm, came to the table to take their drink order. Ian seized the opportunity to flirt with her when it was his turn, by responding with his patented James Bond imitation. He looked up at her and, with all the suavity and cool that a fifteen-year-old could muster, he said, "Sweetened tea, lemon, shaken not stirred."

She grinned and walked back the counter.

"Ian, you moron," Alex snapped, with a mixture of disgust and contempt in her voice.

"That is so stupid, Ian," Brianna added. "They have no idea who you're trying to imitate. You don't know how ignorant you sound doing that."

Clark just grinned through it all. He missed this kind of banter and teasing among his kids. Missed it a lot. If someone had told him five or six years ago just how much he would have missed it, he wouldn't have believed them.

Two "King's Ransoms", pizzas loaded with the works, came hot and delicious, and everybody dug in. They enjoyed the time together, realizing how precious these moments had become. Talk around the table was steady and light-hearted. Near the end of the meal, Brianna winked at Alex, and Clark caught it. Brianna excused herself from the table, saying that she had to make a phone call.

When she returned, Clark was getting a page from the PD. *Oh no, don't tell me I gotta go in for something. Not tonight.* He stepped outside and called the Department. The dispatcher informed him of a shooting incident that had occurred earlier, but injury was minor. No need to go in. "Thank God," he muttered.

Clark returned to the table, as the kids were finishing off the last few slices of pizza. Alex was talking with Brianna about college and upcoming exams. Things a big sister would want her little sister to know about. Clark listened intently to the conversation, as he studied Alex. He noticed that she was wearing the necklace he had given her on her sixteenth birthday. It was an onyx pendant that Clark's grandmother had left him. The necklace was special, and Alex boasted that she had never taken it off.

A few minutes later, the waitress returned. "Can I get you all anything else?" she asked. "How about a refill on the drinks?" They answered no as she tore the bill from her pad. "Here you are," she said, handing it to Clark. She paused a moment to allow all eyes to return to her. Then, slowly, she took a slip of paper from her apron and said, "And this is for you," handing it to Ian.

Caught off guard, Ian took the piece of paper. He gave her a perplexed look, and asked, "What's this?"

Coyly, she replied, "It's my phone number, James."

The girls burst into laughter, clapping their hands as the waitress walked away.

Clark chuckled, looking across the table at Brianna, the culprit. He shook his head and announced, "Only the love of a sister...."

Brianna stared at Ian, and snickered, "James Bond strikes again." She and Alex laughed loudly.

Red-faced, Ian realized that he'd been had. He opened the folded piece of paper and, to his surprise, there was a phone number scribbled on it. He slid it in his pocket.

Clark sat there thinking that this was a perfect evening. It had been a long time since he'd had one.

After dinner, they stopped by Mayberry Ice Cream Shoppe for sundaes. Then Brianna and Ian followed them back to the house. As they pulled in the driveway, a car that Clark didn't recognize was backing out. Then he realized it must be the real estate agent. They parked beside her, got out, and Clark spoke first.

"Good evening, Mrs. Bergen. How are you tonight?"

"Fine, Mr. Dixon. My, it looks like you have the whole crew here."

"Almost the whole crew, I'm short one." Clark liked her. She was a pleasant woman, with a beautiful complexion and beaming smile, who appeared to be in her mid-sixties. He felt that if anyone had to show and sell his house, he was glad it was she. "How did the showing go tonight?"

"Very well," she said, enthusiastically. "There are many things this couple likes about the house. They're transferring here from Charlotte, and the place fits the needs of their growing family. They have two boys and a girl. I really think that they'll ask to see it again."

When she made the comments, Clark began to feel a bit queasy. It was a little like the feeling, he imagined, that a homeowner experienced when he discovered that his house had been burglarized. He and Samantha had raised their family in this home. There were wall-to-wall memories everywhere. There was a story or experience in every stain in the carpets, behind every dent in the walls. As he absorbed these thoughts, he realized Mrs. Bergen was asking him a question.

"Well, would it be okay, Mr. Dixon?"

"I'm sorry. What was that?"

"Would it be all right to show it during the week of Thanksgiving?"

He thought a moment. "Yes, yes, of course. No special plans for the holiday that I know of. Thank you, Mrs. Bergen."

The rest of the evening was pleasant, and everyone relaxed in the den. Clark kept a fire going, as they ate popcorn and watched the old Christmas classic *It's a Wonderful Life*. He carefully followed Jimmy Stewart's character as the spirited father of a struggling, yet loving young family. Instinctively, Clark began to draw parallels between his life and family situation and those of the protagonist.

Near the end of the movie, Clark's mind wandered to the era in which the movie was based: A black and white world with happy endings, where couples kissed and made up, where love and passion always prevailed over pride and indifference. *A black and white world*, as he slowly drifted off to sleep.

After the movie ended, Brianna nudged him. "Daddy, the movie's over. I'm going to bed."

He rose from the recliner and gave her a good night hug.

She kissed him on the cheek. And as if she had been reading his thoughts, she looked him in the eye and said, "Mom's alone too, Daddy."

He started to respond, but decided against it. He looked at her with eyes that said, "Thank you, sweetheart," then he said, "Good night, Bri."

Heading to the stairs, he found Alex on her cell phone and kissed her goodnight. Ian had fallen asleep in the living room playing a video game, so Clark threw an afghan over him and turned off the TV and light. Clark went to bed and fell asleep, almost immediately.

Around 1:30, Clark woke up and couldn't go back to sleep. The more he tried to drift off, the worse his insomnia became. He lay there in a bed that somehow seemed larger and lonelier with the kids in the house. He stared at the ceiling, and bounced his feelings and emotions off it like crazy ping-pong balls. Finally, he decided to get up. He knew the idea was impulsive and inane, but for some strange reason, it was something he was compelled to do. He put on a jacket over his pajamas, crept out of the house, and started his car.

The roads were empty this time of night, so he made good time. He arrived back at King's Inn Pizza in about ten minutes. He passed the restaurant, made a right turn, then a left. He drove several blocks, and then took another right. His heart was pounding, afraid of what he might find. He drove down the street and stopped in front of the beige Cape Cod home, third from the end. He decided to turn into the driveway and, as he did, his lights hit Samantha's car parked at the back of the driveway. Her car was the only one there. *Happy? Relieved? Surprised?*

He was starting to feel old emotions that he thought were dead and it made him nervous. He pounded his head against the steering wheel. "What in the world am I doing here?"

CHAPTER TEN

A light green van with a business logo on its sides slowly pulled over to the curb. The front seat passenger turned down the police scanner which was blaring, and the driver told them they had fifteen minutes, not a minute more. The three men in the back, dressed in black military fatigues, checked their weapons and communications equipment, and synchronized their watches. They placed black hoods over their heads that concealed everything but their eyes. They looked at each other through the eye slits, nodded, and the sliding door opened. They eased out of the van, and ran into a thick wooded lot next to the Harris Teeter supermarket. They were out of view from the road in seconds.

Inside the supermarket, Willie Ferrell, the night shift manager, finished some last minute paperwork and straightened up the office desk. After recounting the deposit, he realized that it had been a busier Saturday than he suspected. He walked to the back of the store to speak with a worker. "Keith, how's it coming along?" Ferrell yelled over the noise of the high-speed floor buffer.

Keith Hall stopped and answered, "Not too much longer." He looked at his watch and said, "Probably another thirty minutes and I'll be finished back here." He pointed to the area that he had buffed. "Does everything look okay so far?"

"Yeah, it looks good, Keith," Ferrell replied, as he inspected the broad area of green and white block tile. The floor had a nice shine to it and showed no sign of the heavy traffic from the busy weekend. Ferrell directed Hall to a spot that he'd missed, and he glided the buffer over to it.

Outside, they moved with stealth, sprinting through the woods like leopards slicing through the jungle. They moved as one, with discipline that reflected rigorous hours of training. They stopped at the tree line, close enough to view the side of the building yet still remain concealed...thirteen minutes.

Ferrell and Hall chatted briefly about the busy evening. Hall, a lanky seventeen-year-old, was one of the store's more dependable employees.

Ferrell had given him extra hours, because he was a good worker and needed the money. Hall was a quiet kid, something of a loner, but Ferrell liked him.

Ferrell went back to the stockroom and cut down the lights in the front of the store. Then he went to the back doors, checked, then re-checked them to make sure they were locked. He was aware of several grocery store break-ins recently in town, including his own store in September. The store manager had made the staff aware of other break-ins to Harris Teeters in Greensboro, High Point, and Reidsville so Ferrell was careful to use all security measures every time he closed the store.

He stopped by Hall's work area and spoke with him once more. "You know the alarm code, right? If you set it off, the Police Department's gonna charge us. Be sure to cut the lights down back here when you're finished."

Hall shouted over the buffer noise, "Yes sir!" He was anxious to finish and get to what was left of Saturday night. He recited the security code, and Ferrell gave him the okay sign and waved good-bye.

Emerging from the woods, they darted up to the south side of the building. The lead man peered around the corner to the front doors, then looked back at the other two. He whispered into his mike, and they raced to join him at the corner. They dashed to the front sidewalk and positioned themselves behind a drink machine and advertisement displays.

The green van had been circling the area when the driver looked in his rear view mirror and noticed a police car approaching him at the intersection. The driver of the van turned right and the police car soon caught up with him. The officer activated his blue lights and, when he did, the driver of the van reached under the seat for a .38 revolver and hid it under his right thigh. He exchanged a glance with the passenger and pulled the van over to the curb. As he did, the police car sped around him and drove away. The passenger radioed a warning to the crew...nine minutes.

Ferrell returned to his office, picked up the moneybag to make the bank deposit, locked the office, and headed to the front door. He looked at the side parking lot and saw his car parked alone in the middle of the lot.

Ferrell walked out and re-locked the door. As he turned to head down the sidewalk, a large black shadowy object swept in front of him. As he felt the blow to his face, his legs buckled under him. The next thing he knew, he was lying on his back pinned against a couple of newspaper racks. His body felt limp; his face was pounding. He shook his head trying to regain his senses. He felt warm liquid trickling down from his forehead, and the cold, hard end of something pressed against his cheek.

In a moment, he was alert enough to know that he was in trouble. He adjusted his vision and looked up at the most evil eyes he had ever seen. But the eyes were all that he could see, against a backdrop of black November sky.

* * *

Clark had an action-filled day with his kids and, to his surprise, Michael had driven in from Carolina. Clark hadn't seen him since Fall Break and it was icing on the cake of a very good weekend. The five of them spent the afternoon shopping in Winston-Salem, and then had dinner at the Outback Restaurant. They ended the evening back in Stuartsboro by going bowling.

Clark slept lightly and dreamed in black and white. In his last dream, he was working at his desk when a group of citizens barged unexpectedly into his office. With angry faces, they shouted at him, but he couldn't understand what anyone was saying. The number of irate people grew quickly, a steady stream filing into his office, and the collective noise was deafening. He couldn't speak, so he stared helplessly at the mob; then he saw the light flashing on his phone. He looked down at it but was reluctant to answer with the tirade in progress. As the phone continued to ring, its volume rose steadily to the point where the ringing now drowned out the crowd's protests. He picked up the receiver and answered but the phone continued to ring, and the ringing grew louder. Slowly, Clark awakened from the dream and realized that the phone beside his bed was ringing.

Clark figured the call was from the Police Department, and that it was going to be bad news. When the telephone rang this late, it was always bad news. The startling, sudden ringing jolted him and caused his heart to break into a sprint. He glanced at the clock, and the bright red numbers were blurry. He focused and read 2:47 as he picked up the receiver, and said hello in a subdued tone.

"Lieutenant, this is Price. Sorry to wake you up but we've had a robbery at the Harris Teeter. I'm here now. We've had shots fired here, and an employee was hit."

Clark took a few seconds to process the information. "Where did you say it was?" Clark asked, still groggy.

Whitaker repeated the location, and continued with his summary. "The employee, a kid, was shot once in the leg and once in the side of the chest. Looks like he fell hard against a counter and was knocked unconscious. He's lost a lot of blood, too. The perps beat the manager up and took the nightly deposit. Then they made him go into the safe. They cleaned him out."

Clark sat up for the answer to his next question. "How bad is the victim?" he mumbled.

"Wilkens is at the hospital with him. Last I heard the boy still hadn't regained consciousness. They've got him in surgery now. The doctors are giving him a little better than a 50-50 chance of making it."

"Through and through shots?"

"No. Hopefully, they'll be able to remove the bullets in surgery. I told Wilkens to hang around for a while just in case he can collect them tonight."

"Does Wilkens need any help at the hospital?"

Whitaker thought a moment. "Uh, I think he's got it covered. He's collected the kid's clothes and he's getting a waiver form signed for release of the medical records."

"Any other victims?"

"Just the manager. He's banged up and a little shaken, but he's refusing treatment. He's more upset about what happened to his worker."

"Go ahead and have EMS en route, just the same. Has the Chief been notified?"

"Yes, sir. But he's not coming out. Capt. Blackburn is on the way."

Good. "Media?"

"Nothing so far. Dispatch is staying off the air, sending us text pages, and we're using our phones."

"Good work. I'm on the way. Be there in a few minutes." He hung up the phone and reached for his slacks on the chair. "Damn! They got us."

* * *

When Clark arrived at the store, several police cars were parked outside the crime scene tape that was flapping in the freezing, early morning wind. He looked down the side of the building and saw the crime scene van, a K-9 car, and an EMS unit.

As he ducked under the tape and headed for the entrance, he was surprised by his sergeant, David Cunningham, who walked over to him and shook his hand.

Clark spoke first. "Welcome back. How was the vacation?"

"Too short. What a way to come back, huh?"

"Good to have you back, really."

At fifty-six, Cunningham was a little older than Clark; he was short and stocky, bald, with a thick black mustache. He had the reputation of being a little slow in his work, never the trailblazer, but he made up for it with dependability, a common sense approach to things, and humorous antidotes. Clark thought Cunningham possessed the proper blend of Sheriff Andy Taylor's wisdom and balance, coupled with Deputy Barney Fife's good nature and quirkiness. He envied Cunningham, a short-timer who was within a year of retirement.

Whitaker joined them at the doors and walked them through the robbery scene. He pointed to the area on the sidewalk where the manager was accosted and gave them his account of the ambush.

When they entered the store, Whitaker said, "We'll go to the office in a second. First, I want to show you the shooting area." He led Clark and Cunningham over to the front of aisle seven and pointed to a number of nine-millimeter casings scattered along the floor leading to the back of the aisle. "My guess is that either the boy heard something at the front and went to check it out, or the perps saw him on the store surveillance monitor. Suppose that's when one of them went after him."

Clark thought aloud. "The victim gets surprised in the aisle by the robber, and he's a sitting duck. The perp opens fire as he runs him down."

Nobody commented.

They walked to the back to the meat counter, and saw a large swath of blood on the floor. "Appears that he fell against this counter, and to the floor here," Whitaker said, as he pointed to the spots.

He paused as he watched Clark and Cunningham conduct their inspection. To the right of the blood, they saw it. A live round. No one spoke as each could read the scene: The perp shot the victim, walked up, stood over him, and attempted to fire a round—at point blank range.

Cunningham presented his theory in a solemn manner. "Our victim is alive for two reasons. The perp's gun jammed, and it was the last round that he had."

They walked up to the office where Ferrell was giving his statement to Capt. Blackburn and one of his men. An EMS technician was attending to the laceration on Ferrell's forehead.

Blackburn interrupted Ferrell and introduced him to Clark.

"Can you describe them?" Clark asked Ferrell.

Ferrell thought for a moment, playing back the scene in his mind. "Hard to say. All I could see were their eyes and the area around them. They had medium skin tones, more dark than light, I suppose." He paused a moment due to the pain. "Thick eyebrows on one of them. I noticed that."

"What about their hands?"

"They wore gloves, at least the two that were in the office. I'm not sure about the one that did the shooting."

"You're doing good, Mr. Ferrell. Sure we can't get you anything?"

"No, I'm okay. I would like to know how Keith is doing." He patted the bandage on his head. "On second thought, a cup of coffee would be nice."

Clark sent one of the officers on the errand; he looked down at Ferrell who was seated at the office desk. *I'm glad you're alive, but I really don't know why they spared you.* Then he continued. "Mr. Ferrell, can you think of anything else that may be helpful to us in identifying these guys? Anything?"

Ferrell paused for what seemed like a minute, and looked up with a strained expression. "No, not really. Well, uh, it was sorta odd the way they spoke."

"What do you mean?"

"While they were robbing me, they hardly said anything. Everything was one-, two-word stuff: 'Move! Open it! Anyone here?' I've been robbed before. It was different this time."

Capt. Blackburn and Det. Whitaker asked Ferrell a couple more questions and then they cued the store videotape. The monitor was an eight-screen system that taped activity in the major areas of the store. The store cameras picked up most of the movements of the robbers, beginning with the manhandling of the manager to the office. The robbers moved quickly, with calculated, confident steps, crouching low to avoid detection from the parking lot. It was obvious that they were carrying long barreled weapons, but the tape wasn't clear enough and movements were too choppy to determine what kind.

There was no camera in the office, so after the tape showed the robbers forcing the manager into the room, the only motion recorded for a couple of minutes was the boy buffing the floor at the back of the store. The detectives kept track of the time the robbers were in the office by the time readout on the monitor screen.

As the tape continued, one of the robbers exited the office after about two minutes. He walked briskly aisle by aisle scanning each as he went. Just as he raised his weapon to fire, the camera switched to another zone in the store. When a camera next picked him up, he was running up the aisle back to the front of store. As the screens changed views, the officers saw the shooting victim lying on the floor, the pool of blood beside him. A minute later, the three robbers fled from the office, and were last seen on one of the screens about ten feet from the front door.

After he was asked a few more questions, Ferrell told the officers that he was knocked unconscious after he opened the safe. When he awoke, he hit the office panic alarm, but he was too woozy to get up. He hoped that Keith had escaped out of the back of the store.

Clark gathered his men together after the interview and processing duties were completed. "Any luck with the K-9 track?" he asked the group.

Whitaker replied, "Afraid not. Sgt. Edwards thinks he picked up a scent along the side of the building, but lost it after a short track. I'd be surprised if a group this organized would run far to get to a getaway car."

Clark added, "I agree. Notice the hands-free mike that one of them had? The way they moved? They were controlled, smooth, and cold-blooded. That bastard shot the kid for no reason, no reason at all." Clark looked around the room, took a deep breath to calm down a little and organize his thoughts. "Anybody know how much they got?"

Whitaker flipped through a couple of pages in his note pad. "Rough estimate from the manager is about $63,000.00."

"Good Gosh!"

"How much?"

"Sixty-three K. Deposits from Friday and Saturday. Most of it came from the safe."

"Busy weekend, big supermarket like this, relatively low level of security," Clark said. "Better, easier than hitting a bank." The others nodded.

"If this gang is that good, then why didn't they take the tape with them?" Whitaker asked.

"Well really," Cunningham answered, "what do you have with the tape? Completely covered and disguised perps. Only in view of the cameras for a few frames. They didn't take the tape 'cause they didn't want it."

Clark shook his head, sighed. "That, and they wanted us to see how good they are." *They'll be back.*

CHAPTER ELEVEN

Clark made some mental notes on the robbery as he drove to the hospital. *Definitely not local stuff.* He knew there were some distinct differences between this one and the typical robbery in Stuartsboro. For one, a robbery with three perps is rare; here, like most places, robberies are one- or two-man. Secondly, most robbers have three objectives: Get in fast, try to avoid hurting anybody, and get out faster. True, these robbers acted swiftly and with purpose, but the perp who shot the kid violated the second objective. He showed no regard for life and the shooting served no apparent purpose.

These robbers didn't waste any movement and, undoubtedly, they had staked out the store; Clark felt certain that they had been in the store at least once before the hit. They appeared to be carrying communications equipment, so there was probably a wheelman. That meant there were at least four perps involved in a violent robbery that could have turned into a murder, and still might.

Clark's cell phone rang, as he pulled into the hospital parking lot. "Hello."

"Lieutenant, this is Cunningham. Did you get the page?"

"Let me check." A pause. "No, nothin' since the grocery store, about an hour ago. Why?"

"I just got one from the PD. Dispatch said that Channel Three's been ringing our phone off the hook. They've got a reporter heading to the hospital. Thought you'd want to know."

"We've stayed off the air pretty well. Wonder how they picked up on it?"

"Probably on the EMS channel."

"Too good to be true, huh, shutting them out?" Clark asked. "Oh well, I'll meet you in the lobby. I'm here at the hospital now." *The media, one more distraction, one more thing to worry with.* Even though the media could be worrisome, Clark had developed a knack for dealing with reporters, and he respected them. He never forgot what former Chief Broward told him on more than one occasion: You treat people nicely who order their printer's ink by the barrel or, in this case, tell your story to a couple hundred thousand taxpayers. Then again, Clark reasoned, some exposure on this robbery might develop a lead, since these perps have most likely hit other cities.

Clark and Cunningham met Det. Wilkens at the emergency room entrance. Clark asked Wilkens, "What's the kid's status?"

"He came to right before they rolled him to the O.R. But like I told Whitaker, he's lost a lot of blood. Doctors had him stable as they prepped him for surgery. I heard from one of the nurses the kid came out of surgery a short while ago and they've upped his chances to 75-25. They removed the bullet from his leg, but the side shot was the one that could've been bad news. They're saying that after the bullet entered his side, it tunneled around, and ricocheted off the forth or fifth rib. By then the bullet's velocity had slowed down and stopped in the chest—no vitals hit—he's really lucky. This particular surgeon didn't have much experience with chest operations. He thought the kid should be more stable before they go in for that bullet."

"Family here yet?" Clark asked.

"Yes sir. His grandmother, he lives with her. A few other people. She's in bad shape, as you might suspect. They had to give her something."

"Where is she?"

"They're in the family room on the right," Wilkens said, pointing down the hallway to the door.

"Ready?" Cunningham asked his lieutenant.

"No. Never am, but let's go."

The family room was comfortable and well furnished, with a large plaid sofa and three matching wing chairs. Clark noticed a floor lamp in the corner, and he wondered if the soft, low light in the room was designed to help ease tension and heartache.

Clark walked slowly over to the family and scanned the room, but didn't recognize anyone. The woman whom he believed was the victim's grandmother, a lady in her mid-to-late sixties, sat in the middle of the sofa. She was anchored by two women and a man who could have been her children. She stared at the Kleenex in her hands, and squeezed it as if gripping it tightly might make some of the hurt go away. Her eyes looked tired and defeated. Her hair was tossed about, and Clark imagined that she had pulled it in the first moments of the shock. The woman beside her was whispering words to her, and patting her on the hand.

Wilkens introduced his superiors. "Mrs. Hall, this is Lt. Dixon and Sgt. Cunningham." She didn't look up, as both officers offered condolences.

Clark continued. "Mrs. Hall, we're going to do everything we can to find the people who did this. You have our word on that, ma'am. We're very sorry."

Slowly, she looked up at Clark, and in a small voice asked, "Why?"

"Why what, ma'am?"

"Why…?" Then her voice broke. "Why…would someone do this to Keith? He never hurt anybody. I don't understand."

The people to either side braced her with their arms. The man to her right looked up at the officers and nodded, as if to say, "Thank you, now please leave us alone, and go catch those bastards."

The officers left the family, found an empty conference room, and continued their investigation. "Whitaker, you're the lead on this, right?" Clark asked.

"Yes sir."

"What's the next step?"

Whitaker referred to his notes, then addressed the group. "Several things. We need to submit the tape to the Bureau for enhancement. They may be able to refine it to the point where we can pick up detail better in the weapons, features in their clothing, stuff like that. Also, we have the casings to submit for latent prints, not too promising, but worth a try."

Cunningham spoke next. "Wouldn't hurt to check with employees for any ideas on suspects; one of the perps could be connected to someone on staff." He panned around the table for a visual cue of agreement. "Need to check with management for employees who've been fired recently, and we should call the other Harris Teeters in the area for a similar case. Perps like hitting stores in a chain."

"Good thinking," Clark said. "Their corporate office is in Charlotte. I probably have the name of their security chief in my files. Anything else?"

"I'll check with patrol," Wilkens offered. "The team working tonight also worked Friday night. Maybe they've seen a 10-60 vehicle in this area, or at one of the other supermarkets. Dispatch may have logged in some suspicious license plates."

They sat silently for a couple of minutes. The wheels kept turning, grinding.

"Any ATM's in the area that may have picked up the vehicle?" Clark asked.

Wilkens lit up and blurted out, "Southwood Village, the First Union ATM."

"Keep our fingers crossed that it's working and can pick up street traffic at night," Cunningham said. He raised his stale cup of coffee in a mock toast.

Clark was next. "Well guys, looks like Stuartsboro just joined the ranks of Piedmont cities hit recently by this ruthless gang. The intel Williams gave us is very consistent with our case, wouldn't you say? I'll give him a call on Monday. Hopefully, the bullets we get from the boy will be good enough to analyze. If so, the lab's I.B.I.S. system may be able to connect our robbery with some of these area robberies. Sarge, how about stopping by the office on your way home and getting dispatch to send a fifty-mile radius message on our case. Ask for positive responses from other departments."

"Right."

Just as Clark was about to continue, there was a knock at the door. A security guard peeked into the room and asked, "Is there a Lt. Dixon in here?"

"Yes. What can I help you with?"

"Sir, there's a reporter out here looking for you."

"Thanks. I'll be right there."

Cunningham looked at him and smiled. "You can run but they'll always find you."

Clark looked around the table at some weary, but committed faces. "This is a tough one, I know you all understand that. Not a lot to go on. But we've got more to work with than other cases that we've solved. You all have full plates right now, but with Thanksgiving coming up next week and the four-day weekend, it's not going to get any better. Anyone off this week?"

"I'm off Wednesday through Friday, Lieutenant," Wilkens said.

Clark mulled over his staffing level. *Great, one less detective next week...that much more work for everybody else... 'Cops were like rats on a tread wheel...no matter how fast they ran, they ended up in the same place'.* "Okay, after you guys get through here, get some rest. Monday will be here before you know it. Thanks."

Clark made a quick call to Chief Brinks to get approval to speak on camera. He filled the Chief in on the case, and the upgraded status of the victim. "Not a lot to go on. The M.O. in this one is different from what we usually get."

"Looks like big-city crime has worked its way west and north to us," Brinks replied. "Williams was on target, I suppose. Have you called him yet?"

"No sir. I was planning on giving him a call on Monday. If this bullet is any good, I'll drive over and see him, and drop it off at their lab."

"Make sure patrol beefs up security checks for the next few days. Grocery stores and shopping centers, especially around closing. Okay? I'd rather you guys investigate a break-in than a robbery, or worse."

"Will do. See you on Monday."

Clark walked out to the hall but didn't see the reporter. He noticed a small group of people gathered outside the family room, and overheard some of their conversations.

One man said, "His old man is a crackhead; never had nothin' to do with Keith or his sisters. His mama comes and goes when she feels like it. If it won't for Barbara, I don't know where these kids would be."

Then the woman next to him spoke. "Keith's a smart boy. He's had jobs ever since he was old enough to work. Not scared to work like his father. Carried newspapers 'til he got the job at Harris Teeter."

Clark pretended to be reading notes from his legal pad as he continued to listen to others. With each comment, he began to sculpt a face and shape a life to go with what, at one point, was only a name and a statistic. The face was that of an average kid working an average job late on a Saturday night, except this kid was around the corner fighting for his life. Why it happened made no sense to Clark. He thought that it could've been his son, Ian. He felt like punching the wall. Kicking the wastebasket.

A few minutes later, Clark saw the reporter and cameraman across the E.R. lobby and approached them. The reporter was a tall, slender, attractive woman with short red hair, wearing a navy blue pantsuit. Clark introduced himself and gave her his business card. They stepped outside and she asked him several questions on camera about the robbery and shooting. To his surprise, the interview was fairly innocuous. The only "no comment" response he gave was to her question regarding the victim's condition.

When he walked back inside to the lobby, he noticed the E.R. waiting room was still packed at the early morning hour.

Cunningham walked up to Clark. "Just had a sexual assault victim to come in. Looks like there may be something to it. Who do you want to take it?"

"Where did it happen?"

"Over in Ann Ruston."

"Whitaker's got his hands full with this robbery. Wilkens is only working the front of the week. Your work is stacked up from being on vacation. Guess Sloan's sweet dreams are about to come to an end. Call Jerry."

Clark and Cunningham saw the Hall family gathering in the lobby, as the surgeon walked up to them. There was an abrupt silence, as he spoke in a subdued tone. Then someone began to wail. Keith Hall had slipped into a coma.

CHAPTER TWELVE

Capt. Blackburn entered Clark's office, caught his breath, wiped dust from his shirtsleeves, and straightened his tie. In a slightly excited voice, he asked, "Can you believe that guy...that anybody could be that drunk on a Monday morning? What ever happened to Sunday as a day of rest?"

Clark looked up briefly from the thick stack of weekend crime reports. "Sounds like he rested on a bottle all night." He was surprised by Blackburn's disheveled appearance. "What happened to you? Don't tell me you were downstairs in the middle of all that."

"Yeah. I heard the traffic on the scanner at the house when I was leaving for work. Call came in that a pick-up truck struck a pole on Main Street. D.W.I. arrest. So when I walked in the back door, I heard the dispatcher announce over the intercom they were having trouble with this guy. Somebody hit the panic strip in processing. I ran in and saw them wrestling with him. I jumped in and down we went...."

Clark interrupted him, using a parental tone, pointing a finger. "Four months 'til retirement. Have you lost your mind?"

"Yeah, probably," Blackburn confessed.

"Okay, so what happened next?" As Clark asked, Detectives Whitaker and Sloan walked into Clark's office and tuned in to the story.

Blackburn continued. "Next thing you know, the guy grabs Lamberth's O.C. spray."

"Uh-oh."

"He's a big guy, and he escapes from under the pile. He jumps up and staggers a little, squares off. Then he points the O.C. spray at us," Blackburn reported in a charged voice, eyes widening, reliving the moment.

Clark moved to the edge of his seat. "Then what?"

Blackburn broke into a slight grin, then a laugh. "The guy aims the canister, presses the button, and sprays himself right between the eyes!" The room erupted in laughter. "There's more, there's more," Blackburn said, as he raised his hands to quiet the crowd. "Susan wasn't satisfied that the guy was under control, right? So she pulls out her Taser...."

"She didn't?" Sloan asked.

"Oh yeah," Blackburn said. "She draws down on him, fires the Taser, and down he goes...like a fly swatted out of air."

"Ouch!" Whitaker exclaimed.

As he continued to chuckle, Clark said, "I gotta ask. Did the guy blow, after all that?"

"No, refused," Blackburn answered. "His third D.W.I."

"You know, this guy's hard-luck story sounds like a bad country music song," Clark quipped.

"How do you figure?"

"Well, you got a drunk, and a pick-up truck, for one." Clark paused to string some words together. "Okay, how about this: Drinkin' her off my mind on Sunday, wreckin' my pick-up truck on Monday. When my drinkin' didn't phase her, I got arrested then got the Taser."

More laughter.

"Definitely George Jones or Toby Keith material," Sloan said.

After a little more conversation, the detectives left Clark's office, and he continued with the police reports. Blackburn sat in a chair across from Clark and joined in on the reading, and he noticed the volume.

"That stack of reports on your desk looks like the Charlotte phone book," Blackburn said.

Clark commented, shaking his head, "What a weekend, huh? Looks like I've got a pot load of investigations to assign this morning. Got the robbery, Wilkens is off on the back end of the week, Cunningham's playing catch-up from his vacation, and Sloan's got a pretty bad rape from Sunday morning that's gonna take some work. Factor in the upcoming Thanksgiving holiday and...oh, by the way," Clark lowered his tone, "thanks for coming out Sunday morning."

"Sure thing. How's the boy doing?"

"Still in a coma last I heard. The surgery went well, considering. No vitals hit. They removed the bullet from his leg, but were afraid to remove the round from his chest, at least until the boy's condition improves."

"Was the bullet good quality?"

"A little deformed but some decent striation marks. I hope the lab can do something with it."

"Hope the kid makes it."

Clark didn't comment as he continued to process the reports. He sifted through several more and was beginning to feel a little overwhelmed. "Car and storage building break-ins, vandalisms, residential B&E's. You name it and we got it." Then he shook his head. "Not enough people to work these cases. I could use twice the staff that I've got." In jest, Clark asked, "Say Richard, how about loaning me a couple of your guys? Just for a few days."

"I love you, Clark," Blackburn gibed. "Just not that much."

Marilyn called Clark on the phone. "Good morning, Lieutenant. How are you?"

"Not too bad for a Monday, Marilyn. Better than I was on Sunday morning."

"I heard about the shooting, Lieutenant. So sad. How is the boy doing?"

"Still in a coma."

"Sure hope he pulls through. Lieutenant, Sgt. Smith is trying to reach you on the radio."

"Thanks." He reached down to turn up the volume on his radio and, when he did, his phone rang again. He decided to answer the phone first. "Lt. Dixon, may I help you?"

"Hey, Lieutenant, this is Katie in dispatch. We've got a unit out at Stuartsboro Jewelry, and they're requesting a detective."

"What do you have?"

"We're not sure. Sounds like a B&E but there's no forced entry to the building. They've got a couple of display cases that were smashed and a lot of jewelry stolen. Sounds like they got hit pretty hard."

Clark looked at his watch, and thought it was a little early for employees to be arriving at work. "Who found it?"

"The alarm activated, and we sent a car. The alarm company notified the manager and he arrived shortly after we did."

Clark was puzzled. "Alarm activation, but no sign of forced entry? Okay, I'll send somebody over there but it'll be a few minutes. Oh, uh, Katie, do you know how the manager's taking it?"

"Real upset," she said with emphasis.

"Finesse, I need finesse on this one…Cunningham," Clark muttered. Cunningham was a supervisor with a good mix of tact and diplomacy. Clark saw those qualities as today's equivalent of the nightsticks, blackjacks, and riot guns of his Stuartsboro PD forefathers. He called the conference room and filled Cunningham in on the sketchy details. Then Cunningham headed to the jewelry store.

Clark decided to call Sgt. Smith on the phone, instead of the radio.

"Sgt. Smith."

"Good morning, Sarge."

"Mornin', Lieutenant."

"If you're trying to contact me about the Stuartsboro Jewelry break-in, I've already got Cunningham en route."

"That's not it, although that one does sound a little odd to me," Smith said and paused a moment. "We've got a 10-67 here at The Meadows. I'm just getting here to the manager's office now, so I don't exactly know what we got. I heard the deceased was an elderly woman who lived alone. Her next-door neighbor found her. Right now, all I know is that the neighbor was hysterical after she found the body. Probably nothing, you know how it goes over here." After a short silence, he said, "Hey, this looks like the manager walking up now. Can you send one of your guys over?"

"Yeah, where do they need to meet you?" Clark asked. He heard Smith talk to someone, then he returned to the phone.

"Apartment 3-14," Smith replied. "It's on the bottom floor on the back side of the two-story here."

Clark hung up, called the conference room again, and Esposito answered.

"Where's Wilkens?" Clark asked.

"He just left for the D.A.'s office; he's got an appointment out there to go over some felony reports that are due this morning."

"Thanks," Clark said, "it'll be right on Brad's way."

Clark called Wilkens on his cell phone and filled him in on the assignment.

"No problem, Lieutenant," Wilkens said, in a forced voice. *Thirty minutes to make it to the D.A.'s office…The Meadows…I should make it okay.* He looked at his watch, tapped the wheel with his fingers, and sped up.

When Wilkens arrived, he noticed there was no crime scene tape around the apartment porch where Sgt. Smith was standing. Wilkens walked up with his processing box and legal pad and shook Sgt. Smith's hand.

"Hey Sarge, have you been inside yet?" he asked.

"No, just got here myself," Smith said. "Brad, this is Howard Simpson, the apartment manager. Mr. Simpson, Detective Wilkens."

The two exchanged greetings, then Simpson walked over to a group of residents.

Smith continued. "There's the next-door neighbor Mrs. Marshall," he said, pointing to a woman standing on the sidewalk in a small group. She was dabbing her eyes with a Kleenex. "Ruby Walker's the name of the deceased. She let Marshall keep a key to her place. Marshall hadn't heard anything out of her all weekend. Walker's car never moved, so she decided to go in a few minutes ago. That's when she found her. Ready to take a look?"

"Ready, warm, and willing."

The two officers stepped just inside the door, looked down, and saw Walker's body. They paused and slowly looked at each other.

"You think we should radio for more help?" Smith asked.

Wilkens didn't answer. He carefully studied the body, which was lying reclined in the chair. She was wearing a blue housecoat, with one hand in her lap, the other on the armrest. A *TV Guide* was open and face down in her lap. To Wilkens, she looked like she died peacefully in her sleep. He guessed she was in her late seventies, although with the severe skin discoloration it was difficult for him to assess. "Sarge, who was the last person to see her alive?" Wilkens asked, as he raised the window behind the chair to get some fresh air into the room.

"Don't know. The last to talk to her was Mrs. Marshall. She said that Walker called her last Thursday evening, right before Walker made a run to the grocery store. You know, to see if she needed anything. Marshall said that was around 5:00, news time. That's the best we can do right now."

Wilkens continued to study details about the body, and the surroundings. "Sarge, if you want to bring your guy in now to start the report, I think it'd be okay."

Smith summoned an officer as they continued to work the room.

Wilkens put on some latex gloves, checked the side pockets of the robe, and found balled-up Kleenex and a throat lozenge. He looked up and noted that the television was on, along with a floor lamp beside the recliner. Beside the recliner was a TV tray and he observed the items on it: Three bottles of prescription medication, the TV remote control, an empty glass, an ink pen, a stack of three *TV Guides*, a crossword puzzle magazine, a bag of hard candy, and four new double-a batteries in a pack. Wilkens took a minute to jot down his findings, then he glanced at his watch again.

Smith checked the bedroom thoroughly and everything looked in place, then he walked back into the living room. "Brad, E.M.S. is on the way. Her bed was made up, the room's neat as a pin."

Wilkens decided to do a quick walk-through of the house before he called his lieutenant. He noticed, overall, the apartment was very neat. In the kitchen, counters were clean, with the typical storage canisters and jars lined in neat array against the wall. There was an oversized black leather handbag on the oval-shaped kitchen table. He reached in the bag, pulled out a matching wallet, opened it, and examined the driver's license. He recognized the woman's picture as that of the lady he met at the community watch meeting, compliments of the large glasses that she wore. Wilkens saw plenty of cash in the wallet, then he put the wallet back in the bag. He made note of the typical items on the table, and also observed a couple of grocery bags.

Wilkens inspected the hall bathroom and bedroom and everything in those rooms was in order. No sign of a disturbance or anything unusual. He made a note that no lights were on elsewhere in the apartment.

"What do you think?" Sgt. Smith asked.

"Everything's looking okay to me," Wilkens said. He then told Smith about the community watch meeting last week, and how he met the Walker woman. "When we walked in, I didn't even recognize her."

Smith looked down at the body, shaking his head. "You know, you live, you die, in the middle you try to have a good time."

"Sounds like the makings of a classic bumper sticker," Wilkens said. "I'll call Lieutenant and fill him in. Can you check with the lady who found her and make sure the door was locked when she entered the apartment? A canvass of the neighbors wouldn't hurt either, and a lot of them are outside right now. I'd like to narrow down the time of death a little more if we can."

Wilkens called Lt. Dixon and took a couple of minutes to fill him in on his findings, trying not to omit any little detail or fact.

"What did you say about points of entry?" Clark asked.

"Hold on a second." Wilkens motioned to Sgt. Smith, who was outside talking with a couple of neighbors, to come over. "Sarge, what's the word on whether the door was locked or not?"

"The lady said it was. The knob lock, though, not the deadbolt."

"Thanks," Wilkens said, and then returned to the phone. "The door was locked, Lieutenant, and all the other points of entry were secure."

"Is time of death matching up with the condition of the body?"

"So far, yes sir." As Wilkens got closer to the body to study it, the stench was more obvious and it caught him off guard. He stepped away and took a deep breath, then re-approached. With his left hand he examined and worked the fingers of the left hand, the wrist, and left arm of the dead woman. "I think so, not much rigor left in the body. That'd make time of death pretty consistent with the last time she was seen, Thursday night, maybe Friday morning. The body has obvious signs of lividity, Lieutenant. Real splotchy patterns consistent with what she's wearing: Darker on the exposed areas, arms, neck, upper chest, lower legs. No signs of trauma."

"Sounds like everything's okay," Clark surmised. "Medical history?"

"She was taking Procardia for hypertension and Coumadin. That's a blood thinner, isn't it?"

"Yeah, stroke patients take it. How old was she?"

"Seventy-eight, a good age to live to. Looks like she died in her sleep. I could think of worse ways to go."

"Me too, Brad. Anything else?"

"No. I think that's about everything. You know, when I walked in, I didn't even recognize her 'til I located her driver's license."

"Why was that?"

Wilkens told his Lieutenant that he met her the previous week, and how seeing a petite woman with such large glasses amused him. "She wasn't wearing them when we found her; but when I saw her license, I realized who she was...."

Smith interrupted Wilkens. "Excuse me Brad, but is that Lt. Dixon you're talking to?"

"Yeah."

"Tell him I just talked to the M.E. and he's released the body to the funeral home."

"All right." Wilkens returned to the phone. "Lieutenant, did you hear Sgt. Smith?"

"Yeah. Sounds good to me. Anything else, Brad?"

"Yes, sir. I really need to head on to the D.A.'s office. Would it be okay if one of the patrol guys takes the photographs?"

"No problem."

CHAPTER THIRTEEN

Clark spent the rest of the morning catching up on paperwork and messages. He reviewed five felony reports that Esposito and Sloan had turned in, then signed off on a stack of case status sheets the detectives had submitted on inactivated cases. Next, he returned a number of phone calls, most of which were media inquiries about the Harris Teeter robbery: Were there any new developments in the case? Was there any change in the status of the employee who was shot? Surprisingly, he received three calls from citizens who heard about all the police cars at The Meadows this morning. They were concerned about the safety of elderly relatives who lived there. *Concerned or just nosey?*

Later, he opened a long list of e-mails and read them, responding to some and routing others. He came to the digital photos that Det. Whitaker had e-mailed him from the Tucker DOA call the previous Friday. For the most part, Price had done a good job with the pictures, covering the important aspects of the death scene. Clark opened each icon, which represented one photograph:

Front and back doors and door jambs.
Pocketbook, loose money and other valuables on bedroom dresser.
Medicines on bedside table, on bathroom shelf, and in living room on side table beside recliner.
Decedent's face (several photos).
View of decedent from several angles in room.
Bathroom, including close-ups of toilet and sink.
Kitchen, living room, and bedroom (several photos each room).
Exterior front and rear of apartment.

As he panned through the rest of the e-mail messages, his pager vibrated. It was Sgt. Cunningham's cell phone number, followed by the number "911". Urgent call. Clark called him.

"Hello."

"David, this is Lieutenant. Just got your page. What's wrong?"

Sgt. Cunningham had a light quality to his voice. "Lieutenant, I'm here at Stuartsboro Jewelry, the break-in. You're gonna love this one."

"How bad?" Clark couldn't tell if the news was bad or worse. Sometimes, David was a little hard to read on the phone.

"I got here shortly after the manager arrived, and he was still fumin'. He had taken a look in the front window and could see the smashed display cases, glass everywhere. Cases looked wiped out. He was pacing back and forth, chompin' at the bit to go in and do his inventory. But we told him we had to search and secure the place first, so he calmed down some. We went in and checked out the showroom area, glass scattered all over the place, like I said. Searched in the back of the store in the storage area and saw a couple sections of ductwork on the floor. We looked up and saw where a hole had been cut in the roof right above the ductwork so...."

"A roof job at a jewelry store?" Clark interrupted. "What's there to love? So far I'm not loving anything, David."

"You will, here's the good part," Cunningham declared. "So Smith calls Barham in for K-9. Barham starts the track in the storage area, below the hole in the roof, and right away Jackson sniffs and hits on a strong scent. He tracks like lightning to the back corner where they keep a few old storage shelves, counters, stuff like that. Jackson's going crazy, starts lunging, sliding all over the concrete floor. I'm thinking if he keeps this up, he's gonna tear Barham's arm off. We run back there and draw our guns and Jackson's barking non-stop trying to paw a sliding door open on a counter. All of a sudden we hear this voice inside the counter hollering, "Git that damn dog back! I give up; git him back!"

"Did it startle you?"

"Startle me? Oh, yeah, a real surprise."

Clark burst into laughter. *What a great morning.* "What was going on? Why did he hide instead of getting out of there?"

"Turns out the guy broke his leg on the fall. He said he thought the ductwork was a ceiling beam when he stepped inside. He put all his weight on it and down he went. Fell through and landed on the floor. He hobbled to the front, grabbed the jewelry, crawled back and hid in this counter. The manager's got all his stuff back. Man, is he thrilled."

Clark said, amidst a chortle, "The one that almost got away. Another happy ending in the little hamlet of Stuartsboro. Nobody got hurt, at least none of the good guys." They laughed again. "By the way, who's the guy?"

"Don't know him. Sandy Chrismon, white male, Winston-Salem address. He's not in our files; Marilyn checked for me." Cunningham told Clark he had some more processing to do and then he'd be clear.

A few minutes later, Clark called the Chief, briefed him on the call, and told him he would be leaving shortly for his meeting with Greg at the S.B.I. office. As he continued checking his e-mail, he ran across the photos from the Harris Teeter robbery. The photos appeared to be in the order of events as they occurred:

Overturned newspaper racks on front sidewalk.
Building front doors and locks.
Office door and office interior photos.
Floor safe; papers, currency, coins strewn about floor.
Office chair overturned.
Manager's face, arms, and overall photos (several angles).
Casings, individual and overall photos.
Aisle where shooting occurred, photos from both ends.
Live round on floor at back of store.
Blood smeared area on back counter where victim fell.
Large bloody area where victim lay.

There were several more photos, but the last one he viewed was enough. He routed the photos to the command staff, to his men, and to Greg in Greensboro. He went to evidence control and signed out the bullet and casings to take to the S.B.I. lab for analysis.

* * *

The headquarters of the Northern Piedmont District of the State Bureau of Investigation was located in downtown Greensboro. The offices were on the fourth floor of a modern four-story office building, in the financial and corporate center. All the operations of the District were located there except for narcotics, special operations, and evidence storage.

The building was completed two years ago to boost downtown renovation efforts, and was also home to insurance and professional services offices. The façade was constructed of deep red brick with green-mirrored windows that reflected a bright afternoon sun. The sidewalk at the entrance was ornate, made of brick, in a stylish basket weave pattern, and rustic wooden benches provided relaxing points for pedestrians. Potted trees with full, even branches, now bare, lined the sidewalks offering a nice, stylish touch. Large water fountains and lampposts decorated the courtyard area. Clark thought the overall scheme was professional, impressive, just like the Bureau. First class.

Clark entered the main lobby and heard the echoing voices of several people, dressed in business attire. He walked across to the elevator doors, pressed "4", and scanned the building directory; he noticed the Bureau offices were not listed. A security measure. Nine-eleven had changed a lot of things, including heightened security of law enforcement offices.

He stepped off the elevator, entered through an unmarked door, and walked over to the receptionist's window. Through the bulletproofed glass and intercom, he spoke with a friendly young secretary. "Hi, I'm here to see Agent Williams."

"Your name, sir."

"Lt. Dixon, Stuartsboro Police. He's expecting me."

"Just a moment please." She then called a number, spoke, and returned to Clark. "Yes sir, he's expecting you. Please come in." As she said that, he heard the door lock buzz.

Clark walked in onto plush dark green carpet and immediately noticed how quiet the area was. He made his way down a hallway furnished with handsome cherry tables and side chairs, and tasteful pictures on the walls.

Williams popped out of his office and met him at the door. "Well, lookie here," Williams said with a smile.

He was dressed in a sharp banker's gray suit, and Clark thought the necktie, regimented stripes of gray, black, and white, looked like it was made for the suit.

"What are you doing all dressed up?" Clark asked. "You're on the blue jeans detail." A reference to Williams' current assignment on the violent crimes task force.

"Court," Williams answered in a subdued tone.

"Sounds like a wasted day. Sorry." Clark pointed to the artwork beside his office door and said, "Say, you guys haven't hit any museums around here lately, have you? Impressive stuff, even for state employees."

Williams laughed but didn't respond to the rib. "I saw the robbery on Channel Three. Sounds like the gang we talked about."

"Looks like it to me, too."

"How's the employee who was shot?"

"A teenager, still in a coma."

They walked into Williams' office and sat down. Clark removed a small plastic baggie from his shirt pocket and handed it to him. "This is the bullet they took out of his leg. There's one still lodged in his chest that they decided was too risky to remove at the time." He looked at the evidence then back to Greg. "What do you think? Good enough?"

Williams put his glasses on and, using plastic tweezers, removed the bullet from the sealed baggie. He studied it, then moved it over to under the light of his desk lamp for closer examination. As he rotated the bullet, viewing it at various angles, he spoke in a slow, deliberate voice. "Looks like nine-millimeter…got some good marks…yeah…some good ones. It's kind of deformed, though. Honestly, may be a borderline classification case. I think you won't have any trouble matching this to a gun, but for I.B.I.S. quality, sometimes it's got to be a notch better. Tell me about the robbery. Enough similarities with the M.O. and the I.B.I.S. findings may be a foregone conclusion."

"Just the same, can you see if the lab will push this through for us?"

"I'll see what I can do," Williams said, "but no promises, okay?" Clark nodded. Williams added, "They're backed up but I think I can justify a rush due to the likelihood that your case is connected to ours. They tend to jump on evidence that's multi-jurisdictional."

Clark laid the case out for Williams, starting with the assault of the manager and ending with the robbers' flight from the scene, and all details in between. He briefed him on the vague clothing descriptions of the robbers, the apparent use of communications devices, what the store videotape revealed, and the statement given by the manager. Clark gave Williams a description of the crime scene, where the casings were recovered, and the theory about why and how the shooting went down. Then he told Williams about the manager's physical descriptions of the robbers. "The manager said medium tones, more on the darker side. One of them had thick eyebrows. White, black, Hispanic, who knows? Maybe a combination. They didn't talk much, very few words, one- and two-word commands."

Williams then spoke. "When you came in, I had just finished looking at the crime scene photos you e-mailed me. Looks and sounds a lot like the robberies in…let me see…." Williams took a minute to browse over the file in his lap.

Clark watched him and was impressed that Greg never seemed to be in a hurry when it came to formulating an opinion or getting the facts right.

Williams continued. "...High Point, definitely High Point...Winston-Salem...maybe two in Charlotte. We've got similar descriptions given by the other victims regarding skin tone. Some of the victims didn't have a clue about race, since these guys were covered head to toe."

"Just curious. Are they saying masks? Hoods? Scarves with stocking caps?"

"All of the above, but mostly hoods. Clark, another thing about your case. They hit you after closing, just like in most of our cases, at or after closing. They hit the safes for the big bucks. Some of the guys on the task force have named this gang, or these gangs, 'The Moonlight Bandits' because of that. Interesting about how few words they use, isn't it? Most other robberies we investigate, the perps aren't that tight-lipped. It's like they enjoy talking trash, street chatter."

"Better words than bullets." When Clark said that, he reached in his pocket and took out several baggies containing the casings from the shooting. "Speaking of bullets, maybe you'll have some luck with these." He tossed them on the desk.

"We'll see."

After comparing a few more notes, they went for a late lunch at a deli a few doors down the street. Over cold cuts, they talked some more about the investigations, and then shifted conversation to several major cases that Williams was working. Although Williams was an assistant supervisor, he had time to carry a small caseload. The most interesting investigation he talked about was a murder-for-hire case involving a minister and his lover in the city of Lexington. Williams spoke enthusiastically about his use of an informant in the case, and how he had gotten some incriminating statements on body wire over the weekend. Clark thought that Williams' work seemed so important. Even glamorous.

As they finished their sandwiches, a group of Williams' colleagues walked in. Clark recognized the two men, but he didn't know the woman, an attractive brunette who appeared to be about forty.

"Who's she?" Clark asked.

"Don't know her name. She's a detective with Siler City."

"Attractive. Pretty hair," Clark commented.

"Hey, Clark, no ring on her...."

"Greg, Greg. Always the matchmaker. Don't you ever give up?"

"Not until I succeed in my mission."

"Don't quit your day job."

* * *

On the way home, Clark reviewed the day's events and felt that it had been a satisfying tour. The morning started with a little humor over the skirmish with the D.W.I. suspect in the arrest processing room. That was one guy that Clark hoped had learned a lesson today, if no one else did. The day improved with the apprehension of the bumbling burglar at the jewelry store. With the probability of so few leads, that case would have been very difficult to solve and the jewelry would have vanished into thin air minutes after hitting the street.

Next, Clark replayed his meeting with Greg and felt good about it. The evidence he submitted could play a large part in solving this case, or at least in tying it to other robberies or shootings. He was confident in the abilities of his men, and had faith they would develop something. Finally, there was no good news about Keith Hall's condition today, but there was no bad news either.

Things on the work front seemed to be going pretty well, pretty well indeed. Even with so many crime reports coming in, his men seemed to be taking everything in stride. The holiday was approaching and that meant a nice long weekend of rest and relaxation for everybody. Then suddenly, the idea surfaced again that he would be spending Thanksgiving alone, or at best part-timing it with his kids.

As he took the Stuartsboro exit off the highway, he mused over the insane late night drive by Samantha's house. He was acting like a shy high school kid the day before the school dance, agonizing over whether or not to call the girl. Then, he thought about Greg and his good intentions to hook him up with someone, and that made him grin. Clark wished he could get out of this rut, this emotional stalemate his personal life was in. If only some door would open for him.

Tomorrow one would.

CHAPTER FOURTEEN

Three down and two to go. Whitaker marked through another name and called the next number.

Officer Larry Barber answered. "Hello."

"Larry, this is Price. How're you doing?"

"Pretty good. Recouping from the weekend, raking leaves, turning the garden over. What's up?"

"Working on the Harris Teeter robbery, mostly."

"Any decent leads yet?"

"Nothing all that significant, but it's early." Whitaker was trying to sound cool and collected, but inside he was pumped with enthusiasm. This was, without a doubt, his biggest case. It was drawing a large community interest, even picked up by Channel Three in Greensboro. And the media was calling daily for updates. Like everybody else, he hoped Keith Hall would pull through, but Whitaker needed to pursue this case meticulously, as if Hall wouldn't. Most of Whitaker's caseload involved juvenile investigations, fights and shoplifters, so this was his opportunity to prove he was more than a "kiddie cop". Then he said, "We're taking all the usual steps trying to generate some leads. Checking similar area cases, talking to local informants, combing over the store employee list. You know."

"Wasn't the victim a kid? How is he?"

"Still in a coma, as of early this morning. Larry, I'm calling everybody who worked the weekend shift to see if anyone remembers logging in any 10-60 vehicles on Friday or Saturday night. I'm trying to see if there were any vehicle stops of interest or if any tags were run that might give us a lead."

"What makes you so sure they had a vehicle?"

"A couple of things. These perps didn't have the look of our locals. Plus, the K-9 track ended abruptly on the side of the building, a good place for a pick up."

Barber pondered for a moment. "You know Price, we rolled from call to call Friday night, real busy. Calls didn't let up 'til around five on Saturday morning. Saturday night was the same way, so busy. I don't remember logging nothin' in."

"Would you've called the tag in to dispatch, if you had seen anything suspicious?"

"Probably not. Not with all the radio traffic that was going on, the dispatched calls, the traffic stops, and all. Tell ya what, I'll run out to my car and check my clipboard. I usually write tags down for later if something comes up. If I have anything, I'll call you right back. Where're you at?"

"My desk for a few minutes, extension 2347."

"Have you called the other guys yet?"

Whitaker referred to the list. "Everybody 'cept Marsha."

"Marsha? She's probably not gonna be much help. She got off early Sunday morning, and she took off Sunday night, too."

"When do y'all come back in? Thursday on days?"

"Yeah. I'm gonna go ahead and run out to the car."

"Thanks for checking. If I don't hear from you, enjoy your time off and I'll see you Thursday."

Whitaker called Marsha O'Connor's number, but there was no answer. Instead of leaving her a message, he decided to page her. As he waited for her to respond, he used Sloan's phone and called the lieutenant.

"Lt. Dixon."

"Lieutenant, Price. If you've got a second, I wanted to fill you on the Harris Teeter robbery."

"Sure, go ahead."

"I've checked with everybody on Hobbs' team, except Marsha. The team only logged in four vehicles for the two nights, and those have been run down. Nothing. I doubt if Marsha has anything, but I've paged her just to make sure. The fifty-mile message didn't yield responses from any department that Agent Williams didn't already tell you about. Uh, Brad checked on the First Union ATM camera but it only runs when the machine's in use. Dead end."

"Did you contact Harris Teeter security?"

"Hadn't had the chance to give them a call yet. The robbery this morning at Paschal's Grocery has put me behind a little."

"Yeah, I got the page on it last night. Any leads on that one?"

"A couple. White male enters the store, no customers in the place. He walks up to the counter to make a purchase. Soon as the clerk opens the register, the guy opens his jacket to reveal a gun in a shoulder holster. The clerk gave him the money and he ran out the door. The K-9 tracked to the entrance of the trailer park behind the store, but that was it."

"Do we know what kind of gun?"

"She thinks it was a revolver, but she's not sure."

"Is it worth doing a computer sketch? Would she make a good witness for that?"

"We can give it a try. Who's qualified to do them?"

"Sergeant and Esposito. It may be a good PR thing to do, regardless of the results, since Paschal's has had their share of robberies."

Whitaker continued. "Clerk said she'd never seen the guy before. He didn't wear any gloves, either. She didn't remember him touching anything but the video shows his right hand on the counter."

"Glass?"

"Yep. Got a half-decent lift that looks like his middle or ring finger. You got a second to take a look at it?"

"Yeah, now's a good time. By the way, did the guy try to hit the safe?"

"Nope, only wanted the drawer and he was two sheets in the wind."

"Come on in and I'll take a look at your lift."

Thirty seconds later, Whitaker stepped into Clark's office and handed him the latent lift card, along with the videotape from the store.

Clark studied the card. "You got some pretty good detail, Price, but I don't know if they'll be able to run it through A.F.I.S."

"Why not?"

"The print looks good enough to compare to a suspect, but it may not be of sufficient quality to run in the computer on a cold search. This looks like a looped pattern, but you need some more ridge detail here," he said, pointing to a smudged spot in the lower left area of the print. "Videotape any good?"

"A little blurry. Not too bad. Whoever knows the guy will probably recognize him and his clothes."

"Well, that's something. Not as bad as it could be. Why don't you make some photos from the tape and circulate them to the media, give some to patrol, and e-mail them to the other agencies in the county. This guy is probably from this area; I wouldn't think he'd come from too awfully far away for such a small take."

After Whitaker walked out, Clark popped the tape in the TV/VCR in his office and watched the robbery. It was just as Whitaker had described. Empty store, robber goes in, confronts the clerk, she hands over the cash and he flees. Lucky if he got more than a couple hundred dollars. Didn't even bother to hit the drop safe. Your classic "grab and run" armed robbery. Same crime and conceivably the same punishment as the Harris Teeter job—until the kid got shot. Only other difference between the two crimes was about sixty grand. The Paschal's robbery represented the typical case they worked, and watching it brought to light the stark contrasts between the two crimes.

* * *

Clark spent the middle of the day with the command staff, taking over three hours to discuss and select the best candidates from the large stack of job applications for three patrol officer vacancies. The pre-employment process was tedious and it took many hours to screen applicants, who nearly all looked the same on the one-page form. The process also required oral boards, interviews, background investigations, medical and psychological examinations, among other tasks. Clark periodically glanced at the clock on the conference room wall. He wanted to end the day at a decent hour so he could get to the gym for a much needed workout.

Back in his office, Clark read several police reports that filtered in over the course of the morning, including some that were from incidents and crimes on Monday. He read the break-in report from Stuartsboro Jewelry and cracked a smile.

Then he carefully read the D.O.A. report relating to the call that Wilkens responded to and investigated. Everything in the half page narrative reinforced what Wilkens had discovered and apprised him of. When a detective wasn't called to a questionable death scene, it was difficult to eliminate foul play or suspicious circumstances with only a couple of paragraphs to read and evaluate.

Clark thumbed through several more reports and was frustrated by the steady flow of car break-ins and outbuilding larcenies. They just kept coming and victims wanted action, not a case inactivation letter. In reality, very little could be done about crimes like these, aside from catching the perps in the act.

He looked at his watch and decided that he had time to catch up on his e-mail before heading to the Y.M.C.A. He checked several messages from the S.B.I. and F.B.I. that related to a national terrorism alert. It was a perfunctory process, reading and deleting these intel bulletins on a daily, sometimes hourly, basis. Threat level warnings, BOLO's, recommended precautionary measures that had nothing to do with Stuartsboro, North Carolina. *If a terrorist event happened here, God help us, they would be happening everywhere.*

His next e-mail was from Whitaker and contained the crime scene photos from the Paschal's robbery. No need to study those so he routed them to the unit and staff. Then he came to the photos that Wilkens sent him from the D.O.A. call at The Meadows. Clark clicked on the first icon, an exterior shot of the front of the victim's apartment. He then opened several more of the icons and looked at photos of:

Front and back doors and door jambs.
Decedent, several photos of close-ups of face, body extremities. Several full-body photos and photos of lap area.
TV tray and items on it, several photos. Also, several photos at angles to include both TV tray area and victim.
Television screen, turned on.
Handbag on kitchen table. Several photos of kitchen table and contents.
Bathroom, including close-ups of toilet and sink.

There were five or six more photos in the e-mail, but Clark was satisfied and decided not to open them. He quickly read several more messages and routed a couple.
He checked his voice mail and had four messages. After listening to the first three, the last one played: *"Clark, this is Sam. When you get the chance, give me a call. I want to speak with you about the family plans for Thanksgiving...Oh, and Clark, Bri's car needs some repair work. I need to talk to you about that, too. Thanks."*
Family plans for Thanksgiving? Wonder what that was all about? He wasn't in the frame of mind to call her, not right now. Bri's car needed work? Money was tight.

* * *

Clark began to feel revived during his workout at the Y.M.C.A. He hit the weight room when it was empty and helped himself to a good chest/shoulder routine. He started with the bench press and completed five sets of five reps, starting at 185 lbs. and working up to 255 lbs. Then he worked some reps on the military press, maxing at 155 lbs. Next, he moved to dumbbell flies and raises, sets of ten. He was working with a good burn by this point, feeling pumped from the release he got by shocking his muscles.
He moved to several sets on the dip and pull-up bars, and finished his routine by hitting the mat for some push-ups. He started with a set of forty,

rested thirty seconds, attempted to do a set of thirty, rested, and continued for several more sets, each set to failure. With the last push-up in each set, his arms and chest trembled with strain as he gave all he could to complete the round. As he fell to the mat with each failure, his chest and arms felt an intense ache, and he gasped for breath. He craved this kind of workout, though, working the stress out of his body, forcing his muscles and stretching them to their limit.

The day was unseasonably warm for mid-November, and Clark decided to take his run outside. It was always his preference over the treadmill. He wondered if part of the reason for feeling that way was due to his belief that the treadmill reminded him too much of his job—all that effort and going nowhere.

As he walked outside, the sun blanketed his face with heat and it felt good, kind of like the first warm, breezy day of March. Short sleeves. Top down on the convertible, listening to the Beach Boys.

He loosened up, did his stretches, adjusted his headphones, and turned on his Walkman. He walked briskly for a block, then he kicked into a jog through a residential area. After about a mile, his wind and legs were adjusted and the jog was easier. Clark enjoyed the songs playing on his oldies radio station, as it paid tribute to the Platters. He ran down through Hillsdale Park, which marked the 1.5-mile point, halfway.

Clark struggled just a bit on a hill that marked the return route to the "Y", but even a rough run gave him a feeling of liberation…no pager…no phone…nobody…just him and the road. As he ran up Maynard Street, he was within a half mile of his destination, so he tried to pick up the pace.

He crossed the intersection, headed north on the sidewalk, and glanced to his right. Suddenly, he saw a vision about thirty feet away, and he was stunned. She stood at the end of the sidewalk sorting through the day's mail. Every stride he took closer to her, the more beautiful she became. She had auburn hair that flowed gracefully in soft curls to her shoulders. The face of a goddess, with soft gentle lines. Her dress was black with a short hemline. It was the kind of dress that looked like it was designed to conceal a curvaceous body and it wasn't doing a very good job. Everything was right. Flawless.

His eyes wandered down to incredibly sexy legs, toned and shapely, with elegant black high heels. As he approached, she glanced his way, meeting him with captivating eyes that caught him and wouldn't let go. He was at a loss when she smiled and said hello, but he managed a quick wave as he passed her. *Whew, how sexy can a woman be?*

He ran another twenty yards and couldn't resist a quick look back. When he turned, she was watching him as she walked up the sidewalk. Clark was a little embarrassed, but he discovered a newfound burst of energy. He broke into a sprint for the quarter mile back to the "Y". Nothing like the sight of a beautiful lady to inspire a middle-aged jogger to peak performance. And she was watching him, too. As he ran to the parking lot and began his cool down, the Platters song "The Wonder of You" began to play on his Walkman. "Now that's appropriate," he said, catching his breath. *She is a wonder.*

After fifteen minutes in the sauna, Clark showered and dressed. He checked his pager and saw a page from the Chief: "*Meet in my office at 4:30 for a short meeting*". Clark had fifteen minutes to get there. What could there be this time of day? Short afternoon meetings had a way of turning into marathons with the Chief, especially on a pretty day, when you wanted to punch out on time. Clark began to speculate about why the Chief was calling the meeting. Maybe he wanted an update on the Harris Teeter case? What a lovely shade of auburn. Perhaps a complaint with the way the Paschal's investigation was handled? Black, and short. A follow-up to the personnel meeting earlier? Incredible legs, definitely a dancer or runner.

Clark looked in the mirror and adjusted the knot in his necktie. *And you're the officer who takes pride in knowing your beat. Looks like you just got thrown for a loop.* Who was she? He was sure that he had never seen her before; her, he would remember. Does she live there? Visiting?

He walked out the front door of the "Y", squinted at generous November sunshine, and had an optimistic thought. *The case of this mysterious woman may take some investigation.* As he crossed the parking lot to his car, he sang, "...a beauty so true, it makes me wonder...the wonder of you."

* * *

Officer Marsha O'Connor received the page from Det. Whitaker and returned his call twice, but she got his voice mail. She decided not to leave him a message. After all, she was off-duty and if he wanted her to contact him that badly, he should have been by the phone. Those detectives could be worrisome about the smallest things. She was trying to enjoy her last two days off before returning to dayshift on Thursday.

Getting off work early Sunday morning and taking off Sunday night had afforded her a little extra time away and it was nice. She was thinking about heading up to Hanging Rock State Park for a day of hiking to take advantage of the pleasant weather.

There were two important things that O'Connor didn't know. She was in possession of valuable evidence in the Harris Teeter investigation. And she was on course to destroy it.

CHAPTER FIFTEEN

"Has he called you back yet?" Bridget asked.

Samantha Dixon shuffled papers on her desk trying not to appear all that interested in the conversation. "No, not yet. But I didn't leave the message 'til late yesterday afternoon. He'll probably call back this morning." She knew that Bridget meant well, but she could be annoying sometimes.

"How do you think he's going to take it, your idea about Thanksgiving?"

Samantha leaned back in her office chair, massaged her neck and took another sip of bottled water. "I don't know, Bridget, but it seems to make sense. I'll have the kids for lunch and he'll have them for dinner. It's fair, nobody gets mad, no feelings get hurt. Then next year we flip-flop. He's got to know that this is an amenable solution to an awkward situation. Right? That's the way it's done." She said it in such a way that sounded as if she were trying to convince herself more than her co-worker.

"Girl, the perfect solution would be for the two of you to sit down together for Thanksgiving with your children, the children that both of you raised. After all, you and Clark are on good terms, aren't you?"

Samantha was checking her make-up in the mirror and gave Bridget a sharp glance. "Please don't start on that again, not today. Why are you always hell bent on trying to get us back together? I told you, it's no good. It was rotten when we ended it and that's how it would start back. Rotten. And worse, it could give the kids false hope that things are on the mend. They've been hurt enough. Things are better now. Everything finally seems to be getting back on track. For them, for everybody." Samantha looked around for eavesdroppers in the hallway. Her cubicle didn't afford her much privacy and Bridget always seemed to get louder as conversations developed.

Bridget countered. "Are you sure that it's the kids that you're worried about getting false hope?"

"What's that supposed to mean?"

"Come on, Sam, it's so obvious. I mean look at you. Since your divorce, you haven't dated, hardly any. You've turned down dates with a couple of the biggest babe magnets in the office. You work, you go home, you work, you...."

"Stop already. I get your message...look, I thought I'd be out of this funk by now, but I'm not—end of story. I'm not forcing anything. When I'm ready to go out again, I'll know it. Right now, though...." She paused a moment, leaned over to Bridget, and lowered her voice. "Right now, I'm concentrating on this promotion. You know that. I've worked hard for it, and I've got to sink a lot of time into this to make it happen."

Bridget saw the opening and pounced. "Concentrating on promotion? Sink time into your work? Seems like you were shooting venomous darts at a certain police lieutenant about two years ago when he was *concentrating* on making captain."

"Foul, Bridget. Not fair. It's different now. I don't have a spouse. Back then, he did, and his job was his first love, and I was second or third—or whatever place I was. It's no good, trust me," she said, shaking her head, then placing several hanging file folders in her side drawer.

"Oh, come on. It couldn't have been that bad."

"Yeah, it got that bad. 'Cause you know what's worse than animosity or bitterness?"

"No, but I think I'm getting ready to find out."

"Indifference. That's right, indifference. And that's what happened to us. We grew apart, slowly, kind of the way your favorite houseplant, sitting on the windowsill, gradually dries up, wilts, then dies. Except this kind of death is slower, much slower. You don't even feel it or notice it when the blooms fall or when the leaves drop. You don't hear a sound, don't see a thing. Then one day you realize the plant is dying and all the sunlight, water, fertilizer you give it isn't enough," she said, slamming the drawer shut.

"And Clark feels the same way?"

"Who knows? We still don't talk. Kind of like we're still married, huh?" Samantha said sarcastically.

"I bet he still loves you. And I noticed that you, my dear, never actually said in this conversation that you don't love him."

"You, Bridget," Samantha said, as she shook her head, smiled, and leaned back again. "You should be writing soaps or romantic cards for Hallmark."

"Love you girl, gotta run," Bridget said, patting her on the shoulder.

Just as Bridget walked away, Samantha's phone rang. "Protective services, Dixon."

"Hey Sam," Clark said. "Got your message yesterday but I had a busy afternoon. How's your day going?"

Samantha sighed. "Not too bad. Just got through watching a soap opera."

"What?"

"Nothing," she sniffed. "Thanks for calling back. Bri needs some work done on her transmission. Tom at Vogler's Garage said that if we don't get it done now she's going to have some major problems. With the low mileage on the car, he said he'd definitely have it fixed. He gave me an estimate of $620.00 but said that was a rough estimate, could be more or less. Can you pay half on it?"

"I get paid early, next Wednesday, since Thanksgiving's next week. Can it wait 'til then, or did he say?"

"He said that we need to have it done pretty quickly." A pause. "I tell you what, she'll just have to ride in every day with me and she can use my car when she has to work." Another pause. "Clark, I wanted to check with you to see if you've had any ideas about Thanksgiving."

He knew the statement meant that she had something in mind. "No, I haven't really thought much about it."

She got straight to the point. "How would you feel about the kids eating lunch with me and dinner with you?"

"I suppose that'll work." He really didn't know what else to say. Sam had been fair about the holidays. And that's pretty much the way things were when it came to compromise and resolution. Just verbal agreements—no referees. He knew from some of the divorced guys at work just how bitter and ugly things could get, and how broke they were at payday. Ironically, Clark almost wished she would display some kind of aggression, some emotion. Maybe if she did, it would jumpstart things, one way or the other, between them. He hesitated briefly, then decided to ask it. "Say, uh, Sam, I was wondering if you might be interested in getting together one evening for dinner?" He gazed out the window and braced for her answer.

A long silence. Caught off guard, she paused a moment, thinking that saying "no" could mean "no forever", and saying "yes" could mean "yes, people are going to get hurt, again". Then she suddenly blurted out, "Clark, there's trouble with a customer in the hallway. I've gotta go. I'll call you back."

Click.

Slowly, he placed the phone on the receiver and wondered what *really* happened. He considered calling back and checking on her story, but let it go. He felt like an idiot, vulnerable and desperate. He sat there and took a moment to question his motives for asking Sam out. Why now after all these months?

Was it she whom he really wanted to be with? Or was it just a case of his romantic interest, in general, being rekindled by seeing the beautiful stranger yesterday? Either way, Sam said she'd call back, and she was good for it. *Guess the guy's invited the girl to the dance. Now comes the sweat.*

* * *

Chief Brinks gave them an inquisitive look and asked, "Anything new at the S.B.I. intelligence meeting?"

Capt. Blackburn took his cue from Clark to go first, and began. "Overall, it was a good program. The 'Who's Who' in law enforcement was there. Most all the RAC's and SAC's from the Bureaus and the D.E.A., the Chiefs from Winston, Greensboro, Charlotte, I think High Point. It was well-attended, about seventy-five there."

"Who actually presented the program?" Brinks asked.

"The RAC from Charlotte, Lawson. Sharp guy, gave a PowerPoint presentation on current strategies of Al Qaeda, and shared some theories about why they haven't hit again. It was really interesting; it's a subject everybody keeps asking about. He offered some pretty plausible theories."

As Blackburn continued, Clark daydreamed, tuning in and out, just as he had done at the intelligence meeting. His mind wandered along parallel tracks, Sam on one and this beautiful stranger on the other. He wondered what Sam's response to dinner was going to be? How she felt about him now? He also wondered if he would ever run into the mysterious woman again. Which did he hope for more? And why?

The Chief seemed focused on Blackburn's report. "Which theories impressed you the most, Richard?"

"For one, Al Qaeda has always shown that it's more than willing to wait a good while, years if necessary, to execute its plan. Lawson gave the example of the two strikes on the World Trade Center—seven, eight years apart. We think in terms of months or holidays, the terrorists think in terms of years. Another theory is that Al Qaeda has tried to attack us, but failed; the French Intelligence Service has helped intercept several planned strikes that were developing overseas against us. Most of these cells were discovered and disrupted due to their efforts, along with the British." Blackburn looked at Clark, turning the floor over to him.

There was a pause. The Chief looked at Clark and asked, "Well, what about you?"

Clark looked at Blackburn, then to the Chief. "I was impressed with the theory of why the tactic of suicide bombers doesn't work here. You'd think that this kind of low-level attack would have been easy to pull off by now. One bomber on a crowded street or at a high-profile event could send our country into upheaval. The experts are saying the terrorists may hate our lifestyle, but they may learn to accept us and may change their minds about murder. They have to integrate in the community because isolated terror cells could bring attention to themselves. And when they're forced to integrate, they see people more as human beings and less as targets."

Clark explained further. "The way they pick and deploy their suicide bombers brings this key point of isolation to light. When they choose the bomber candidate, they'll send him on his mission within a day, usually that quickly. Then overnight, they isolate him in a room and work him into a frenzy by shouting dogma, quoting verses, pumping him up, that kind of thing. Isolation is the key."

As Blackburn resumed the conversation, Clark drifted again. Terrorism talk may impress Brinks, but it wasn't high on Clark's agenda. He had a lot more, much closer to home, to worry about. Like making some arrests in all these car B&E's and assaults they were having. He wanted to nail this violent robbery gang, before it struck again. And he was concerned about Keith Hall, who was still in a coma; every day, Clark faced the grim possibility that the kid might not pull through. He was also concerned about the sharp increase in crime and if his men could keep up, keep their morale up. These things bothered him more than terrorism. These were the relevant issues.

On the drive home, there was something that kept nagging at him, but he didn't know what it was. Something he had overlooked? It was the kind of feeling he had whenever he left for a vacation and wondered if he turned the stove off or remembered to pack everything. Was it a phone call he failed to return? An e-mail he forgot to send? *Nagging feeling.*

* * *

Mario Slade slipped a blunt under the table to his cellmate, as a guard walked by. Slade spoke in a low voice, "Easy, bro, easy. Eyes on us." He looked at his mate, grinning, and asked, "Where's my shit, man?"

"I'll get it, you know what I'm sayin'. Wait 'til we get to the rec room. That dude up there," he said, nodding to an inmate trustee at the entrance, "he's holdin'. Just chill, you know what I'm sayin'."

Slade continued eating his lunch, thinking about how badly he wanted to get out of the place. His bond had been lowered to $10,000.00, but he still needed some help. Another day in this hellhole, and he was going to have to kill somebody. He wanted to get his girl and he wanted to get high. Made no difference which order. As he took another bite of his sandwich, he overheard two inmates talking at the table directly behind him. At first, he was drawn to their conversation by the low volume. Then he was drawn to what they were saying:

"They…out of…boro…A couple of stores…come off looking like…Shooting up the…cleaned out the…."

One voice was deep and throaty and the other was more like his. As he strained to eavesdrop, he could only understand a few words. He didn't dare look around, not until he had a reason to. He decided to hurry and finish his plate, before they did, so he could get up and get a look at them. He continued to listen:

"…Uzis and some kind…don't play…Hit three or four…make…by using…Black military…Uzi shit."

Slade listened intently as he gulped his last bite. He rose from the table, looked at his cellmate and said, "Later."

"What about your shit?"

"I'll get it. Tell him to hold it for me." Then, Slade walked up to the window and slid his tray through the opening. He turned around and walked slowly to the exit. As he did, he cut a look their way. He knew the shorter one with the beard; they called him "Fatmeat." Slade didn't know the white dude, but he'd find out, and quick. He was looking at his ticket out. He could almost feel his girl in one hand and a cold thirty-two-ounce brew in the other.

CHAPTER SIXTEEN

The Dragon Garden Restaurant was not that busy when they arrived. Capt. Simmons called Capt. Blackburn on the radio, "We're 10-23 if you want to join us. They don't look too 10-6."

"10-4," Blackburn responded, "I'm a couple of blocks behind you. Be there in a minute."

As they pulled into a parking space, Simmons turned off the car and asked Clark, "Just want to wait here for him?"

"Nah, let's go on in. He gets sweetened tea. I'll order for him."

"Hey, Clark, we got interrupted a while ago. So how do you feel about what she said?"

Clark reflected for a moment. He could talk to Simmons. Dan was a decent guy, who had been through a divorce several years ago, a sloppy one that nearly cost him his bars. A voice of experience Clark could use. "Guess I should've expected it. Don't quite know what got into me. Divorced nearly a year, and then I go and do this. What a fool," he said, with a nervous laugh.

Simmons laughed. "A woman can make a man do some strange things, Clark. Happens to all of us."

Clark unbuckled his seatbelt and glanced out the window. "You know, Dan, maybe I need to push myself back out there and start playing the field a little, make something happen. Damn, it's been so long, seems like forever ago."

"Guess the last time you dated, Eisenhower was President?"

Clark laughed. "Not quite that long ago." A brief pause. "She said not right now, that it was a bad time. Said she didn't think it'd be a good idea."

"Hey man, you know women. Who ever knows? Heck, Clark, no harm, no foul. If you feel like it, call her again in a few days, maybe after Thanksgiving. Do you think there's some kinda chance for you two?"

"I doubt it," Clark replied. "It's just that some of these old feelings have come back. A couple of weeks ago, I would've told you that things were as through as the day we signed the papers. Finished—which makes no sense that I asked her out. Right? It's like any time I spend time with the kids it's great, nothing like it. But there's a piece of the puzzle..." then he cupped his hands together to demonstrate, "...a three-dimensional puzzle, where a wife is missing on this side, a mother on this side, on this side a confidant is...." He didn't finish the sentence. After a slight pause, he continued, "One miss, but in a lot of places, I guess. It's tough," he said, clearing his throat, "tougher than I would've thought."

"Least you're looking at it for all the right reasons. Me, I tried to make it work with Portia to keep the house, the cars, all that. Jerome was almost out of school, old enough to understand things weren't working out. At some point, you may have to let go. Are you seeing anybody?"

"Not exactly."

"By not exactly, you mean 'no', right?"

Clark didn't answer.

Simmons looked in the rear view mirror and saw Capt. Blackburn pulling into the parking lot. "Richard's here. You ready?"

"Ready. Hey, Dan?"

"Yeah?"

"Nothin'."

The three of them walked in, and Traci met them with menus. "Well, if it ain't the three wise men," she said, teasingly.

"Funny, Traci. I wasn't in the mood to tip today, anyway," Blackburn cracked. He thought Traci was cute, and the guys always enjoyed her ribbing. Expected it. Sometimes it was better than the wonton soup.

Traci pointed to each man as she sounded off, "Unsweetened tea with lemon, sweetened tea no lemon, and ice water, lemon."

They laughed.

Clark shook his head and grinned. "You know, I think Traci is God's way of telling us we've come here way too much." They laughed again.

"At least she didn't say 'three wise-asses'," Simmons said.

The meals were delicious, something they could always count on. Conversation, as usual, centered on work. Complaining about the lack of officers to do the job, unrealistic deadlines to meet, citizens that couldn't be satisfied.

Blackburn looked at Clark. "How're the chicken wings?"

"Great, as usual. Your sesame chicken looks good."

"No complaints."

Simmons chimed in, "I got an idea. Let's split everything, make a little buffet here." Traci brought them a couple extra plates and refilled their drinks. They passed their servings around the table, scraping portions onto their plates.

Clark took a bite of the twice-cooked pork that was Simmons' contribution. "Awesome, Dan. We got the better end of this deal."

Talk shifted to holiday plans for Thanksgiving and Christmas.

Midway through the meal, Clark looked up and saw Sloan and Esposito walking in. Clark hoped nothing was wrong, but he could tell, with the deliberate steps that Esposito took toward his table, something was up. The captains got quiet as the young detectives approached.

Esposito spoke. "Lieutenant, we just got a call from the hospital about Keith Hall."

Clark felt his heart racing. He braced himself for bad news.

"He came out of the coma a little while ago," Esposito said. "The nurse said he's doing good. Surgery maybe in three or four days. Thought you'd wanta know."

Everyone exchanged a look of relief, and then Esposito and Sloan went to another table. Cunningham and Wilkens, who had just walked in, joined them.

Clark continued his meal, thinking about Hall. Whether they solved the case or not, Hall was just about out of the woods, and Clark felt a burden removed. He noticed that even the food tasted a little better. News of the kid's recovery sparked talk about the investigation, so Clark updated the captains.

After a minute of quiet, he switched conversation. "By the way, do I owe either of you anything? A reply on something? Do something for you?" He sputtered, as he seemed uncertain how to properly phrase the question.

"Not me," Blackburn replied. "Why?"

"Whatcha talkin' about?" Simmons asked.

"Probably nothing. I got this feeling like I forgot to do something," Clark said. "If it's not something for either of you, then it's probably no big deal."

"What about the Chief?"

"Nah. Only time I spoke with him yesterday was when Richard and I briefed him on the training we went to." Clark asked Blackburn, "He didn't ask us to do anything, did he?"

"Uh-uh."

Suddenly, the guys at the other table burst into laughter.

Simmons turned to check it out. "Wonder what that's all about?"

Clark answered, "My guess? Jerry probably tried to hit on Traci and got egg drop soup in his lap."

As they chuckled, the light moment was interrupted as Blackburn raised his hand, "Shh. Listen." Radios at both tables blurted: *"Repeat, all units available, 10-65 silent alarm, Bi-Rite Grocery Store, 2282 Riverside Road."*

Without a word, officers sprang from both tables, as Cunningham dropped a glass, shattering it on the floor. Startled customers turned to look, as the seven men sprinted for the door. Blackburn jogged to his car, and shouted to Esposito to take the rear of the store. Clark and Simmons hopped in Blackburn's unmarked Chevrolet, as they could hear a couple of patrol sirens in the distance.

"Damn!" Blackburn yelled. "They need to cut their sirens before they cause a hostage situation." Blackburn radioed the order to the officers, then he screeched tires pulling onto the street.

They were about twenty blocks away.

Clark advised headquarters that the three of them were en route to the call. "Units 3, 4, and 7 are 10-17."

Cunningham did the same for their vehicle. "Units 19, 24, 26, and 35 same traffic."

Headquarters acknowledged, *"10-4 all units."*

Esposito had the jump on Blackburn as the two sedans darted in and out of thick noon hour traffic. They barreled onto Richardson Drive.

"You guys thinking what I'm thinking?" Clark asked. His adrenalin was pumping like a Texas oilrig. "Can't be."

"They wouldn't come back this quick," Simmons said, trying to offer reassurance.

"Could be a false alarm," Clark said. "Nearly all of 'em are."

"Keep those positive thoughts comin'."

"All units responding to Bi-Rite, be advised there is no answer at business on call-back. Be advised no answer on call-back."

"Shit! So much for positive thoughts."

Patrol Lieutenant Edd Johnson then radioed instructions to his responding units. "Unit 23, take position for north and west sides; unit 31 take south and east."

"31, 10-4."

"Unit 23, 10-4."

Blackburn nearly rammed into a garbage truck, which had cut in front of him, and then passed it. "Dumb-ass!" he shouted, as he tried to keep pace with Esposito. The two cars veered onto Courtland Avenue. On the sharp turn, Blackburn's notebook and walkie-talkie slid across the dash and dumped to the floorboard.

Nine blocks away.

Within two minutes, units 23 and 31 radioed that they were approaching the area.

"Unit 23 to headquarters, I'm turning onto Riverside now."

"31's a block away."

"*10-4, 23 and 31.*"

"This don't fit them, busy, middle of the day," Clark said. He made the statement as if he believed that words of logic and reasoning might magically alter the course of anything bad that was about to happen. Clark grabbed the mike and called Lt. Johnson, "Unit 12, two unmarked units will be 10-23 in a minute. Where do you want us?"

Four blocks away.

"Unit 23 has a visual, headquarters."

"County 47 to Stuartsboro, your channel. We have two units five minutes out."

"Shotgun in your trunk, Richard?"

Lt. Johnson responded to Clark, "If you can, park where you can observe traffic at the front and rear."

"*10-4, 23. 10-4, County 47.*"

"10-4, 12," Clark replied to Johnson's request.

"Uh..." Blackburn mumbled, but had to think for a second, "...in the trunk, shotgun's in the trunk." He turned right, hot on Esposito's bumper. "I'll pop the trunk when we pull in the lot and you grab it. We'll be out of view, safer to do it there. Clark, you're plain clothes. This may be your day."

Clark responded sarcastically, "Thanks a lot, Richard."

Blackburn replied in kind, "You detectives get *all* the fun stuff. Seriously, everybody be careful. This may be it."

One block away.

Clark radioed their arrival. "Units 3, 4, and 7 are on Riverside, check us 10-23."

"Unit 31 has a visual, headquarters."

"*10-4, all units.*"

"Headquarters, we need to have a K-9 en route."

"31 to 23, do you see anything yet?"

"*Traffic for headquarters, repeat.*"

"Unit 12 to headquarters. Any contact, yet?"

"*Unit 12, were you requesting K-9 at the scene?*"

"Negative, headquarters," Johnson snapped. "Have you made contact yet?"

"Negative, unit 12. Still trying to make contact."

Lt. Johnson called Capt. Blackburn on the tactical channel, "Captain, you guys there yet?"

"We're here in the parking lot now," Blackburn replied, as Simmons got out and grabbed the shotgun from the trunk. The shopping center parking lot was packed, typical for mid-day. "I'll advise you of something shortly."

Simmons jumped back into the backseat and racked a round in the Remington 870. Blackburn unsnapped his holster.

Clark switched the radio back to channel one and announced that they were on-scene, and Esposito did the same.

Blackburn called Esposito. "26, what does it look like back there?"

"So far, so good. Everything looks 10-4. Got a couple of delivery people back here. Stockers unloading a truck, regular stuff."

Blackburn eased into a parking space a couple rows from the front, as the three of them watched the front doors like eagles from a perch. They knew the perps could look like anybody, trying to blend in, especially at this busy time of day.

"All units on scene. Be advised that customers seen coming and going. Everything appears 10-4 at the moment," Clark radioed.

"Unit 12 to headquarters, any contact yet?"

"Negative. Still trying. The line was busy on the last attempt; now it's ringing again."

After another minute, Blackburn looked at Clark, "That don't sound good. What do you make of it? If the hold-up is in the office, wouldn't a customer have made 'em by now?"

"I doubt it," Clark said. He reached down, unsnapped his ankle holster, drew his .380 Sig, and slid it into his coat pocket. "Give me your radio. I'm going in."

Simmons reached over to the front seat. "Here, take mine."

Clark radioed to Cunningham to make entry in the rear. "Take off your coat and necktie. Make sure to hide your stuff. Work your way up easy to the front of the aisle closest to the office. Be careful." Clark turned the volume down on the radio and put it in his inside coat pocket.

Blackburn kept a watchful eye on the store. "Still looks okay. Hey Clark, anything happens to you, who gets your leftover chicken wings?"

Clark flicked him, giving him a wry smile.

"Be careful," Blackburn said, and then he radioed the entry plan to the other cars. "All units, be advised that traffic in and out of store still appears to be 10-4. Plainclothes officers are out on foot now."

Clark knew that even in a crowded store, he could be recognized if the perps were local. As he approached the front doors, people were pushing grocery carts out in a steady stream, some carrying bags. Everyone seemed to be walking in slow motion, and those who passed him appeared to be staring at him. He started to take his sunglasses off but, as an afterthought, decided to leave them on. His mouth was dry and he could hear that pulsating sound in his ears. *This could be it.* Slowly, he walked into the front area of the store and began to lose his sense of hearing as if he were entering a silent movie.

The store was packed; people everywhere. Quickly, he scanned the checkout area, right to left, seven aisles. One by one, he glanced at each, while he reached for a shopping cart: Money changing hands. Friendly conversation. Scanning groceries. Scanning groceries. Empty lane. Bagging groceries. More scanning.

He rolled the cart to within about fifty feet of the office door, as several shooting scenarios raced through his mind. His lips felt very dry, his legs a little shaky. He looked to his right and saw Cunningham gradually working his way to the front of the aisle. As Clark slowly pushed the cart, he realized that he forgot to remove the police badge from his belt. At that precise moment, a man in a black uniform, standing at the office door, turned and glanced his way. Clark made eye contact with Cunningham and nodded to the office. Cunningham nodded in reply.

Clark buttoned his coat to hide his badge and he reached into his right coat pocket. He fumbled for his gun and positioned it for a quick draw. Then, Clark saw a second man, dressed in the same uniform, walk over to the door from inside the office. The two men looked at each other and then at Clark. The second man was carrying a long object by his side, probably a rifle. Clark knew that this was going to be bad. He'd never used his gun in his career, but this was it. His heart was banging in his chest. He reached in his pocket and gripped the gun. His hand was sweaty. *I've gotta let them get out of the store so nobody gets hurt...but if I have to shoot, it's gotta be quick, accurate. All these innocent targets wandering around.*

Suddenly, he was startled by a voice behind him. He turned to look. Capt. Blackburn was walking his way.

"Clark, did you copy the radio traffic?"

"What?"

"Everything's 10-4. False alarm. They're working on the alarm system; the guys over there," he said, pointing to the men at the office. "Headquarters finally made contact. We tried to reach you on your radio."

Clark froze in his steps and gave Blackburn a bewildered look. Then he glanced at the office, and back to Blackburn. "Alarm company?"

Blackburn noticed Clark's paled expression and nodded. "Alarm company."

* * *

The temperature was a notch below freezing when Clark walked in the back door, so the aroma of fresh coffee brewing was pleasing. He entered the kitchen and heard Alex coming down the stairs. A big taco salad was on the counter and it looked good. He was starving.

"Hey, Dad, you're right on time. Did you get fired?" Alex asked jokingly.

"Funny, little lady. I'd ground you but I know how great your coffee is," he said as he reached over and kissed her on the head. "How was school?"

"Good. You need to sign those forms," she said, pointing to some papers on the counter. "They're due tomorrow. If I don't turn them in on time, I get docked a letter grade."

Clark held up his right hand in a mock-injured pose. "I hate that for you, sweetheart. You see, I hurt my hand today, real bad and it hurts so," he said with a grimace.

Alex smiled. "All right, all right. Truce."

Clark put on his reading glasses, walked over and picked up a form. He browsed over the document and signed it. Then he took his glasses off, placed them on the counter, and washed his face and hands.

It was a ritual for him, washing the day from his face. A sign that no matter how bad the day was, at least it was over. He meandered back to the alarm call at the grocery store, replayed the scene in his mind, and wondered if he had done things the right way. He knew that being bound to an office chair meant losing a little of his edge in tactical situations. That was a concern for him, but, at the same time, the call was exhilarating.

Unfortunately, though, the incident at the grocery store seemed to underscore the shortcomings of his life's work. What he was lacking was the dramatic shoot-out, the "Okay Corral" thing. Guns blazing, where the bad guys fell to the ground and the good guys saved the day. Instead, he felt like he was trapped in a career of responding to false alarm calls and writing above average memos.

The taco salad was tasty and Clark went for seconds. He returned to the den and put the plate on the tray beside his recliner. Alex was getting a fire started. "Any luck with it?" he asked.

"Yeah, I think it's catching," she said. She stood up, brushed her hands, and headed back to the kitchen. "You need a refill?"

"I'm good for right now, thanks sweetie." Clark put his plate on the tray and enjoyed a couple sips of coffee while it was still hot.

Alex called from the kitchen. "Daddy, you didn't sign this other form." She walked in and handed him the paper.

"Sorry about that," Clark said. He turned to the tray, and put his coffee cup down. Then, he reached for his glasses, but they weren't there; he had left them on the kitchen counter.

Then he froze for a moment.

He studied the items on the tray. One by one. His dinner plate, coffee cup, two magazines, and the TV remote control. And suddenly it hit him—*like a load of bricks*. That thing that had nagged at him for two days. That feeling that he had forgotten something. He continued to stare at the tray as photo images and words began to replay in his head.... "*...amused by her energy...large glasses...she wasn't wearing them when we found her....*"

So where were Ruby Walker's glasses?

Clark was interrupted by Alex. "What's the matter?" she asked.

Slowly, he turned from the tray back to her and said, "Nothing, nothing, dear." Indeed, he was hoping that it was nothing. He didn't like the alternative.

CHAPTER SEVENTEEN

Sgt. Cunningham crunched the numbers as he walked into Clark's office. He didn't see any big surprises. "Here you go, Lieutenant, hot off the press. Wilkens leads the league with twenty-six cases. Next is Esposito with twenty-three, I'm carrying nineteen, and so is Whitaker. Sloan's got sixteen. Overall, we're in pretty good shape. Better than I suspected."

Clark was glued to his computer screen and didn't look up. He responded slowly, obviously preoccupied. "Not bad, David. Frankly, I'm surprised the caseloads are that good, with all that's been going on. Wilkens will be back Monday, right?"

"Yeah, Monday." Cunningham could see from his side of the desk that his boss was intently studying some photos, looking at one, going to the next, and then clicking on the previous photo again. Cunningham re-lit his pipe, took a draw, and craned his neck to get a better view of the screen but he didn't recognize the photos. "Whatcha lookin' at, Lieutenant?"

After two more clicks, Clark turned to him, took a sip of coffee, and asked, "Any idea where Wilkens is? Did he go anywhere, I mean?"

"Not sure. He said something about going to Virginia to visit his wife's folks. Why? What's up?"

Clark thought for a moment. "Do you remember the 10-67 call Wilkens went to on Monday at The Meadows apartments? Elderly woman."

"No, why?"

"Oh, that's right. That was the morning you took the jewelry store call. Anyway, Festerman, uh no, no, it was Smith. Smith called for a detective at the death scene and Brad handled it. Neighbor found the body. Looked like she died the previous Thursday or Friday, from what I remember. Brad worked the scene and it looked okay, nothing unusual about the body—it'd been there awhile—the place was secure. She was in her mid-to-late seventies."

"So is there a problem?"

"Probably not. But something's been nagging at me and I figured out last night that it was this case, something about it that wasn't adding up."

Cunningham trusted his addition. "What is it?"

"Well, in looking at the photos of the scene, I don't see the woman's glasses. Not in any of the photos. Not on the tray beside her, not in her lap. Who knows? Maybe they fell on the floor, or something."

"How do you even know she wore glasses?"

"Brad called me from the scene. He said that he didn't recognize her when he arrived, not 'til he got a look at her driver's license and saw her wearing glasses."

"Maybe she wore contacts, too."

"At her age? Maybe. The living room and porch lights were on and she was wearing a housecoat, so there's the indication that she may have died at night. Assuming that, contacts at night instead of glasses?" He clicked on the first picture of the dead woman to show Cunningham. "You'd think if she put on her nightwear then she would have removed the contacts as part of that routine, wouldn't you?"

"Maybe, maybe not. The glasses could've been in her purse, on a counter or something."

"Yeah, could've been. But wouldn't she lay them some place accessible, kitchen counter, bedside table, or bathroom counter? Wilkens didn't find much in her pockets. I've looked at all the photos and haven't run across the glasses." Clark then clicked on a couple of photos, one that showed the dead woman's lap, the other that showed the TV tray beside her body. Cunningham leaned over Clark's desk to more carefully examine the screen. Clark allowed him a moment to study, then he carried on. "Here's something else. See the *TV Guide* in her lap, opened. Obvious she had been reading it, right?"

"Yeah, I guess. Oprah Winfrey. So?"

"The woman died last week. I was curious about something so I called my mom to check it out. She's one of those who's got to have her *TV Guide*. Like the TV won't work without it. The cover last week was Tom Cruise."

"And...?"

"The week before that was Jessica Simpson, and before that, Bill Clinton."

"So she's looking at a *TV Guide* that's two weeks old."

"Three. Doesn't mean much, I know. And if you're right about her wearing contacts, then this is probably much ado about nothing. But if she only wore glasses, wouldn't they most likely be in her pocket or on the tray beside her?"

"Knowing old folks like I do, I'd say yeah. They keep everything at arm's reach."

"Precisely. The recliner is their throne. The TV was on when they found her, so you'd think she was watching it when she fell asleep or died. But there's more." Clark clicked on another icon and brought up a picture of the kitchen table. "Looks like bags of groceries here."

"Yeah."

"Wonder why didn't she put them away? Isn't that what most people do, especially seniors, before they relax or move on to some other activity? She went shopping in the early evening which strengthens the likelihood that she died that night."

"Maybe she was interrupted. I don't know, forgot to do it, got sick or something."

"Maybe. But she took the time to change clothes from her shopping trip, didn't she? Wilkens carried on about what a neat place this woman kept. She was a neat freak, everything had its place." Clark clicked on several room shots to prove his point to Cunningham.

"See what you mean. So what do you think? You're not saying foul play, are you?"

Clark sniffed. "The apartment was secure, best I can recall."

"What about medical history?"

"Nothing extensive, for her age anyway. Obviously she could get around. Wilkens ran into her somewhere a week or two before this call."

"But why would anybody want to…?"

"I'm not saying they did."

"Anything missing from the apartment?"

"Nothing that was obvious. Her wallet had money in it. Keys to the car were on the table. What else does a senior have to steal?"

"Autopsy?"

"At her age? With no sign of foul play? You know our M.E.—it's hard enough to get one with a knife stickin' in the back."

"Where's the body?"

"Let's see. Found on Monday, probably buried on Wednesday, Thursday at the latest."

"But still no motive," Cunningham said. Clark shook his head. "What's the next step?"

"Just to play it safe, I better call the Chief, let him know what's going on. You try to run Brad down. He doesn't have to come in, not yet anyway. But if he can point us to his notes, that would help. First thing we need to do is find out where the body is. Oh, by the way, how did the reports look this morning?"

"Uh, not bad. Four assigned. Whitaker got a break-in at the high school; they broke into the library, stole several computers, about $4,000.00, trashed the place. Whitaker had to run to juvenile court. Sloan got a forgery case. I took a vandalism case from the country club, and I assigned Esposito a larceny case, not much to go on, PR sorta thing."

"Doesn't sound too bad. Meet me back here in twenty minutes. We'll ride over to the crime scene together. We gotta do this low key. Don't want to cause an uproar in a senior village, right?"

Cunningham grinned. "Sure."

Clark noticed his reaction. "Okay, David, what's so funny?"

"Nothing. Just that when you started this conversation five minutes ago you referred to it as a death scene. Now, it's a crime scene."

"Freudian slip."

Cunningham turned and walked out of Clark's office, and nearly ran into Officer O'Connor. "Excuse me, Marsha."

"Sarge, you seen Price?" she asked.

"Yeah, he's in court. He got called over on a case this morning, last minute thing."

"He paged me Tuesday or Wednesday, but I've had trouble getting him. You don't know what he wanted, do ya?"

"No clue, Marsha. He ought to be clear by lunch, if you want to stop back by."

"Thanks," she said. *I've done my part. If it's that important, he can call me.*

* * *

Clark and Cunningham arrived at the office and met with the manager. It was late morning but Howard Simpson was already working on a greasy hamburger. "Thanks for taking time to see us," Clark said. "We won't take but a minute, Howard."

"Have a seat, please," Simpson said, as he directed them to a couple of chairs. "What can I help y'all with today?"

"The lady that passed away last week, Ruby Walker, did you know her well?"

Simpson looked at Clark, then Cunningham, and back to Clark. "Why, sure. What's goin' on?"

Cunningham quickly interjected, "Just routine follow-up. Routine stuff, that's all."

"I suppose I knew her 'bout as well as anyone here. Let's see. She got around real good, knew everybody, lotsa energy, active. Hard to believe she's gone. She was in here last week, brought me some brownies. She looked, seemed fine, no complaints about anything. I never got to return that container to her," he said, pointing to the green Tupperware on his file cabinet.

Clark's pager buzzed and he recognized the number as that of Citty Funeral Home. "Excuse me just a second," he said. Then he whispered to Cunningham, "It's the call we've been expecting."

He stepped outside as Cunningham continued the conversation. "Sounds like a really sweet woman, I mean anybody that brings you brownies...."

Simpson chuckled. "Brownies that came with a cost, but they were delicious just the same." He looked up again at the container.

Cunningham played along, smiling. "What do you mean 'a cost'?"

"Well, I'm not gonna speak bad of the dead," he said, holding his hands out in a defensive position. "Ruby was a sweetheart, but she was the nosey sort. Always prying into things. She came in last week, Tuesday, Wednesday maybe, with the brownies, asking questions about recent move-ins."

"Questions?"

"Said she was drumming up interest in her community watch meetings. Wanted to know who our new tenants were so she could invite 'em." He said with a smile, "She really was a sweet old gal, but loved to pry."

As he said that, Clark re-entered the office, and he gave Cunningham a grim look, combined with a subtle shake of the head.

Cunningham then looked back to Simpson and asked, "Mr. Simpson, did Walker wear contact lenses, that you knew of?"

"Contacts, no. Why?"

"Are you sure?"

"Absolutely," Simpson said, then grinned. "Ruby was blind as a bat without her glasses. Now that you mention it, I never saw her without them. Not even once."

Clark picked up with the interview. "Did anyone here go to her funeral yesterday?"

"I don't know. I wanted to go but there was too much going on around here. Repairs, paperwork due by the end of the month."

"Has her apartment been cleaned out yet?"

"She has a daughter out in the county, last name of Wheeler; she's supposed to take care of all that. We usually give them to the end of the month on the clean out. No big rush."

"Has anybody been in the apartment since the body was removed?" Clark asked.

"Just the daughter."

"Did you give her a key to the place?"

"Actually, no. I let her in a couple of times, once to get Ruby's pocketbook, another time to get her things for the funeral. You see, for liability reasons we have to keep control of the place, you know, so things don't walk away." Simpson took a huge, overdue bite of his burger, chili dripping from the other side. He wiped his mouth, and looked at the detectives. "This isn't a routine look-see, is it?"

Clark paused a moment, contemplating just how much to tell him. Come to think of it, there wasn't that much to tell at this point, so he eased into it. "There are a couple of things we need to run down, Howard, things that may have been overlooked that day. Can we borrow the key for a few minutes?" Clark tried not to look so eager.

"Sure, help yourselves. Anything else that I can do?"

"Maybe one more thing," Cunningham offered. "The new tenants that Mrs. Walker inquired about, could you get those names for me? If it's not too much trouble."

"Be glad to."

"Thanks," Clark said. He started to walk out of the office, but turned back to Simpson in a cautioning tone. "Oh, and Howard, we need to be sure we don't cause any undue worry among the residents here. You know what I mean?"

"Now there, Lieutenant, you're preachin' to the choir," Simpson replied. "But you gotta know they don't miss a trick around here. You know how many of 'em realize that the police are here at this very minute?" he asked, grinning, as he handed Clark the apartment key marked "3-14".

"Then it looks like you may be getting some more brownies this afternoon, huh?" Cunningham quipped.

"Brownies?" Clark turned back and asked.

"I'll fill you in on the way," Cunningham said, laughing, as he patted Clark on the back. "We'll be back in a few minutes with the key, Howard."

"Take as long as you need," Simpson said. "It's the far building, the two-story, on the back side. Her car is still there, too, the gray Buick. Park Avenue."

As they drove to the apartment, Cunningham filled Clark in on what he missed at the office. "She was nosing around the day she was at the office, mid-week, trying to find out who the new neighbors were. Who knows why? Said she wanted to invite them to some watch meeting. The new neighbors' names were the ones I asked Simpson for. Maybe one of them knows something."

Clark looked preoccupied. "Didn't wear contacts. She's reading, watching TV, so where were her glasses?" Before Cunningham could answer, Clark added, "And now she's in the ground, so we're talking court order to exhume."

"Whoa there, boss! Jumping ahead, aren't you?"

"Yeah. It's what I do, lots of jumping and worrying. Better have more than a missing pair of glasses and a hunch to put on a court order, else the D.A. will have an order for me, like a mental commitment paper. I know there're valid explanations for my concerns. After all, elderly woman, no signs of trauma. No forced entry. No robbery. Here, here in Quietville, U.S.A."

They gave the apartment a quick once over and it looked as it did in the photos. Neat, in order. Clark began in the living room and he noted that everything looked the same in the area where she had been found. The TV tray, its contents, everything looked untouched. Clark searched thoroughly around the recliner, on the floor, under it. No glasses. He even leaned the recliner over and searched under it, and in the sides of the cushion where the glasses could have slid. No luck. Maybe the daughter found them, needing them for the funeral.

Cunningham inspected the kitchen and noticed that everything looked about the same. The woman's pocketbook and grocery bags had been removed from the table. He inspected the counters, looked in cabinets, even glanced over some photos held by magnets to the refrigerator. He walked over to the garbage can, lifted the lid and surveyed the contents at the top in the garbage can; he saw a grocery bag.

When he reached for it, Clark walked in and asked, "What do you got?"

Cunningham opened the bag. "Somebody threw eggs away."

"So it was eggs in one of the bags on the table? Gotta wonder why she didn't put them in the fridge when she got in. You know, David, bits and pieces."

Cunningham dug a little deeper in the bag, pulled out a receipt that was a foot long, and scanned it. Then he opened the refrigerator and saw a couple of nearly empty shelves. "Whatever she bought, it ain't in here."

"Maybe she got mostly dry goods."

"Look at the receipt, look at the meats, dairy products on it."

Clark started to feel that forty-pound bag of sand weighing down on his back again.

Cunningham picked up the car keys from a basket on the table; they went outside to the car and unlocked the doors. They saw very little after searching under the seats and in the glove compartment.

"Clean, just like the apartment," Clark said. There was an umbrella in the front passenger's floorboard, and a Bible and box of Kleenex on the backseat.

Clark went to the trunk, opened it, and they looked inside. Then they slowly turned to each other.

Cunningham said, "I know, I know, bits and pieces."

"We better give her daughter a call."

CHAPTER EIGHTEEN

The late November fog was thick, making driving treacherous on the winding country road. Suddenly, Cunningham swerved his sedan to avoid two deer sprinting across in front of him. He recovered and said, "That was close," as he and Clark turned to watch them disappear into the woods. "Shame that Jerry and Steve aren't here. They'd be foaming at the mouth for a clear shot at that buck. Nice rack. There's deer everywhere out here. No wonder the County guys are always getting their cruisers banged up."

Clark was mildly amused by the excitement. Then he returned to Ruby Walker's checkbook, examining the ledger entries. "Steve?" he asked as an afterthought. "I didn't know he liked to hunt."

"Oh yeah. Remember a couple weeks ago when they took off Thursday and Friday?"

"Sorta."

"Jerry took him deer hunting. Steve's virgin voyage, got his first taste of blood. They hunted for three solid days, out on Almond's farm, killed two bucks and a doe. Coulda got more, but you know Sloan. He's somethin' of a prima donna when it comes to hunting. Beneath him to kill just any doe, has to be something special. He's got a reputation to uphold around here, you know." As Cunningham approached the city limit, he noticed Clark was a little preoccupied. "What did you think of the Wheeler woman, and what she had to say?"

"She seemed like a really nice lady," Clark said, after a moment to think about it. "Kinda quiet, but sweet. Obviously still upset over her mother's death. I don't think she bought it that we were 'tying up loose ends' though, do you?"

"Not really, Lieutenant. But, then again, she's probably like us, thinking that there's no way anybody would want to hurt her mother. Honestly, a woman her age, living in a retirement village. No robbery. Insurance policy of $20,000.00."

"It's more plausible to think that what happened to Walker was just a situation where an elderly woman became disoriented, confused, lost track of what she was doing. So she stretched out on the recliner, never woke up," Clark surmised, his eyes shifting to Cunningham for a reaction.

"Except we can't find...."

"I know, I know. I was hoping in the worst way her daughter had them," Clark said, disappointment obvious in his voice. "That would have resolved everything, closed the case. There's got to be a valid explanation. Indications that she was watching TV, reading." After thinking about what needed to be done, Clark continued. "We need to pick up with this thing low key, so we don't send The Meadows into a panic. Wouldn't help our image all that much either, on the heels of the Harris Teeter robbery, amidst all the other things going on."

"By 'other things' you mean unsolved crimes?"

Clark answered cynically, "Of course. When you live in a town that averages one or two homicides a year, everybody expects you to wave a wand and wrap things up all nice and neat. David, you know as well as I do that the *Sentinel* will eat us alive on this one. I can read the headline now: 'Bungling Keystones Overlook Homicide'."

"I can't believe that she was...that foul play was involved."

"No motive," Clark said deliberately, evenly as he shook his head. "Where are her glasses?"

"So what do we do next?"

"What did you find out about Wilkens?"

"He and his family are traveling in Virginia. Went to visit the in-laws, but they're sightseeing, too. Pagers don't reach up there, so we'll have to wait. I did leave a message on his answering machine at home. Left a message on his voice mail too, in case he checks it over the weekend."

"What kinda sick guy checks his office messages while he's away on vacation?"

"Well, you're looking at one," Cunningham confessed.

Clark grinned. "Me too, I'm ashamed to say." He placed the checkbook in his satchel and collected his thoughts. "Okay, first thing we do when we get back is to comb over the apartment, side to side, top to bottom." He began to create a mental list of things that needed to be done. "We need to retrace her steps. How about getting Esposito to check at Lowe's Foods where she shopped on Thursday or Friday. Maybe they've got her on camera. See how she was acting, if anybody was following her, paying her a little too much attention. See what she was wearing, how she paid for her groceries."

"Steve had to get off this morning. He only had a couple of hours left in his work cycle."

"Not having overtime money is killing us. So...uh, guess that leaves Price, Jerry, and you." Clark paused. "Can you handle it? I need your experience on this. If we've already made a mistake on this one, we can't afford another."

"Roger that. What else?"

"Did you get the list of names of tenants from Simpson that he gave Walker?"

"Not yet, but I'll call and see if he's still in. How do you want to handle the processing detail at the apartment?"

"It'll be dark soon. See if Halbrook can come over from the Sheriff's Department in an unmarked and process the place." Clark hesitated, then said, "On second thought, tell you what. Why don't I follow up on the grocery store lead, and you help Halbrook. Clean as her place was, it'll be more of a fact-finding mission than an exercise in crime scene collection."

"There ya go with that 'crime scene' phrase again. What are we looking for anyway, I mean besides the obvious?"

"I wish I knew," Clark said as he pondered. "Just anything that looks out of place or missing. Look for any notes she may have left lying around. See if you can tell where she's been lately, check her mail. Look through her garbage; if she's got an answering machine, check it. Collect her medications." Then Clark thought aloud, "Uh...let's see...what else? What are we missing?"

Cunningham pulled into the rear lot of the Police Department and asked, "What about interviewing the tenants? How do we go about doing that?"

"There's the rub, I'm afraid. How to do that without causing a stir. Why don't we pick up with the tenant interviews on Monday? We'll wear casual clothes, soft knock and talk, relaxed. Maybe that'll minimize the excitement. I'm afraid there's no easy way to do it, unless...."

"Unless what?"

"One idea that might fly." He paused, crafting his idea. "We need a smoke screen. What if we told the tenants that Walker may have gotten her meds mixed up, had some bad reaction? So what we're doing is checking with people who may have had contact with her to see how she was acting. How does that sound?"

"Medicine? Bad reaction?...maybe that'll work."

"I'll give you a call if I run across anything of interest at the grocery store. Other than that, we can crank it back up on Monday. Things won't change much between now and then. Plus, Wilkens and Esposito will be back. Fingers crossed for a quiet weekend, huh?"

"Yeah, especially with only three workdays next week with Thanksgiving."

As they headed to the back door of the building they ran into Officer O'Connor. She was leaned across the seat in her patrol car with the door open.

"Hey Marsha, did you ever find Whitaker from when you were looking for him this morning?" Cunningham asked.

She looked over her shoulder. "No sir. He's been tied up in an interview in his office ever since I got clear from lunch." She returned to making some adjustments to her in-car camera and, as she did, the recorder made a whining noise and began to rewind on its own. "Shit!"

Clark and Cunningham laughed.

"What's the matter," Clark teased, "you didn't break it, did you?"

"Just give me a hammer." She paused to turn a knob on the panel. "This camera hasn't caused me nothin' but trouble the last couple of weeks."

"What's the problem?"

O'Connor sat up in her seat and wiped her hands on a rag, as she answered Cunningham. "Sometimes when it runs for a while, it automatically rewinds and erases vehicle stops behind it. I've got a D.W.I. and a couple of drug searches on here from last week that I'm gonna need for court. If they get erased, the D.A.'s gonna erase me."

* * *

Cunningham went to his office and made a call to the County to set up the apartment search.

Clark walked down to the Chief's office to fill him in on the interview with Walker's daughter, and his ideas on the case. The Chief was on the phone when Clark entered so he took a moment and surveyed his lavish surroundings. It struck him that Brinks' office resembled something of a small museum—a place where people paid to come and gaze at handsome furnishings, adore the stylish paintings, and speak in soft whispers. Everything was in perfect order. Golden accessories sparkled on the large, shiny mahogany desk. Small stacks of papers placed neatly at ninety-degree angles. Clark noticed the surroundings didn't match the perturbed look on his boss's face.

Brinks hung up the phone and gave it a lingering stare. "Have a seat, Dixon. That was the City Manager. I've been on the phone with him for the last twenty minutes. He's getting a lot of heat from several of the councilmen on recent crimes, all at a time when they're recruiting some serious business prospects to the city."

Not this again. "Any crimes in particular?"

"Yes. Particular crimes," he said in a biting tone. "The Harris Teeter shooting, two or three recent business break-ins, a sexual assault that Detective Sloan is *supposed* to be working," and then he paused for dramatic effect. "A vandalism case at the country club where four golf carts were wrecked, a break-in at the high school, several computers stolen. What do you say to all that, Lieutenant? Is that particular enough for you?"

Clark could feel his temper rising, but he kept it under control. The comment about Sloan was enough for him to reach across the desk for Brinks. Clark was already feeling the extra pressure from the Walker case and he knew that being defensive was what the Chief would probably expect—and want. At times like this, Clark wanted to cuss him out because, if for nothing more, Brinks seemed to be out of touch with how overworked his men were, how limited personnel resources were, and how many crimes they had to investigate. *Careful, easy, I need him on this Ruby Walker thing.* As he structured his reply and proceeded, Clark tried to ignore the Chief's polished, immaculate desk, and his polished, immaculate appearance. He needed to concentrate.

Clark spent the next couple of minutes going over the status of the cases. Most of his explanation seemed to satisfy Brinks. "Part of the problem, as you know, is that my guys run out of hours on the Wednesday or Thursday of the last week in their twenty-eight-day work cycle. That means most every week, there's a detective who runs out of hours on Thursday or Friday; he has to take time off because there's no overtime to pay him. His cases sit, and more reports drift in for the others to work." Clark hoped that he had presented the facts well, but knew this was nothing the Chief hadn't heard before.

"Look Clark, you know the City's, and our, financial situation right now. Your men will just have to work smarter."

Smart this. The Chief loved that slogan: Work smarter. It was one of those canned phrases that he loved to recite in lieu of using creative problem solving. Clark knew there was no use in challenging the Chief's advice. They had butted heads on more than one occasion over this same staffing issue. Clark shifted to the Walker case and where they were on the investigation.

Brinks stood and leaned over his desk. "Clark, how in the hell could something like this happen? Do you honestly think that someone would and could do harm to this old woman? Why? What about motive, for Christ's sake?"

Clark began to feel foolish, even impetuous, because he didn't have an answer to the question regarding this most basic element of a crime. Motive. "We don't have a motive. Not yet, anyway."

"So let me get this straight, Lieutenant," Brinks said, raising his voice and extending his left hand out to the side to facilitate his point. "On this hand, we have a dead woman, close to eighty, health and medical problems. We have her residence secured, no sign of force. No robbery, no trauma to the body, and…" his voice got louder, "…oh yes, we have a pair of missing glasses!" Then he held out his right hand. "And on this hand, we have all these cases that need solving, need arrests made; a crime wave, of sorts, is sweeping through Stuartsboro. And here you are trying to make a murder out of a routine natural causes case, the end result of which will send our community into a frenzy and cause irreparable embarrassment to our Department. How am I doing so far, Lieutenant?"

"With all due respect, granted, it's a small point, the glasses. But it's something that has to be explained, along with the other minor points I mentioned to you. I have a feeling about this one, Chief. We'll know a lot more, hopefully in the next couple of days."

Brinks thought about Clark's instincts. He trusted them, but he wasn't about to acknowledge that, not in this round. Here, now, it was more important to show superiority, to drive his point. Brinks put his glasses back on as if to continue his deskwork, then looked over them for emphasis. "Lieutenant, let's do this quick and quiet. Understood?"

Clark nodded and left the room. Stalemate. But he needed to stay focused on the work at hand. *The Chief can expend energy on these pissing wars. It's what he does. I've got crimes to solve, questions that need answering.*

Back in his office, Clark called Lowe's Foods and spoke with the manager. Luckily, they still had the tape from the period in question and Clark arranged to go by and view it in the next few minutes. He felt a little buzz from the anticipation of getting some conclusive answers. He saw the tape as the beginning of the process of retracing Ruby Walker's steps. Tapes were hard proof, irrefutable evidence.

As Clark began to construct a "to do" list for the investigation, Det. Whitaker walked in.

"Lieutenant, good news," Whitaker said. "I just got two confessions on the car B&E's on Walters Street from last week."

"Who were they?"

"A couple of middle school kids, from the neighborhood. I'm going to recover a couple of CD players from them. Kids have never been in trouble before, not that we know of."

"What are you thinking, Teen Court?"

"Probably."

"We don't solve too many of those cases, and that area has really been hit lately. You know, we might make a detective out of you, yet," Clark said in a proud, somewhat paternalistic tone. He knew Price was pressing to make a name for himself in the division; with a college degree, he was pushing hard to make the next sergeant.

Whitaker smiled and turned to walk away. As he did, Clark remembered something and called to him.

"Price, Marsha O'Connor was looking for you. Did she find you?"

"No, but it's no big deal. Sergeant told me she was hunting me down from when I tried to reach her first of the week on the robbery. Meanwhile, I checked the computer activity report and she was tied up on a D.W.I. about the time of the robbery, plus she got off early that night. Don't think she'd know anything. Thanks, anyway."

Whitaker turned again to walk away, as Clark returned to his list and looked at the last item he wrote: "Lowe's Foods videotape". Videotape. That triggered his memory to the conversation a short while ago with O'Connor.

"Hey, Price, one more thing. Just curious. Do you know where she stopped the car that night?"

"The D.W.I.?"

"Yeah."

"No, but hold on a second." Whitaker walked at a brisk pace to his office, and returned with the printout. "According to the C.A.D. here, she stopped it on Turner Drive at…looks like 1:37 a.m." Whitaker was catching up.

"Turner Drive? That's only a block from Harris Teeter. What time was the robbery called in?"

"2:08 a.m. 'Course it happened a little earlier. The manager was knocked out, we assume, for a few minutes. After he came to, he hit a panic alarm, which called the alarm company which, in turn, called the PD."

"I know it's a long shot, but it sounds like O'Connor was right there at the time of the robbery, a block away, possibly closer. Maybe she's got something on her car-cam, a person, a vehicle, something. It wouldn't hurt to check it."

"We should be so lucky."

"We need to be so lucky. But you better get her on the radio, fast. She's having problems with her recorder rewinding and erasing."

Whitaker ran back to his office.

* * *

On the way to Lowe's Foods, Clark decided to take a short detour by way of Gordon Street. He thought a lot about the woman he had run into earlier in the week. He had driven by the house several times over the last couple of days, but no sign of anything. He couldn't get her out of his mind, a silly thing. She was a stunning beauty, and that he couldn't get over. Who was she? Why was she there?

Clark had done research on the house and the owner was William Everhart, a retired businessman. Clark had heard of him, but that was about it—there wasn't any room for cops in this neighborhood. Gordon Street was lined with old oak trees and old money. Dating back to the late 1800s with the founding of Stuartsboro, Gordon Street was established by prominent businessmen, doctors, and attorneys. It was *the* place to live.

He approached the old white Victorian house on the opposite side of the road and noticed a gold Acura backing down the driveway. His heart began to race. He couldn't believe his luck. Could it be her? He passed the Acura as it backed into the street and he studied the license plate on the car. Then suddenly, he looked ahead and saw the car in front of him stopped in traffic. He slammed on his brakes, coming to a screeching halt, almost ramming into the car. Clark looked over his shoulder as the Acura, now in the street, was driving away. He could see the auburn hair, but that was all. He felt like an idiot, but it was worth it.

A license plate was a good place to start. *Beautiful hair.*

CHAPTER NINETEEN

With the threat of an ice storm, the grocery store was busy, but Clark finally found a parking spot. He was a little early, so he headed to the back and waited for the manager. In a couple minutes, Clark saw a boy who couldn't have been more than eighteen or nineteen walk over to him. He looked more like the neighborhood newspaper delivery boy than the manager of a supermarket. When the kid got close enough, Clark read his nametag and saw that he was one of the assistant managers. *God, is everybody less than half my age now?*

"Lieutenant Dixon?"

"Yes."

"I'm Kevin Roland. We spoke on the phone."

"Nice to meet you," Clark said, while they shook hands. "Thanks for fitting me in, too. I can see you're really busy."

"Yes sir, pretty hectic at the moment," Roland said, guiding Clark into the office with an arm. "If you'd like to wait here a minute, I need to approve something up front. I've got the tape queued to the day and time you asked me about. Feel free to get started, if you like. I'll be right back."

The kid was nice, polite and that impressed Clark. He took a moment to study the color photograph of Ruby Walker. This could take a while, depending on how frequently the store cameras picked up a roving senior citizen. He knew from the lengthy cash receipt that she had been in the store awhile.

He looked at his watch and decided to wait for the manager before he proceeded. After all, with watching eight screens, four eyes would be better than two. Besides, there was an important call he wanted to make, concerning some information he was dying to find out. He called the PD.

"Stuartsboro Police, this is Hudson."

"Sidney, this is Lieutenant Dixon. How's everything going so far tonight?"

"A couple of disturbance calls, a wreck, that's about it. Not bad, but it's early."

"The last weekend nights you worked weren't kind to your squad, from what I remember. Here's to a quiet night."

"I'll drink to that," Hudson said, chuckling. "Hey, can you hold on a second? I got two lines ringing."

"Sure, take your time." Clark waited a minute.

"Okay, sorry."

"No problem. I need a 10-28 on a North Carolina tag, if you got a second." Clark gave him the number. He could hear Hudson pecking on the computer keys as Clark reached for his pen.

"Let's see, Lieutenant...uh...here it comes...a 2007 Acura Legend to a Lana Marie Demarko, 3117 Oakview Drive, Reidsville. Tag's valid."

The tag came back to a woman, not a couple. That information provided a good starting point, and perhaps it meant that she was single; he began to feel a tinge of excitement. *Lana, pretty name...the actress from the fifties, Lana Turner. Demarko. Italian?* Reidsville was about thirty miles to the east.

"Lieutenant?"

Clark continued to reflect. *Real nice car. She must have a pretty good job—or be married to someone who has one.* Clark had been to Reidsville on many occasions. He spent wonderful summers there as a kid visiting his grandmother. Oakview Drive was in one of the nicer areas. His thoughts drifted back to the woman.

"Lieutenant, are you still there?"

"Uh, yeah, Sid, sorry. How about running a 10-27 on that name for me, would you?" Again, Clark heard Hudson typing in the info. Clark unconsciously mimicked him by tapping his fingers on the office desk. The manager returned to the office, and Clark whispered to him that he'd be off the phone in a minute.

"Here it comes, Lieutenant," Hudson said. "Come on...she's a little slow tonight on 27's.... Okay, license on Demarko is valid, Class C, address same as the...no, it shows a Greensboro address on the license, 217 Vanstory Road, Greensboro." Hudson read off the date of birth. "Anything else, Lieutenant? I've got a line ringing."

"No. That's it, Sid, thanks. Have a good night. Oh, Sid?"

"Yeah, Lieutenant?"

"Would you make me a printout of that and put it in my box?" When he hung up, Clark did the math and, assuming the woman he saw was Demarko, he figured that she was forty-eight. That surprised him. He would have guessed forty, forty-two at the most. He wondered which address was current for her, though. And was she planning still another move to Stuartsboro? *An asset, she would definitely be an asset to this town.* Back to present, he turned to the manager. "Okay, ready to go hunting?"

"Yes sir, ready."

Clark showed him the picture of the woman they would be searching for on the tape. He noticed the kid looked a little eager, perhaps excited about playing detective. For the next few minutes, they ran the tape, play and reverse, play and reverse, watching the monitors, trying to locate her. Clark knew her checkout time was 6:24 p.m., so he figured she came in thirty, forty minutes prior to that. Finally, they located Ruby Walker in one of the aisles at about 5:47. She was wearing a brown coat, over a dark blue turtleneck. He definitely noticed her glasses. "Those damn glasses," he muttered.

"Excuse me?"

"Oh, nothing, nothing. Kevin, I know you're busy; I can take it from here. We'll need to take this tape, just for a while. Okay?"

"No problem. If you need me, I'll be up front. You can call me at extension 12."

"Thanks," Clark said, handing him a chain-of-custody form to sign. "Say, don't suppose I could get a cup of coffee around here, could I?"

"Cream and sugar?"

"Just cream. How much is it?" Clark asked as he reached for his wallet.

"Don't worry about that. Be right back."

Clark spent the next thirty minutes studying the screens, making notes of little points, and the places on the tape where those points occurred. He sipped his coffee, which was good for vending machine brew. As he watched Ruby Walker move about the store, loading her cart, he couldn't help but wonder: Was he viewing a woman whose heart simply gave out a few hours later? Or one who was about to be murdered?

Clark also speculated about the time of death. Their best estimate was nothing more than an educated guess. If she died this particular night, though, he was really puzzled. She moved about the store with the spunk and vigor of a woman much younger. He viewed her as she stopped and spoke with a couple of other customers. From time to time, she studied labels on items. She zigzagged through aisles and around other shoppers with the precision of a NASCAR driver.

He continued to watch the monitors for segments including her and, gradually, he became amused. At one point, she reached for an item on a shelf just as another woman did, and Ruby came away the winner. Afterwards, she appeared to look at the other woman as if to say, "Ha, ha. I got it." Ruby Walker must have been some kind of character, with all that he'd heard about her. As he watched her place the item in her cart, Clark spoke in a slightly morbid tone, "Guess that's about the last good deal you'll ever see, Ruby."

He stopped the tape and called Cunningham to check on his progress at the apartment.

"Cunningham."

"Hey, it's Lieutenant. How's it going?"

"So far, nothing. It's neat as a pin here. This woman was some kinda housekeeper. Everything in its place. We could've used this gal in the PD locker room. A list maker, a labeler. Nice and tidy, I'm tellin' ya."

"But no...?"

"Nope. We even checked the pavement around her car, thinking maybe she slipped and fell. Nothing. We did find what looks like an old pair of reading glasses in the back of her desk drawer. That's the best we got. We searched through the garbage, nothing."

"Anything else?"

"Yeah. We checked her answering machine. She had several messages, mostly 'Call me' stuff. There were a few messages on it from a Margaret Rierson, who was checking on her. Sounded kinda pressed for her by the second or third call. The calls came in on a Friday morning. Looks like Walker may have died Thursday night, early Friday morning."

"Make sure somebody interviews Rierson. That may give us something." Clark digested Cunningham's information and a sick feeling began to develop in his stomach. From what he could see, this woman didn't show any visible sign of being in distress. "David, did you have trouble getting in the place, I mean, anybody see you?"

"You know how it is in these retirement villages. Never a soul around, but you get out of the car and feel like a million eyes are on you. We're probably okay. Parked right at the door and closed the blinds."

"Not much here on my end with the tape." Clark then filled him in on what he had watched and how Walker carried herself in the store. Clark even told him about the contest she won at one of the shelves.

"Doesn't sound like her ticker would go out on her that quick, but you never know. You remember your idea about using the bad medication thing as our ruse for conducting these neighbor interviews?"

"Yeah?"

"Well, what if it really was something related to her medicine? Wouldn't that be a real kick in the ass?"

"I can think of worse alternatives."

After Cunningham paused a moment, he voiced another theory. "Maybe she slipped, banged her head walking from the car to the apartment. Didn't it snow Thursday night, or was it Friday?"

Clark considered Cunningham's idea and retraced last Thursday in his mind. He remembered working late that day, the command staff meeting. Then he recalled the snowfall when he left the building. "Thursday, it snowed Thursday. Slipped, huh?" He weighed the probability of the idea in his mind. Then Clark shifted the conversation. "David, it appears in the tape she was wearing a brown coat and a dark-colored turtleneck. How about checking on that. Meanwhile, I'm going to page Price to see it he found anything on Marsha's car tape."

"What's she supposed to have on her tape?"

"She made a traffic stop down the street from the robbery at Harris Teeter, about the time of the robbery. It's a long shot, but I told him to check with her on it. That case is dying on the vine and we could use a fresh lead."

"Yeah, we could. Let me go check and I'll page you back. Black turtleneck?"

"Navy blue, maybe black." Clark hung up, then paged Whitaker to the office phone. And while he waited for a response, he thought over the Walker case. Maybe it was much ado about nothing. Perhaps the Chief was right. Maybe all this manpower and time could be better invested on some of these violent robberies and shootings where real people had real injuries. It probably didn't matter anyway. He knew the reality of the situation with the Walker case; unless they uncovered something substantial, it was going to be shelved. And they were running out of leads as fast as they were running out of time.

Clark resumed the tape with Ruby at the checkout line. He noticed the tape didn't show the bagboy, and he wished that it did. Then the office phone rang and he answered it.

"Lieutenant, this is Price. You page me?"

"Yeah." Clark asked him how it went with the viewing of O'Connor's tape. "Any luck?"

"Hard to say. We located the D.W.I. stop that she made, but not a minute too soon. Two stops after that had been erased. Anyway, as O'Connor was making the stop, she passed around a black compact car and a green van. We could make the tag on the car and it's a local. The van, the glare was bad and we could only make out the first part of the tag. Looked like some type of plumbing business logo on the back doors. Afraid that's about it. Want me to keep the tape?"

"Get Capt. Blackburn to make you a copy of it. O'Connor will need the original for court. Did you say a black compact?"

"Yeah, black compact."

"Probably nothing to do with the robbery, but you still need to run it down. I'd think the perps would use something bigger to haul three gunslingers around. The van sounds interesting. So you got the prefix on the plate?"

"Alpha and the first numeric."

"Commercial tag?"

"Uh-uh."

"Wonder why not?"

"Hmm, don't know. Didn't think about that."

"Make and model?"

"Ford E-150."

"Good. Get headquarters to contact the S.B.I. and request an off-line search." Clark's pager vibrated, it was Cunningham. "With a partial like that, Price, they can give you a list of possibles." *A little odd for a commercial van to be running around in the early morning hours*; he wasn't familiar with a local plumbing business that owned a van that color, either. Why no commercial plate? Clark didn't have to tell Whitaker to get right on it; he could smell his enthusiasm through the telephone.

"Got it. Talk to you later."

Clark knew they could use a break in the case. Breathing room. Needed it. Clark called Cunningham. "How'd it go?"

"Found the turtleneck. It was on top in the dirty clothes hamper. Looks like she wore a solid-colored suit, matching slacks with it."

"What else?"

"No...wait a second."

"What?"

"Oh nothing. Just checking to see if...label says 100% wool, dry clean only. Maybe she hand washed stuff like this."

"Who knows? But this woman strikes me as the kind who would even dry clean her socks."

"So why put the outfit in here with the regular stuff?" Cunningham looked deeper in the hamper. "Towels, underwear...mean anything?"

"Yeah, bits and pieces. But I'm afraid that's about it."

***

Earlier that afternoon, lab tech Rosalie Lawson entered the office of Parker Hubert, the Supervising Agent in Charge of the Northern Piedmont District of the S.B.I. An hour before, she had delivered him a routine e-mail message, indicating a match on a bullet she had analyzed and entered; the bullet matched several entries recently submitted from other departments. The department that submitted this bullet would now be connected to a number of other departments investigating violent crimes committed with the same gun. It sounded like very good news, and she was proud of that. She cleared her throat and tried to speak assertively. "Sir, you wanted to see me?"

Hubert swiveled around from his computer. "Yes, Rosalie, come in and have seat. Would you get the door, please?"

He was cordial in his tone, but Lawson remained on her guard. Hubert was in his late fifties, stocky, with a thin head of red hair and a strong, forbidding jaw line. He had the reputation in the Bureau, certainly in this office, for being as tenacious as a pit-bull. Some believed his ferocity prevented him from ascending to an Assistant Director's position in Raleigh. Too much aggression, not enough polish.

"I received your message a while ago, concerning the I.B.I.S. hit on the projectile," he said. "Great work, Rosalie, very nice."

"Thank you, sir," she said sheepishly, relaxing a little. Usually, she was a nervous wreck around him. He was a large, burly man, who spoke with a deep, resounding voice.

"Didn't your message state that this was Agent Williams' case?"

"Yes, sir, Agent Williams."

"What department submitted the case?" He asked sharply, as his tone shifted, on a dime, from cordial to all business.

"Stuartsboro Police."

"Have you notified Agent Williams of the hit?"

"No sir, I haven't had the chance yet, honestly. You see...."

Hubert held his hand out to interrupt her. "That's okay, Rosalie. That's all right. Have you informed anyone else of your finding?"

"No, sir." She wanted to ask "Why?" but she didn't dare. She caught herself squirming in her chair.

"You're sure about that?"

"Positive, sir."

Hubert paused for a moment. His phone began to ring, but he ignored it. "Rosalie, I need you to keep this test result of yours confidential, strictly confidential. Absolutely no one, I mean no one, must learn of this finding of yours. You are to keep this to yourself, only discuss it with me, and only in this office. Do you understand?"

"Why yes, uh, why...?"

Hubert's tone eased up, but only a little. "I can't get into any details right now, but at some later point we will be able to talk about it. For now, bring me everything you have on this submission. Delete all your files and messages relating to the examination and entry. Destroy everything else you have, lab notes, everything. Understood?"

"Yes sir."

"Thank you, Rosalie, that's all. Get me the file ASAP."

"Yes sir, right away." She was baffled. She had worked for the Bureau for almost seventeen years and had never heard of such a request. All her orders always came from within her unit. The Bureau was very regimented that way. Why wasn't her supervisor involved in this? Or more importantly, why *was* the S.A.C. involved in it? Something was wrong.

As she walked over and opened the door, Hubert called to her. She closed the door and turned back to him.

"This is a very serious matter, Rosalie. I have to know that I can trust you." Hubert stood, removed his glasses, and put them on the desk. "You know, I'm retiring within the year. And my recommendation for laboratory supervisor will be based on the person who is most competent and trusted. The person who can pass the test. Are you that person?"

Rosalie lit up. It was a job she'd had her heart set on for years, and she'd been passed over twice for it. "Yes, Agent Hubert, I am that person. You have my complete and total trust on this."

"I'm counting on that. This may be your test, Rosalie."

"Oh, one question, sir."

"Yes?"

"What should I tell Agent Williams about the examination? He was expecting my report. He's already called today inquiring about the results."

"Tell him it was unclassifiable. Will that be a surprise to him?"

"I don't think so, sir. This projectile was a borderline case. He would realize that, assuming he's even looked at it. What should I do about testing the casings?"

"Stall on that until I get back with you. All right?"

"Yes, sir."

Hubert watched her turn and walk down the hallway and then he waited a moment. He sat down, picked up the phone and called an out-of-state number.

"Yes?"

"Add Stuartsboro to the list."

CHAPTER TWENTY

Three…four…five…ahh…feels great. Clark replaced the bar on the rack. Any time he bench-pressed 245 with sets of five, it was the sign of a strong workout. In his routine, the chest and shoulders were the exercises that counted the most. He enjoyed his lengthy workouts on Saturday mornings at the "Y", and today the weight room was almost empty. Resting between reps, he watched one of his favorite movies, *Casablanca*, on the overhead TV.

After his third set, Clark moved on to the dip bar. He felt a nice stretch, dropping as low as he could, then slowly raising, leaning forward to work his chest, until his arms were fully extended. Moving slowly, good technique, taking his time. After the fourth set of ten, he rested a few minutes before going on to the military press.

"Mornin', Dixon. How's it going?" Charles, a workout buddy asked as he walked in.

Clark, resting on a bench, recovering, looked up. "So far, so good. You just getting started?"

"Yeah, gotta get a quick one in today. Things to do with family coming over for turkey day," he said, loosening up.

Clark looked down, tightening the Velcro on his gloves, still panting. "Well, least you're here. Who's coming over for Thanksgiving?"

"My brother. You remember Bruce, don't ya?"

"Oh, yeah," Clark said, walking over to the squat rack.

"He's coming up from Wilmington. My sister and mom's comin'. Aunts and uncles, the whole gang."

Clark raised the Olympic bar, starting his military press at 100 pounds. "How's everything in the produce business?" he grunted.

"A little slow 'til recently. Picking up now with the holidays and all. Been reading about your business lately. It's booming, ain't it?"

Clark did several of the presses behind his head, then got his breath. "Booming and then some. Too much work, too many distractions. Wish I was in the grocery business. Ah, now there's a steady job," he said, smiling. "Good hours, low risk." Then he got on the floor and did some push-ups.

Charles was finishing a set of sit-ups, straining. "I noticed you didn't say great pay."

Clark collapsed after thirty quick ones. "Well, you can't have it all." A few seconds to recover. "Sure was good news about the Hall boy, wasn't it? Lucky kid."

Charles was lying on the sit-up bench, staring at the ceiling, recuperating from the set. "Yeah, it upset a lot of people at work. Everybody's rallied together, set up a fund for him. He lives with his grandma and from what I hear they struggle to make it. Keith's a good boy, works hard. Respectful."

During the conversation, Clark made up his mind to run by the hospital, a block away, and visit Hall. "That's really nice of y'all to do that. Everything that I've heard about the boy has been good." He strained on his last set of presses, as Charles did a set of pull-downs. Afterwards, Clark rested a minute. "How much is everybody giving to it, Charles, the fund?"

"Corporate in Salisbury got it started. They donated $5,000.00."

"Nice start."

"Yeah. Most everybody at the store's given $10.00, $20.00, others more. Some of the other stores in the area have even taken up collections. We've had truck drivers, salespeople, a lot of customers giving to it."

"That's a good story," Clark said in a slightly surprised, elevated tone. "Hey Charles, when I leave, I think I'll drop a little something at the front desk for him."

"That's kind of you. I'll make sure it gets there."

"I'll put it in an envelope and leave it with Abby. How's that?" Just then, Clark's pager buzzed on his shoe. He hooked it on his shoestrings when he worked out, since it wouldn't fit on the weight belt. The page was from Whitaker.

"Y'all made any progress on the case?"

Not enough. But he was hoping that this page might tip the scale that way. He gave Charles his patented response. "We've made some, but not that many leads to go on right now." That was putting it optimistically. However, one plus on this case, Clark believed, was that Whitaker was a good man to be working it. Young and energetic. Hungry.

"They won't leave you alone, will they?" Charles said with a grin, while Clark re-clipped the pager on his shoe.

"Like I said, what I need is a job working in produce. Don't you have an opening somewhere, maybe in lettuce and carrots?" Clark grinned and headed to the front office. He found a private phone and called Whitaker's number at the PD.

"Detective Whitaker."

"Hi, Price, got your page."

"Sorry to bother you on a Saturday, Lieutenant, but I got a response on the partial tag from the S.B.I. Thought you'd want to know about it."

"On a Saturday? You got a response on a Saturday?"

"Yes, sir. Evidently, they got a unit now that works 24/7 on certain requests, including these off-line searches, when the targets are violent gangs or watched groups."

"Nine-eleven."

"What? Oh, yeah. Well, anyway, they ran all the info, the three alphas and one numeric we had. Turns out there are only three possible registrations in the state to match this partial on a Ford E-150. One plate's registered in Mitchell County, one in Fayetteville, and one in High Point."

"Mitchell County and Fayetteville are a good ways off. High Point, huh?"

"High Point. The plate was reported stolen two days after the Harris Teeter robbery. Stolen off a van at a local car repair shop."

"Repair shop? It's perfect."

"What is?"

"Their plan. They steal a plate off a vehicle getting repairs so the theft goes unnoticed for maybe two or three days. That gives them time to pull off a robbery. But they're careful, they steal one off a vehicle that's the same make and model."

"Why is that?"

"If police run their tag for any reason, it comes back to a Ford E-150, like the one they're driving. It's safe. They probably are even so careful as to steal the tag off a van that's the same year as the one they're driving."

"Does it mean that this van…?"

"Is the perps' van? Got to be. A van fits what they're doing. Real coincidence that it happened to be on the perimeter of the store, late at night, at the precise time of the robbery. Yeah, I'd say excellent chance that the van you're looking at in that tape is our boy. And tied to no telling how many other robberies and shootings in the area."

Whitaker was silent for a few seconds. He was trying to absorb the magnitude of the case, and the potential for solving some of the most violent robberies in the state. *This case could put me on the map. Good timing with an opening coming up for sergeant in a few months.*

"Price, quick as you can, get an e-mail and memo out to our people and send out a fifty-mile BOLO on the van, with all the description that you have on it."

"Even the tag?"

"Yeah. They'd be fools not to have trashed it by now, but you never know. Chances are they still have the van and, by now, have either parked it or stolen a tag off another Ford. But we have to go with what we have, so…tag and all, get it out. Make sure you indicate 'No Stop' on the van. Right now, we don't want them to know we're on to them, since we don't have enough for an arrest. In the BOLO, make sure to indicate: 'If sighted, please develop intel and contact this Department ASAP'. All right?"

"Got it."

"Price, you said the van had some kind of business logo or sign on the back of it?"

"It's a little hard to make out, but it looks like a plumbing business. Hard to tell because of the glare from Marsha's headlights."

"Then how about sending another fifty-mile message. Inquire if any department can advise if there's such a business in their jurisdiction with that kind and color of vehicle. If I were you, I'd make a call to High Point PD on Monday. Could be that if the van is stolen, it's their case, maybe Greensboro's. We may have to hit the yellow pages on this one," he said with a chuckle.

"Good thinking, Lieutenant. Any responses to our messages, do you want me to page you?"

You betcha. "Please do." Clark was beginning to feel a little better about this one. *Maybe these bastards have finally run out of luck…in my city, and all because a patrol officer stops a drunk early on a Sunday morning. Boy, this could be sweet. What are the chances?* But he knew they were a long way from solving the case. If this van was the perps' and they still had it, then the chase was on. Now, if only Greg would call with some good news about the evidence they were analyzing. Hopefully, that would connect Clark's case with other departments; it may provide further leads, like the general area of where the perps' base was and where their next strike might be.

Clark finished his workout, pumped up from the news. He did a series of alternating push-ups, dumbbell flies, and lateral raises. At the end of it, he spent twenty minutes in the sauna, the dessert at the end of the main course. He loved the feeling of the intense heat: Sweat dripping from his face and arms, streaming down his back. He took an occasional drink of water from the bottle, letting some of it trickle down his chest.

After that, he showered, applied lotion to his face, and dressed. He checked out at the desk, and left an envelope with Abby.

* * *

A large number of visitors were passing through the area as Clark approached the nurses' desk. He noticed an attractive nurse, who looked up from behind the counter and greeted him.

"Hey, can I help you?" she asked.

"Yes, good morning," Clark said, as he instantly noticed her beautiful blue eyes and warm smile. "Could you tell me what room Keith Hall is in?"

"Hall. Let me see here." She looked at a chart, then back to Clark. "Room 310, on the left," she said, pointing to the left wing.

"Thanks a lot."

"My pleasure." Her answer caught him off guard. Another lovely smile.

Clark turned and headed to the room. *I gotta do business up here more often.*

When he was out of earshot, the nurse, Olivia, turned to a co-worker. "Do you know who that guy was who was just here?"

"What guy?" Julie asked.

"The one I gave the room number to."

"No, I didn't see him. What did he look like?" Julie asked, as she looked down the hallway trying to spot him, but there were a number of visitors strolling and mingling.

"I don't know, I didn't get that good a look. I guess about 5'10", green eyes, short, wavy blonde hair, mustache and beard thing," she said as she stroked her chin with her fingers. "Green turtleneck, nice chest."

Julie gazed at her for a moment, grinning.

"What?"

"Nothing. What a shame, you didn't get a good look at the guy."

Olivia, smiling in return, responded in a high-handed tone. "I take customer service very seriously, Julie."

"Oh, you do, do you? Just how far would you take this customer service commitment of yours?"

"Anything for the hospital and Director Gibbons. I'm a company girl," she said proudly, as they both laughed. She looked around for listeners. "All right, he was sexy."

"Wouldn't do for a nurse to be running a fever on duty."

"He's in 310. Go sneak a look for me."

"Olivia."

"What?"
"You're drooling on my medicine chart."

* * *

Keith Hall was propped up in bed, and his grandmother was reading a magazine in a chair beside him. A couple of teens were leaving as Clark walked into the room. Clark nodded to them and then said hello to Keith and Mrs. Hall. As she began to rise from her chair, he told her to keep her seat. Clark stepped over and shook Keith's hand, and noticed the boy looked even younger than he expected.

"I'm Lt. Dixon, Keith. It's real nice to finally meet you."

"Thanks," he said, weakly. He looked up at Clark, studying him, as if trying to figure out why he was there.

"Thought I'd stop by and say hello. I've heard some good things about you."

Hall didn't know what to say. He slowly managed a smile.

They chatted for a minute, mostly about school and how Keith was feeling. Clark was careful not to mention anything about Keith's job or the store. While Keith spoke about his plans for college, Clark was sidetracked in thought, thinking it was a miracle that the boy was alive. He knew how close to death Hall had come. As close as a jammed nine-millimeter bullet, and that's about as close as they get. Clark also wondered about the follow-up surgery and hoped it would be routine, without complications.

He shook Keith's hand and stepped outside the room to speak with his grandmother. He briefed her on the case without getting into too many specifics. He did tell her that there could be a promising development in the case.

"Thank you for coming to see Keith, Mr. Dixon. And thank you for what you're doing on his case." She squeezed his hand as she spoke.

Clark assured her they were doing their best, but he knew better than to make any promises. He learned about that pitfall, the hard way, early in his career.

Clark returned to the desk, over to the pretty nurse. He spoke, almost in a whisper. "Excuse me, ma'am, can you tell me if they've set a date for Keith Hall's surgery, yet?"

She met his eyes. "Sir, are you in the family?"

"I'm with the Police Department," he said, drawing and displaying his wallet badge. "We need the evidence that'll be recovered in surgery." He didn't say the word "bullet". He was superstitious that way.

She referred to the file, and as she did, Clark happened to glance down the hall, in the direction of the elevator, and thought he saw her. *Was it her?* The nurse was saying something, but his attention was diverted, as he tried to spot her in a crowd, walking away. He saw the back of her head, and noticed she was wearing a long teal coat. Then he looked back to the nurse. "I'm sorry, what was that?"

"The doctor is planning the surgery for first of next week, providing the boy can get his strength back. So, you're a detective?"

Clark never heard the question, as he hurried off to the elevator. He rounded the corner, and saw the elevator doors close. He wasn't sure if it was her or not, but he had to find out. *Second sighting in two days*? The elevator light indicated down and Clark hit the stairwell. Three floors down, and he hustled. Steps, turn, steps, turn. More steps.

He landed on the first floor and took a deep breath as he opened the stairwell door leading to the hallway. Several people were waiting for the elevator as he casually walked to the back of the group. The elevator doors opened, several people exited. No teal coat.

* * *

Mario Slade was weaving his way through the crowded jail recreation room, when someone reached out and grabbed his arm.

"What's up?" asked the guy who was known as 'Fatmeat'.

Slade was slightly startled, but he recovered and said, "Callin' my old lady. What's it to ya?"

"That's cool, man. Just looked like you was in a hurry. You been askin' a lot of questions around here lately, 'bout me and my boys, shit goin' on in the big city. Stuff like that. You ain't leavin' us, are ya? Bondin' out?"

"Look, man, I ain't all that when it comes to readin' code. What you tryin' to say?"

Fatmeat held out his arms in a non-threatening pose. "No big thang, Slade. We cool man, we cool."

Slade watched as Fatmeat walked away. The room was packed but one of the payphones was finally available. He knew he didn't have a lot to tell, but he hoped that what he knew was enough to get Esposito's ear. Slade had nosed around as quietly as he could, and evidently Fatmeat had heard about it or noticed it. But nobody really took Fatmeat seriously, he was all mouth. He was almost a joke on the street.

Slade looked around, walking up to the phone. He called the PD.

"Stuartsboro Police, this is Sacrinity."

"Yeah, uh, this is Mario Slade. Uh, I need to speak to Det. Esposito," he said in a low voice, carefully looking around.

"Sir, he's not in."

"Where's he at?"

"Sir, he's not in. Unless this is an emergency, you may want to call back on Monday."

"Look man," he started to raise his voice, but then caught himself. "I need to speak with him. Can you page him to…?"

Suddenly, Slade felt a sharp piercing pain in his lower back, and he gasped. It felt like a burning spear had been thrust in and it took his breath. He tried to recover, get his wind, but couldn't. He clung to the phone and dropped to his knees. The pain was intense, and everything was becoming splotchy. The cinderblock wall in front of him seemed to move back and forth. He tried to yell for help, but the pain overtook him. After a moment, Slade dropped the phone, fell to the floor on his face, and blacked out.

"Hello? Hello sir?"

The phone was placed back on the receiver.

* * *

"Rosalie?"

No reply.

"Rosalie?"

She looked behind her slowly, with a vacant expression. "I'm sorry, what?"

"Are you okay?" Anita asked.

"Yes, why?"

"Are you finished then?"

"Finished with what?"

Anita looked down at the copy machine as if the answer was so obvious it was humorous. "The copy machine, are you finished running your copies?"

"Yes, sorry," Rosalie said, trying to regain her composure. She realized she was deep in thought, and she was thinking she might be deep in something else, too. The lab supervisor's position was a goal, an obsession of hers. But she was content with her job if it were compared to an active jail sentence. Jail was not an option. Am I overreacting, she asked herself? SAC Hubert was an ethical man, as far as she knew. Why in the world, though, would he want to conceal information of this nature, not only from the submitting agency, but from one of his own agents, too? His assistant? It was totally frustrating for her, because she was forbidden to discuss the matter with anyone or seek any answers. What was so significant about Stuartsboro? About its connectivity to these other North Carolina towns?

"Rosalie," Anita said, laughing now. "Should I go somewhere else?"

"Oh, let me move. Sorry, Anita." She grabbed her papers and scurried off to her office. At her desk, she deliberated over this code of silence with Hubert. Was there anyone in the office in whom she could confide? Anita? Probably not. Anita was her best friend, really her only friend, but she liked to gossip…loose lips. Fran was her most trusted colleague in the lab, but definitely competition for the supervisor's job that she wanted. What about Greg Williams? Greg was a great guy, more than likely the next appointed SAC. Plus, it was his case. And if it leaked out that she told him about it, she could always deny it, saying that it was a misunderstanding. After all, she had a reason to talk with him about his case.

Just as she was formulating a plan about how to broach the subject with Williams, her computer beeped with a message. She turned around from her desk and clicked on the message. It was the mirrored response from Washington on the hit she made on the Stuartsboro bullet with the other North Carolina agencies: Charlotte, Greensboro, High Point, and Winston-Salem. She hadn't worked these cases that she could remember, so it must have been Fran. Washington maintained the Bureau of Alcohol, Tobacco, and Firearms I.B.I.S. files, so when any state made and then entered matches between agencies, Washington was notified. Then, if there were matches to other states, the national file would make connections of cases between states. The national file was the conduit that brought all the states together on bullet matches.

She made a hard copy, against Hubert's directive, and locked it up in her desk drawer. Next, she deleted the message just as she was ordered. She shifted back to thinking about her predicament. The more she thought about it, the more she worried. Perhaps this was an internal test of her trustworthiness, loyalty to the Bureau; Hubert did say that this was a test. Then again, maybe the Bureau or A.T.F. ordered silence because they were working a major investigation, and didn't want local interference. Maybe they were about to make arrests. But was this level of secrecy necessary?

As she continued to think and scratch out some ideas, her computer beeped again. She turned around and clicked on the message. This time it was a message marked "Urgent". It was a positive response from Washington on the Stuartsboro entry. The Stuartsboro bullet matched an entry submitted by the Columbia, South Carolina, PD. *Now that's interesting, another state involved. That means the gun used in the Columbia crime has also been used in Stuartsboro. This could make it a case for the feds.* She was beginning to feel a little relieved now that she was developing a perfectly logical rationale for the secrecy demand imposed upon her. She repeated the process of making a hard copy, and then deleting the file.

She turned around to continue her work. She was behind on the day, with all its distractions. After a couple of minutes, she leaned back in her chair and tried to rub the stress from her neck. As she was attending to that, it happened. The computer. Beeping, beeping, again, and again. She turned around, staring at the blank screen, almost afraid to click on the message. After a pause, and then a sigh, she clicked on the icon, and there they were. More matches:

Macon…Miami…Tallahassee…Richmond…Charleston…Nashville.
Knoxville…Lynchburg…Atlanta…Jacksonville…Several more.
"Oh my God!"

CHAPTER TWENTY-ONE

As they chatted, Greg Marcellus rolled over to Det. Wilkens and refilled his cup.

"Thanks, that's good," Wilkens said. "This is great coffee Mr. Marcellus, especially on a day like this." Wilkens watched his guest turn and roll into the kitchen to return the coffee pot to the counter. Wilkens noticed that Marcellus was having some trouble maneuvering his wheelchair.

"More cream or sugar?" Marcellus asked from the kitchen. He decided to pour himself a cup, thinking that it might convey a message that he was being cooperative, supportive.

"No, this is fine, thanks," Wilkens answered, taking another sip.

Marcellus tried not to be obvious, as he carefully studied the detective. *I've got to play this just right, can't appear to be too interested. We've come too far to let anything like this stop us now. Not these small town rednecks.* But Marcellus knew that Wilkens was no redneck. He was impressed with the way Wilkens carried himself, with measured steps and poise, and he possessed a large athletic build, looking sharp in his navy blue suit. He was articulate and intelligent, and struck Marcellus as someone who was better than good at what he did for a living. *Maybe I'm the one who's being studied here.*

Then Marcellus continued. "So that was about it, Detective. She seemed to be a nice woman. She asked me if I would be interested in going to a community watch meeting next month."

"Was that the first time you met her?"

"Yes, first and only. I don't get out very much," Marcellus said, gesturing to his wheelchair. "She even brought me brownies. Nobody else around here has ever bothered to stop and say hello. A nice lady."

"When she came by, did she act okay? I mean, did it look like she was having any problems?"

"Problems?"

"Yeah. Did she make sense with what she said? Speak clearly? Ramble?"

Marcellus began to sense where the detective's line of questioning was leading. "Well, that's hard to say, not knowing her. She only stayed a minute, seemed all right. But I did notice one thing about her, now that you mention it."

Wilkens leaned forward. "What was that?"

"Well, I noticed that she seemed to perspire a lot. Every minute or so, she wiped her face and forehead with a handkerchief."

"Really?"

"Yeah. I asked her if she was okay, if she needed anything. I figured maybe it was too warm for her in here. I'm a little cold natured."

Wilkens took another sip, thinking. "What did she say?"

"Oh, she shook it off, said it was no big thing. Said she debated over going to the doctor for it but otherwise she felt fine. I was a little worried about her." Then Marcellus added, "I even offered to follow her back to her apartment, but she said she was fine. That's really all I remember."

Wilkens wanted to wrap up the interview; this canvass was turning into a dead end. While Marcellus was talking, Wilkens kept glancing down at his notes. The Davenports had said that Ruby Walker never stopped by. The Hampton guy wasn't in when Wilkens went by his apartment. That meant that he'd have to waste another trip and come back for the interview. He was beginning to feel some pressure. The PD had another busy weekend of reporting and he needed to get back to the office.

When Marcellus finished his answer, Wilkens asked, "You say you followed her back to her apartment?" Wilkens had not been paying close attention.

What's he trying to do? He's on to me. He responded in a slightly defensive tone, "No, I said I offered to do that, but she said she was all right." Marcellus' hand started to shake so he shifted his cup.

Wilkens noticed, and wondered if Marcellus was getting a little emotional over the death. He decided to move on to friendly small talk before leaving, a way of showing appreciation for the hospitality.

"So Mr. Marcellus, how do you like living here? Looks like a good situation for you."

"It's nice, it's quiet. Most everybody minds their own business. The manager seems like an okay guy."

Wilkens had detected a slight accent at the outset, but didn't want to appear to be too inquisitive. "Where are you from?"

Marcellus answered cautiously, "Uh, Ohio, Cleveland area."

"Ohio," Wilkens repeated. "Then you like the milder winters down here, I imagine."

"That's one of the things that attracted me to this area."

"What else?"

"I have family in Charlotte." Marcellus felt his voice quivering a little, and wondered if the detective noticed. "I lived with them for about a year, but the city got to be too big for me. The traffic was a hassle. I got tired of the crime. Friend of mine in Charlotte had lived in this area, and it sounded like what I was looking for, something smaller."

"Traffic and crime? I'd say we're two up on Charlotte in those respects. Is that where it happened, Mr. Marcellus, your accident? I had heard something about it," Wilkens said, softening his voice, glancing sympathetically at Marcellus' wheelchair.

"Yeah, Charlotte," Marcellus blurted out. He was caught off-guard by the question, but he hoped that his answer would work.

"How long ago?"

Damn, when's he gonna stop? After a slight pause, Marcellus stammered, "Three, uh, four years ago."

Marcellus seemed a little on edge to Wilkens. *Maybe it's still difficult for him to talk about it. Better break it off.* Then Wilkens said, "Hey, Mr. Marcellus, thanks again for the coffee. It was kind of you." He placed his cup on a side table and reached into his coat pocket for a business card.

"Any time. Pleasure to meet you, Detective," Marcellus said, beginning to feel a little relief. He tried to regain a cool, even look.

Wilkens handed him his card, then shook his hand. "Thanks again for your time."

Marcellus wheeled his chair over to the door, following Wilkens. "Good luck with your case. By the way, there's nothing suspicious about Mrs. Walker's death, is there?"

Wilkens was taken aback by his question. Odd. It's the kind of question that he would expect a concerned neighbor to ask out front, not on the exit. To this point, Marcellus had shown no interest in why Wilkens was there. No curiosity. He had answered every question, yet never asked one.

Wilkens rebounded, as he turned back to Marcellus. "No, not at all. Just routine stuff. It's a chance she may have taken some bad medication, or had a reaction. Health related. Maybe the sweating you saw was the beginning of some problem."

"If I can help with anything else, give me a call."

When Wilkens left, Marcellus closed the door and rose from the wheelchair. Two men appeared from the darkness of the hallway. One of them removed the silencer and re-holstered his semi-automatic. The other one gave Marcellus a look of contempt.

* * *

Wilkens headed to the Police Department and called Clark on his cell phone.

"Hello."

"Lieutenant, this is Brad."

"Hey, are you at The Meadows?"

"Just finished up, actually. I got something on Walker that may make you a little happier. I've been trying to track down the three residents on the list that the manager gave us. One couple said she never stopped by to the see them that day. I checked on some other guy who wasn't in. But I just interviewed a man who saw her that Wednesday or Thursday. His name is Marcellus; he lives above where she lived. Black male, mid-to-late twenties, in a wheelchair."

"Any help?"

"Maybe. He said she stopped by that day as a kind of welcome to the neighborhood type thing. Even brought him some brownies...."

"And?"

"Marcellus said she only stayed for a couple of minutes. Invited him to a community watch meeting. Get this. He said he noticed she was perspiring pretty badly. He even asked her about it, but she waved it off."

"Interesting."

"Yes, sir. Thought you might say that. He was concerned enough about it to offer to follow her back to her apartment."

"Did he?"

"No. She said she was fine. Wrote it off as no big deal."

"Did he see her again, after that?"

"No. He said that was the only time he ever saw her. He's handicapped and doesn't leave his place much."

How ironic. The medicine, our explanation for doing the canvass, just like David said. That would suit me just fine. "Well, that's a start, Brad. That's the first information we have that she may have been having some sort of trouble. Sweating, huh? Means nothing to us but, you know, it may mean something to her doctor. You got time to check it out?"

"Sure."

"Where are you headed to now?"

"En route back to the PD to check on my new cases. Did you pile it on me this morning?" Wilkens asked, half jokingly.

"I went easy on you. Assigned you a drug shooting. The vic's okay, bullet wound to the arm, says he can I.D. the perp. And, uh…seems like one more…oh yeah, the break-in at Strader's Mart, another cigarette smash and grab. Newspaper carrier got a pretty good vehicle description. Overall, not too bad a weekend. By the way, how was your trip?"

"It was great. Weather up there was nice for this time of year. Kids had a ball; the in-laws live next to a horse farm, and we got to do some riding. The kids didn't want to leave. They treated us really good, but then they always do. They spoil the kids something terrible."

Clark thought that anybody would be lucky to have Brad for a son-in-law. "Good. Good to have you back, too. We're over here at Nick's All-Seasons. They got hit really bad, we think probably late last night."

"Not again? Did they ever get their alarm system fixed from the last break-in?"

"Afraid not, and the owner, old man Evans, is in his usual form."

"Did patrol find it?"

"Uh-uh. But it would have been difficult to spotlight that side door through the chain link fence. Perps also knocked down a section of the back fence and our cars can't see or patrol back there."

"Who all's there with you?"

"Sloan and Sergeant are doing the processing."

"I'm close by, I'll see you in a minute."

"See ya."

On the way to the scene, Wilkens reviewed the information he received from Marcellus. They finally had some first-hand information that Walker could have been experiencing a medical problem.

Still, in the back of his mind, he couldn't help but wonder. Wonder if he may have committed the most egregious of sins as a detective—overlooking a foul play death scene. It was even worse than losing a murder trial. At least with the trial, you, or somebody else, could always get the asshole the next time around. With a questionable case like this, you never really knew what the score was. And the answers may be locked away forever, six feet under.

Wilkens was a little troubled with Marcellus. He was a likeable guy, for sure, but he seemed out of place. Smooth hands, too, for a guy that wheeled around all day. And the way that Marcellus responded to a couple of his questions was a little unusual. *Probably nothing. Maybe it's because he's not from around here....* He pulled in the parking lot of the business, and saw Lt. Dixon huddled up with the other guys.

Cunningham walked up to Clark, who asked, "How bad's the damage?"

Cunningham gave him a disturbed look, then referred to his clipboard. "According to their inventory, looks like nine chainsaws, six lawn tractors, and," Cunningham paused, then said, "three utility tractors."

"Utility tractors?"

"Three. Somebody had good taste. Stole the 6003 Series, 98 horsepower, 9F/3R transmission."

"My gosh. What do they retail for? Twenty?"

"Try twenty-five, and that's low end."

"What did they haul them with? A flatbed?"

"Probably two, unless they had a tractor-trailer."

"How long were they here?"

"An experienced crew? Six, seven minutes."

"Where was patrol?"

Cunningham hunched his shoulders.

"Got an estimate, yet?"

"Close to $120,000.00." When Cunningham said that, he noticed the manager, Mr. Evans, pacing their way.

Clark saw him approaching, too, and he cautioned his men to be on their guard. "Back to the dog and pony show, guys," he said in a low voice. "Here comes the attack dog now." Then he spoke up for Evan's benefit. "How did the tire casting turn out?"

Sloan answered. "One of the tires left a pretty good tread. The dental stone needs a little while longer to set up." He pointed to an area near the damaged fence. "Looks like they backed the truck up right there. They probably...."

"You boys got any leads, yet?" Evans asked, his voice shook with emotion.

Cunningham placed a hand on Evans' shoulder in an effort to calm him down. Then Cunningham took a minute to explain what had been done, and what follow-up measures would be taken.

Clark walked over to Wilkens and asked, "So we got somebody who said Walker may've been having some trouble?"

"That's what he said," Wilkens carefully replied.

Clark noticed that he sounded a little preoccupied. "Something wrong?"

"Nah. How's everything going here?"

"Same ole, same ole. We may have a decent cast of one of the tires on the perp's truck," Clark said, pointing toward the fence. "All we need now is a truck to go with it. Looks like a hit of close to 120K."

Wilkens whistled.

"Multi-purpose tractors, lawn tractors…'Tis the season. Chainsaws, a little something for everybody. We could've seen this one coming just by looking at the calendar. Somebody will be getting a nice Thanksgiving present."

"I think I'll cut out. See you in a little while, Lieutenant."

"Where're you going?"

"Back to the office. I need to make a call to Charlotte PD to check on something."

* * *

"Detective Esposito."

"Steve, this is Mike at the jail. How's it going?"

"Ah, typical Monday. How about you?"

"Not too bad. Court's out this week for the holidays, so that's good. Say, I, uh, just wanted to give you a call and let you know that Mario Slade was stabbed here in the jail over the weekend."

"Mario Slade, huh? What happened?"

"Don't know for sure. He got it in the back while he was on the payphone. We've heard a couple of things, gang stuff, somebody looked at somebody the wrong way. You know."

"How bad is he?"

"He'll probably make it, too mean to die. Looks like he took some kinda pick in one of his kidneys."

"Thanks for the call. Just curious, though, why are you calling me?"

"Your name was on the visitors' log, you and Sloan. We're required to notify all badges of stuff like this, in case it's your arrest or you got something going on with 'em."

"Oh yeah. Knowing Slade, he probably ran his mouth one time too many. What do you think?"

"Yeah, he's a real smart ass, all right. Hey, can you tell Jerry about it, save me a call?"

"Sure, Mike. Take care, and thanks for the call." After Esposito hung up, he reflected on Slade a moment, staring at the phone. He returned to his report. *A little jail justice.*

CHAPTER TWENTY-TWO

Rosalie Lawson spent a sleepless weekend agonizing over Hubert's mysterious order to falsify her findings. She tossed her conscience around like a lottery ball, wondering why he swore her to silence and what she should do.

Of all the ideas and theories she bounced around, the lottery ball always slowed to a stop on this number: The simple fact was that she was told to manipulate analysis results from a violent crime, and then lie to a fellow agent. In all her years of working in a state lab, she had never seen so many connections of shooting cases between so many cities. The same firearm had been used in a number of cities and not just in North Carolina—all over the Southeast United States. What was going on? What in the world could she do?

She walked down the hall, passed the administrative offices, and noticed that SAC Hubert's office lights were out and his door was closed. She entered the break room and, as she was pouring water for a cup of hot tea, she stepped over to the daily calendar to check on something. Just as she suspected, Hubert was on vacation all week for the Thanksgiving holidays. She gazed at the calendar, and as she did, she heard a telephone ringing in the adjoining office. As she listened to it, an idea popped into her head. A way to resolve her predicament, protect her career, and finagle around the lie that she was being forced to tell. *A simple solution!*

She stood there evaluating her plan, staring at the calendar like a misbehaving student facing the chalkboard. She was unaware that Anita had walked in the room.

"Rosalie, your heartthrob's looking for you."

No reply.

"Rosalie?"

Slightly startled, she turned to her friend. "Oh, hey. Didn't hear you come in," she said, steeping the tea bag. She was already feeling a little better about her quandary.

"Did you hear me? I said your heart throb is looking for you."

Rosalie grinned sheepishly. She knew exactly to whom Anita was referring. Everybody in the office knew that Rosalie buckled at the knees whenever Agent Greg Williams was within a mile of her. "Did he say what he wanted?" she tried to ask in a cavalier manner.

"No, but he was in his office about ten or fifteen minutes ago. You can probably catch him there."

They chatted for a few minutes about work assignments.

"You have any plans for Thanksgiving?" Anita asked.

"I may go to my mom's in Danville." *So Greg's in his office.* Maybe she should stop by and see what he wanted. That way, she could go ahead and give him the bogus test results in his Stuartsboro case. Get it over with. She stepped over to the sink and added a little cold water to her tea. While she did that, she took a moment to fluff her hair and check her lipstick in the mirror.

Anita noticed and grinned. "We'll probably do the same thing we did last year. Have lunch at my folks' place in the country and then go to Tony's parents' for dinner. That's a lot of traveling for one day, but you know how it is splitting the holidays with the in-laws." Anita realized what she said a moment later and wished she could take it back. Rosalie had no idea what that was like, because her mother was really the only family that she had. "Rose, you look great. Better hurry, your knight awaits."

"Give it a rest," Rosalie said. But she really did like the attention that Anita gave her. Most of the others in the office didn't ever seem to have much to talk with her about, except work.

A few minutes later, Rosalie passed Agent Williams' office and saw him on the phone. She stood in the hallway, within earshot, waiting. When he hung up, she took a deep breath and walked over to his doorway. "Hey, Greg, were you looking for me?"

He looked up and smiled. "Yes, good morning Rosalie. Come in, please," he said as he stood and offered her a seat. "How was your weekend?"

Pure hell, I may go to jail. Did you know that? She replied, "It was okay, I suppose. I did some reading, early shopping for Christmas. How about you?" she asked, lowering her eyes to his mouth. *You have the sexiest lips.*

"Nothing special, really. Weather was kind of crappy. I did some reading, too. Caught a movie, we went out to eat. It was okay, I guess. I was hunting for you to see if you've had the chance to run the ballistics test on the Eden suicide-homicide yet. The Chief called me again this morning and the media's hounding him for more information. He'd love to get some kind of answer before the holiday break this Thursday, if possible. That is, if you're able to, Rosalie."

She loved the way he said her name. And then she heard her voice say, "I should be able to get to it this afternoon or tomorrow morning at the latest. How does that sound?"

"You're the best."

She shifted in her seat. "By the way," she said, looking down at the file in her lap, "I have the results on the Stuartsboro bullet you gave me a few days ago."

He knew what was coming. He could tell by her tone, but more by her expression. "Please, give me some good news. Remember, it's Monday."

"Sorry, but it was too deformed to qualify for entry. Not quite enough striation marks. Wish I had better news for you. Now if you can get me a gun to go with it, I can match it up, no problem." She hated seeing the disappointment register in his eyes, not to mention feeling the disappointment in herself for the lie she had just told. Had a criminal cover-up just begun?

"Thanks for the effort, just the same. Anything on the casings, yet?"

"Hope to get those tested right after the holidays." Rosalie decided to investigate a little. "Let me ask you something, Greg. What's the greatest number of departments you've ever heard of being connected on bullet matches in our state? Or any state, for that matter?"

"Hmm, good question, let me think," Greg said, pausing. "A buddy of mine in the Coastal District worked a case several years ago that ended up with bullet matches in three or four cites, plus two in South Carolina. That was *some* case."

"Sounds pretty impressive. Do you know any of the details?"

"Only that it was a bank robber traveling along I-40. He never shot anybody, but his M.O. was that in every bank he hit, he'd fire shots just to frighten everybody and gain control. But the calling cards he left turned out to be his undoing. Poetic justice, huh?"

"And you say the lab got two other hits from South Carolina?"

"Yeah. He had hit a bank and some superstore down there. Moved up here and went on his spree."

"But you've never heard of a three-state match?"

"Can't say that I have. Three states would be pretty extraordinary, but I'm sure it's happened somewhere. Most shooters typically don't travel that much, you know, between states." Greg was beginning to wonder why

Rosalie was so interested in what he had to say. This was the longest conversation he could ever recall having with her. For some reason, she had difficulty carrying on a decent conversation with him. He had assumed that she didn't like him very much, but he didn't know why. He knew he had a way with most women around the office.

Rosalie pushed further. If she ever got in trouble for what Hubert had strong-armed her into doing, then maybe Greg would remember this conversation as her attempt to seek help. "Well, let me ask you this. What if you had a case with multiple state hits? What kind of case would it be?"

"I suppose it could be some kind of serial killer type. They're known for extensive travel. Or, uh, could be some organized gang. Of course, they'd have to score big hits to justify so much travel. Know what I mean?"

She nodded. That gave her something to think about. "See you, Greg. Again, sorry about your case. I guess that won't be good news for Stuartsboro, will it?"

"Afraid not. Their case sounds a lot like several we're investigating, and I think they need a break. Getting a bullet match could've been that break in a nowhere case. When you get enough departments working together, sharing resources, comparing notes, before you know it, the case picks up momentum. Think I'll make the call and get this one over with. Thanks again, Rosalie."

She walked out of his office and heard him pressing a number using his speakerphone. She stood in the hallway and eavesdropped, as he spoke with an officer, named Clark, and gave him the negative results on the bullet. She could tell by the conversation that the two were good friends. While she listened, a couple of agents walked her way, and she pretended to be busy. *Actually, I guess I am.* She was writing down "Clark-Stuartsboro". She had a phone call to make, too.

* * *

Back in the office, Clark was getting on with the chores of the day triggered by the weekend crime reports. The All-Seasons break-in was another piss in the wind. A huge hit with practically nothing to go on. It seemed like crime the last month had jumped to a level he had never seen in his ten years in C.I.D. His phone rang and he could see on the screen it was the Chief calling. "Lt. Dixon."

"Good morning, Clark, this is the Chief. I just got a call from Mr. Evans, the manager at Nick's All-Seasons."

"Yes sir, I left there a short while ago. They took a big hit, about $120,000.00. The perps stole three utility tractors; somebody knew what they were doing." As he said that, Marilyn appeared in his doorway, evidently to tell him something. Clark acknowledged her, then gave the Chief a synopsis of what was done at the crime scene. "Chief, can you hold on a second?"

"Yes, but only that. I've got to be in the City Manager's office in five minutes."

"Yes, ma'am?" he asked Marilyn.

"I'm sorry to interrupt you, Lieutenant, but I have Price on the phone for you. He sounds excited. Says he's calling from the GPD. What should I tell him?"

"Tell him to hold on about thirty seconds, then transfer him to me."

Marilyn nodded and left.

Clark returned to the Chief. "Sorry, I've got Whitaker on hold for me. He's at the Greensboro PD and he may have some good news on the Harris Teeter case. He took the O'Connor tape that I told you about over there for enhancement. He's also inquiring about the van while he's there." Clark paused. "Where were we?"

"Processing at All-Seasons."

"Oh yeah. Well, that's about it. We may have a good cast of a tire, but you know how useful that'll be after the truck's been driven another few hundred miles."

"Doesn't sound like you have much in the way of leads, then."

"Unfortunately, no."

"Mr. Evans is upset about a couple of things, Clark. He felt like patrol should have found the break-in. And, he said that you were rude to him when you were there a while ago."

"Rude? What could I have done that he considered rude?"

"I know that he's upset. But he said when he walked over to speak with you, that you turned your back to him and walked away. Is that true?"

Clark recalled the encounter. "I think I know what he's talking about. I was mulling over the case with the guys and he walked up. When he did, Sergeant Cunningham took over and I went over to Wilkens to get briefed on his canvass at The Meadows. But I wasn't rude to him. I'd been there awhile and already spoken with him a time of two. As far as patrol finding the break-in, you know the layout of the place; the points of entry were the side door and the back fence. It's difficult for our guys to see glass breakage when they flash their spotlights through the chain-link fence, and they can't see the back fence from their cars. The real problem is that they still haven't gotten their alarm system fixed from the last B&E when their wires were cut. Evans didn't like it when I said something to him about it. That's probably why he's complaining. I told him something that he didn't want to hear."

Silence, and Clark wondered what was next.

"I know Evans. I'll handle him. What did Wilkens develop on his canvass?"

Clark filled him in on Wilkens' findings and as he did, Marilyn reappeared at the door to remind him of the pending call. He smiled and waved his hand in acknowledgement. Quickly, Clark informed the Chief of the concern that Marcellus had about Walker during her visit. Clark could feel the Chief wanting to say, "I told you so."

"That's another thing, Clark. I just got a call from Sammy Joyce, the owner of The Meadows. You may have heard that he's proposing an expansion of the apartments. He's getting calls this morning from some residents who are concerned about what we're doing over there. I guess he's referring to the search you conducted the other night, maybe the canvass this morning...."

"Chief, I've got Whitaker on the other line. Do you...?"

"I know you have to go, but listen. I warned you the other day about keeping things low key over there. Remember? Do this. Put a couple of guys over there for the next two or three nights, so I can tell him we've got everything under control. It'll make them feel safer. Doesn't have to be a marked unit. Hell, I don't even care if they sit in their car and do paperwork the whole time. Just so I can tell Joyce that we have some badges over there. Understood?"

Before Clark could answer, the Chief hung up. "Mr. Personality," he muttered to himself. How had the residents picked up so quickly on what was going on?

Clark called Marilyn. She transferred Whitaker to him and he answered.

"Lieutenant, this is Price."

"Sorry to keep you waiting. Crazy Monday."

"I'm over here at the GPD. They ran our tape through their video-enhancement equipment. They've been really generous and bumped our case over a bunch of theirs. This equipment is really impressive."

"High-dollar stuff. Any luck?"

"Not a great deal. The tech was able to reduce the glare on the back of the van to the point where we could see the entire license plate. Turns out it *was* the one that was stolen from High Point. That much we know."

"What else did you get?"

"The business name on the back looks like it's 'H and B' or 'H and R', or something like that. They can't make out any better with the second letter. The last word is 'Plumbing'. 'H and B', or 'H and R', or 'H and whatever Plumbing'."

"Is there a business by that name over there?"

"Not that we've found. We checked here, High Point PD, Guilford County Sheriff's Office, but no record. The problem is that there's no consolidated list of plumbing businesses and no clearinghouse where there's an all-inclusive list of them."

"I see what you mean. Any other ideas?"

"One. The lady that works records here said we ought to focus on the license plate more and maybe something will come up on the van eventually. The business name could be bogus anyway."

"Good point. What did she mean by focusing on the tag?"

"Well. Your theory is that the perps are stealing a tag from a van like theirs, just before they hit, right?"

"That's right."

"Okay, she said that we could contact the S.B.I. in Raleigh and have them flag every theft entry that they receive that is in the ballpark for what we're looking for. So, we give them the Ford E-150 info. When they get such a stolen entry, their computers can actually be programmed to page us. Could be that when we get the page, they've stolen a tag and are getting ready to hit another store."

"But if the tag is discovered missing a couple days later, then we may get the page too late, as well."

"Hey, it's not perfect, but it beats looking for a needle in a haystack. At least we can start to get a general idea of where their theft radius is. That is, assuming they're using the same van. We already know they stole the tag from High Point, to the east."

"Of course, we're still assuming that this van is the one involved in our robbery, a pretty fair assumption."

They talked a few more minutes about the case, and Clark instructed him to contact the S.B.I. and furnish them with the details.

"It's a long shot, Price, but it may work. Give them all of our pager numbers, will you? Who knows what time of day we may get the page on one of these stolen tags."

"What about radius? How far away do you want the responses to come from?"

Clark considered the question. "Let's make it two counties, all directions. Anything farther away probably won't be relevant to us."

"Sounds good. Two counties every direction."

Clark hung up. *Wouldn't that be something? These imbeciles steal a tag, the tag's reported stolen, then Clark and his guys get a page from Raleigh. They issue a hot area BOLO on the perps and catch them in the act. A long shot, but some plan's better than none.*

A few minutes later, he called Esposito and Sloan and lined them up for The Meadows patrol that night. *Babysitting...What a waste of precious man-hours.*

CHAPTER TWENTY-THREE

Esposito switched on his wipers to delay speed to clear the light coating of sleet from the windshield. He was tired of listening to Sloan's music, so he scanned to one of his favorite stations for some classical. Next, he looked at his watch and sighed. It had only been fifteen minutes since the last time he checked it. This assignment, the sheer boredom and waste of it, reminded him of some cold autumn nights on patrol, where the only thing out there to fight was sleep.

Sloan saw Esposito staring at his watch. "Man, I've been on some boring damn assignments in my life but this has to make the top of the 'Don't Fall Asleep' list. Between your choice of music, the sound of the sleet hittin' the car, and this dead village, it's about all I can stand. What in the world are we doin' over here, anyway?"

"First of all, there's nothing wrong with my music. It's classical. Timeless. Haven't you ever heard of Bach? Beats that country crap you listen to."

"Oh, yeah? Did you know that country's the most popular music in the United States, 'specially in this area? It's what the South is all about. You want to be an expert deer hunter, don't you? Well, country music is part of that whole package," Sloan said, in a way as if he were lecturing a teenage son.

"Look man, I'm trying to inject a little culture in your life." When Esposito said that, he smelled a foul odor emanating from Sloan's side of the car. "Damn, Jerry, what did you do?"

Sloan had a mouthful of sandwich and he started to get tickled.

"Man, roll your window down. Now, you pig!"

Sloan continued to giggle, to the point where he couldn't stop long enough to swallow the bite of sub sandwich. Again, he tried to speak, but was still too humored. When Sloan finally regained his composure, he snickered, "How's that for some culture?"

"Do you know how common you are?"

"Well, think about it this way. Since I have trouble expressing my true feelings to you, I send you this. Kinda like a bouquet of flowers, huh? Only cheaper."

"Man, you suck," Esposito said, then he unscrewed the thermos lid, as steam rolled out, and poured some more coffee. "Refill?"

"No, I'm good, thanks. How much longer?"

"About thirty minutes. Lieutenant said when we get through here to check around Nick's place for a little while, since they got hit so bad. Is that your case?"

"Yeah."

"Good luck. You know there's no pleasing Evans, don't you?"

"Yeah. Lieutenant said Evans had already complained on him by the time he got back to the PD this morning. Evans is a real piece of work. These guys have these million dollar inventories and no working business alarms. What a bunch of idiots. Wonder how he can afford insurance, with all the hits he's taken over the last few years?"

The sleet began to pick up. Esposito turned his wipers to low speed and took another sip of coffee. As he did, Clark called on the radio and informed them that he was en route to meet with them.

"Wonder what he's doing out this late?" Esposito asked.

"Beats me. Probably trying to get to a good stopping point for the holidays. A lot of stuff going on lately, all the reports and everything."

"That, and there's no Mrs. Dixon to go home to."

"Wonder if he ever goes out?"

"I never hear nothing."

"Come to think of it, I've never even heard him talk about anybody."

"He's a pretty private guy. You remember the tidal wave it sent through the Department when he and his old lady split up. I mean, after all those years, you think you could put a marriage on autopilot and coast on in to the golden years, wouldn't you?"

Sloan responded emphatically. "Let me tell you something. If I had an old lady and we split, I'd be right back out there bangin' away the next day. The best way to get over one woman is to get on with life and go find someone else. Not sit around moping, taking anti-depressants, and sobbing all over old wedding photos."

"You know Jerry, you just may be the most sensitive and tender guy I've ever known."

Sloan continued his philosophical pitch. "Steve, can you imagine seeing this buck, big twelve pointer, trudging through the woods, looking down and out, whining, sniffling, over breaking up with some doe? See how crazy that sounds?"

Esposito glanced at Sloan, slightly humored by such a ridiculous analogy.

Sloan added, "Not a chance. He gets right back out there and prowls around for another doe."

Esposito smiled and shook his head. "And to think we give you a gun." Then he countered. "What you're saying about our friend, the buck, isn't that usually the beginning of his demise? Mating season? He puts his brain in the wrong place, gets careless, reckless, then wanders out in the open trying to sniff them out?"

He's got a point there. Sloan offered in a conciliatory tone, "Yeah, but could you think of a better way to go?"

As Sloan asked that, they looked to the right and saw headlights coming their way. The vehicle slowed down when it approached them, and then they realized it was their lieutenant. Clark pulled into the space beside where they were backed in, as both men sat up in their seats.

"Fellas, how's it going?" Clark asked.

"Doing hard time, Lieutenant. About as much fun as visiting the in-laws," Esposito said.

"I know, I know," Clark said. "Have you been able to get any work done?"

"A little something," Esposito said. "I was able to finish the Dove burglary you asked me about today. All I gotta do is download it. Should have it on your desk in the morning."

Clark looked at Sloan, who said, "I've got caught up pretty good on my case status sheets."

"Good," Clark said. "Glad this assignment hasn't been a total waste of time. Just one of those things."

They talked a few minutes about the Ruby Walker case.

Esposito asked, "So what do you think about what Wilkens' found out from Charlotte PD on this Marcellus guy?"

Clark stroked his chin, thinking. "Hard to explain. No record of anybody by that name being involved in a car accident. They even checked back seven, eight years."

"Charlotte's a big town, Lieutenant," Esposito said, "could be any number of things. What if Marcellus' accident was outside the city limits and S.H.P. investigated it?"

"Brad asked them about that. Turns out when the PD and Sheriff's Office merged several years ago, they went to a county-wide computer system. If a wreck is investigated anywhere in the county, they enter the data. They've got an all-inclusive database."

"Okay," Sloan said, "so maybe he's switched up his name, interchanged the first and middle. Added a name. Or maybe his name was entered wrong."

"That's a lot of maybes. Afraid Charlotte doesn't have anything close to his name. And the names of accident victims who are even in the realm of possibles either aren't the same race as our guy or they're way out of the age range. Or the Marcellus in question had no injury in the accident, things like that."

"All right, he's lying about where the accident happened, or about his name. Why?" Sloan asked.

"That's what we need to find out," Clark said. "Maybe he's wanted somewhere."

Esposito offered a theory. "Maybe he gave a false name to hide a criminal history that would've kept him from getting a place at The Meadows."

"That's feasible," Clark replied. "And that makes it interesting for us. As of this moment, he's the last person we know of who spoke to Walker."

"Ain't it convenient that Marcellus just happened to notice something wrong with Walker?" Sloan asked.

"Yeah, I've thought about that, too," Clark said. "We need to get a make on this guy, but I'm not sure where to start." Clark paused for a moment. "We need to do a thorough check on him, confirm his name, see where he's from. Maybe he's legit; if he's using an alias, then we may have to get creative and get his prints, somehow. Get the manager to let us in his place one day when they're doing an inspection or something, print a drinking glass."

"Isn't that illegal, boss?" Esposito asked.

"It would be if we were using it as evidence in a criminal case against him. But this is only for our intel purposes. All we have to do is get in his place, brush a little powder around, lift a print, get out."

"By the way, where's his apartment?" Sloan asked.

Clark pointed to the two-story apartment building to the east. "He's on the back side, top floor."

Esposito's police radio blared with traffic.

"What was that?" Clark asked. "Mine's turned down."

"A car just struck a pole," Esposito said. "Sounds like a transformer's on fire. Looks like the sleet's starting to make things rough."

"Think I'm going to head on in," Clark said. "If it keeps coming down, y'all go ahead and close up shop here. Don't worry about patrolling around Nick's place, either. Maybe it'll be a quiet night with the bad weather."

"Thanks," Esposito said. "I don't think Jerry will be able to stomach any more of my music. And I don't think I'll be able to stomach any more of Jerry."

Clark turned up the volume on his police radio and heard more traffic on the wreck. "Sounds like a mess. They're calling for the rescue squad. Betcha somebody's pinned in. Did you catch where the wreck is? I may go by and check it out on the way home. They may need some help with traffic."

"Somewhere on Gordon Street," Esposito answered.

"Gordon Street?" Clark asked.

"Yes, sir."

Now he was sure he'd drive by and check it out. Lana Demarko. Lots of emergency lights at night and all the related commotion tend to bring the neighbors out. Maybe this would be his lucky night.

"Y'all be careful, see you tomorrow."

"Night, Lieutenant."

A few minutes after Clark pulled out of the parking lot, the sleet began to pick up, along with the wind.

"Time to head on in, partner," Sloan said. "I think we've both had enough of this for one night."

"Me too, big guy," Esposito said, as he cranked the car.

When Esposito revved up the engine, Sloan noticed some headlights coming from behind the two-story building. He continued to watch and saw that it was a van coming their way. He touched Esposito on the arm as he was shifting into drive.

"Hey, hold up a sec," Sloan said. "Put it back in park. Quick, take your foot off the brake."

When Esposito looked at Sloan to ask him why, the headlights shined on them and, instinctively, they ducked down in their seats. They heard the sloshing of the van's tires as it passed, and then they sat up.

"What's that all about?" Esposito asked.

"Kinda strange, don't you think? I mean, here? This time of night? This weather? Come on, let's tail it. We're leaving anyway."

Esposito pulled out slowly, without headlights, and followed the van. "Dark color," he said. "Can you make the tag?"

"Not unless you get closer. Where's your field glasses at?"

"Draped over the back of your seat."

Sloan grabbed the case, removed the binoculars, and began to focus them. The sleet made it difficult, but Sloan could see that the van had a handicapped license plate. "Oh, this is too good."

"What?"

"Can you get a little closer?"

"It's kind of hard without any lights, and this ice." He sped up a little, trying to gain some ground. He ran off the right shoulder a couple of times but kept control of the car. "What is it?"

"You ain't gonna believe it."

"What?"

"This van may be our...."

Suddenly, the two officers were jerked forward, Sloan dropped his binoculars, and his head slapped against the dash. Esposito's face hit the steering wheel, and the collision caused him to reflex and slam on the brakes. The car slid on the slippery road, but when Esposito recovered, he was able to bring it under control and to a stop. "Damn!" he yelled. "We hit something!"

"More like something hit us," Sloan said, applying pressure to his forehead to relieve the pain. "You okay?"

Esposito regained his composure, then put the car in reverse, backing slowly. Sloan lowered his window and the sleet pelted him in the face. He flashed his light over to the right shoulder as Esposito continued the slow speed in reverse. Sloan saw the deer lying on the side of the road, breathing heavily and bleeding. Esposito turned on his headlights but noticed the right one was out.

They got out and inspected the front right corner of the vehicle which, surprisingly, didn't look bad. They looked it over, and Esposito said, "Six, seven hundred bucks—no pun intended. Coulda been a lot worse."

"Yeah," Sloan said, walking over to the injured deer. He shined his light on the doe, panting heavily. "This one's had a bad day, I'm afraid."

When he said that, Esposito drew his Glock .45 from his holster, and held it at low ready.

Sloan looked at Esposito, and lightly touched his arm. "What do you think you're doing?"

"I'm gonna shoot it. Put it out of its pain."

"Think about it, Steve. We're standing here within earshot of The Meadows, where all these seniors are already freaked out about what they think is going on. That'll be all she wrote if they hear a gunshot. 'Fore you know it, we'll be pullin' permanent night shift over here."

As Sloan said that, he reached behind his back, lifted his sweater, and drew his knife from its sheath. Esposito watched carefully, absorbing the moment. Sloan bent over the doe, which kicked a little, and placed the sharp point of the knife against her throat. "Steve, you put it right here in the middle of the deer's neck, right where the windpipe is." When Sloan said that, he slowly and methodically sliced a neat, clean line. Blood gushed, and almost instantly the deer stopped breathing.

* * *

Three blocks from the accident site, Clark could see the impressive light show. A number of fire trucks, E.M.S. and rescue squad vehicles, utility trucks, and police cars dotted the area around the collision. The red, blue, and yellow emergency lights blinked, rotated, and pulsated in the freezing night. The sleet had slacked up somewhat, so neighbors and curious passing motorists poured into the already congested area. Clark activated his blue lights to bypass the long stream of cars.

He drove to within seventy-five feet of the wreck, got out, and began to sift through the crowd of onlookers. Clark surveyed the scene; it appeared that the car that struck the utility pole initially hit another car head on. Then that vehicle ran into a ditch and overturned. The larger crowd had migrated to the car at the pole, where a rescue squad volunteer was using a chainsaw to cut the pole away from the smashed door. Clark could see the driver stirring inside the car, and he looked like he was all right. *Must be a drunk driver, they always pull through in bad wrecks like these.*

Clark noticed that the wreck was four doors down from the Victorian house where he had seen the woman. He began to scan the crowd of about forty, hoping to see her, but no luck. He spent the next few minutes chatting with one of the patrol officers, who was trying to keep the crowd at a safe distance.

About ten minutes later, his attention was drawn back to the Victorian house when the front porch light came on. A woman came out and it looked like it could be her. He watched from the other side of the crowd, as she walked carefully down the sidewalk to the street. She joined a couple of bystanders, and appeared to be socializing with them as she continued toward the accident scene. It was her.

Clark glanced her way periodically, and felt that this could be his chance to meet her. Since he first saw her, he couldn't help but think about her every day. But over the last few days, she was consuming more and more of his thoughts. The mystery of her. Who she was and what she was like. Where she was going.

Fifteen minutes later, the excitement at the scene began to die down and so did the crowd. Clark glanced her way and saw her walking back in the direction of her house. He decided to make his move. He flipped open the cell phone that was clipped to his belt and turned it off.

She walked up the sidewalk to the porch, and Clark picked up the pace, getting to within thirty feet of her. *Not too close, don't want to scare her...here goes.* He took a deep breath, heart in a sprint, and called to her, "Ma'am, excuse me, ma'am."

She turned to him, but she didn't say anything. She looked around for a nearby neighbor, and then back at him, regarding him carefully.

CHAPTER TWENTY-FOUR

He stopped at the end of the sidewalk and displayed his badge. "I'm Lt. Dixon, with the Police Department, and that's my car," he said, pointing to the unmarked sedan with its blue lights flashing.

"Yes?"

"I just received a page from headquarters, and my phone's dead. Do you mind if I use your phone to make a quick call to the office?"

She stood there for another moment, evaluating him, then she looked at the car. "Sure, come on in," she answered, waving him to the house.

He walked to the porch, climbed the steps, and introduced himself. "I'm Clark Dixon."

"Lana Demarko." She studied him closely, with an inquisitive expression. "Have we met?"

Do dreams count? "I don't believe so," Clark said, as they shook hands. He noticed her hand was soft, yet her handshake was firm, confident. An alluring smile, beautiful brown eyes. He was standing face-to-face with his fantasy; he was impressed, just like he knew he'd be. "Thanks for letting me use your phone. I really appreciate it. These phones are useless sometimes," he said, nodding to his phone, "especially in weather like this."

"Anything to help Stuartsboro's finest," Lana said, good-naturedly, leading him into the front entrance. "It looks like your colleagues have their hands full down there with that terrible wreck. Do you think the drivers are going to be okay?"

"Yeah, I think so. The guy in the overturned car was very lucky. Banged up with a few scratches. The guy who hit him and then the pole, he's got some bad lacerations, probably a broken bone or two. You always get these bad wrecks right after the ice starts. People haven't adjusted their driving yet because they don't realize the roads are that bad." Clark wasn't exactly sure what he was saying, but he hoped that whatever he said sounded impressive. He was having a little difficulty concentrating, because he felt like he was watching himself walk across the threshold of a door that led into a dream.

They entered a large hallway that Clark found to be impressive. "Here's the phone," she said, directing him to the credenza. "I'll be right back." She walked down the hallway, and turned out of view.

"Thanks," Clark called out, "I won't be but a second." He surveyed around him and glanced into an adjoining living room. He was a bit overwhelmed by his surroundings. The hallway was larger than Clark's own den, with a winding staircase and elegant chandelier. *So this is life on Gordon Street.* Well-crafted, old furnishings lined the hallway and portraits in oval frames hung on the walls that were papered in a large floral print design. Dimly lit by light sconces, the hallway looked unchanged and unspoiled by anything in the last half century.

As he walked across the hardwood floor, his steps echoed throughout the long hallway. He picked up the phone, wondering if there was a husband or boyfriend in another room. He listened but he couldn't hear anything. She sounded like she was still in a back room but, nonetheless, he went through the motions of pretending to make a call. When he placed the receiver to his ear, she reappeared and gave him a hand towel. She smiled and returned to the back.

Then Clark spoke. "Hey, it's Lieutenant, I got your page…Yeah, we'll probably need to check with Reidsville. Their case sounds very similar to ours…No, I didn't…It can wait 'til tomorrow. I don't think there's any need to call them tonight…Sure…We need to send the locate message, and Reidsville needs to clear it…No problem…Okay, bye."

He put the phone down and dried his hair with the towel. He took a few steps toward the back hallway and, as he did, Lana met him.

"I'm having some hot tea. Would you like some?" she asked.

"Sure, thanks. That's very kind of you."

"Come on back," she said, and he followed her.

He noticed that she had taken off her coat and was wearing a pale orange sweatshirt with blue jeans. *The color of the sweatshirt and her auburn hair, very lovely. Does everything she have look great with her hair? Nice pair of jeans. She is gifted.* He followed her down the hallway, intently watching; he likened her moves to those of a prowling cat. "You have a beautiful home, Ms. Demarko, very nice."

She turned left through French doors and led Clark into a spacious study. "Thank you, but it's not mine. It's my uncle's. He lived here for over forty years." She stopped near the center of the room, placing her hands on the top of a wing chair. "He always loved this room. He proudly claimed that some of his biggest, most successful deals were made in here. He was a businessman. Real estate, investments." She glanced at him, then around the room. "Do you like honey or sugar in your tea, Lieutenant?"

"Honey sounds great."

"Make yourself at home. I'll be right back."

He ambled around the study and, although it was spacious, he found it to be cozy and comfortable. A dying fire. A couple of table lamps that cast light into corners. The walls were rich wood paneling with floor-to-ceiling built-in bookcases. Stately. A large rust-colored leather sofa dominated the center of the room.

Clark felt as though he had stepped back into the 1940s. If for just this moment, he was the leading man in one of those black and white movies that he loved to watch. He had the feeling. It was as if he was called upon as a last minute stand-in for Cary Grant in *My Girl Friday*. All he needed was the pipe and the smoker's jacket, and the cameras could roll.

He stood with his back to the fire, and its warmth drew him to it like a magnet. He continued to listen for activity in other parts of the house, but the only noise he heard was the crackling fire behind him. Surely there was no other man here, or else she wouldn't have offered him to stay for tea. Would she?

He loosened his necktie and enjoyed watching the firelight dancing about the ceiling. Shortly, Lana returned to the room.

"Here you go," she said; "it's a little hot. Be careful."

"Thanks," he said, "this is really kind of you. In my line of work, it's not too often that I get invitations for tea. Come to think of it, this may be a first. I could get used to this." He reached for the cup and saucer, glanced down, and noticed that she was barefoot. Her feet were beautiful, her toenails manicured and painted red. Sexy. It stirred him a little.

"Then maybe you've been working the wrong areas of town," she said jokingly, showing a bit of a sly look.

He liked her quick response. It was obvious that she was sharp, a nice sense of humor. "Well, to tell you the truth, I kept waiting for the job opening to come up for the Gordon Street walking beat, but it never posted." Then he handed her the towel. "Thanks for the towel, it feels good to be dry again."

"Would you like to sit down for a minute?" she asked, showing him to the sofa.

"Sure, why not." Clark went over and sat at the end closest to the fire. He tried to sip the tea, but it was too hot.

She walked over to the hearth, stoked the fire, and then placed a couple of small logs on it. "I love this fireplace. I remember as a child coming here and visiting Uncle Bill and Aunt Nancy at Thanksgiving, right about this time." She gazed at the fire for a moment, as if in a trance. "My sister and I used to rake leaves up from the big oak tree to the side porch and jump into the pile all afternoon. We had a ball. When it got dark, we'd come inside and he'd always have this nice fire burning. We'd have so much fun toasting marshmallows, and...." She stopped abruptly, catching herself reminiscing a little too much in front of the visitor.

As she spoke, Clark was taken by the childlike expression on her face and enthusiasm in her voice. It was refreshing to him. She retold the event like she was sharing the experience with her third grade classmates at the Monday morning show-and-tell.

"Sounds like a great time," Clark said. "And I know what you mean about a nice fire. Nothing like one at the end of a rough day. Seems to smooth everything out."

"I imagine in your line of work, you have your share of them, rough days."

Clark paused for a moment, unsure of how much he wanted to reveal to her. "I've been at it so long that they all kind of seem the same to me. Bland. Not necessarily good or bad. I'm just glad when the whistle blows." He took a sip of the tea. It had a nice flavor. "This tea is delicious."

"Glad you like it. I drink way too much coffee during the day at work. I think tea's a nice change of pace in the evening. I would think that you drink a lot of coffee on your job. Is it true, the stronger the better?"

"Depends on whether you're on or off duty and how strong a drink you want it to be."

"How strong do you like it?"

"Like I got it now, but not a bit hotter," he said, chuckling a little.

As they talked, he kept trying to see if she was wearing a wedding band. It didn't look like she was, but it was a little too dark in the room to be sure. The fire was picking up gradually and, as it did, her loveliness grew in the glow cast by the flames. But the left side of her face, the side in the shadows, he found just as intriguing. He took another sip. "Your uncle, you spoke of him in the past tense, is he, uh...?"

"No, no he's not. But he's not doing well. He's in the skilled care unit at the hospital. He suffered a stroke back around the end of September, and he's gotten progressively worse over the last couple of months. I'm here for a few days to look after some things with the property, and handle some business.

Aunt Nancy passed away in March, and now it looks like Uncle Bill may not see Thanksgiving."

"I'm sorry. I know that aunts and uncles are really special people. I've lost some of the best in the last several years that a guy could ever have. Cancer. Nothing's easy about that."

Lana continued. "Bill and Nancy never had any children, so they spent a lot of time with my sister and me. They were so good to us. We used to spend wonderful summers here."

"Well, I guess our paths probably have crossed at some point in the past, because I've lived here all my life." He sipped his tea, leaned forward and said, "Hey, wait a minute."

"What?"

"You do look familiar to me now."

"I do?" she asked, surprised.

"Yeah, you do. Didn't you break in front of me in line at McDonald's in 1968?"

She took a moment, resisting the smile, and decided to play along. "Well, if I confess now, am I going to be arrested?"

"Oh, I reckon the statute of limitations has run out. Tell you what, let's split the difference. I'll consider this cup of tea to be your community service." Clark was having a great time, and couldn't believe how enjoyable the conversation was with her. Instant attraction?

"I couldn't help but overhear when you were on the phone, you said something about Reidsville?" When she asked that, he noticed that she was gently gliding her finger around the rim of her cup, back and forth.

"Reidsville? Oh yeah. We're working a couple of cases that may be connected to something that they're investigating."

"I live in Reidsville."

"Oh, really?"

"I was wondering if there was anything that I should be concerned about."

"Nothing more going on there than what's going on in most places these days. Sad to say, but it's the truth."

"Bad as it may seem, I know it's an improvement over the way things were when we lived in Greensboro. All the murders and gang shootings. Gangs are getting to be a big problem there. That was one of the reasons for the move to Reidsville. You know, I thought I'd mind the commute to work to Greensboro every day, but in some ways I like it. Helps to wind up, wind down. We live on the south end of town, so the drive to work isn't all that bad. Twenty,

twenty-five minutes most mornings. We had a beautiful home in a quiet neighborhood in Starmount, but at some point you get so tired of all the traffic, all the lines everywhere you go. My daughter, Whitney, goes to U.N.C.-G. It would have been nice to still live there for that reason, but she comes home most weekends."

"Greensboro? Too big for me, too. Love shopping and going out to eat there, but that's about it. I couldn't afford the taxes. Reidsville sounds like a nice place to live, from what I've heard. Close to the big city, but not too close. By the way, I know a couple of supervisors in your Police Department. Went to school with one of them, Captain Wray. How long have you lived there?"

"Going on two years now."

"Are you from Greensboro originally?"

"No, I'm a Durham gal. But let me make it perfectly clear before you ask. I'm not a Duke fan."

"Glad you made that clear. Speaking of Reidsville, when I was a kid, I used to go there to visit my grandmother. She lived in a two-story gray house on Vance Street. Talk about fond childhood memories…the fun times in the backyard. Neighborhood games like 'Fox and the Hounds' and 'Kick the Bucket'. Endless hours of playing whiffle ball. Walking to the neighborhood store and buying baseball cards and a pocket full of candy for a quarter." The talk of it pulled him, for an instant, back to that time, the feel of it. For that moment, he looked up and past her.

"If we could go back for just one day," she said, as she noticed a sparkle in his eye. "Sounds like we're traveling down memory lane tonight, doesn't it?"

"Yeah, I guess it does."

"Nice, don't you think?"

"I suppose so, unless the lane you're traveling down happens to have a dead end."

"Most everybody's got a few of those," she said, sipping her tea.

From the conversation, he still couldn't determine if she was married or not. He decided to take the lead. "So you have a daughter at U.N.C.-G.?"

"Yes. Whitney's a sophomore."

"I've got two in college. Michael graduates from Carolina next spring and Alex goes to the community college here. She lives with me. My other daughter and son live with their mother in Rallingview."

"Four kids?"

"That's right. I came from a family of five kids, so it seemed natural to have a big family."

"My older daughter Jennie goes to Carolina. Did you say your son's a senior?"

"Yep, he graduates in May. He's studying to be a teacher. I'll actually have a tax-paying child in the work force."

"Jennie's a junior. She loves it at Chapel Hill."

They chatted a little longer, mostly small talk, which didn't seem so small to Clark. He finished his tea, thinking it should be his cue to leave. He had felt so relaxed, sitting on the plush sofa, enjoying hot tea and a surging fire. Talking with her seemed so easy. Clark had made a career of being able to read others, and he believed that she was having a good time, too. He stood up and said, "Thanks for the tea, Ms. Demarko. It was a pleasure to meet you. And thanks for letting me use your phone."

"Any time. It was nice to meet you, as well."

As she turned to lead him to the hallway, he reached in his back pocket and pulled out his small mag-lite. With her back to him, he quietly placed it on the coffee table. He followed her to the front door, and took a business card from his coat pocket. When she opened the door, he handed her his card and said, "Thanks again."

"So we're even on the McDonald's thing?"

"Even Stephen. If you ever need anything, give me a call." As she looked down at the card, he looked at her left hand. No ring.

"Thanks, I will. Good night, Lieutenant," she said, smiling, and they shook hands once again.

"Good night, Ms. Demarko," he said, and walked out. Clark went down the porch steps and headed to the street. Then it dawned on him. This was the exact spot where he first saw her a couple of weeks ago. This visit *was* like a dream. He did get to meet her, after all. She was a beautiful woman. He got to chat with her, even share a cup of tea and a couple of laughs. But he wanted more. *The story of my life.* Clark headed to the car.

* * *

Three hours later, seventy miles away in Salisbury, the night manager of the Super-City Department Store lay severely wounded in the parking lot. His hands trembled, as he looked up, trying to keep the rain out of his eyes. The gunman stood over him, the end of the rifle barrel pressed against his blood-soaked face.

"You are very weak. You are pitiful," the gunman said in a cold tone. Then he pulled the trigger. Twice.

* * *

Later that morning, at 11:15, all the pagers in Clark's unit buzzed with the S.B.I. phone number in Raleigh.

CHAPTER TWENTY-FIVE

Clark leaned against the shower wall, took a deep breath, and relaxed. Then he turned around and allowed the hot water to beat against his neck and shoulders; he stood there reveling in the moment. While he did, he rehashed the events of the previous day. The break-in at Nick's All-Seasons was a big loss—typical of cases with nothing to go on. Almost like clockwork, All-Seasons would take a hit every year around Thanksgiving. There were preventive measures the owners could employ to minimize their chances of getting hit, but they didn't. *Maybe nobody gives a shit; why should we worry about it?* The insurance company would settle, and business was back to usual. In the end, the Police Department would take criticism for being incompetent or indifferent. Old man Evans would bury them every morning on the biscuit circuit, starting at Chaney's Restaurant and ending up at Farmer's Table.

As Clark showered, he thought about the Harris Teeter case and the stolen license plate strategy. He realized that the plan they were using to catch the robbers hinged on timing. But was the green van really connected to the case? If so, were the perps still driving it? Still stealing tags just before their robberies? Would the next stolen tag be reported by the victim in time for Clark and his men to get notice from Raleigh, get the word out to other departments, and set up? How much would other departments even care about the BOLO?

He walked over to the closet to get dressed and thought about the enjoyable time he had with Lana Demarko. She was kind and friendly. Why? She was one of those rare women who had the gift of making a guy feel so important. On the chance that he might see her today, he wanted to look his best. He decided to pick a suit in a color that Lana might like, one that she would wear. He reached for the dark brown one and got dressed.

In the kitchen, Alex was pouring a cup of coffee when he walked in, over to her, and kissed her on the head. "Morning, sweetheart," he said. "What're you doing up so early, with school out this week?"

She put two pieces of bread in the toaster. "Lauren and I may go shopping after a while. I want to go ahead and get in an early workout. Get that out of the way."

"Well, aren't you the smart one," he said, sipping his coffee. "Ahh, good stuff, girl."

"Have you made a list of what we need for Thanksgiving yet? It's only two days away."

"A list?"

"Yeah, a list. You know, a grocery list."

"Well, uh, no. I was planning on getting that together today."

She gave him a suspicious look, and then grinned. "Just what did you have in mind? How big a dinner are you thinking about?"

She asked the questions with all the savvy of an expert interrogator, scanning her target for signs of deception. Clark deliberated a moment. "Since you're going to have a big lunch at your mom's, I was thinking about something lighter for dinner. Snacks, like chicken wings and potato salad. Maybe some salsa and chips, stuff like that. How does that sound?"

"That sounds good," she said, slightly surprised. "Want me to run by the store and get some of the things while I'm out?"

"Hey, that would be great, sweetie," he said, reaching in his wallet. He pulled out a twenty-dollar bill, but angled his wallet so she couldn't see that he only had five dollars left. "If you need some more, let me know."

"Daddy?"

"What?"

She hesitated. "Are—are you sure there's no way we could all get together for lunch on Thanksgiving?" Her voice was subdued. "What would that hurt?"

Clark put his cup down on the counter. "Honey, we've been over this." He paused, trying to be sensitive, then explained, "It's just the way things are. I'm sorry. I...look, I called your mom...I've tried to...." Then he caught himself, realizing he had said too much.

"You've tried to what?"

"Nothing."

"You've tried to what, Daddy?"

"Nothing honey," he answered. But then he made a mistake. He looked at her and saw that expression. That expression. The one he first saw in her toddler years—when she used to reach desperately for him with her arms, begging him to rescue her from the playpen. The one that he never quite learned to turn down. He crumbled. "Look, maybe you ought to know. I called your mom a few days ago. I asked her if she may be interested in going out for dinner. Before I asked her, I'd given it a lot of thought. It was just going to be friends together over dinner. That's all."

"What happened?"

"Nothing. She hung up, some office emergency. Evidently, your mom doesn't think that it's such a good idea. And she's probably right. With that said, it would be unfair to force anything like a Thanksgiving meal on her. We, I need to respect the way she feels. Don't you see? It doesn't mean forever, Alex. Maybe later, things will...."

"She never called you back?"

They talked a couple more minutes. Of the four kids, Alex seemed the most affected by the divorce. She also seemed like the one who was the most optimistic about reconciliation. Kids should never give up. When he was a child, he never did.

* * *

Later that morning, Sgt. Cunningham walked into the conference room, and saw Clark jotting some training information on the laminated calendar. He handed Clark a piece of paper. "Here ya go, Lieutenant."

"What's this?"

"The estimate on Steve's car. M&H had the lowest figure of the three shops."

"$1,175.00. Nothing low about that. But no choice, we have to get it fixed. Why don't you see if they can take it today or tomorrow? That way it can sit over the Thanksgiving weekend and it'll be ready for Esposito to pick up on Monday."

"Okay."

Wilkens walked in and took a seat at the table with a file. "I heard about Steve and Jerry. What happened last night?"

Clark smiled. "Well, let's just say that Esposito won't be getting the 'Safe Driver of the Year Award' this year," he said, shaking his head.

"How bad was it?"

"Not very. They were wrapping up their assignment at The Meadows, when they saw your buddy, Marcellus, leaving and they followed him. They got no farther than a half-mile from the complex when Rudolph dashes out in front of them. Smashed the right front corner of Steve's car."

"They're okay, though?"
"Yeah."
"What time did it happen?"
"Around 9:00, 9:30."
"Wonder where Marcellus was going to that time of night?"
"In that ice, too," Clark added.
"What did you say Charlotte PD found on him?" Cunningham asked.
"Nothing. Nada," Clark replied. "They had no accident report with his name, either as a driver or passenger. Didn't even have him in their master files. They checked city utilities, everything." Everyone was silent for a moment. Then Clark spoke. "You know, I was nearly ready to hang it up on this Walker thing. Even considering the missing glasses, questions about the death scene, the store videotape. But now, now with this Marcellus guy, about the last contact she had…we catch him in an apparent lie. Add to that a mysterious late night drive. Questions seem to be popping up again."

Cunningham followed. "So maybe we need to put a tail on him for a couple of nights and see where he's goin' to at such late hours."

"Looked to me like Walker died in her sleep," Wilkens said, "peacefully. But let's assume Marcellus was involved in her death. What's his motive? She wasn't robbed, that we know of."

"Maybe a sexual assault," Cunningham suggested. "Hey, Lieutenant, what does the Chief say about all this?"

"I haven't told him about last night yet. He's not going to be too happy about the damage to Steve's car. As far as the foul play theory, I had him hanging on, but only by a thread. However, now with these issues surrounding Marcellus, maybe he'll give me a little room to nose around some more."

"I don't know," Wilkens said, shaking his head. "It was something about Marcellus that made me wonder. Something wasn't right. You want me to pay him another visit, check him out some more?"

"Better not," Clark warned. "We don't want to spook him. If he's on the run, he's already super sensitive to us. We have to play it below the radar. What we need is his prints. If we can get his prints and run them through A.F.I.S., then we'll know more about what we're dealing with."

"You mean 'who' we're dealing with," Cunningham said.
"Right, 'who'."
"How do you plan to get his prints?" Wilkens asked.
"That'll be the easy part," Clark said. "I think our deer slayers will be able

to accommodate us on that. All we need is for Marcellus to take another spin in the next few nights and we'll be good to go."

Clark walked back to his office to get caught up on paperwork. He noticed his voice mail light was burning. He had been checking his messages frequently over the course of the morning, hoping that Lana would find his flashlight and call him. The phone screen indicated that he had five messages. The first message was from the reporter at the *Sentinel*, wanting an update on the accident on Gordon Street and the break-in at Nick's All-Seasons.

The second message was a hang-up.

Then he played the third message: "*Hello, this is Olivia. I'm the nurse you spoke with on Saturday about Keith Hall's surgery. I had a note in the file to call and notify you that his surgery is scheduled for tomorrow morning, first thing. My supervisor said you need to get the medical information release form and have it signed, prior to getting Hall's records. If you can call me by 11:30 this morning, I'll be more than happy to run it by your Department on my way to lunch.*"

At the end of the message, she left her desk number. *Oh yeah, the nurse with the beautiful blue eyes. So Keith's going back for surgery.* Clark was a little surprised. He didn't think Keith looked all that strong on Saturday. Clark hoped that the bullet to be removed would be in good enough condition to compare to a gun and enter in the I.B.I.S. system. They were "0 for 1" in the latter category.

As he was checking his next message, his pager buzzed. He glanced at the page, noting that it was a long distance number, a 919 area code, Raleigh. The voice message continued to play: "*...just called me and told me about your conversation this morning. Clark, why the hell did you tell her that you asked me out? That was private, between us. She's upset with me. What are you trying to do? Pit her against me?*" After a pause, she continued, her voice angrier: "*If you're trying to use Alex to get back with me or to get back at me....*" Click.

"Didn't that go well," Clark muttered. He hadn't counted on Alex confronting her mom with the matter. Maybe he should have kept it to himself. Too late now.

Then he played the last message: "*Hello, this is Lana Demarko. I think you left your flashlight in the study here last night. It's a small black flashlight. If it's not yours, you can disregard this message. If it is yours, call me on my cell phone and we can arrange for you to stop by and get it. My number is 555-0328. Talk to you later.*"

He had forgotten how smooth and sexy her voice sounded. Hearing the recording of it made him reminisce about last night. He wondered when he should call her back. At the end of the day? That way he could stop by without being interrupted by work. Would she be different? More business-like?

Clark was deep in thought when Whitaker walked into his office.

"Lieutenant, did you get the page from Raleigh?"

When he asked that, Esposito and Wilkens walked in too, evidently for the same reason. Then it struck Clark what the page was related to. "Yeah, have you made the call to the S.B.I. yet?"

"Sure did," Whitaker answered enthusiastically. "D.C.I. said that they got a stolen tag entry a few minutes ago from the Rowan County Sheriff's Department."

"Anything else?"

"I called the Sheriff's Department and got the story. The detective I spoke with said the victim reported that the plate was on his van when he went in to work Monday evening, third shift. When he got off work this morning, he realized that it was stolen."

"What kind of business was it?"

"A textile mill, outside of Salisbury."

"These have got to be your boys," Clark remarked.

"What now?" Cunningham asked.

"You've got the broadcast message prepared, right?" Clark asked Whitaker, who nodded. "Let's roll on this. Get dispatch to send the message to all agencies within a 100-mile radius. Label it 'Urgent Message' my authority. Also, put special attention for areas where there are supermarkets, superstores, places like that. Put emphasis on times of day at and after closing. I'll give Capt. Blackburn and the Chief a call, to see if we can beef up patrol for the next couple of nights. They could very well come back here and hit us again. I think I'll call Williams at the Bureau." Then Clark turned to Esposito. "What are you using for a car since yours is down?"

"Would it be okay to drive one of the narcs' cars? They're off for the holidays."

"Yeah, that's fine. I'll let Captain know. Is Sloan planning on helping out again tonight?"

"He's gonna ask for the night off, but you didn't hear it from me."

Clark turned to Wilkens. "Can you fill in for Sloan on The Meadows assignment tonight?"

"I should be able to. Let me make a call and I'll let you know shortly."

"Thanks, Brad. If Marcellus goes mobile, then there's something I want y'all to do. If you clear from it at a decent hour, then afterwards, you and Steve can patrol around and help out with the BOLO for the green van."

"Will do."

"If you stay out much past midnight, get some rest and don't worry about getting here right at eight in the morning. We'll manage 'til you get in. Wednesday's our last work day."

As they left his office, Clark's phone rang again. The screen read "William Everhart". A little nervous, he took a deep breath. "Lt. Dixon, may I help you?"

"Lt. Dixon, this is Lana Demarko. I left you a message earlier about your flashlight."

"Yes, thanks for the call. How are you?"

"I'm very well. And you?"

"Doing good. Hey, I appreciate the call. That is my flashlight. I didn't even realize it was missing 'til I got your message."

"I saw it on the table in the study this morning."

"Yes, and I think we may have a problem."

"Excuse me?"

"Well, if you recall our conversation last night, I was willing to overlook the disorderly conduct incident at McDonald's several years ago. However, now you turn around and steal my police flashlight. I don't know what to say. Theft of police property is a felony. I don't think I can help you any longer."

Lana giggled. "This sounds serious. But I'll have you know, Lieutenant, I've got good attorney friends and special people in high places. I can have your job."

Clark laughed. "First of all, the phrase 'good attorney friends' has got to be an oxymoron. Secondly, if you had my job, then you wouldn't have much more than that flashlight you're holding."

Lana played along. "I better not say anything else until I can confer with legal counsel. I will tell you, though, that I'm running to Reidsville for a while, and I'll be back later this afternoon. I'd be glad to drop the flashlight by the Police Station now, or you could stop by later on your way home and get it. I didn't know if you'd be needing it now."

"If it's okay with you, I'll stop by on my way home. I'm kind of in the middle of something. Would that be all right?"

"That'll be fine."

"I'll call first. Thanks, again."

When he hung up, he thought about Lana. She liked to joke around. And laugh. Laughter was definitely something he could use more of. Clark felt that beautiful women usually didn't score all that well on the personality test. She, however, was making straight A's. He thought about when he'd be stopping by later to see her. Then he began to fantasize about a romantic rendezvous, slowly unfolding. His phone rang and snapped him to present. "Lt. Dixon."

"Yes, listen carefully," the voice hummed. No regular voice. Some kind of electrical device was disguising it. "I have information about your robbery at Harris Teeter."

"Who is this?"

"Your robbery is tied to several others: Charlotte, Greensboro, Winston-Salem, and…"

"How do you know…?"

"…and High Point," the voice snapped, and grew louder. "And not only that, but your case is connected to cases all over the Southeast United States."

"How do you know about all this?"

"Trust me, I know."

"Are you involved in some way?"

"No."

"Then why should I believe you?"

"Call these agencies and examine their case files. You can see for yourself."

Clark was scribbling notes as quickly as he could. "Will you give me a call-back number? I promise that I won't try to trace it. You have my…."

Click.

CHAPTER TWENTY-SIX

"Give me a minced barbeque, hot dog everything but onions, large fry, large coke," Capt. Blackburn said.

"You want slaw on the barbeque?"

"Yes, please. Apple turnover to go with it."

The waitress smiled and repeated both orders. They nodded and she walked away.

"Watching that cholesterol, huh?" Clark asked.

"Hey, what do you expect in this place, anyway? Grilled salmon with steamed vegetables?"

"Better watch that size eight figure of yours, Richard. Four months to go to retirement. You want to make sure you can still get into your uniform, look your best at your farewell dinner."

Blackburn grinned. "Ah yes, four months. I like the sound of that…rings true in me ears. Along about the first day of spring, marching out of here. I'll be thinking about you guys, Clark." Blackburn slid some keys across the table to him. "Here's the keys to the car you asked for. Tell Dale Earnhardt, Jr. to go easy tonight, will you? I can't afford to put another car in the garage. I already have one out of service. Hey, want some action on the Packers and Lions game on Thanksgiving Day?"

"You know I'm a diehard Packer man from way back."

"So are you in or not?"

"Nah. I'll wait for the Super Bowl to throw in my bet." Clark's pager buzzed and he checked it. "Thanks for the loaner. This security detail over at The Meadows may uncover something interesting for us."

"Who's your page from?"

"Sloan. He wants to stop by and tell me something about Marcellus." Clark called Sloan and gave him his location. "We're at Short Sugar's. Come on by, we just ordered." Then he hung up.

"Marcellus? He's the one at The Meadows that you're talking about?"

"Yeah. We need to check him out." Clark peered over his shoulder for an eavesdropper, then spoke in a lower voice. "He may have had something to do with the Walker woman's death."

"So now you're back to thinking that she was murdered? You've waffled more on this case than a politician, haven't you?"

Clark took a sip of water, ignoring Blackburn's questions.

"If she was murdered, what's the motive?"

"I knew you were going to ask me that. Don't know. That's the piece missing in this puzzle."

"Big piece, Clark."

A few minutes later, the waitress brought their food and they dug in.

Clark took a bite of his minced barbeque sandwich. "Delicious. This is absolutely the best, better than Fuzzy's or Stamey's. Why do Lexington and Smithfield brag about their barbeque? They got to know they can't compete with this. How's yours?"

"Good stuff," Blackburn said, taking a bite. "Say Clark, what's the matter with Whitaker?"

"What do you mean?"

"I passed him in the office right before I left to come here, and he looked like he'd lost his best friend or something. He barely spoke to me. He's usually a pretty friendly guy."

"He's a little down over the Salisbury murder/robbery."

"Salisbury?"

"Yeah, haven't you heard?"

"Uh-uh."

Clark took another bite of his sandwich, then continued. "Price had this plan, and it almost worked. A few days ago, he contacted the S.B.I. in Raleigh and had the license theft people flag all stolen plate entries where the vehicle was a Ford E-150, like the one we think our suspects are using."

"Sounds like a pretty good plan."

"We all got a page on it this morning. Price called Rowan County and learned that a tag was reported stolen off a van just outside of Salisbury. The problem was that we got the notification too late. The theft occurred overnight and the perps committed the robbery in Salisbury, evidently, shortly after the theft. So our page came a few hours too late."

"Damn. Half a day late, and a dollar short."

"Yeah. If the perps had waited and committed the robbery after the plate was reported stolen, we would've gotten the page and at least been able to alert the area. Who knows, maybe Salisbury would have picked up their patrol and caught them. Now they've got a murder." Clark paused, looked around again. "Headshot. At least we know now that the van is our guys."

"Same M.O.?"

"Yeah. Large department store. I heard the store video shows three, four guys, dressed like our suspects, going in and robbing the manager after closing. At some point, he broke away and ran for it. They shot him in the back, caught him, and for good measure they executed him, point blank. Just like our case, but our kid got lucky."

"Well, so two things we know. The perps are still using the same van and game plan. Their luck'll run out."

"I hope ours doesn't run out first." When Clark said that, Jerry Sloan walked in the restaurant, over to their booth, and slid in beside Blackburn. Clark asked Sloan, "How was your meeting in Greensboro?"

"Not bad," Sloan said, and as he did, the waitress came over and took his order. When she walked away, Sloan eagerly watched her, and whispered, "I'd like to barbeque that."

Blackburn laughed.

Clark shook his head, grinning. "Focus, Jerry, focus."

Sloan turned back to his lieutenant. "I am, believe me, I am." Then he leaned over a little closer to Clark. "What would you say if I told you we may be able to make this All-Seasons break-in and this thing with Marcellus may help us do it?"

Clark lit up. "Then I'd say that you have my undivided attention and Capt. Blackburn has your lunch."

"Here's the deal," Sloan said. "I took the case file, along with the others you asked me to, and shared them at the intel meeting. Turns out that Reidsville has a snitch who has made some pretty big cases for them. He says that there's a theft ring operating out of our area that hits lawn and tractor places, just like Nick's. They hit this kind of business all over the state and the Southeast, and haul off big numbers. They score fast, use lookouts and radio communications, high tech stuff."

Sloan continued his briefing for a couple more minutes, until the waitress brought him his food, then he paused until she left. "They even take orders in advance, for equipment that they steal. We're talking heavy equipment, too, like they got at Nick's."

"Sounds interesting. So where's it going to?"

"The snitch said most of it goes somewhere out in the Midwest. Some of it's even being hauled overseas and sold to third world countries for outrageous prices."

"The Midwest?"

"Yeah, and get this," Sloan's tone became more excited, "the ringleader is supposed to be some guy who is from the Midwest, where some of the goods are going."

"Cleveland," Clark said in a low voice.

"What?" Blackburn asked.

"Cleveland," Clark repeated. "Marcellus is from Cleveland, at least that's where he says he's from."

Sloan beamed with excitement. "So what do you think?"

"You said the snitch said the ring is operating out of this area. 'This area' could mean here, Charlotte, High Point...."

"I know," Sloan said, interrupting. "But that's the best they got right now. The reason the snitch thinks they're based in this area is that a couple of the dudes are seen from time to time, hanging around Reidsville, Greensboro. That's right up the road."

"Marcellus does have the extended van. Maybe the handicap is a cover," Clark said.

"That and living in The Meadows. How much more low key could you get?"

"Out of state orders," Clark said. "That could involve the F.B.I."

"How do you figure?" Blackburn asked.

"Interstate theft. When I heard 'utility tractor', I knew we were up against something organized."

Sloan continued. "The F.B.I. was at the meeting. The agent said he's taking it back to the Greensboro office to his boss."

"Good luck, there," Clark said in a pessimistic tone.

"Why do you say that?"

"You see how much help they are now on bank robberies, don't you? This terrorism thing's caused them to shift all their assets, especially manpower. A theft ring would have to be huge, before it grabs their attention. Of course, this one sounds like it could be that large." Then Clark asked Sloan, "You're off tonight, right?"

"Yes sir, if it's okay."

"Yeah, it's all right. I think I'll tell Steve and Brad to concentrate on Marcellus, tail him if he goes out. It looks like our perps hit last night in Salisbury, so I think we're okay, at least for a couple of days anyway. Famous last words."

BLOODY NOVEMBER

* * *

On the way to Lana's house, Clark called a number.

"Special Agent Williams."

"Oh yeah, what's so special about you, Agent Williams?"

"There aren't enough hours in the day to answer that one."

"I can't believe you're still in the office at five 'til five. Are you up for your annual appraisal?"

"Funny, Clark. You're keeping me from getting to the parking lot, plus you're abusing a state telephone line. What's going on?"

"Need a favor."

"Fire away."

"Our Harris Teeter case, the kid's going to be operated on tomorrow and they hope to remove the other bullet. If we rush it over there, can you have it analyzed for us tomorrow, as well?"

"Hey Clark, you know tomorrow's the last day of the week with Thanksgiving."

"I'm asking a lot, I know it's a big favor, but I also know our robbery is connected to some others. Did you hear about the Salisbury murder early this morning?"

"No, I didn't. Salisbury's in the Southern Piedmont District. What happened?"

Clark filled Greg in on the details. He also told him about Whitaker's strategy with the S.B.I. in Raleigh, the notification of the stolen tag, and how it was several hours too late. "Salisbury's sounds a lot like ours. It really would help us to identify some other agencies in the same hunt for these guys."

"Ah, I see what you mean. Hubert *is* on vacation," Williams said thoughtfully. "How quickly can you get it over here tomorrow?"

"The surgery is scheduled first thing in the morning. We'll be waiting to catch it as soon as the surgeon has his mitts on it."

"I'll get Rosalie, our lab tech, to be on stand-by. Get it here ASAP, okay?"

"Thanks, Greg. You know, your kindness humbles me. It makes me feel a little guilty for trashing your locker our senior year."

"That's okay, Clark. I'm the one who put the rubber in your hotdog at the awards picnic."

Clark chuckled, and then switched to a businesslike tone. "Maybe this bullet will be a little better quality than the last one."

"Frankly, I was kind of surprised that the last one wasn't good enough for I.B.I.S., but I'm no expert."

"Hey, one more thing and I'll let you go. I got a weird call this morning. Anonymous caller, couldn't tell male or female because he used some sort of amplifier to disguise his voice."

"What was it about?"

"The caller told me that our Harris Teeter case, the one you and I are talking about, is connected to robberies and shootings all over the state and the Southeast U.S."

"Probably some crackpot."

"Nah, I don't think so."

"What makes you say that?"

"A couple of things," Clark said as he glanced at his note pad, then back to the road. "It was the words he used, words like 'agency' and 'case file'. You've got to admit that these aren't typical words used on the street."

"Go on."

"He mentioned that our case was related to robberies in Greensboro, Charlotte, and other cities. He used specifics. Another thing was the way he phrased his statements. I get crank calls every so often, but they're nothing like this one. I'm telling you, this guy was detailed, talked intelligently. And the disguised voice, why?"

"Because either you know him, he knows you, or he thinks that you may meet. Your line's not taped or traceable, is it?"

"No on both counts."

"Well, maybe this bullet you're going to get us will answer some of these questions. Get it over here and we'll see what you have."

"Thanks, Greg. I'll call you tomorrow."

"Take care."

A couple minutes later, Clark pulled into Lana's driveway, drove up to the iron gate, and parked beside her Acura. He had been looking forward to this moment all day. The lights were out at the front of the house so he decided to use the side door where lights were burning. He climbed the stairs to the porch.

As he crossed the porch to the door, he heard a crunching sound under his shoes. He looked down and saw broken glass and a box-cutter knife on the floor. Then he saw the window was broken out of the upper half of the door. Alarmed, he suddenly realized that Lana might be in trouble. Never taking his eyes off of the door, he knelt and drew the .380 from his ankle holster.

CHAPTER TWENTY-SEVEN

Clark eased up to the door and listened for sounds or movement. *Should I get back to the car and call for back-up? How long would it take for them to get here?* He'd have to turn his back to the house, and he didn't particularly like the idea of a bull's eye painted on his back. His heart was pounding. It bothered him that he couldn't hear anything.

He waited a few seconds and decided to try the doorknob. He turned it slowly, finding that it was unlocked. He glanced inside to a room that looked like a parlor, and everything appeared to be in order. Why was so much of the glass on the outside of the door? He studied the box-cutter another long moment.

Clark continued to listen and heard a thud that sounded like it was coming from upstairs. He decided to go in. He opened the door and entered, cautiously stepping over some glass on an area rug. He held his gun at low ready and tried to step quietly across the parlor, but the floor creaked about every other step. Clark paused and looked up, as he heard footsteps above him. He stood at the doorway to the hall, looked to the left and right, and saw no signs of ransacking or struggle. He scanned the hallway floor for blood, thinking that the intruder may have cut himself. Suddenly, his pager buzzed loudly, and it startled him.

He froze for an instant, unsure of his next step. If he took the winding stairs, he would commit to that "fatal funnel" where he would be vulnerable to an attack or a shot. If he called to Lana, the perp might panic and do something drastic. Then he had an idea. He backed out of the doorway and tucked his gun in his waistband. He grabbed his cell phone and called her number.

The phone in the hall rang: One ring…two rings…three rings, nothing…four rings, five rings, still nothing.

"Hello."

"Lana?"

"Yes, who is this?"

"Clark, Clark Dixon," he said in a whisper.

"Oh, hey. Are you stopping by?"

"Actually, I'm here."

"Here where?"

"I'm downstairs in your parlor. Are you okay?"

"Downstairs? Yes, I'm okay. Why do you ask?"

What if she's being held at gunpoint? "Lana, if something's wrong, if you're in trouble, then say a number, any number."

She laughed. "What? No really, I'm fine. Why do you ask? What's going on?"

He could hear her steps getting closer as she made her way to and down the front stairs. "Your side door," Clark said, "the glass was broken...I saw a box-cutter on...." He continued to hold the phone to his ear, when she came into view, appearing at the bottom of the stairs. He walked out to the foyer to greet her, and noticed that she was smiling. He sighed, then smiled nervously.

"Sorry about that," Lana said. "I had a couple of rooms of carpet removed from upstairs today and the workers got a little clumsy carrying the rolls out the door. I decided to replace those worn-out pieces with a couple of Kara Stan rugs. Didn't mean to scare you."

Clark reholstered his gun and forced a grin. "No problem. Really, glad everything's okay."

Lana watched him. "Isn't that an unusual place for a policeman to carry his gun?"

"It suits me with my desk job. On my ankle beats wearing it on my side and pulling on my slacks all day."

"Well, we wouldn't want a cop sagging, would we?"

"We sure wouldn't. To tell you the truth, I'm sagging enough these days without five more pounds of help." For some unexplainable reason, the stress of the moment had put Clark at ease. He felt relaxed standing there with her, but not so relaxed that he didn't notice the dark blue v-neck blouse that she was wearing. Her hair was pulled up, and it was a little tousled. Natural look, and he liked it.

"Say, I'm curious about something. Suppose that I'm in trouble, I mean real trouble, and you answer the call. Are you a good enough shot with that gun of yours to rescue me?"

"I rarely miss..."

"Good."

"...the victim."

"Hey, wait a minute! That's not funny. I'm serious—are you the right man for my potential damsel in distress call?"

"Don't worry, Ms. Demarko, I always shoot the bad guy. It's just that the bullet sometimes has to travel through the good girl to get to him. I admit that it's not a perfect system, but you've got to say the end result is pretty neat, huh?"

"Very funny." She smiled warmly, showing perfect teeth and pouty, sensuous lips. "Please, call me Lana."

"And I'm Clark. So, you're fixing up the place?"

She scanned the foyer, as if viewing it for the first time. "Actually, the house is in fairly good order," she said, wiping her hands with a rag. "All the fireplaces are functional; there are four of them. The roof was checked out recently, and structurally the place is pretty sound. That is, for a house built in 1893."

"1893?"

"That's right. Stuartsboro didn't even have electricity back then, but it was added to the house in the late twenties, or so I was told." Her voice resonated in the foyer. "Would you like the twenty-five-cent tour?"

"Sure. You know, I think a Victorian-style home is fascinating, all the special features." He knew that was a white lie. What he really meant to say was that he thought the woman in the Victorian-style home was fascinating. "These stained glass windows are beautiful. The house faces east, doesn't it?"

"That's right, east."

"So the morning sun has got to look magnificent streaming through these windows."

She gave him a pleased look. "I remember one summer night years ago when my sister and I were eight or ten, we spent the night here. We stayed up all night just to sneak down stairs and look at the sun shining through this window," she said, pointing to one in the turret at the stairs. "We played make-believe that if we gazed at the window long enough, we could make any wish come true."

"Did it work?"

"Well, you tell me," she said in a thick Southern Belle accent, smiling coyly and batting her eyes. "I made the wish that I wanted to become the most beautiful woman in all the world."

"My, my, then I would say that this window does, indeed, possess mysterious and wonderful powers. Any chance I can rent a room some time, stay up all night, and make a wish of my own?"

"And what would you wish for?"

"World peace."

Lana laughed. Over the next few minutes, she showed him around the house, beginning with the upstairs, and then working back to the first floor. She told him little stories and facts about each room. He noticed the furnishings looked rich, heavy, and expensive. Everything looked impressive, like some large antique shop. Dark wainscoting lined the front and back staircases, as well as the parlor, foyer, and dining room.

Lana ended the tour by showing Clark where the original kitchen was located, on the porch, and how it was accessed through the back door. He liked the tour but he really enjoyed her company. The v-neck that she wore was a little revealing and her lovely shape made it difficult for him to concentrate. Clark believed that he had performed well, judging by her reactions to his questions and comments.

They sat at the kitchen table and chatted. Lana poured Clark a cup of coffee and asked, "How was your day?"

"Not bad. Trying to squeeze as much as I can out of a three-day workweek, so I can take it easy over the holiday." He took a sip of the coffee and complimented her on it. "Speaking of work, you said last night that you work in Greensboro."

"Yes, Cone Hospital."

"What do you do?"

"I'm a hospital administrator."

"What's that like?"

"Well, like most admin jobs, maybe even yours, I do a lot of things. I handle the budget process, community assessment surveys, feasibility studies of what the community's needs are. I'm responsible for recruitment efforts. Work with the physicians on staff…now there's a challenge."

"Egos?"

"That, and then some. I guess it'd be like you having to answer to and pacify a small band of Chiefs of Police. How does that sound?"

"Like purgatory."

"I've thought about transferring to a smaller hospital, maybe even the one here. Cone is so large, so impersonal. You know? The time that I've spent here at Memorial with Uncle Bill, I've really been impressed with the staff. They seem very caring. Sounds kind of sappy, doesn't it? Unless you're the one who's getting the wonderful treatment, then you're a believer."

"How large is Cone?"

"We have about 3,000 full-time employees, but we're getting bigger all the time, merging with other hospitals."

"Don't you mean 'buying out'?"

Playfully, she replied in a snobbish tone. "It sounds softer, more genteel the way I say it, don't you think?"

Clark laughed.

They meandered around the downstairs, while Lana shared her ideas for remodeling the rooms. They walked into the parlor and felt a burst of cold air pouring through the broken window.

"What are you going to do about this tonight?" Clark asked, looking at the door.

"The carpet people are taking care of it. Someone with a local glass business is stopping by in a while to repair it."

"Would you like some company while they're here?"

"I think I'll be all right, but thanks anyway. If they turn out to be bad guys, I'm not so sure I like your shooting tactics."

"This coffee's fabulous. Want to go for a short walk while I finish it? It's really a mild evening, and I hate to waste a good cup of coffee. That's a felony in our city and I don't think you can survive another charge."

"You sure have some odd laws here. I'd hate to spend Thanksgiving weekend in jail." She paused for a moment. "Let's go. I could use the fresh air." She grabbed a maroon and beige plaid sweater from the hall tree.

They took a stroll down the sidewalk, under the glow of the streetlights, and talked about their jobs, their children and plans for the holidays. As she spoke, he noticed how dreamy her eyes appeared under the pale white lights. It reminded him of the way she looked last night beside the fire. Different light, same captivating look.

The night air was clear and a little chilly. The sky was starry, and Clark looked for the big dipper, finding it overhead. Every so often, a gust of wind swept gold and orange leaves across the sidewalk, and Clark and Lana shuffled through them. The smell of dried leaves and the feel of a crisp fall night. A train passing through town, blowing its whistle. It was beautiful.

Clark spoke next. "So this is Gordon Street. Nice place to walk, isn't it?"

"It's quiet, peaceful that's what I enjoy about it. Who knows, I may decide to move here eventually."

Finally, Clark got up the nerve. He turned to her and asked, "Are you married?"

She looked at him, took another stride, and then crossed her arms. The pause was uncomfortable for him. Finally, she answered, "Twice married, divorced."

"Oh," he said, and then he was at a loss for words. *Clever line, Clark, think of something, quick.* "Uh, how long have you been divorced this second time?"

"Not long enough," she said cynically.

"One of those, huh? What about your first?"

"The first marriage was good for a while. We had two beautiful daughters, started a home, all the trappings. But we grew apart. He traveled a lot, a drug rep, very successful. He opted to go for more travel, which meant more pay. And the distance between us, literal and figurative, got to be too much."

"And the second marriage?"

"A real lesson for me. I jumped into another relationship before I was ready. Not a lot of happy times before he developed a pretty bad drinking problem. And when he got drunk, he wasn't very good to me. My problem was that I stayed in it too long. He was strong, physically. Latin temper. You're a police officer, do I have to go any further?"

"No further than you want to." Clark then talked about his divorce. He noticed that Lana appeared to be listening attentively; she seemed to really care. "I know there are things that I could've done differently. Less time at work, that sort of thing. You just can't see it when it's happening, can you? Do I need to go any further?"

"No further than you want to," she said, in kind.

When they arrived back at the house, a work truck with a "B&G Glass" sign on the door pulled into the driveway.

"Looks like your repairman is here," Clark said. "Perfect timing."

Lana stopped and turned to him, but didn't say anything. She glanced away, and then back to him again. Her eyes met his with a kind of warmth that radiated in the cool night. "Sometimes, timing is everything," she said. "Do you believe that, Clark?"

A long pause. A smile. He didn't answer. There was no need to.

Across the street, and two blocks down, smoke drifted from the window of a burgundy Altima. A minute later, the cigarette was tossed out, landing on the street with several other cigarette butts.

CHAPTER TWENTY-EIGHT

Wilkens had drifted off to sleep, when Esposito punched his arm. "Brad, get him on the phone!" he said, excitedly. "Tell him it looks like Marcellus is on the move."

Wilkens stirred a little, and sat up. "What time is it?" he asked, reaching for the SPD officer roster and searching for the cell number.

"A little after ten. You dozed for a few minutes."

"I see what Jerry meant about this detail," he said, sighing. "God, this is awful." Wilkens called the number, and Patrol Officer Walter Hunt answered.

"Hunt."

"Hey, he's on the move."

"Dark-colored van, right?"

"That's it. Handicap license plate. Don't wait too long to make the stop. We're on the edge of the city as it is."

"You want me to make a righteous stop, don't you?"

"Look man, you're not running for 'Officer of the Year'. We'll be close by. Be sure to call us before you're finished with him, in case we have to stage out of sight."

"10-4."

"Hey Walt, on second thought, how about staying on the phone with us. This shouldn't take long. We're coming out of Farmington Estates now. Can you see us yet?"

"Uh-uh."

"You will in a minute."

Esposito followed Marcellus at a careful distance, catching his taillights at various turns out of the development. "Wonder where our man is heading?"

"Kind of late for a shut-in to be running around," Wilkens said. "Likes the cover of darkness for some reason. Maybe tonight we'll get some answers."

They drove another mile and were heading for the highway.

"Well, if a lawn and tractor dealership gets hit tonight, then Jerry will be looking pretty darn smart."

"We may be...."

"I think I see the van now," Hunt said, interrupting Wilkens. Then there was a pause. "Okay, now I see your car. Hey, don't you guys look really nifty in that narc car."

"Bite me, Walt."

After another minute and a couple more turns, Hunt pulled in behind Esposito, and said, "Okay, let patrol take over, boys. Time for the big dawgs to go to work." Esposito pulled into a driveway, as Hunt sped around him and caught up to the van. Hunt followed the van for a quarter mile, then activated his blue lights.

Esposito turned to Wilkens. "Get on the phone to Lieutenant. Tell him that it looks like Marcellus is heading out of town. See how far he wants us to go outside the city on the tail."

Wilkens called Clark, told him about the stop, and where Marcellus appeared to be heading. After a short conversation, he hung up and turned to Esposito.

"Well, what'd he say?" Esposito asked.

"Afraid he gave us some limits on how far we could go."

"Like how far?"

"Something like the Outer Banks to the east, Richmond to the north, Myrtle Beach to the south."

"Blank check, huh?"

"Yeah, he wants the make on this guy. I could hear it in his voice."

"All right, green light."

The road was fairly clear of traffic so, after a minute, they drove slowly to the area of the stop. When they saw Hunt's blue lights, Esposito pulled onto the gravel shoulder of the highway, cut off his headlights, and waited for the call.

Officer Hunt walked carefully up the side of the van, flashing his light in the cargo area. He noticed a large object, but the tinted windows made it difficult to see. He stopped at the driver's window.

"Good evening, sir. Can I see your driver's license, please?"

"What's the problem, officer?" Marcellus asked. He reached in his wallet, pulled his license out, and offered it to him.

Hunt stood there for a moment, writing on his clipboard, while Marcellus continued to hold the license. Still looking down, Hunt replied, "I noticed you were weaving a little in your lane." He took the license, glanced at it, and then to the driver. "Is everything all right, Mr., uh, Marcellus?"

"Yes officer, I'm fine. I've been on the road for a while. Guess I got a little sleepy and didn't realize it. Sorry."

"You haven't been drinking tonight, have you?"

"No sir, I don't drink."

Hunt stared at him for a few seconds with the flashlight aimed at his upper chest, then he panned the light briefly over to the passenger's side. "I'll be back in a minute."

Hunt headed to his car and, as he did, tried to take another look in the side window of the van. He got in his squad car and was busy for a minute. Afterwards, he called Wilkens on the phone.

"You in position?" Hunt asked. "I'm finished."

"Ready to go. How's things on your end?"

"Great," he said. He filled Wilkens in on the details.

Hunt already had some of the warning ticket filled out prior to the stop, so he quickly completed it and returned to the van. He handed Marcellus his license and the warning ticket, and drove off.

Marcellus, relieved, pulled out his phone and made a call.

"Hello."

"I'm going to be a few minutes late getting there."

"Why?"

"A traffic cop stopped me."

"Why did he stop you?"

"He said I was weaving."

"What happened?"

"Nothing. Everything's fine. He gave me a warning. That's it."

"Did he question the license?"

"Not a word. He gave me a warning ticket and drove off."

"You cannot be attracting attention. We have told you that."

"I tell you, everything's all right," Marcellus said, pulling back onto the highway. He headed east on Highway 29.

Esposito pulled back onto the road and kept his distance. "He's heading toward Greensboro."

Wilkens called a number and waited. "Lieutenant, it's me again…Couldn't have gone better…Right thumb and index…Walt said they looked perfect…Yeah…Okay…Right, 'bye."

They followed Marcellus for about twenty-five miles, all the way into Greensboro, and they were surprised when he pulled into a small shopping center. Marcellus parked in a space in front of an all-night grocery store. They parked several rows away where they could watch him leave and return to his van.

"I think I feel a miracle coming on," Wilkens said.

"What are you talking about?"

"Just watch, you'll see."

After a minute, Marcellus stepped out of the van and walked across the parking lot to the store. Esposito and Wilkens looked at each other and grinned.

"Damn, I knew it!" Wilkens said. "I knew something wasn't right about this guy. Didn't I tell you?"

"The crippled to walk again. What now?"

"We sit and wait."

"Think we oughta call the Lieutenant again?"

Wilkens looked at his watch. "It's kind of late, don't you think? We'll fill him in on everything in the morning. Let's see what else happens."

By now, the parking lot was thinning out. Esposito had to move a couple of times as customers returned to their cars and left, leaving his car exposed.

After about forty-five minutes, Marcellus exited the store, pushing a full grocery cart. A bagboy pushed a full cart behind him to the van, and then helped him load the groceries in the back.

"Looks like he's fixing some kind of Thanksgiving feast."

"I'll say."

Marcellus got in his van and drove past Esposito's car, as the two detectives ducked low. Esposito waited until Marcellus pulled out of the parking lot, and then followed him; Marcellus took the same roads back to the highway.

"Looks like he's heading back to Stuartsboro," Esposito said.

"Wonder where to?"

About thirty minutes later, Marcellus approached Stuartsboro and, instead of taking the exit back to the city, he made a turn onto a road a couple miles outside of town. They followed him for about a mile as he made several more turns.

"This is hooking around the city, isn't it?" Wilkens asked.

"Yeah. We're basically looping around the southwest side of town. You know, we're not all that far from The Meadows here. I figure maybe a couple miles, if that much."

Marcellus turned down a dirt road where a dead-end sign was posted, so Esposito didn't follow.

"Where does this go?" Wilkens asked.

"I'm not sure. I think there's a couple of dairy farms and a trailer park or two down there."

"What do you say we hit the lights and see where he's going?"

"Nah. Too risky. Betcha we're on to something big here. Marcellus looks like he's a gopher for some people. And he's gone to some kind of painstaking efforts to conceal his game. We can't afford to blow this. Maybe Sloan's getting ready to bust open a huge theft ring. You may soon be addressing him as 'Sergeant Sloan'."

"Now there's a scary thought."

"Let's take this back to the lieutenant."

CHAPTER TWENTY-NINE

"Firearms, Lawson."

"Hey, it's Greg. Are you busy?"

"Not bad."

"Stuartsboro dropped off their bullet for you to examine. Remember? The case I told you about yesterday. Is now a good time? Rose, it looks like a beaut."

Rosalie had worried about this moment since the previous day. She hoped that the bullet would be less than quality grade, but evidently it was superior. *What if I can't get out of this one? Hubert's on vacation, so I can't go to him for advice...I can't stall or refuse Greg's request; he's in charge in Hubert's absence.* Greg was sharp, and if the bullet was that good, then he'd know something was up if she claimed that it was not. If she were forced to do her job and do it right, Hubert would understand, wouldn't he? She began to think that maybe this was an escape from her predicament. On second thought, why not tell Greg she entered it with no match? As long as he didn't check behind her, everything would be okay. She'd be off the hook.

"Rose, are you still there?"

"Uh, yeah Greg, I was in the middle of something. Sure, bring it on over. I'll run the test for you."

Five minutes later, Greg walked through the double doors of the lab, evidence bag in hand. He gave her the chain-of-custody sheet to sign, and placed the evidence bag on the counter beside her stool.

"What did I tell you, Rose? How much better shape could a nine be in?"

Rose was so nervous that she signed the wrong side of the sheet. She scratched through it, sighed, then signed on the correct side.

"I need to pay attention, don't I?" she said. "Rushing a bit, I guess."

Greg offered a reassuring smile, and he noticed that she was acting a little more stressed than usual. "Rose, thanks for working this case in. I know you've got a heavy day today. I appreciate it. This is a favor for a longtime friend of mine."

His words were sincere and soothing.

She smiled, looking at him. *You know, I could melt in your arms right now...you smell heavenly.* Then she said, "Glad to help out. Call anytime."

He moved closer to her, and her heart leaped. Today, he happened to be wearing one of her favorite neckties. Occasionally, she fantasized about loosening it for him, at the end of a date, or after a long, hard day at the office.

He touched her gently on the arm. "I'll be in my office. Just holler when the test is done." Then he left the room.

When she got up the nerve, she cut a look at the bag and, sure enough, the bullet was in pristine condition. It showed very little deformity and the striation marks were clear and defined. She had to think, and fast. As she scanned her options, Hubert's words rang in her ears.... "*Absolutely no one, I mean no one, must learn about this finding of yours...delete all your files on this case...I have to know that I can trust you. My recommendation for lab supervisor will be based on the person who is most competent and trusted...are you that person?*"

* * *

Chief Brinks put Clark on hold for a few seconds, then returned to the phone. "Where is Wilkens now?"

"He's checking around out in Sudbury Lane," Clark replied. "He and Steve didn't want to get burned following Marcellus that late at night, not knowing what or who was down there. That and realizing it was a dead-end road, too."

"Make sure the County knows that he's out there. If we're nosing around on their turf, they need to be made aware of it."

"Already done."

"What's your thinking at this point on Marcellus?"

Clark filled the Chief in on Sloan's theory that Marcellus may be involved in a professional theft ring. "One thing's for sure, he's not faking the handicap only to get the cheap rent at The Meadows. He's lying real low for some reason," Clark said, finishing off his breakfast bar with the last of his coffee.

"By the way, I received another call from Mr. Evans at Nick's today. He wanted an update on his case, see how you're progressing with your leads. He's going to worry us to death on this thing."

"Did you ask him if they've fixed their alarm system yet?"

"I sure did, and you may want to take a seat if you're standing. He informed me that they're working on that and also looking into a perimeter alarm for the yard."

"Well, that's good. As far as suspects on his case, it's like this. We're either hot on the trail of the perps or we don't have a clue who did it."

"I don't mind telling you that I like the sound of your first possibility much better. We've taken a lot of hits lately, Clark. So do you still think that Marcellus is connected to the death of the Walker woman?"

Clark sighed. "I don't know, Chief. Undoubtedly, we've got some warning flags surrounding her death. If he's tied to it, I don't have a clue what his motive would be. Not a clue. Walker may just be one of those unexplainable things."

Then the Chief switched gears. "How's the Hall boy doing since his surgery?"

"Last I heard he was doing well. Sometimes there's no substitute for youth, is there?"

Brinks laughed, a rare occurrence. "I suppose you're right about that. A captain that I had at BPD would disagree, though. He had this saying that he used a lot: 'Age and treachery will always overcome youth and brilliance'."

Clark chuckled.

"When are you planning to take the bullet over to the lab?"

"You know Whitaker, my resident jumping bean. He was ready for it as soon as they brought it through the O.R. doors. I called in a favor with Williams and they're analyzing it today for us. In fact, I got a voice message from him a few minutes ago. He hopes to get the results of the examination in the next hour, or so." Clark then filled Brinks in on the traffic stop last night and the latent prints that Officer Hunt lifted.

"How long will it take to get an I.D. on them?"

"If we put them in the mail today, the lab in Raleigh should get them by the first of the week, at the latest. But as far as when an examiner will get to them, who knows. Latent probably has a backlog of several months. Is there any way you could make a call to rush them up?"

"I know the supervisor of molecular genetics Bob Goodman. I'll see what I can do. But right now, so I understand it, we don't have any paper on Marcellus. Just suspicions, right?"

Clark tried to think of some way to finesse around the point, but what the Chief said was correct. "I'm afraid that's it. But it'll only take them a few minutes to run the prints through A.F.I.S., once they bump our case up. If

Marcellus is involved in this theft ring, it's supposed to be organized and sophisticated, and a number of agencies are affected. That's one of the criteria for the lab to push cases up, multi-jurisdictional."

"True. But theft theory aside, I don't think he's quite out of the picture on this elderly woman's death either, do you?"

"No, I don't. I'll let you know if Wilkens comes up with anything today. By the way, do we need to continue with The Meadows security detail tonight?"

"I don't think it's necessary. But, if you would, how about making a P.R. call to the manager, and touch base with him. Anything else, Clark?"

"Yes, one other thing, if you have a minute." He briefed Brinks on the Salisbury robbery/murder and how it was the similar to their Harris Teeter case. He also conveyed his belief that the attacks by this group, assuming it was the same group, were widespread. He had a notion to tell the Chief about the anonymous caller the day before, but Clark didn't want to spoil a positive phone call.

"Is that everything, Clark? I may head in early today, get a start on the holidays. We're going out of town."

"That's it. Have a nice Thanksgiving, Chief."

"Thanks, you too. Oh, Clark?"

"Yes, sir?"

"Good work."

Where's a taped line when you need one?

* * *

Wilkens wore casual clothes, careful not to draw attention to himself, and he decided to drive the narc car that he and Esposito had used the previous night. He was anxious to check out the road that Marcellus drove down, but he really didn't know what to expect. He discovered that Sudbury Lane was longer and more populated than he remembered, and there were several secondary roads off of it. Even though the road was just outside of town, the PD rarely backed up the Sheriff's Office on calls there because it was an isolated area with no direct connecting road to the city.

It was a typical rural area with farm houses and tobacco barns, small framed homes, and trailers set back off the roads, secluded by droves of scraggly spruce and cedar trees. Wilkens realized how close he was to the city limits when the bells of First Baptist Church, next to The Meadows, rang at ten o'clock.

Before coming here, Wilkens had driven by The Meadows to check for Marcellus' van, but it wasn't there. Maybe Wilkens would hit the jackpot today and find the van parked where Marcellus went last night. He drove slowly up and down the road a couple of times, surveying both sides and making mental notes of the area.

He decided to take some of the secondary roads off of Sudbury. He turned down a steep dirt road and came to a cluster of small-framed houses that dotted a large tract of land that had been farmed that fall. When he drove by one of the houses, one with light blue siding, he noticed an open shed at the back of it. There were a number of pieces of machinery under it, so he picked up his field glasses to take a closer look. When he focused, he saw a combine, an old pick-up truck, a tractor and something else that caught his eye: Two John Deere lawn tractors that looked relatively new. "There sits about six grand," he muttered. He checked at the road for a mailbox but instead there were about fifteen of them perched on a wooden rail. Most of the rusted boxes didn't even have names on them; he had no clue which box belonged to this house.

He sat there trying to focus on the license plate on a car parked next to the house, and heard a rumbling noise. Looking in his rear view mirror, he saw a cloud of dust coming down the road toward him. He had to be careful because Marcellus could recognize him. When the vehicle got closer, he could see that it was a late model sedan, and it slowed to a stop behind him at the mailboxes. Wilkens decided to get out of his car, approach the driver and see what he could find out. He walked back to the car, as the driver was taking his mail from a box, and spoke to him.

"Hey, good morning."

"Good morning."

"Nice day, isn't it?"

"Yes."

"Maybe you can help me. I'm with Farm Bureau Insurance and I'm looking for a Linda McKinney. Does she live here?" he asked, pointing to the blue house.

"I am sorry. I do not know who lives there."

"Thanks, anyway," Wilkens said, waving to him as he walked back to his car. He decided to check a couple more of the side roads and then head back to the office. It didn't look like it was going to be a very successful mission.

The driver of the sedan opened another envelope and kept a periodic eye on the stranger's car until it was out of sight. Then, he decided to pull onto the dirt road across from the mailboxes. He parked, picked up his cell phone and called a number.

"Hello."

"A man was just here, on the main road. He said he was an insurance agent, but he looked like your friend, the black detective."

"What was he doing?"

"He said he was looking for someone and thought she may live in the house here at the postal boxes."

"Are you sure it was the detective?"

"Fairly certain. I believe he is looking for you. Isn't it too much of a coincidence that you were here last night and he is here today? Are you sure the police did not follow you last night?"

"Yeah, I'm sure. I went to Greensboro after they stopped me. Remember? There's no way they would've followed me all the way over there, and then here."

The driver paused for a moment. "He is getting too close to us. We need to divert their attention or our plan will be ruined."

"What do you mean by 'divert'?"

"Divert their attention and energy to some other objective. It will take their concerns from you. They are small force. It will not require too much to occupy their time."

"What are we going to do?"

"Listen carefully. Do this. Call this detective to your apartment this afternoon. Tell him that it is urgent, that there is something that you suddenly remember. Something that may be very important concerning the elderly woman whose death he was investigating."

"What do I tell him?"

"Think of something to tell this man. Make sure that he arrives at your apartment at fifteen or ten minutes before the four o'clock hour. Tell him that you have to be somewhere, an important appointment, and you must leave your apartment at four o'clock."

They discussed their plan for several minutes and then they synchronized their watches. "Have him there, and we will take care of the rest."

* * *

Greg went to pick up their order, while Rosalie sat wide-eyed in the booth. She couldn't believe that she was actually having lunch with him. She knew it didn't officially count as a real date, but it was as close to one as she had been on in a long time. She kept hoping other employees would show up, just so she could have eyewitnesses to the event. Anita ate here two or three times a week, and Rosalie hoped that she would show up today.

Greg placed the tray on the table, handing Rosalie her basket. "Enjoy. Hope it's what you wanted. They slip up on orders sometimes, but their mistakes are as good as what you ask for. Guess it's because they're always so packed at lunchtime."

As they began to eat, Greg labored over the Stuartsboro case. He couldn't figure for the life of him why Rosalie wasn't able to classify this second bullet. It was in excellent shape. He knew that Rosalie was a great tech; he wasn't questioning her ability. *I wouldn't mind a second opinion, but it'll have to wait until next week, since she's the only analyst working...maybe I'll have Fran take a look at it Monday.*

"This is great, Greg, thanks for inviting me to lunch. It was very kind of you."

"So the sandwich is good?"

"Very good."

Greg barely heard her words, continuing in thought. "You did say Diet Coke, didn't you?"

"Yes, and it's good too."

They talked a few minutes about current events and projects they were involved in, but Greg couldn't resist a re-approach on the examination. "I don't get it, Rose. The bullet in the Stuartsboro case was terrific quality. What does it take to make it entry-worthy in this I.B.I.S. system, anyway?"

Rosalie began to get nervous again. She knew Greg was an experienced interrogator. He made his living distinguishing deception from truth, and in breaking the suspect down to a confession. *Make your explanation short, and stay as close to the truth as you can.* She had heard the agents say in their office war stories that smart criminals did just that—stayed as close to the truth as possible. *Here goes.* "Certain manufacturers' bullets are not as compatible, for whatever reason, with the software we use. Remington manufactured this bullet, and their ammo is one that we have trouble with. It has to do with an area of metallurgy that I'm not real familiar with. Our software company is trying to address the problem. I'd say that with ideal bullets like this one, we're able to successfully classify seven out of ten from Remington, maybe eight." She felt her story was a little shaky, but she hoped he bought it.

They ate and chatted a few more minutes, while Greg continued to ponder the situation. He had a theory, implausible as it may be, and there was something that he wanted to check out. He looked at his pager.

"Rose, this is from Clark, my man in Stuartsboro. He probably wants to know about the results. I left my phone at the office, mind if I use yours to break the news to him?"

"Sure." She pulled the phone out of her purse and handed it to him.

"It's kind of noisy in here. I'm going to step outside. Be right back."

Rosalie felt a little better and started to relax a bit. This would all be over soon. Hubert would be back on Monday and, no doubt, proud of how she dodged the situation. A couple minutes later, she was thrilled to see Anita walk in.

Anita waved and, with a surprised look, walked over to her. "Hey, what are you doing here?"

Rosalie proudly explained that she was having lunch with Greg.

"You're joking," Anita said, then slid in beside Rosalie, who filled her in on the details of how the invitation came about.

Shortly, Greg returned to the booth and the three of them chatted.

"Well, guess I better run get in line. It's getting longer by the minute," Anita announced. She stood and said, "See you all back at the office," giving Rosalie a wink.

After they finished their sandwiches, Rosalie said, "Greg, this was really good. Your invitation to lunch was a nice surprise."

He looked at her and smiled. "I'm glad you enjoyed it, Rose. You know, I can't tell you how surprised I was," then he leaned toward her, "when I began pressing the number to Stuartsboro PD and saw that your phone book already had the number listed. And judging by the list, I'd say you made the call in the last day, or so."

Rosalie was caught completely off guard. She looked at him, then quickly reached in her pocketbook as if she were fumbling for something.

After an intentional pause, he asked, "May I ask why you called Stuartsboro?"

"Why I called Stuartsboro?"

Repeating my question, sign of deception. Then he said, "I could check on the time and date of your call there, Rose. I would wager that my research would reveal that you made the call yesterday, in the afternoon. And perhaps to a Lt. Dixon?"

Still, she didn't look up. Instead, she reached for a Kleenex.

He placed his hand on hers and said in a low voice, "Let's get back to the office, Rosalie. We really need to talk."

CHAPTER THIRTY

Cunningham placed the file on the front corner of Clark's desk, and tamped the tobacco in his pipe. Then he opened the next file. "All right, let's see here. This is the drug dealer shooting that Wilkens worked. He's got one witness willing to testify against the shooter, but the problem is that he's a thug, too. We collected some blood from the victim's car that is most likely the shooter's. But we'll need a search warrant to get a sample from the shooter. Is it worth it?"

"Who's the perp?"

"Name is Tyler Cannon, white male, thirty-two."

Clark repeated the name. "I don't think I know him. Do you?"

"Nope, unless he's related to the Cannons on Clifton Street. If he is, then he's trouble."

While Cunningham continued, Clark stared at his phone, the way he had for the last couple of hours. Hoping that Lana would call. He debated over calling her, just to say hello, but he wondered if he was being too pushy. He had even picked up the receiver twice to call her, and decided against it. He smiled at his own shyness and uncertainty. He wondered what she thought about him. He didn't hear Cunningham's question.

"So what do you think, Lieutenant?"

"What?"

"What do you think?"

"Level of injury?"

"Treated and released. I can easily see this being pled down to a misdemeanor in district court."

"How about getting with the narcs. See how big this Cannon guy is on the street. If he's big enough to the narcs, then go for the search warrant."

"Another case of one more drug dealer puttin' another one in jail. Snuffing out the competition."

"Hey, whatever it takes." When Clark said that, his pager buzzed and he checked it.

Cunningham paused, until Clark was ready for the next file. "Everything okay?"

"Yeah, it's Wilkens."

"Anything good?"

"Possibly. He may have a location on where Marcellus went to last night. He thinks he may have spotted some of the stolen property from the All-Seasons break-in."

"Hey, that's better than good news. Where is it?"

"Down off Sudbury Lane, outside of town. His page says he spotted a couple of new lawn tractors at the back of a house. He must be paging me through dispatch. Sorry for the interruption, David, what's next?"

"The High School break-in. Remember all the computers and stuff that was stolen? Nowhere to go on the case. Bennett wants to know if you want to raise the Crimestoppers award to two thousand."

"Any suspects?"

"Nothing. We've kept a close watch on the pawnshops, and had Rallingview PD and the County looking out for us. The *Sentinel* ran an article on it, but no luck. Nothing on the street, either."

"Raise it, then."

Cunningham laid the file on the desk and opened the next one. "This one is Strader's Mart, the smash and grab. On this, we had the...."

They were interrupted by some commotion in the hallway. Suddenly, Esposito ran by Clark's door, backed up when he saw them, and yelled, "Alarm at Bank of Stuartsboro! No answer on callback!"

Cunningham tossed his remaining files on the desk and Clark jumped from his chair. They raced out the door and down the back stairwell.

Esposito was a flight below them, and shouted up to them, "Brad and Jerry are on the way!"

"Anybody on-scene, yet?" Clark yelled. As he asked that, he glanced out the stairwell window and saw two patrol cars roaring out of the back lot. He reached for his keys while he ran down the stairs and fumbled for his car door key to have it ready. He had run this drill countless times in his career as a detective. Racing down the stairs, blood pumping, bursting through the back door, getting the keys ready on the run. He looked at it as a good drill and he considered the false alarms a way to prepare for the real thing. Like today?

They hopped in his unmarked car and backed up, nearly striking a vending truck that was pulling in the back of the building. Clark could hear sirens wailing in all directions in the cool fall afternoon; the screaming seemed to ricochet off of the low, gray clouds, making their sounds louder and more eerie. Clark pulled onto the street and Cunningham turned on the siren. "Who's the patrol supervisor today?" Clark asked over the noise.

"Let me think," Cunningham said, and, in a moment, he heard "Unit 12" on the radio. "12, that's Johnson."

In a steady flow, several other officers announced they were en route as Johnson advised them to cut sirens near the bank. "Good move, Edd. David, get on the radio and tell them we're coming."

Cunningham picked up the mike. "19 to headquarters."

"*19, go ahead.*"

"7 and 19 are 10-17."

"*10-4, 7 and 19. Unit 12?*"

"12, go ahead, headquarters."

"*I've received a call from an unknown source that shots have been fired in the bank, but this is not confirmed. There is still no answer in the bank.*"

"Shit!" Cunningham shouted.

"Headquarters, unit 23 is about three blocks away."

"Unit 36 same traffic."

Clark barreled onto Holden Road, barging through an intersection. "All our guys are en route, right?"

"Whitaker's still in...." Cunningham was interrupted.

"12 to headquarters, I'm 10-23 in the area. Stand by for status."

"*10-4, 12. 10-4, units 23, 36.*"

"Whitaker's still in Greensboro. Didn't Steve say that Brad and Jerry are 10-17?"

Clark's adrenalin was pumping as he darted around a thick line of traffic a mile from the bank. Questions raced through his mind. How many were shot? How many were dead? The same perps that hit the Harris Teeter? He spoke loudly over the yelping of his siren. "Make sure dispatch has E.M.S. en route and have them put the E.R. on standby."

Cunningham called dispatch but was put on hold.

"Better go ahead and hit the siren."

"26 is 10-23, headquarters."

"24 same traffic."

"*10-4, both units.*"

"3 also."

"*10-4.*"

"12 to headquarters, have you made contact inside the bank yet?"

No response.

"12, I'm 10-23 in the shopping center on the opposite side of the parking lot. Can you advise?" unit 36 asked.

"3 to 12, do you have a canine in service?"

"Standby, 3. Headquarters, any contact in the bank, yet?" Lt. Johnson repeated his question.

Clark slammed on the brakes at the four-way stop, half a block from the bank. "Come on, Sheila, answer your lieutenant."

Then, for several seconds the radio was silent.

"Which route would they take out of the city?" Clark asked.

"Probably Terri Street. That's the quickest way to the by-pass. Hey, I just remembered something."

"What?"

"Esposito's wife works at this bank."

"Didn't she transfer to the main office?"

"Uh-uh. I guess he's really on edge about now."

Several more seconds of radio silence that seemed like hours.

"Come on Sheila, tell us something," Clark pled. "What's taking so long?"

Lt. Johnson radioed to his units to set up observation points to cover the four sides of the bank. "Unit 23, take north and east, 36 take south and west. Advise if you see any traffic in or out of the bank."

"10-4," acknowledged unit 36 first, then 23.

"12 to headquarters, can you advise anything yet?" Lt. Johnson's voice was loaded with tension.

Clark's hands were sweaty as he gripped the steering wheel. "Still no response...I hope that doesn't mean what I think it does."

"What's that?"

"That we got here too damn fast and now we got a hostage situation. You wearing your vest?"

"Afraid not."

"I got a tact vest in the trunk. When we pull over in the parking lot, I'm going to grab my shotgun and you can get the vest, okay?"

Finally, headquarters called Lt. Johnson. "*Unit 12.*"

"12, go ahead."

"*I've made contact in the bank. Everything is 10-4. Inside phone lines were cut and an employee had to call by cell phone. Suspects are three males, race unknown, dark clothing, masks and hoods, armed with handguns. They fled through the bank side doors. No vehicle description given so far.*"

"Can you advise on injuries?" Johnson asked.

"The caller isn't certain. She's very upset and there's a lot of background noise in the bank. It's hard to hear."

"Headquarters," Johnson called, "try to get a vehicle description, if possible. Also, notify the Sheriff's Office, and send out the fifty-mile radius message." Johnson then directed two units to two nearby intersections, possible points of flight, and told them to stand by, in case a car description was developed.

Officers cautiously entered both sets of bank doors with guns drawn and ordered all the employees and customers down to the floor. Clark and his men made a security sweep of the second floor offices as the patrol team checked the first floor and attended to a couple of elderly customers. Crime scene tape was draped around the building and police cars were repositioned in the parking lot to serve as an extended barrier around the crime scene.

When Clark and Cunningham returned downstairs, calm was restored, for the most part. A couple of tellers were sobbing and being consoled by officers. He saw Esposito over by the water fountain talking with his wife, who seemed composed. E.M.S. techs were making their way into the bank, as Sgt. Maloney yelled for everyone to be careful not to touch anything.

Johnson walked over to Clark; Captains Blackburn and Simmons then joined them.

"Upstairs clear?" Johnson asked.

"Yeah," Clark said. "Everybody okay down here?"

"Shook up, but okay," Johnson replied, and then called to his sergeant, "Maloney."

"Yes, sir?"

"Get the K-9 track started before the area gets too contaminated. Make sure the squad cars aren't running, so the exhaust doesn't throw off the scent."

"Right."

Then he called to one of his officers, "James, canvass the surrounding businesses for a witness on their getaway. See if anybody caught a look at them or their vehicle."

"Okay."

"Also, check around for any businesses with cameras aimed to the outside, that may have caught them coming or going."

Johnson turned to Clark. "We're a little short today. Can one of your guys help him on the canvass?"

Clark gave Sloan the assignment.

Wilkens came over and joined the huddle. "Nobody's hurt out of all this. It's a miracle. Shots were fired over here." He led his supervisors over to the side doors. "When the robbers told everybody to hit the floor, a young guy made a run for it. He's really lucky, made it out. That's him over there talking to Neville."

"Exactly how lucky was he?" Capt. Blackburn asked.

"Six shots' worth, as I count them," Wilkens said. He pointed to three bullet holes in the wall beside the doors and another three in the glass doors. They studied the scene, while the crime scene tech placed I.D. markers on the floor beside the casings, and began to take measurements.

The manager walked over to Clark and gave him a brief summary of the robbery.

"What about the tape?" Clark asked.

"They took it."

"You say they didn't go in the vault?"

"That's right, they did not. But they knew enough to ask for the money from the lower teller drawers."

"Did your tellers get a chance to put a dye pack in their bags?"

"We don't have dye packs."

Clark looked at Cunningham and said, "This one's yours. You okay with it?"

"Yeah."

Clark called Wilkens and Esposito over. "You guys start the interviews." He gestured to the side offices. "Why don't you use them for privacy? It'll help clear the floor so we can get on with the processing. I'll call the Bureau and see if they can get an agent rolling over here to help us."

Capt. Blackburn walked over to Clark when there was a lull in activity in the center of the bank. Blackburn had a grin on his face, and Clark gave him a puzzled look.

"What's so funny, old man?" Clark asked.

"This whole thing. It's your fault."

"How do you figure that?"

"Remember lunch at Short Sugar's yesterday?"

"Yeah. So?"

"You were talking about the Salisbury hit and you said we'd be okay for a few days, since that robbery looked like our perps. You jinxed us man, you didn't knock on wood."

"Thanks, Richard. What a true and dear friend you are," Clark said with a smirk. "How would you like an early retirement gift?"

Blackburn chuckled, knowing what was next.

Clark opened his coat, used it to shield his right hand from the crowd, and flicked Blackburn.

CHAPTER THIRTY-ONE

When Clark knocked on the bank doors to re-enter, Sloan and Esposito were lying in wait. As he stepped in, they were applauding, teasing him for the television interview he had just conducted in the parking lot.

"Sir, may we have your autograph? Oh, please sir," Sloan pled.

"Funny, Jerry," Clark said. "Why don't you re-channel some of that comedic talent of yours and go find us a couple of bank robbers."

Cunningham was amused by the scene and walked over to Clark. "How'd it go with Channel Three?"

"Ah, I guess okay. I never feel like the interview ever goes that well. You know me, if I don't say 'no comment' at least a couple of times then I feel like I've told all. Overall, okay. She did ask me about crime here over the last few weeks, and if we've seen any increase."

"What'd you say?"

"No comment."

Cunningham laughed. "The news lady's quite a looker. Redheads, my weakness. I've never seen her before. Is she new?"

"Nah, not brand new. She interviewed me a couple weeks ago at the hospital on the Harris Teeter robbery. You're right, she's cute, nice legs. High heels must be a lost art around here." Clark dropped his tone a notch to business level. "So how's everything going?"

Cunningham browsed over his notes. "Lady over at the DMV office a few doors down saw a white SUV speed away from behind the shopping center right about the time of the robbery. Said it looked like there were four or five adults in it. She can't do any better than that, but we're still workin' the canvass."

"I know they didn't have a dye-pack, but what about marked bills?"

"Afraid not. When the perp shot at the kid, it freaked out the tellers so bad that they lost it; one of 'em passed out. They didn't think to put the marked stuff in the bags."

"K-9 track?"

"Zilch. By the time the dog got here, the place was infected with people. Too many cars in the area, that sorta thing."

"Prints?"

"Gloves."

"Can any of them be I.D.'ed?"

"Masks."

"David, do you ever want to get promoted around here?"

He shrugged his shoulders. "Hey Lieutenant, you can't make chicken salad outta chicken...."

Wilkens interrupted the conversation, grabbing Clark by the arm. "You got a second, Lieutenant?" He had that urgent look about him that Clark had learned to recognize.

"Sure, what's...?"

"Lieutenant!" Esposito yelled from a nearby desk, where he was on the phone. He gave them an emphatic wave and they hustled over to him.

"Brad, hold on a second," Clark said. "Let's see what he's got."

"Great news," Esposito said, "you're gonna want to hear this." Then he put the caller on hold.

"Let me guess," Clark said. "Three masked men just turned themselves in at the PD. They've got handwritten confessions, they refuse to speak with attorneys, and they want to return all the money they stole."

"You're close, check this out. We may be able to solve the Harris Teeter robbery before you take your first bite of turkey tomorrow." Clark didn't respond, so Esposito continued. "I'm on the line with a Charlotte detective. They raided a motel this afternoon and took four guys down on one of their robberies. A Harris Teeter that was hit a week before ours."

"Why are they calling us?" Cunningham asked.

"They got the BOLO's that Whitaker sent out," Esposito answered.

"So they think these may be the same perps that hit us?" Clark asked.

"A lot of stuff about it sounds like ours. The officers seized black hoods, masks, fatigues, a couple of Uzis. And these guys are some bad asses, like the ones we're looking for. They took a couple of shots at the Charlotte officers, but missed. One of the perps got clipped, though."

"Man, that does sound promising," Clark said, "assuming, of course, that the perps who hit here today aren't our Harris Teeter robbers."

"Do you think they could be?" Cunningham asked.

"I have a feeling they aren't," Clark answered. "These robbers were more amateurish. They seemed too satisfied with the little take that they got. Our

Teeter robbers wouldn't have stopped with the teller drawers. And another thing's for sure."

"What's that?"

"They wouldn't have missed the kid who escaped."

"White or black?" Sloan asked Esposito.

"Both. Plus, these guys were driving a van. The police found radio equipment, police scanner, the works. One of the perps is talking, too. Sounding good, you got to admit."

"Is the van the E-150 we've been looking for?"

"I asked, but he doesn't know. He's checking."

"Where are they from?" Clark asked.

"Hold on," Esposito said, returning to the phone for the information. Then he put the detective on hold again. "Sounds like all over the place. One's from Atlanta, one's from Asheville. All of them are wanted."

Clark turned to Cunningham. "That does sound interesting. Being from all over fits their large hit area, too. We need to send somebody down to Charlotte quick before the perp lawyers up. Strike while the iron's hot."

"Hard to believe that the Harris Teeter case may just about be solved. Prospects looked pretty dismal," Esposito added.

"Yeah, they did. Nice to think that we've got some casings and bullets to compare to their guns, too," Clark added. They took chairs and sat for a breather. The promise of clearing such a violent case seemed to provide an instant of relief for them during what turned out to be a very stressful afternoon. Clark shook his head in thoughtful repose. "Hard to believe. What great news, really great."

"Lieutenant, I'm sorry to interrupt but I have some good news of my own to tell you," Wilkens said.

Clark looked at him and smiled. "Sure you don't want to save it, you know, ration it for a rainy day?"

Wilkens glanced at his watch and said, "Wish I could but this one's got a time limit on it." Esposito returned to his call, and they huddled around Wilkens. "You'll never guess who just called dispatch and wants to speak to me?"

No guesses during the pause.

"Marcellus."

"You're kidding."

"What's that all about?" Clark asked.

Wilkens continued. "He left a message with dispatch about ten minutes ago and said he remembered something that may be important to us in the

Ruby Walker case. I spoke with Sheila at the desk. Marcellus told her he's got some kind of family emergency and he's got to leave town in a few minutes. He said if I couldn't make it to his apartment by about ten of four then he'd catch me later."

Clark and Cunningham exchanged a perplexed look.

"What do you think?" Cunningham asked.

"I don't know," Clark said. "Maybe he made you guys on the tail, and he's trying to throw us off his track."

Sloan spoke up, "I doubt it. We really laid back last night. Maybe he does remember something about Walker."

"Wouldn't it be great if he did have something good for us?" Clark asked. "Some small detail or clue that would guide us in a clear direction. Putting the Teeter and Walker cases down, both in the same day. Imagine that."

"Hey, Lieutenant," Cunningham said, "we ain't even had Thanksgiving yet and you're already lookin' for Santa Claus."

"Well, what do you think, Lieutenant?" Wilkens asked. He was getting a little edgy for an answer.

Clark evaluated the situation. "Go ahead, Brad. But I want you to take back-up with you. Jerry, are you through here?"

"Yes sir. I was waiting for Steve to finish on the phone, so we could run this evidence to the station and log it in. Then I'll be ready to saddle up."

Clark looked at his watch. 3:20 p.m. "That's going to cut it too close. Can't Steve handle it and you go on with Brad?"

"Sure, if somebody could give him a hand."

"We'll take care of it," Clark said.

Clark and Cunningham conferred on the final wrap-up at the bank.

"If you've got everything under control here, I think I'm going to head back to the office and get the media release started," Clark said. "Looks like another case where we can use some help."

"And some luck."

On the way back to the office, Clark mulled over the surprise call from Marcellus. A call right out of the blue. Was Marcellus trying to shake them? Or could he have some legitimate, useful information about Walker? What could it be? If it were something substantial, would it be enough to obtain a court order and exhume Walker's body?

Clark checked his voice mail and, already, the media was hot on the trail of this one. Bank robberies were one crime that proved too irresistible for reporters. Funny, Clark thought; the average haul from them was only a few thousand bucks. The All-Seasons theft was ten times the loss of this one, but a John Deere tractor just didn't carry the glamour or sexy appeal of a bank heist. Toss in a few shots fired and Stuartsboro was in the on-deck circle on the six o'clock news.

He was typing a media release when his phone rang. "Lieutenant Dixon."

"Listen carefully," the caller said in a low, somber tone.

Clark grabbed a pen and paper during a short pause.

The voice continued. "I'm being held hostage at this very moment. I need the best marksman in the Stuartsboro Police Department to take a shot at this kidnapper who has me in a choke-hold."

Clark shook his head, smiling. What a nut. "Tell ya what, lady," he said, "I'm on a doughnut break at the moment. Why don't you call back in, say, an hour, and I'll see what I can do to help you out."

"Thanks a lot, Clark," Lana said. "Did you know it was me?"

"Sorta."

"Can a doughnut be that good?"

"Obviously you've never had a jelly-filled, or you wouldn't be asking that question."

"So how's your afternoon been, I mean, before the doughnut?"

They talked for a few minutes and then Clark told her about the robbery.

"Will it be on the news tonight?" Lana asked.

"I'm afraid so."

"Which channel?"

"Three. But you can't look at it unless you promise not to laugh at me when you see it. You got to know that my make-up artist was off today, and I'm sure I looked as stupid as I sounded."

"I doubt that," Lana said. "Even on a bad day, George Clooney or Brad Pitt would have to take a back seat to you."

Before they hung up, Lana invited Clark over for breakfast on Thursday morning. She explained that her daughters were going to the beach with friends and that she was having Thanksgiving dinner in Durham.

"That sounds great. Can I bring anything?"

"Just you…and maybe some of those jelly doughnuts of yours. If they're that good, I can't wait to taste one of them."

When Clark hung up, he sat there enjoying a peaceful moment, and relishing the compliment that Lana had given him. It had been quite a day. For that matter, it had been quite a couple of weeks. So many things going on professionally and personally. Even in this small town, things seemed to rock all the time. There was more than enough crime for five men to investigate. Recently though, crime in the area seemed to take on a different character, a different texture. The robberies and shootings were more violent. People were getting hurt and shot by thugs who seemed more aggressive and calloused than those in the past. Somebody was trying to make a statement with their crimes, and they were using bodies for exclamation points.

It was hard to believe that Thanksgiving was tomorrow. Lana had invited him over for breakfast and he was excited about it. He had been hoping that she would call and, sure enough, she did. Lana seemed to have it all: She was beautiful, witty, sexy, charming. Kind.

But in the midst of this pleasant thought, he was interrupted by an odd feeling. Something pricked him about Wilkens' meeting with Marcellus. He looked at his watch. 3:50 p.m. He decided to head over to The Meadows, and then he'd call it a day, but he sat there for another minute. He scanned his office, glad he wouldn't have to see this place for five days. Not this desk. Not these file cabinets. Thank God not this phone.

He'd get to see Lana tomorrow and spend the latter part of the day with his children. It was nice to have something to look forward to. His eyes wandered over to the credenza and he gave it a long, lingering look. He got up, walked over to it, and picked up the picture of Samantha. Studied it. Then he placed it in a drawer, flipped off the lights, and left.

* * *

Sloan pulled into a parking space on the opposite side of the building. Wilkens got out and said, "Give me a couple minutes to get upstairs to his apartment. Then you can drive around to the back and park. Take a look around and see if everything looks okay."

"Be careful, man. Remember, we know he's got friends."

"Don't worry, I got my radio. Let's go to channel two."

They switched their radios to the channel, then Wilkens shut the car door and headed to the breezeway, which led to the back.

He had already worked his way through a thick wooded area at the corner of the church property. As he weaved through a gauntlet of branches, the back of the apartments came into view. He picked the spot, squatted, and opened the hardened plastic case. With workmanlike speed, he took the Heckler and Koch MP-5 out of the case, extended the stock, and locked the scope onto the receiver. He knelt on his right knee and propped his left elbow on his left knee. He checked and adjusted the sight for the 125-yard distance. Then he looked at his watch...3:56 p.m.

Wilkens knocked on the door, and Marcellus opened it almost immediately and greeted him. "Hello, Detective. Thanks for stopping by."

"Not a problem, Mr. Marcellus. What's up?"

"I apologize but I've had an emergency to arise in my family that I have to leave for now. Can we talk on the way down?"

"Sure thing." Wilkens tried to get a look in the apartment, but Marcellus closed the door too quickly for that. "So what is it that you wanted to talk to me about?"

As they headed for the stairwell, Marcellus gave him the bogus information.

He unhooked the strap from the rear butt stock and wrapped it around his left arm, just above his bicep. He placed the butt of the rifle against his right shoulder and cupped his left hand under the front hand guard. When his left arm was positioned at the front of the rifle, the strap tightened. The weapon was now as steady as if it were on a tripod. He looked through the scope and, as he focused, he grinned when the red dot appeared on the officer's face...3:59 p.m.

"I didn't think much of it at the time," Marcellus said. "But later it hit me that it was unusual that a salesman would ask Mrs. Walker such a question. Don't you agree? Maybe it's nothing, but I thought you would want to know about it. You could ask some of the other neighbors if he approached them."

"Did you actually see this man?"

"No, I didn't."

With the red dot zeroed in on his target, he went methodically through the mental drill: Breath...Relax...Aim...Squeeze...Fire...4:00p.m.

Wilkens thanked Marcellus for the information, as the church bells across the meadow began to ring. They shook hands and Marcellus watched Wilkens turn to take the back steps. On the third ringing of the bell, he took a third step, then a fourth. On the fourth ringing of the bell, there was a loud, echoing noise followed by an awful clanging sound. Wilkens spun around and saw that Marcellus had fallen out of his wheelchair. "Mr. Marcellus?" he called out. Wilkens topped the steps, hurried over to him, and saw blood pouring from Marcellus' face. His right eye was missing.

Instinctively, Wilkens dropped to the balcony floor, drew his Glock .45, and scrambled over to the brick wall beside Marcellus' wheelchair. He got his breath, fumbled for his radio, and dropped it. He picked it up and shouted,

"Shots fired, headquarters, shots fired! Man down! 10-33! I've got a man down, officer under fire!" Sloan sprinted around the building with his gun drawn, looking in all directions, but he saw nothing.

As quickly as he assembled the rifle, he removed the scope, collapsed the stock, and placed it in the case. The spent nine-millimeter casing was picked up and put in his pocket. He evaluated his assignment, walking briskly back to his car. He had logged hundreds of hours of paramilitary training with this weapon. He was an expert sniper who rarely missed. He smiled as he drove away.

CHAPTER THIRTY-TWO

Within five minutes of Wilkens' cry for help, nearly every blue light in Stuart County converged on The Meadows. It was four o'clock, and many officers who were heading home, including sheriff's deputies and highway patrolmen, heard the radio traffic on their scanners, and raced to the aid of a fellow officer. With each passing minute, police cars continued to pour into the crime scene; a logjam resulted as officers had to park their cruisers on the sides of the only road leading into the complex.

Officers from the other agencies didn't operate on the same radio channel as the Stuartsboro PD, so they entered the scene with sketchy details. They jumped from their cars and ran to the heart of the complex with shotguns, automatic weapons, and handguns drawn. Eventually, officers filtered over to the crime scene; Capt. Blackburn routed some of them to a door-to-door canvass to pry information from the terrified residents. Capt. Simmons assigned others to establish a perimeter around the property, because it was too large to cordon off. He carefully directed them away from the area of the police canine search that was beginning.

In the next ten to fifteen minutes, another wave of cars converged on the scene. Reporters from the local newspapers and TV stations moved as closely as they were allowed to the action, milling around hungrily for details. A helicopter from Channel Three hovered over the area, panning for fresh footage for the six o'clock news. Three Councilmen, the Mayor, and the owner of The Meadows arrived next, magnets for the curious on-lookers.

At the corner of the upstairs breezeway, Marcellus' body was covered with a white sheet, a large crimson stain at one end. Aside from that, and the overturned wheelchair, there was no other cue indicating what had taken place a few minutes earlier. Standing in a small group, Clark, Cunningham, and the other key players were sifting through the details as Wilkens fielded a barrage of questions: *Where did the shot come from? Did you see anyone? Did you hear a car door? See a car leaving? What did Marcellus tell you? Exactly where were you when he was shot?* Still visibly shaken, Wilkens did the best he could with his answers. He re-enacted his movements and his position at various stages.

"Who's doing the track?" Clark asked Lt. Johnson.

Johnson pointed to the canine team out in the grassy area adjacent to the parking lot. "Edwards and Kobey."

"Why is he working him on lead?" Esposito asked.

"My guess is that he wanted this search to be a sure bet," Johnson answered, "not miss anything, and on-lead is the way to go." The officers watched intently from the second floor balcony while the leashed German shepherd methodically sniffed in grid formation, weaving back and forth.

Blackburn walked into the breezeway from the front of the building and approached the group. "I've got a team set up on perimeter patrol and one started on a canvass, Lieutenant. Can you think of anything that I've overlooked that we need to be addressing right now?"

Clark considered the question, as he continued to watch the canine working in the field. There was so little to do on a case that was so important, and he knew it: No items to fingerprint, very little to sketch or measure, no one to interview that they knew of. He shook his head, saying, "I can't think of anything else. I hate to say it, but I'm not counting on much of anything to come from the door-to-door. That search there," he said, pointing to the canine, "may generate our only lead."

They all turned to study the activity, while Clark continued. "From the building here to the edge of the parking lot is what, about twenty-five yards? The field, another fifty? The brush beyond that another twenty-five to thirty? What does that make it? About a 100-yard shot? Captain," he said, turning to Blackburn, "you're the S.R.T. man. What do you think?"

Everyone was quiet, a show of respect. Blackburn was the resident expert on this sort of thing. He was a well-trained tactical and firearms officer and had the kind of military background that made him the perfect fit for the S.R.T. Commander position.

"From what you guys are telling me, there's a lower likelihood that the shot came from the parking lot, right?" Blackburn asked.

Cunningham spoke up, "That's the way I see it. Look at the angle that a shooter in a vehicle would have had to fire from. And if he was hiding behind one of those parked cars, he would've taken a chance of being seen by somebody. Too risky. On top of that, I think when Brad was walking down the stairs he would've noticed a vehicle or person moving across the parking lot. Right there in his field of vision. A quiet lot like this one, don't you think it would've caught his eye?"

"I agree," Sloan said. "Not to mention that the shooter would've had to haul ass outta here fast, if nothing else, to keep Brad from returning fire. I would've seen or heard something."

Capt. Simmons walked over and joined the huddle. He scanned the area and said, "Hey, I just thought of something. Where's the Chief? I mean, with all these cameras and reporters around here."

The group chuckled, trying to seize the light moment.

Blackburn sported a devilish grin. "He left town for the holidays. That makes me 'da man'."

"There is a God," Clark said.

"Yeah, well don't get too excited," Blackburn said. "I still got to give him a call shortly and make him aware of all this, plus the bank robbery."

"Can't you wait about forty-five more miles before you do it?" Clark pleaded.

All eyes returned to the wooded area, as K-9 Kobey worked diligently, maneuvering his way to the brush area next to the tree line.

Blackburn continued with his theory. "This area is pretty wide open, as you can see, and there's nowhere to hide. On this kind of shot, they would certainly have to be patient, take careful aim. Anybody taking a shot at a cop would want to be well concealed so he could study his target, not worry about being seen. My guess is he shot from that closer tree line," he said, pointing to it and pausing for a second.

"Why do you say that?"

"Mainly because of Marcellus' wound," Blackburn answered. "It looks larger than a twenty-two; I'd say the round was a nine-millimeter or maybe a .223. With a gun like an AR-15 or an M-16, that would mean a shot from that closer point. That looks like about a 100 yards, and that's a fairly long shot for a nine," he said slowly, as he studied the range. "Now, if the shot came from one of those farther areas, then you're talking an assault rifle with a more potent round, like a 7.62. If that were the case, there would've hardly been enough of Marcellus' face left to recognize him. And it definitely would have been a through-and-through shot. Marcellus only has the entrance wound, right?"

"Yeah."

"No exit."

Clark turned to Capt. Simmons. "You do have officers on the other side of the woods securing the area?"

"As best as we could. It's a lot of ground to cover. Spans from the church over to the back of Elm Street. My guess is, though, that the shooter parked at the church. Nobody's gonna go walking through a neighborhood with a rifle in his hand. I've got a couple of officers keeping a close eye on the perimeter of the church."

An officer called to Capt. Blackburn from down in the parking lot. "Captain, I've got the Chief on the phone. Can you come down and take it?"

Clark turned to Esposito. "How about checking down at the office with the manager, see what information he has in his files on Marcellus. I'm sure most all of it's bogus, but who knows? Perps use aliases and bios close to the real thing. Maybe he got sloppy and we'll get something useful from his file." Esposito nodded and as he walked away, Clark called back to him, "Steve."

"Yes sir."

"How about heading to the PD after that and rapping out a search warrant for his apartment and van. We may as well get on top of this, and quick."

Whitaker, who had just returned from Greensboro, walked up to Cunningham and got a quick summary of the shooting. "How did everything go at the bank?"

Cunningham sighed. "Helluva day, Price, I tell you that. What do we average? Two, three bank robberies a year? And I can't remember the last time a Stuartsboro badge had a shot fired at it. Now, both happen in one day—a few minutes apart." He paused to organize his answer. "We were at a good stopping point at the bank. We got all the interviews done, collected some good bullets. Got a thorough canvass, it's just that we didn't get any real good stuff from it. Maybe a vehicle description, a white SUV. I'm glad the bank's closed for the next couple of days."

Clark overheard the tail end of the conversation, stepped over, and said, "Price, looks like your Harris Teeter case may finally be cleared. Did you hear about the Charlotte arrests?"

"Yes, sir. Steve told me about the call. It'll be nice to get a match on the ballistics and close that one, with all the time we've spent on it. Was the detective able to confirm that the gang was operating the Ford van that we identified? Steve didn't know."

"No word on that yet. Are you ready to head down there and jump in on the interrogation?"

"Yes, sir. I need to run by the house and pack a quick bag in case I need to stay overnight. Okay?"

"Yeah, but get back home early tomorrow for Thanksgiving. If you don't, you may not have a home to come back to."

Whitaker looked puzzled, not quite sure how to take the advice of his lieutenant.

"Personal experience, Price."

"Lieutenant," Esposito called, walking over to him. "They checked and re-checked the parking lot. No casing, nothing."

"I was afraid of that," Clark said, then he turned to Lt. Johnson. "If Kobey gets to the woods and hits on a trail, will it be difficult for him to track through those thick pines?"

"Not really. Actually, it'll help him. Dogs generally do better in those conditions because there's plenty of debris, leaves, pine needles on the ground to disturb. Everything about a good track has to do with disturbance. My guess is that, if the perp did shoot from that cluster of trees, then he just about had to park in the church lot and walk through the woods to his spot."

"Have we got somebody checking at the church for witnesses?" Cunningham asked.

Just then, the church bells rang at five o'clock. It startled Wilkens, who turned and spilled his coffee. Clark saw it and walked over to him.

"Hey, are you all right?"

No response.

Clark placed a settling hand on Wilkens' shoulder. "Listen, if you need to go home, we can get you a ride. You don't need to hang around here if you don't want to. We got it covered."

"I'm okay," Wilkens said, in a slightly shaken voice. "That ringing brought it all back for an instant."

"I'll tell you something, Brad, although I don't think it's going to make you feel any better. I'm beginning to think that shot wasn't meant for you."

"You don't? Why?"

"Because somebody shooting from that far away, assuming they did, really knew what they were doing. I think they may have wanted to make it look like they were trying for you and missed."

"What makes you say that?"

"Marcellus and the shooter set you up, needless to say. But if the shooter gave a rat's ass about Marcellus, he would've waited until you were clearly away from him before he took the shot. The shooter would've had plenty of time and chances to get his sights on you, when you were farther down the stairs, or even when you stepped down to ground level."

The theory seemed to put Wilkens a little more at ease. "Still, that's too close."

"No argument there."

"Lieutenant Dixon," an officer called from the parking lot.

Clark walked to the rail.

"Capt. Blackburn is calling you on channel two."

Clark switched his radio to the channel and called him. "3, this is 7, did you have traffic?"

"10-4. I just spoke with the Chief and filled him in on the cases. He said for me to handle the news media on this. I'm heading across the parking lot now to knock out some interviews."

"10-4, that'll be a big help. Thanks."

"He also wants me to contact the City Manager."

"10-4." After Clark answered, he heard radio traffic from the officer who was assigned to shadow the canine team. The officer stated that the canine had entered the woods and, according to his reaction, hit a strong scent. Clark stepped over to the group. "Looks like Stuartsboro has a sniper on its hands."

"Yeah," Sloan said. "If this was meant for Marcellus, I wonder what he did? Somebody really good wanted him really bad."

Clark and Wilkens chatted some more about the information that Marcellus gave just before the shooting.

"We still need to run down his information about this salesman," Clark said, "determine whether it's true or not." Then he added, "If it was a lie, that leads us back to Ruby Walker. Could seal the deal that something happened to her. Too many coincidences."

"Could be that Marcellus ran out of places to hide from a past crime or debt," Capt. Simmons suggested. "Maybe Walker discovered something about him when she visited him."

Clark's pager buzzed; it was Greg's number at the S.B.I. office. He called the number and, while he waited, he noticed that with overcast skies, it was getting darker more quickly and blue lights were shining brighter by the minute. He looked to Johnson and Cunningham and said, "We gotta move on this search, it'll be getting dark soon."

"If our theory is right about the shooter," Johnson said, "then he probably parked at the church. It's not that far from the tree line to the parking lot. The dog ought to be there shortly."

After several rings, an answer. "Special Agent Williams."

"Greg, it's Clark. I got your page."

"Yeah, hey, how's it going?"

"You picked a bad day to ask that."

"Why?"

Clark filled Greg in on the shooting, then on the bank robbery.

"Wadsworth told me he was coming over to assist on the crime scene," Greg said. "I can't believe that you guys had shots fired on another robbery."

"Luckily, nobody got hurt."

"What is it with these trigger-happy bastards? Seems like they're getting more violent by the day. Tell you what, though, I'm glad Wilkens is okay."

"His cage is a little rattled, but whose wouldn't be? We figure he was close enough to hear the bullet whistling by his ear. We did get a real good piece of news while we were at the bank robbery, though."

"About what?"

"Esposito talked to a Charlotte detective about a big collar they made today on a Harris Teeter robbery they had a week or so before ours. It sounds like it could be our guys." Enthusiastically, Clark filled Greg in on some of the details and similarities between the cases.

Greg cleared his throat. "Actually, Clark, that's why I'm calling you. I know you got your hands full at the moment, but there's something that I found out today about this very case. But I have to tell you this in strictest confidence. Okay?"

Clark was a little curious. "Yeah, sure, what is it?"

"There's something going on over here in our office that I don't understand. Hubert's on vacation and, for a reason unknown to me, he ordered one of our lab techs to lie about the analyses on the Harris Teeter bullets that you submitted."

Clark was stunned. "Lie? What for?"

"I don't know. But you know me well enough to know that I'm going to find out. There must be some secret directive from Raleigh, maybe something from the federal level. I'm clueless. Hubert tells me everything. Something's going on that he evidently has been sworn to secrecy over."

"You said your tech lied. Does that mean she got hits on the bullets?"

"Did she ever. Unprecedented hits. Whoever hit your store has hit stores in Charlotte, Greensboro, High Point, and all over the Southeast United States. I've never...."

"Damn! Just like my anonymous caller said."

"My lab tech *was* your anonymous caller. She's a good girl, Clark. Hubert pretty much gave her an ultimatum and she was stuck. Didn't know what to do."

"Looks like we're about to clear some pretty big cases."

"I'll say. If these Charlotte dudes are your robbers, it looks like they traveled the big city route, keeping to the interstates. But for some reason, they got off the beaten trail and hit your town. Now, that ought to make you feel real special."

"One of my guys is on the way down to Charlotte now to jump in on the interrogation, hopefully get a confession. One of the robbers is talking."

"So why did this Marcellus guy get popped? Do you think they were really shooting at your man?"

Clark offered his theory. "I think we may have gotten close to an organized theft ring stealing farm machinery and Marcellus was involved, somehow. It looks like he was somebody's errand boy, and he became expendable. Either that or he was on the lam and somebody caught up with him."

"I know about the theft ring. I sat with Sloan at the intel meeting when they presented the case. Maybe by finding your shooter, you'll clear up the thefts, as well. Too bad it's a holiday, though, you'll have to wait until next week to get Marcellus' I.D."

"What are you going to do on your end about the situation there?"

"I'm going to poke around quietly. There's a reason why Hubert didn't want me to know about this arrangement, and I don't want to blow whatever it is that's going on."

They exchanged ideas for a couple more minutes and planned their moves for the first of next week. When Clark hung up, he walked over to the group, listening to his radio for an update on the canine track. "What's the latest?"

Cunningham had a bit of a frown. "Just as we suspected. The dog had a pretty decent track through the woods to the parking lot of the church."

"And?"

"And nothing. The scent died. Strong indication that the shooter got in a vehicle."

"Did they recover anything?"

"Yeah. A couple of cans, cigarette butts, that sorta thing. But the items looked like they'd been laying there awhile. I doubt that somebody as good a shot as that guy was would leave his prints or DNA behind."

An hour later, the crowd of on-lookers and reporters had dwindled, as well as the number of officers from the assisting agencies. At least on the surface, The Meadows was once again a quiet, peaceful village.

Clark discussed the case with his men and the patrol supervisors, then they wrapped it up.

He got in his car and headed out of the parking lot. He was exhausted. Drained. Today he had literally come within inches of losing one of his men, and his division added a violent bank robbery, with few leads, to a growing list of unsolved cases.

He turned on the car radio to listen to some music, hoping for a shift in his thoughts and emotions. A Christmas song was playing, and he turned it off. *I'm not even ready for Thanksgiving and they're already celebrating Christmas.*

He pulled out of The Meadows, and didn't notice the headlights in his rear view mirror. The burgundy Altima followed him. All the way to his house.

CHAPTER THIRTY-THREE

On Thanksgiving morning, Clark walked up the steps to Lana's front door and couldn't help but grin—as two ideas struck him. He thought back to his last visit, when he saw the broken glass and suspected that Lana was in danger; he preferred the uneventful approach that today offered. Secondly, he noticed how the bright morning sun struck the beautiful windows on the front of the house. *Gordon Street, what a life; she lives in a world of stained glass and I live in a world of stained Styrofoam cups. It's nice to be stepping into her world.*

Lana came to the door wearing a coral silk blouse with crème wool slacks. "Good morning, may I help you?"

"Very cute. Happy Thanksgiving," Clark said, handing her a colorful green box with a red bow on it. "These are for you."

"Oh Clark," she said, dramatically, "you really do know how to sweep a woman off her feet, don't you? One dozen jelly-filled Krispy Kreme doughnuts. What can I say?"

"How about 'Would you like one?'" He walked in behind her and told her to look at the card that was tucked under the bow.

She read it aloud, "'For the woman who thought she had everything, now she does'." Lana laughed. "Well, these ought to perk up our omelets. Come on back." After a few steps across the foyer, she turned back to him. "Oh, by the way, I can't tell you what a privilege it is to have a TV celebrity in my home. Any offers from Hollywood yet?"

"Yeah, one. *America's Funniest Videos*. Okay, so you saw the interview. Was it bad? Be honest. I'm a court-certified expert in deception detection."

"No," she said, with a giggle. "You did a good job. Talking into a camera isn't easy. I know, I have to do interviews every so often at the hospital."

"For what?"

"Usually when we promote a community outreach program. Or if the hospital is undergoing a big renovation project. If we've acquired some new technology of interest. Things like that. You came across well, Clark."

"Kind of you to say that. Assuming it was okay, what was your favorite part?"

"I'm sorry, I can't comment on that."

"Why can't you tell me?"

"No, silly, that was it," she laughed. "When you told the reporter 'I'm sorry, I can't comment'. You said it like you were really in control, not the least bit intimidated. That was kind of sexy."

Clark grinned. "The truth is out. So you like a man who's in control? Excuse me while I pull out my notepad and jot that down."

"You're almost correct." She pointed to herself and said, "I like a man in control when I put him there. The secret is he doesn't know that I put him there."

"Your secret's a secret with me."

"Do you have any leads on your bank robbery?"

"No, afraid not." They stood in the foyer and talked another minute, as Clark talked a little about the case. When he shared his work with her, it seemed to help him put things into proper perspective. And that made him feel better about his cases. She was a good listener.

Clark could smell breakfast cooking and the closer he got to the kitchen, the more pleasing the aroma became.

"You did say you liked omelets, didn't you?" she asked.

"Oh yeah. I haven't had a hot, sit-down breakfast in ages. This will be so good, there's no way you're gonna fail."

"Sounds like I'm doomed to succeed then, doesn't it?" She began to pour Clark's coffee, then stopped herself. "Oh, I almost forgot. Would you help me with something upstairs for one second before we dig into breakfast? I need a big strong man to help me move a dresser in the guest bedroom."

"Sure, let's do it."

They went up the back staircase to the bedroom. At her direction, Clark moved the dresser, straining a little, to an opposing wall. He brushed his hands, panting. "That's one heavy piece of furniture, Lana. Oak?"

"Yeah, oak. Looks better here," she said, evaluating the move. "Kind of gives balance to the room, don't you think?"

Clark got his breath. "Well, if my answer entices you to want to move it again, I'm only good for one move per holiday." She grinned, and he backed up a couple of steps to study the dresser. "Yeah, I agree with you. Looks good there, I do believe." When he turned to her to make the comment, he was closer than he realized. Close enough to smell her perfume, and the scent was glorious.

They looked at each other for a long moment.

"We better get downstairs before our omelets get cold," Lana said. She showed Clark to the hallway bath, where he washed his hands, and then they headed down the front stairs.

When they reached the landing, the sun was beaming through the stained glass windows in the turret. They stood in the alcove and paused to admire the brilliant rainbow of colors that poured in.

"Here's the magic window," she said softly, almost with a childlike fascination.

He looked at the radiant blend of blues, yellows, reds, and greens that seemed to surround her in a cloud of color. Before he realized what he was doing, he reached over and kissed her gently on the lips. A slow, deep kiss and she took him aback by her soft, yielding mouth. When he finally pulled away, he gazed into her eyes, and then kissed her again, longer and deeper. When they separated, he placed a hand on the side of her face and whispered, "Now I believe in magic windows."

They stood on the landing a little longer and glanced once more at the window. They looked at each other, and their eyes exchanged the message of how wonderful the kisses were, because words wouldn't be sufficient.

She led him back to the kitchen where they shared an enjoyable breakfast with steady conversation. She poured him a second cup of coffee as he took the last bite of his omelet.

"Honestly, Lana, this was delicious."

"So glad you liked it."

She was working on her second jelly doughnut, when a bit of jelly spurted from the doughnut onto her chin. She wiped it quickly and licked her finger.

Intently, he watched her.

"Oh my gosh," she exclaimed, "these are out of this world. I think I'm addicted. Hey everybody, my name is Lana and I'm a doughnut-aholic."

Clark played along. "Hey Lana."

"So this is why you couldn't answer my call for help yesterday. Can't say that I blame you now."

They chatted about how they planned to spend the next four days.

"Your daughters have deserted you for the beach?" Clark asked.

"I miss them, but I understand. They've had a tough semester and need to have a good time. Besides, we haven't had that many happy family holidays lately. Maybe their attitude about them would be different if we had."

"I know what you mean. This Thanksgiving will be different for me, too. But the kids have been real good about it. Especially Alex."

"She's the one who lives with you?"

"She's the one."

Lana paused for a moment. When she looked down at her cup, Clark could tell that there was something on her mind. He was still thinking about her kisses. They were incredible, and he wondered if there would be another this morning.

"Clark, there's something that you need to know, something that I feel like I need to tell you," Lana said in a subdued manner. Another pause. "My ex, he's been giving me a little trouble lately. I just wanted you to know, so you could be prepared."

"Prepared?"

Then, she looked up. "He's been following me, from time to time. Not every day, maybe two or three times a week. I'd be out running errands, shopping, and I'd see him, watching me from his car. He was calling me, too, but that seems to have stopped. I kept getting hang-ups, until I finally changed to an unlisted number."

"Did you ever report any of this to the police or get a phone trace?"

"I came close to doing it, but I was worried if this thing ended up in court that it might impact my job. I'm in one of those public relations positions where image counts for a lot. Besides, he would've been too smart for that. He found a way to maneuver around caller I.D. and *69. I think he used those disposable phones and phone cards. He knows how to cover his tracks."

"Where does he live?"

"Greensboro."

"Has he stalked you at home or here?"

"No. He knows better than to do that. I think he believes that I'd take action against him, if he did show up. He only follows me in public. That way he can always say it was a coincidence or that I was imagining things. Bastard."

"Have you spoken with an attorney?"

"Not yet. Hopefully he's getting bored with this game, and has or will move on. I found out after our divorce that he did this very thing to his first ex."

"What made him decide to leave her alone?"

"He married me."

"Oh."

"I'm trying to think positive about this thing. Like I said, I haven't seen him in the last couple of weeks, so maybe he...."

"But you've been here. Does he know about this place?"

"I'm afraid he does. Clark, the reason I told you about this is that I want you to be careful. He just may appear out of nowhere. Carl has a bad temper; he's very strong. And violent. Extremely jealous."

"Still jealous of you?"

"It's about control. He doesn't think that I should get on with my life. Not until he gives his blessing, on his own time and schedule." She still appeared troubled.

"What's the problem?"

A longer pause. "The last man I dated, Carl tracked him down and...."

"Don't worry, Lana," Clark said in a comforting tone. "I know guys like him, and I'm a big boy. Everything will be all right. Nothing happens to you on my watch."

* * *

Alex and Brianna had settled in the den to watch a movie with a couple of their friends. Clark could hear them from the dining room table while he chatted with Michael. The girls seemed to be talking on the cell phone and giggling far more than they were listening to the movie. He asked Michael, "Have you applied here yet?"

"I haven't, but I will. Our counselor told us last week that Guilford County is giving five thousand dollar signing bonuses for math and science teachers."

"What's the catch?"

At the moment he asked the question, Ian yelled from the living room. "Yes! Touchdown! Dad, Mike, touchdown Green Bay!"

"What's the score?"

"Hold up." A few seconds of silence. "The point is good! Yes! Packers 35, Detroit 14."

"How much time left?"

"A little over five minutes in the third quarter. Favre is on fire. Y'all are missing it."

Clark and Mike returned to their conversation. Shortly, Alex came in and reached over her dad for a bowl of chips and salsa. When she did, she kissed him on the head.

"Wow, what's that for?" he asked.

"For being the greatest dad in the whole world," she said, heading back to the den.

"Thanks, sweetie." He turned back to Michael. "Are there any conditions tied to the bonus?"

"You have to agree to work five years for them. Still, that's not bad. Their supplement is better than what's offered here, too."

Brianna came into the kitchen with a tray of glasses to refill their drinks. "Daddy, this is Amber."

Clark turned around in his chair. "Hey Amber, how are you?"

"Fine, thanks."

"Would it be okay to drive Amber home after the movie?" Brianna asked.

"Sure, just be careful, and buckle up."

"And Daddy, while I'm at Amber's...."

"Yes, Bri?"

"Well, I may as well go ahead and spend the night, don't you think? Stay off the road. Drunk drivers are terrible over the holidays, you've always said that."

"Now aren't you the sneaky one."

Clark and Michael enjoyed their coffee and pie in the living room, joining Ian in front of the television.

On his way back to the kitchen to reheat his coffee, Clark stopped and looked at the Thanksgiving tablecloth. It was a beige linen cloth that he and Sam had bought when the kids were toddlers. Every Thanksgiving, they would place it on the table, and give each child the same color magic marker from the previous year. They would write a short sentence, with the year beside it, about something they were thankful for. By now, the cloth was just about covered with little scribblings from each child and, over time, it had become priceless to Clark.

He sipped his coffee, reading and walking slowly around the table. It was adorable to Clark how the writing and ideas matured and differed with each child. It was an emotional stroll for him, as he read some of the notes:

"*I am very thankful for our wonderful house*"—Brianna—'99

"*I enjoy spending my time at home, so I'm thankful for my home*"—Ian—'02

"*I am thankful for friends and family*"—Michael—'00

"*I am thankful for the good times spent with my friends and family. I'm also thankful for my house and church*"—Alex—'04

He read over several notes that the kids had written when they were younger. Sweet notes about being thankful for their parents, the family dogs Jackson and Cody...thankful for straight A's...for a baby doll...for a team winning a championship. He remembered that with this writing ritual, Alex was always the private one. For some reason, she would wait until after the meal, when no one was around, and she'd sneak back to the table and write.

When Clark wandered around the other side of the table, his eyes fixed on a cluster of writings that were next to his. Then he read:

"So proud of my children and so thankful for my wonderful husband! Grateful for good jobs, a nice house, and peace"—Mom—'02

CHAPTER THIRTY-FOUR

Lana was drying the last couple of pans when the phone rang. "Hello."

"Hey, it's me. Whatcha doin'?"

"Trying to get a decent start on my day, so I can finish some projects before I go back to work next week. I've got a long list of things to get done."

"After all these years, still the list maker. I thought you'd have grown out of that by now. That must be some kind of compulsion for you."

"You should never, ever talk in such a disrespectful manner to your big sister," she said, lightheartedly. "Show me a little respect."

"That'll be the day," Lynda said. "You're not in the middle of breakfast, are you?"

"Lord, no. I need to fast for a few weeks after that feast last night."

"I'm still stuffed. I had a good time, but it wasn't the same without your girls; they're the life of the party. They remind me of us at their age. Did you enjoy everything?"

"Yeah, too much. I can feel the chess pie and sweet potato casserole on my hips this morning. Oh gosh, they were good. Momma looked well."

"She looked all aglow, what with her favorite daughter there and all."

"I know you're talking about yourself."

"Have you been up to see Uncle Bill this morning?"

"Not yet. I'm going up after a while and spend some time with him. I know he doesn't even know that I'm around. I just want to be there for him, with him, you know, when he...."

"Well, do you think I ought to come up?"

"That's up to you, Lyn. But I really don't think he's got much longer. The good thing is he doesn't look like he's suffering."

"Are you looking forward to going back to work?"

"Like the Black Plague. I tell you I've enjoyed my vacation. You need to take a day off and come see the place. I think you'd like some of the improvements and changes I've made. I've concentrated mostly on the upstairs for right now, getting one room at a time. I moved some furniture around yesterday in the guest room, hung a couple of pictures. Added some accents. I think it looks better already."

"Speaking of moving furniture around, so tell me. This Mr. Muscles that you were talking about, what's he like? You didn't say much about him last night. What does he do? What does he look like?"

"Slow down, Joan Rivers."

"Let's have it."

"Well, uh, he's a little older than me."

"Yeah?"

"And he's a little taller than I am."

"Yeah? And?"

"And he's a little heavier than...."

"Stop it. Come on now, tell me. What does he do?"

"He's a policeman. Here in Stuartsboro."

"A cop? You're seeing a cop?"

"You make it sound like I'm a hooker or something. And by the way, I'm not 'seeing' anybody. We're just friends. Well, maybe between friends and good friends. It's not the way you may think. He's really nice, not like anybody I've met."

"How do you mean?"

"I don't know, different things. He's got a neat sense of humor and he likes to laugh. He's handsome, works out a lot. Nice, soft eyes. He makes me laugh, too."

"Hurry up, Lana, you're putting me to sleep."

"Cute. He came over for breakfast yesterday, and we had a good time. We did."

Lynda picked at her. "Just how good a time did you have?"

"Not *that* good. But do you remember that magic window we had when we were little?"

"The window? Of course, I do."

"Well, let's just say that it worked its magic yesterday morning." Lana paused for a reaction. "Now, that's all you're getting out of me today." After she said that, she turned from the sink and noticed the doughnut box on the table. She began to miss him a little.

"A cop, huh? That's probably a good thing for you. Did you tell him about Carl?"

"Yes, as a matter of fact, I did."

"What did he say?"

"Not a lot. He told me not to worry about things, and you know something, for the first time, I'm not. I feel safe when he's around."

"Does 'he' have a name?"

"Clark Dixon." They chatted a few more minutes then Lana hung up and got busy with the housework. After finishing in the kitchen, she decided to take a short break and go get the morning newspaper. When she walked out the side door to the porch, she started down the steps and something caught her eye. She saw where a large pile of leaves had been raked up beside the porch. And on top of the pile, in the center, was a bag of marshmallows. *If this is what policemen do, I should have stolen a flashlight a lot sooner.*

* * *

Clark pulled into The Meadows and drove over to the back of the building. He parked beside Esposito's car and noticed Sgt. Cunningham's SUV a few spaces down. The apartment door was open and he walked in. "Anybody home?"

"Back here," Cunningham hollered from the bedroom. He walked out to the hall to meet Clark. "You just couldn't stand being away, could ya?"

"Hey, how was your Thanksgiving?"

"Not bad," Cunningham said, patting a bulging stomach that was not well concealed under a tight knit pullover.

"Good gosh, David. Looks like you could use a couple days on Slim Fast. Any luck here?"

"Not so far. How did you know we were here?"

"I called dispatch to check on the overnight reports. Katrina told me you were here."

"How did she know? We didn't check on-duty or nothing by radio."

"You should know by now that Katrina is all-knowing," Clark said, shaking his head. He looked around him, slightly puzzled. "What's going on? Didn't Steve execute the search warrant here Wednesday night?"

"He did, at least he got started."

"What happened? Why didn't he finish the search?"

"Something came up on the bank robbery, and it could be good news. Steve had started the search on Marcellus' van when a Crimestopper's tip came in on the bank robbery. I needed some help on chasing down the lead, so I decided to put this on hold. Since I had to pull him away from here, we installed the mobile alarm and kept a marked unit outside. I hope you don't mind. I was gonna call, but I didn't want to bother you. Tell ya the truth, I think this is gonna be a bust."

"You're probably right. What's the tip on the robbery?"

"We found out the bank fired one of its tellers recently for dipping in the till. Somebody called in and said that her boyfriend did the bank. We checked and he's got a pretty good record. It may lead us somewhere."

"Sounds better than what we had. Where's Steve?"

"Back here in the bedroom," Cunningham said, leading Clark to it. "He's trying to get into Marcellus' computer."

"Computer?"

"Yeah. Steve says it's a nice one. He found Marcellus' password so he's nosing around now, trying to get into some files."

They entered the room, and Esposito was hard at work; Cunningham filled Clark in on the sweep of the apartment. "It's obvious this guy was keeping secrets. The place is void of the usual bills, financial records, photos, any kind of record of a past. It's as bare-boned as a motel room, you know, Gideon Bible and phone book."

"He expected Wilkens was going to get it and he prepared for our knock on his door."

"Hi, Lieutenant," Esposito said, looking around from his seat. "Happy holidays."

"Yeah, ain't they, though," Clark replied. "You having any luck?"

"Not so far, but I'm sure the Bureau will make short work of this thing." Esposito looked at the monitor, tapping keys, whispering, "Come on baby, speak to me." Then he looked up at Clark and said, "This guy had good taste…this is a Dell Optiplex Pentium Six…looks like he had it password protected with encryption…whatever he has in here, he didn't want just anybody seeing it."

Cunningham continued with his summary of the search. "This place is squeaky clean. It's almost like he didn't stay here. Just gave the appearance of it. No letters, correspondences from anybody, no checkbook. Even his phone book is spotless."

"Speaking of phone books, how about getting a court order on Monday for his phone service. Surely he made some calls to his associates, family. That is, unless you've found a cell phone."

"Yeah, as a matter of fact we did. In the van. Might as well get a subpoena for that too, huh?"

"Once we do, I think part of this mystery will be over and we'll start making some progress toward an arrest."

"Speaking of the murder, is Wilkens okay?"

"I called him late Wednesday night, and he was doing all right."

"I bet he'd like five minutes with this sniper. Do you think he's the guy who lives in the Sudbury Lane area?"

"Who knows. But once we find out who lives there, we're a step closer to solving this homicide. And maybe the Nick's case, too."

"What's your plan for scrounging around out there?" Cunningham asked.

"The area is a nightmare if you're trying to find anybody. First, you got a language barrier with the colonies of migrant workers spread all over the place. Then, there are the trailer parks. I don't have to tell you how transient those tenants are. Most of them don't even have the credit to put utilities in their names, so record searches would only reveal the owners' names. A lot of the houses are rentals, which means we'd have to hunt down a slew of owners to see who the renters are. Plus, if we go checking door-to-door, we'll stand out like a sore thumb and surely scare off whoever it is that we're looking for. Assuming he or they haven't broken camp already."

"Yeah, maybe they ran when Marcellus went down. Personally, I don't like the idea of snooping around in a place where a sniper may be sittin' up and waitin' to take a pop at me. That is, if this sniper lives out there."

"Well, the one thing that may be in our favor is that whoever lives off Sudbury doesn't know that we know they live there. Element of surprise, right?" Clark looked at Esposito, working through several screens. "Any luck, Steve?"

"Not yet. Hey, Lieutenant, guess who I got a call from on Thanksgiving Day? Mario Slade."

"Slade?"

"Yes, sir. A few days ago, he got knifed in the back. He called me collect from the infirmary and, like a fool, I accepted the call."

"What'd he want?"

"Help. And money."

"Money? For what?"

"He told me when he got stabbed, he was on the phone with the PD, trying to track me down. He wanted to pass me some info he heard in jail. He thinks he knows the name of one of the robbers who's hit stores in this area, maybe our Harris Teeter."

"Ain't it a shame that our case is all but solved? Else, we could've made Slade a rich man."

"How did Whitaker do in Charlotte?" Cunningham asked.

"Nothing grand," Clark answered. "The guy confessed to ours but he didn't seem to know enough about it to satisfy Price."

"Maybe Price is expecting too much."

"Maybe."

"I bet these guys hit so many stores, they can't even remember all the details of each hit," Cunningham said.

"Could be. Maybe we'll get some definitive answers on the ballistics test. Our bullets plus their gun equals ten years."

Esposito's back was to them as he continued his efforts to access the computer files.

Clark tapped him on the shoulder. "So what was the name that Slade gave you?"

Esposito stopped typing for a moment, and tried to think, staring at the computer screen. "Senior moment, wait a minute…uh, some kind of Bible name…Abel, Cain, uh Cain, yeah, Cain somethin'…Cain Mims, that's it."

"Where'd Slade get his information?"

"He got it from a guy he hung with in jail who was from High Point and knew some details about one of the robberies over there. He bragged about getting in on a major crack deal with this Mims guy after the robbery. Sounds like the cash from the robbery was used to finance the drug deal."

That struck a chord with Clark. He couldn't tell them, but Greg had told him that High Point was one of the other cities hit by this gang. *Maybe there's something to this Cain Mims.* "Steve, how about calling Price when you get through here and give him the name. Maybe it'll click with something he learned in Charlotte. From what I've heard about Slade, he's been right on the money with some stuff."

"So you think that this guy that's rolling over in Charlotte is legit?" Cunningham asked.

"I don't know. If they're the gang who killed the employee in the Salisbury robbery, he may be trying to save his ass from the death penalty. Confessing to stuff he didn't do just to make himself look good." Clark pondered for a few seconds. "Wonder why they haven't found the Ford van yet?…Maybe they ditched it, got too hot. Cain Mims. We'll have to look into that."

"Hey, check this out," Esposito said. Cunningham and Clark gathered at his shoulders. "Looks like he's got some mail pending." Suddenly the computer beeped and the screen went blank. "Damn! Can't check his e-mail. He even had that password protected."

"Keep workin' sport, you can do it," Cunningham said. Then he looked at Clark and noticed the preoccupied expression. "What're you thinking, Lieutenant?"

Clark concentrated for a moment. "Thanks, Steve," then he looked back to Cunningham. "He just gave me an idea for the Sudbury canvass on Monday."

Esposito turned around. "What did I do?"

Clark grinned. "It's what you said…you've got mail!"

* * *

That night, Clark went to bed early. The last couple of days had been an emotional roller coaster for him. First, there was the tense response to the bank robbery; for a dreaded instant, he thought they had a hostage situation, and shortly thereafter learned that a young man barely escaped being shot. Then, on the heels of that, Wilkens missed death by inches and the PD was stuck with a classic "whodunit". The victim was as much a mystery as the sniper who gunned him down.

Thanksgiving Day was a treasure. The time with Lana was exciting and a welcomed change of pace to the week. Unforgettable kisses. The evening with his children was fun and relaxing, a good finish to a special day. He did have a lot to be thankful for. He fell asleep thinking about the tablecloth and the precious writings on it. Then he dreamed:

He walked into a room where she was and she smiled at him. Slowly, she unbuttoned her blouse and invited him to beside her. He glided his hand along her leg up to her thigh, and the sight and touch excited him. He lay beside her and they kissed. Deep, long kisses that seemed to last until next week, but were still too short. He kissed her neck, softly biting as he worked his way to her chest. He smelled her perfume in all the right places. That intoxicated him. He wanted more, and finally he couldn't take it any longer.

Clark woke up aroused, sweating. He looked over at the clock, and he cursed that it was so late. He wanted to call her and tell her how he felt about her. He lay there debating for several minutes, and then he decided to do it. He just hoped that he wasn't going to make a complete fool of himself.

He called the number and, on the third ring, she answered sleepily, "Hello."

"Hey, it's me. I'm sorry to be calling so late."

"Clark?"

"Yeah, it's me."

"Why are you…hey, is something wrong?"

"No, nothing's wrong. I know it's late, but I just wanted to hear your voice. That's all." They talked for a couple minutes, and he told her that he had to see her. Now, and it wouldn't wait—now, and he wouldn't take no for an answer.

When she spoke, her soft tone was sensuous and inviting, and that rekindled his desire.

He sped to her house, arriving in ten minutes. When he got to the door, he started to knock, but she was already there. She was wearing a short, white gown, sheer, and the hall light at the stairwell cast a shroud of desire around her. Neither of them spoke a word as she took him by the hand and led him upstairs. He watched her eagerly from behind as she slowly climbed the stairs and entered the room. The lights were off, and a single candle flickered on the dresser. Soft music played on a side table.

They lay down on the bed and made love. The kisses were passionate, soft and wet, and they hungered for more. She poured warm oil on her hands and rubbed his chest. Then he did the same to her. Over the next few minutes, they exchanged playful touches that gradually became more aggressive. And when they could take no more, their desire surged to a point of no return and, finally, they were spent.

"That was phenomenal," she said, after catching her breath.

"Phenomenal isn't the word; there's no word for it," he said, panting. "You look lovely tonight."

She smiled, as he stroked her hair.

They lay there and talked in whispers. Revealing everything about their feelings and hiding nothing. Every once in a while, one of them offered an intimate touch or a soft probing tongue. He swept the hair from her face. "I have a confession to make."

"What's that?"

"Do you know when I decided I really wanted you? I mean *really* wanted you?"

She grinned. "When?"

"You're gonna laugh."

"No I won't. When? Tell me."

"Remember the voice message you left me at the office the other day?"

"Which one?"

"The one where you jumped down my throat because I told Alex that I had asked you out."

"Yeah, I remember. Why did you like that?"

"The fire. I knew the fire was back."

Sam looked at him, with a sleepy, sexy look. "What is it about you men that you like to be scolded?"

"I don't know. I suppose it's got to do with man's desire for a real challenge. You know, the competitive spirit of the hunter."

"You've met your challenge, and you know it," she said as her tongue darted playfully against his lips.

They made love again.

CHAPTER THIRTY-FIVE

Downtown Stuartsboro was bustling with a festive spirit Monday morning, following the Thanksgiving weekend. City employees went about the annual 'Monday-after' ritual of hanging Christmas lights on trees and decorations on utility poles. Store employees and customers sauntered out to the sidewalks on South Scales Street to watch, as if doing so would inoculate them with a healthy dose of Christmas joy.

In stark contrast, reporters and cameramen flocked to City Hall to intercept the Mayor and City Manager on their way in to the building. The two were peppered with a barrage of questions about the recent upsurge in violent crime; the bank robbery and murder last Wednesday dominated the volley. City Manager Butler did the best he could to answer questions off the cuff, but the reporters were relentless. Mayor Donovan managed to slip to the back of the crowd and call Chief Brinks, who called Capt. Blackburn who, in turn, called Clark to respond ASAP to the scene. The chain of calls resembled the water line of the old days where firefighters passed a metal bucket from hand to hand to douse a blazing fire.

Clark was working at his desk when he got the call. He stepped outside and walked next door to the back of the crowd on the sidewalk. Butler saw him coming, just as the reporter from the *Stuartsboro Sentinel* asked a question. "Are there any leads on the bank robbery?"

Relieved, Butler yielded to Clark, who stepped up and confidently addressed the reporter. "We have a couple of leads in the case, and we're aggressively working those leads."

"Can you elaborate any further?"

"No, I'm sorry, I can't comment." Clark wished that Lana were listening; she liked that line.

"Why not?"

"Because doing so would compromise the integrity of the investigation." Clark liked that line.

"Would you rather comment on the recent surge in violent crime here?" the reporter retorted.

Clark gave him a cool look before answering. "We are very concerned about the increase in violence in our city, but it's an epidemic in this entire region. We're placing as many resources as we can on these cases, and hopefully we'll be able to make some arrests soon."

The reporter from the High Point television station shouted next. "Lieutenant, in your opinion, was the officer at The Meadows the intended target of the shooting?"

"I'm sorry, no comment."

"Can you comment on why he was there? What he was doing?"

Before Clark could respond, the other media people unloaded: "Are you pursuing any leads in the shooting? What can you tell us about the victim? Have you established a motive in the shooting?"

Clark went with the last question. "We're looking into some theories for the shooting, but saying anything at this juncture would be premature on our part."

Then the reporter from the *Sentinel* struck again. "Do you believe that these crimes are connected in some way?"

Clark decided to throw him a bone. "There's a possibility that a couple of these crimes may be tied to shootings and robberies in other cities. We're working closely with the S.B.I. and other police departments in our efforts to draw a connection between cases. We have some critical evidence that is being examined that may be instrumental in solving some of these cases." He pared a couple more questions and the reporters, no longer smelling the scent of fear, started to pack up.

When the interview was over, Clark spoke briefly with the City Manager, and headed back to his office. And, as he did, his thoughts shifted to Sam and the night they shared. With each step back to the building, he wondered what their next step might be. He realized that he never really stopped loving her. And then, as an extension of the same thought, words of an old country classic filtered though his mind: "*Back in your arms is where I'll stay, What a fool I was to walk away, For us last night was a brand new day, Back in your arms is where I'll stay...*" As he opened the front door to the building, he saw his reflection in the glass and he couldn't help but smile.

When he returned to his office, he opened the drawer, took Sam's picture out, and placed it back on the credenza. He deliberated for a long moment and then moved it back to the corner of his desk, where pictures of her sat for a lot of years.

He walked in the conference room, as the guys were pouring coffee and enjoying sausage biscuits, leftovers from the holiday. They spent the next half hour reviewing the high profile cases, and then discussed lower level investigations that developed over the busy four-day weekend. Clark looked around the table. "I forgot Jerry's off today. When does he come back?"

"Wednesday."

Clark turned to his sergeant. "Any progress on the bank robbery?"

Cunningham began by bringing Whitaker and Wilkens up to speed on the Crimestopper's tip that he and Esposito worked. Then he addressed Clark's question. "Steve and I did some more checking on this guy over the weekend and he's lookin' like a definite maybe. He's got a lengthy record, mostly larcenies and burglaries, but no robberies. One interesting thing we've heard, though, he runs with a drug dealer from out in the county who drives a beige SUV."

"Beige SUV?" Whitaker asked.

"Yeah," Cunningham answered. "A witness from the canvass told us she saw a white one pulling out about the time of the robbery from behind the shopping center."

"Oh yeah, I forgot."

"Are you going to run the bullets and casings to the lab this morning?" Clark asked Cunningham.

"Soon as I clear out my morning calls. Let's see, what other evidence do we need to take? Marcellus shooting, the bank...any more?"

Clark asked Wilkens, "Brad, what about your drug shooting? Wouldn't hurt to take your casing."

"I'll run down to the evidence room and get it."

Esposito was next in the rounds, and he briefed the unit on the Marcellus shooting. He reported that the canvass yielded nothing, to no one's surprise. "We checked at the church and the staff was running daycare on the other side of the building at the time of the shooting. None of the residents on Elm Street would have had a clear view of the parking lot."

"What about the stuff seized from the woods?" Cunningham asked.

"Nothing. We dusted the cans but all we got were smudges. What if we send the cigarette butts to the lab and they develop DNA samples, then run them through the D.O.C. database?"

"Worth a try," Clark said. "Let's do it." Then he turned to Brad. "You ready to play mailman?"

"Soon as I check out the evidence for Sarge, I'll hit the road."

Whitaker looked baffled, which caused Esposito to chuckle, so Clark explained. "I called Postmaster Bullock this morning and he okayed for

Wilkens to ride shotgun with the mail carrier in the Sudbury area. Who knows more about your business than an inquisitive mail carrier?"

Whitaker raised a brow and nodded his understanding.

Clark continued. "If we're right about Marcellus' contact, he or they are probably lying even lower than Marcellus did. That could mean that they get very little mail, if any, or maybe they've received suspicious mail or packages. Fingers crossed, the carrier's seen Marcellus' van in the neighborhood. If this strategy doesn't work, we'll just have to come up with something else."

Esposito spoke up. "Lieutenant, what about Marcellus' computer? You want Sarge to take it with him when he goes to the lab?"

"Yeah, thanks Steve," Clark said, and then he looked at Cunningham. "Might as well take it, too, and get it on their waiting list. It'll take them some time to get to it. They're so backed up on computer cases."

* * *

Thirty minutes later, Wilkens met the mail carrier, a friendly little blonde in her mid-twenties named Rachel, at a convenience store near Sudbury Lane.

"The Postmaster told me that one of you guys was looking for someone and that I needed to help you," she said. "That's all I know."

Wilkens got comfortable in the backseat. "That's about all there is to it. Tell you the truth, Rachel, this is confidential—something we're helping the military with. We got a call from Fort Bragg this morning. They're trying to locate one of their soldiers who went AWOL a few weeks ago. They believe that he may be hiding out in the Sudbury area, based on information they received."

"What's his name?"

"Robbie Carter, but we don't think he'd be stupid enough to use his real name. Maybe since he's hiding out, laying low, he doesn't get very much mail."

"Then this oughta be easy."

"Why do you say that?"

"'Cause. Most everybody gets a similar amount of mail on a rural route like this. I can take you right now to three, maybe four houses in that area that get less mail, and I betcha one of 'em's gonna be your man. That is, if he's there."

"Great, looks like we're ready to get rolling. Remember, confidential."

"You want me to take you straight to the houses I'm talking about?"

"Nah, better run your regular route. We don't want to draw any attention."

In five minutes, Rachel pulled into the neighborhood and began her deliveries. She made fast work of the area, and Wilkens started to get a little nauseated with all the stop-and-go driving. Most of the mailboxes were in clusters, so the accelerating and braking was steady and constant.

"I couldn't do your job," he said to her.

"That makes two of us, 'cause I couldn't do yours, either."

There was quiet for a minute, four or five quick stops, and then he could feel the car making a turn.

"Okay, here's one of the houses I was telling you about," she said. "They ain't getting any mail today, so I'm gonna stick this extra flier in their box to give you time to take a good look."

"Smart thinking, Rachel. Maybe we ought to put you undercover with us for a while." He peeked out the window at the small white frame house set far back off the road. "Who lives here?"

"Most all the mail goes to a Dennis Mark Peters. He only gets the usual bills, rarely personal letters. Never any packages. A lot of days I don't stop here. Think this may be your soldier?"

"What? Oh, hard to say. You ever see anybody around here?"

"Can't say that I have. But you know our work—or maybe you don't— soon as we get through with the route, we're through for the day, so we hustle. Not much time for sightseeing."

"Ever see a dark or black van here?"

"Not that I can remember. I tune in to people more than cars."

Wilkens wrote down the name and address and they continued with the route. Over the next fifteen minutes, Rachel made deliveries and pointed out five more houses. Only one of those houses received any mail today; at the other four, she also stuffed their boxes with the flier. He drew a rough map of the locations and wrote the names and addresses on the back of the map. At each house, he repeated the questions about seeing people around it or seeing the van, and each time she answered 'no'.

After she finished deliveries, she drove him to his car.

"I bet you anything that your man lives in one of those houses I pointed out to you," she said confidently. "It's really obvious when a house gets very little mail."

Wilkens thanked her for the assistance and started back to the PD. As he drove away, he glanced at the six names on the piece of paper and wondered if one of them was the lead in the murder. He also wondered if one of them was the shooter who came within inches of killing him.

* * *

Jerry Sloan finished his workout, walked out the front door of the PD, and ran into Officer Leon Lucas on the steps. Sloan asked him, "Did you get to go hunting last week?"

"Naw. It didn't work out. I got subpoenaed for superior court and was placed on close stand-by all day Tuesday and Wednesday, so I got screwed."

"What did you have?"

"D.W.I. It was the guy's fourth offense. That's why he appealed it."

"So he pled out?"

"Hell yeah. They took a plea right before the trial."

When Lucas said that, Sloan noticed a striking woman walking down the sidewalk, heading their way. She had dark skin and deep, penetrating eyes, with jet black hair that was wavy and shoulder length.

"Whoa! Check that out," Sloan said.

At the very moment Lucas turned to see, she glanced up to see them ogling.

"Damn, Leon, do you have to make it so obvious?"

"Well, how about giving some kinda warning next…?"

"My God, look at those legs," Sloan whispered, noticing the short hemline to her navy skirt and high heels that gave an accent to toned, very sexy legs. "Hey, she's coming this way…I'll take this. Watch and learn, my brother."

She climbed half way up the flight of steps and said good morning in a slight accent. "Excuse me, is either of you an officer?" Sloan checked her out from head to toe, and was very impressed. Her only blemish was a thin scar, about two inches long, between her left cheek and temple.

"Yes, I'm Detective Sloan. What can I do for you?"

She handed him her business card and, as he read it, he couldn't help but glance over the top of the card at the most gorgeous legs he'd seen in recent memory.

"I'm supposed to meet with your Chief at 11:30, and I need to run a few errands first. I don't know my way around here. Could you tell me where the nearest office supply store might be?"

Sloan gave her directions to Office City on Freeway Drive.

"Thanks so much. Would there be a coffee shop on the way? I'm a bear without my morning cup."

I'd like to see you bare. I'd give anything. Then Sloan said, "It's kind of tricky from here. How about I lead you to it?"

Lucas gave him a look of pure envy.

"Well, how nice of you, Detective. But only if it's no trouble, and the coffee's on me. That's my car over there."

"There's mine," he said, pointing to the red pick-up truck in front of them. "Just follow me to that light there, and we're gonna take a right."

She smiled, thanked him, and crossed the street to her car.

Sloan elbowed Lucas, started down the steps, and boasted, "The master at work."

As she walked away, he absorbed everything. "Delicious, just look at that," he said as he eyed the tight skirt. "Jerry," he muttered to himself, "it do pay to show up at work on your day off." He got in the truck and read the card: Piedmont Communications, Sophia Bagio, Sales Associate.

A few minutes later, they took a booth at the Sanitary Café, and talked over coffee. When she removed her jacket, he noticed how endowed she was, wearing a white blouse that she filled out very well; he tried to catch a look every chance that he got. They talked a couple minutes about the café, which she seemed to like, and about her appointment to see the chief. She told Sloan that she was presenting a sales proposal for new walkie-talkies that, she claimed, were a little more expensive per unit, but had greater range than what they were using.

"We've sold these to Kernersville, High Point, Lexington, and Eden," she said. "They've been very satisfied with them."

"How much are they?"

She pulled a calculator from her bag and asked him how many officers there were in the department, so she could figure the price break.

"We've got about forty-six sworn, and six civilians who are also assigned a radio. Chief would probably want to order fifty-five to have some extras. Oh yeah, he'd need eight or nine more for the reserves."

She seemed to light up as she punched the numbers and did some figuring. "I could get you a break on sixty-five for $575.00 per unit. How many relay antennas do you have on towers around the city?"

"Five. Without them, our range would be pitiful. You'd almost have to be next to the car you're talking to in order to be heard."

"I know. But our radios are ten watt, not five, so they have greater range. If you switched to them, then I'd say that you would only need two antennas for the entire city, one north and one south."

"That'd save the PD a load on maintenance costs and repairs."

"And that's one of our biggest sales points," she said, while she continued to scribble some notes. "Do you know the locations of your antennas?"

Sloan flipped his paper place mat over, drew a rough map, and marked the locations. She studied the map for a moment, then took her pen and drew two X's on the map, charting proposed sites.

She asked him several more questions about their radios, mutual channels on which they converse with other police departments, and a few tactical questions. She tucked her notepad back in her purse and said, "I think we can make a very competitive offer to your chief." Then she looked at her watch. "I've got to run if I'm going to make it to the chief's appointment. I want to thank you, Jerry, for being so kind to me. And so helpful," she said, offering her hand across the table.

"It was my pleasure," Sloan said, holding her hand a little longer than he should have.

"I'd like to return the favor if you'd allow me to."

"Oh, that's not necessary," he said, wondering what she had in mind.

"I'll be in this area again in a couple of days; I have a meeting with the chief in Rallingview. I'd like to treat you to lunch if that would be okay. Here's my cell number."

Sloan took it. "I'm looking forward to it. Very much."

She smiled at him. A very sexy smile.

* * *

Behind his closed office door, Greg and Rosalie read and discussed the hard copies of the I.B.I.S. information that she kept against Hubert's directive. They bounced theories off each other about why Hubert ordered the secrecy, why Greg was excluded, and why Stuartsboro was on a list with much larger southern towns that were hit.

His phone rang. It was the A.F.I.S. tech from the fingerprint section at the S.B.I. lab in Raleigh. She had run Marcellus' prints and made an identification. Greg listened, jotting some notes, but Rosalie could tell by his serious expression that something was wrong. Greg slowly hung up the phone, and looked at her. Without saying a word, he called Clark's number.

"Lieutenant Dixon, may I help you?"

"Clark, it's Greg. Glad I got you. I've got some news for you from the lab."

"Great. The I.D. on Marcellus?"

"Yeah."

"You work fast, man. I owe you one."

"Clark, I'm afraid this is one of those infamous good news-bad news calls."

"Okay, let's have it."

"The good news is that we made an identification on Greg Marcellus."

"And the bad?"

"The bad news is that Marcellus' real name was Falsain Hamim. He was a converted Muslim, an extremist, and he'd been on an F.B.I. watch list for some time."

CHAPTER THIRTY-SIX

"Clark, are you there?"

Silence.

Clark was stunned and took a moment to recover. "Extremist? Did you say F.B.I. watch list?"

"That's right. Your guy Marcellus was really a man named Falsain Hamim; he had a violent criminal history dating back to the late nineties when he was a teen living in Cleveland. He went to federal prison on drug charges and that's where he converted to Islam. His file says that he hung out with an inmate who had ties to an extremist group out of the Detroit area. When he got out of prison four or five years ago, he crossed the lake and joined the group."

"How did you get all this? Have you spoken with the F.B.I.?" Clark heard himself ask.

"The tech gave me the intel attached to his fingerprint file. She's got more information for you when you give her a call."

"You think I should contact the Greensboro field office or the anti-terrorism squad in Charlotte?"

Greg chuckled. "You won't have to, Clark. I'm surprised they're not knocking your door down this very moment to see why you ran the prints in the first place."

"Huh?"

"The anti-terrorism unit in an area is automatically notified any time prints or inquiries are run on one of these 'Watch List Targets'."

"But, why in the world would a guy like that be living here in Stuartsboro?"

"How long did you say he'd been there?"

"About six months, at least that's how long he lived at The Meadows."

"You still think he was looking good for the farm machinery theft ring?"

"I don't know now. With this information about his background, and the fact that it was probably a sniper hit, it makes me wonder."

"Where are you on identifying his contact?"

Clark told Greg of Wilkens' assignment. "I'm expecting him back within the hour. Hopefully, he's narrowed the field down. It's a big area he's canvassing and a little difficult to nose around in. But, then again, whoever Hamim was associated with there may have already left town."

Greg gave Clark the contact information for the technician at the lab. "Give her a call. I took the liberty of giving her your e-mail address. Call me back when you get a chance."

"Thanks. Hey, before you go, any idea when you may have the ballistics comparisons on the bullets we brought you? I'd really like to nail our Harris Teeter case on the Charlotte gang. Who knows, maybe even the bank robbery we had, assuming all the gang members didn't get taken down."

"Let me think. Charlotte PD is supposed to run their tests today or tomorrow, so we ought to be able to compare our results with theirs by then. If I were you, though, I wouldn't get my hopes up too high on a match. The gun used in your Harris Teeter robbery might not even have been seized in the Charlotte bust."

"Hey, I'm trying to be optimistic. I believe the shooter in my case really enjoys killing people, has the taste for it, and I bet he's the one who's done most of the shooting for this gang. Guys like him never get rid of their weapons. You know that. Their guns are like family."

"I'll see what I can do. Hopefully, I can get you an answer in the next two or three days."

Clark hung up, called Raleigh, and spoke with the fingerprint tech. She gave him more information, including an interesting fact that Hamim had accidentally disclosed to Wilkens, that he had lived in the Charlotte area for a short while. The tech informed Clark that around the same time, Hamim had evidently fallen off the federal surveillance radar.

After speaking with her, Clark notified the chief, who called a meeting of the command staff. They discussed the information at length, and Clark filled them in on the strategy to locate Hamim's contact in the Sudbury area. Everybody seemed relieved that Hamim was out of the picture, but they were left with the troubling question of why someone would want to kill him. Or Wilkens.

When Clark returned to his office, the e-mail from the lab tech had arrived. He scanned over the info, then studied the aliases that Falsain Hamim had used over the last several years:

Hammil, Farley	Marcellus, Greg
Marbury, Henry	Marcellus, Harry
Marbury, Hilton	Marcellus, Henry

Clark read the e-mail and was surprised by the volume and detail of the classified intelligence collected on Hamim, who was considered only a fringe member of a radical group.

A few minutes later, the chief called Clark and, just as Greg had predicted, an agent from the F.B.I. office in Greensboro was on conference call. Clark jogged back to the chief's office and saw that Capt. Blackburn was already there.

Over the next few minutes, Clark informed the agent, Pat Pegram, of what they had on Hamim and, more importantly, what they needed. "We became interested in Marcellus, uh, I mean Hamim, when the death of an elderly resident became suspicious."

"Where are you on that case?" Pegram asked.

"We probably have enough now surrounding her death to get an order for exhumation, but it'll have to wait a few days. We're covered up right now with shootings and robberies."

Pegram chuckled, then spoke in a suave, polished tone. "I don't mean to hurt your feelings guys, but I have been hearing and reading a lot about Stuartsboro in the news lately."

Everybody took a moment to laugh in an otherwise edgy gathering.

"Where are you on locating Hamim's connection?" Pegram asked.

"We hope to narrow the search down to a few places, but we have to be discrete," Clark said.

Pegram continued. "As far as we can tell, Hamim had 'wannabe' spread all over his file. Guys like him are a dime a dozen. They get pumped up for these radical causes in jail, get converted, then they get used up and thrown to the side. Sooner or later they rejoin the mainstream, and you never hear from them again. Even though we think he may have been behaving himself lately, I wouldn't want to bet my paycheck on it. Is there anything we can do to assist you?"

Clark glanced at Chief Brinks and Capt. Blackburn, who were looking at him for an answer.

"I think at the moment we're okay," Clark said. "We'll try to develop something on Hamim's contact and take it from there."

"Please keep us posted, Chief," Pegram said. "I'll contact our SAC in Charlotte and tell him what you've got going on there. Our office is going to be tied up the rest of the week preparing for the President's visit on Friday here and in Winston. We've already received several threats, so we're throwing everybody we have into the project."

A short while later, Wilkens went to Clark's office, and briefed him and Cunningham on the mail route.

"Did she go for the AWOL story?" Clark asked.

"Yeah. Never a question about it. I stressed the confidentiality thing to her. I think she's okay."

"Did the van mean anything to her?"

"Afraid not. These carriers roll all day. Barely stop nearly enough to toss the mail in the box, then they're off to the next one. Stop and go, stop and go. I came close to heavin' a couple of times in the back floorboard."

Cunningham laughed.

"How'd it go?" Clark asked.

"I've got six names here, Lieutenant. The mail carrier said that, without a doubt, these addresses are the ones that receive far less mail than the others. So if your theory's correct...."

"She's sure?"

"Absolutely. She said it's that obvious. It's a deal where most everybody out there gets about the same amount, these get very little," Wilkens said, handing the note and sketched map to Clark. "Good chance our man or woman is on this list."

Clark read over the names. Then he cross-checked them against the list of Hamim's aliases on his computer screen. After studying both lists, a smile slowly surfaced on his face. He tossed the list on his desk, as Cunningham craned his neck to read the names:

Dennis Peters
Juan Rodriguez
Billy Childrey
Wallace Madden
Harris Hamilton
Victor Spring

"Beautiful. There's our man," Clark said confidently, pointing to the name.

"What now?"

"Brad, go see if the surveillance van's available," Clark said. "Sarge, get Capt. Blackburn to let you in the narc office to get the body wire. I'll call next door to Code Enforcement and see if they can give us a loaner.

***

An hour later, Esposito drove into the Sudbury area, and the surveillance van lagged behind about a quarter mile. Esposito gave them a test count and Wilkens acknowledged by radio that he and Clark could hear him loud and clear on the body wire microphone. Esposito referred to the refined map that Wilkens drew, taking the three turns as indicated.

He advised them that he was approaching the residence. "Okay…the house is set back off the road…grey siding, one story, frame. The driveway's kind of long, looks like about a hundred and fifty feet…I'm pulling in now."

Wilkens pulled the van over to the shoulder of the main road, got out and raised the hood. Then he walked over to Clark's window.

Esposito parked the Code Enforcement pick-up behind a small sedan. "There're two cars in the driveway…I can't read the tag on the front one. This one's Edward-Robert-Robert-4-3-3-7…nobody in the yard…I'm getting out."

Clark called dispatch on his cell phone and requested registration information on the license plate. After he hung up, he looked at Wilkens.

"Who does it come back to?" Wilkens asked.

"Not in file. Could be a new tag and the info hasn't made it to Raleigh yet."

They listened as Esposito walked up the steps to the front porch. The transmission was so clear they could hear him breathing.

"Here goes," Esposito said, knocking on the door. "Don't hear anything on the inside."

"Come on, come on," Clark mumbled, after a strained pause.

After about fifteen seconds, Clark and Wilkens heard a louder knock.

"Never fails," Wilkens said, "you get all this tech stuff together and lined up, and then nothing."

"Harris Hamilton," Clark said whimsically, "come to the door. We know you're in there."

Wilkens spoke next. "If the landlord's waiting on Hamilton, aka Marcellus, aka Hamim, to get this month's rent in, then I got bad news for…."

"Shhh, listen."

Wilkens turned up the volume on the receiver and they heard Esposito walking.

"What's he doing?" Wilkens asked.

"I don't…." Clark was interrupted.

"Hey, how you doing?" Esposito asked.

A muffled response.

"I'm with the Tax Department. Name's Cruz," Esposito said.

"What do you want?"

"We're working this area over the next few days, checking properties for tax revaluation. Do you live here?"

A pause. "No, I don't. I'm visiting a friend."

"Is your friend here? I'd like to speak to him briefly if I can."

"He's gone, he had to run an errand."

"According to our records, this house is owned by a Mr. Curt Thompson. He has a Harris Hamilton listed as the renter. Is Hamilton your friend?"

"Yeah."

"Any idea when he'll be back?"

"No. He went into town."

The sound of pages being turned. A dog barking.

"Hey, he doesn't bite, does he?" Esposito asked.

"Nah, he's friendly, unless you mess with him."

"I've had more than my share of those on this job. Mind if I give the outside a quick look over?"

"Help yourself."

Wilkens turned to Clark. "Esposito's smooth, isn't he, Lieutenant?"

"As silk," Clark replied. "All that narc undercover work he's done."

Esposito spoke in the mike. "Okay, I'm walking around the house now. The dude is staying in the backyard. He's moving some boxes to the house from a shed...he's a little uptight...never seen him before...looks Italian, Mexican."

Then Clark and Wilkens heard more walking.

Silence for half a minute.

"Hey, I think I saw a curtain move on the east side of the house here."

Wilkens gave Clark a look of concern. "He's not going inside, is he?"

"Go put the hood down," Clark snapped.

Esposito yelled to the man, "I'm about through here!" A few seconds of silence. "Hey, I just got a page from the office. Mind if I use your phone for a quick local call?" A faint noise. "Thanks, man. I won't be but a second." Another muffled response.

More walking, taking steps. A door opening, then closing.

"It's right there."

"Thanks a lot," Esposito said. Then he pressed a number.

Clark's cell phone rang. "Yeah," Clark said, angling the phone so Wilkens could listen.

"Hey, this is Cruz. I'm out in the Sudbury area, working Regal Road. Yeah, that's right. Are we supposed to fill out the new 5-2B form or do we use the old one? Yeah…I was told that there were no more 10-60 exemptions…Only one maybe two…Okay…I'll do the best that I can…Thanks." Esposito looked around as he hung up. Then he called the Tax Department and hung up after a ring.

"What was all that, Lieutenant?" Wilkens asked.

"Hey, man, thanks a lot," Esposito said. "Will you tell Mr. Hamilton that I came by? I'll be sending Mr. Thompson a revaluation notice. He should be getting it in the next thirty days."

"Yeah."

Then Clark answered Wilkens' question. "'5-2B form'—it's a five-room house with two bedrooms. 'No more 10-60 exemptions' means nothing looks suspicious at the moment. 'One, maybe two' means he thinks he heard or saw somebody else in the house."

Clark and Wilkens heard a door open and close.

"Okay, I'm outside now," Esposito said. "I think I heard a door close in the front when I entered the backdoor at the kitchen. Nothing looked out of the ordinary, that I could see."

Esposito got in the truck and started it up. Then he called them on his radio. "Did you copy okay?"

"Yeah, good job, Steve. So you think there was somebody else in there?"

"I coulda swore I heard somebody."

"Could you make the tag on the lead car?" Clark asked.

"Uh-uh, didn't have a chance. It looked like a light blue Chevrolet. That's all I could tell. Did you run the tag on the one that I gave you?"

"Yeah. It comes back not in file. What kind of car was it?"

"A burgundy Altima, late model."

"We'll meet you at the convenience store up the road."

"10-4."

As the truck backed out of the driveway, Yasin, who had hidden in the front bedroom, limped noticeably out to the den. He looked at Sa'diah, and asked, "What did he want?"

"He's with the Tax Department. They're surveying properties in this area."

"Why did he come inside?"

"He had to use the phone. I listened to his conversation. Everything is okay."

Yasin hobbled over to the phone and pressed the redial button, and let it ring. After someone answered, he hung up. "Have you ever seen this man before?"

Sa'diah paused, and coughed. "No, not that I recall. Why?"

"Why don't you follow him up the road to see if he stops at other houses."

"I will. After that, I'm going into town for a couple of things. Do you wish to come?"

"No. I will stay here, in case the others try to call us."

Sa'diah went out and got in the Altima. He reached in the glove box and pulled out his .45 semi-automatic. He dropped the magazine to check it and then fed it back into the gun. He did recognize the taxman; Sa'diah had seen him at The Meadows the afternoon of the murder. Sa'diah knew that he was a policeman, but Sa'diah didn't want Yasin to know about it. Sa'diah would have to take care of this himself. *I've worked hard on this project...over a year...made too much progress...sacrificed too much to let these chicken thieves get in the way.*

He had to make a move on these detectives. And fast.

CHAPTER THIRTY-SEVEN

Esposito pulled up beside the van and asked, "What do you think, Lieutenant?"

Clark leaned over to Wilkens, who was in the driver's seat, and said, "We need to contact DMV about the license plate and see if they can tell us who the owner is. Maybe it's the guy you spoke to. It could be that DMV has the information, but hasn't entered it into their system yet. Did you say it was a Nissan?"

"Altima, late model, had the new taillights. What's the next step?"

"The landlord?" Wilkens asked.

"We need to find out what he knows about these people," Esposito said. "At least, we know the guy I talked to is lying about Harris Hamilton."

"True," Clark said. "But we got to be careful how we move on this. Let's get back to the office and throw some ideas around."

"I'm on the way."

Sa'diah sped down the road, trying to catch the truck. He figured the officer was heading back to the police station and Sa'diah knew where that was. He approached the city limits and saw the truck about four cars ahead of him. After two more turns, he gained some ground on it. He was now one car back, and a white van was between him and the truck.

The truck entered the downtown business district, and Sa'diah noticed that the van continued to follow it. *Must be his back-up.* Now it was obvious that they were traveling together.

After several more blocks, as he suspected, the two vehicles pulled into the back of the Police Department. The municipal lot was large enough for Sa'diah's vehicle to blend in so he pulled up to the City Hall side. From a distance, he observed the officers get out of the two vehicles: The older man whom he believed was the supervisor, the black detective from The Meadows shooting, and the one who posed as the tax office employee.

They stood in the middle of the parking lot huddled together for a minute. Then he saw the supervisor walk over and put something in the gray

Chevrolet, the same car that Sa'diah had followed on several occasions. The three officers then entered the back of the building. Sa'diah needed to catch the supervisor out somewhere, isolated from the others, and then he could make his move. It was a little after one o'clock, and Sa'diah thought that the supervisor might leave soon for a late lunch. He looked at his watch again and decided he would wait thirty minutes. He lit a cigarette and slumped back.

Inside, Clark and his men discussed the results of the assignment, and Esposito's voice was charged with enthusiasm.

"For one, this guy looked out of place; he spoke with some kind of accent. I could tell he was hiding something, the way he acted."

"Not to mention he was lying about Hamilton."

"And I know there was somebody else in that house; I heard something. We've run across some kind of operation. It's the greatest place in the world to hide out, and until Marcellus was killed, they even had someone running their errands. They're careful and they're organized."

They tossed some ideas around and returned to their offices.

Clark checked his voice messages and one of them was from Lana. She was in town on short notice and invited him over for dinner. He had missed her company, but things had changed so suddenly in his life. Though he hadn't known Lana very long, he thought too much of her to deceive her. He had never been in this kind of predicament before, and he needed to give this situation a lot of thought. Getting involved with Lana would be an easy thing to do. Way too easy.

Next, Clark checked his e-mail. He replied to several messages, routed others, and took some extra time to view the digital photos from the bank robbery and murder. If he didn't learn anything else from the Ruby Walker case, he learned the importance of paying better attention to photos. He studied every one from the bank robbery, especially the one showing the bullet holes in the wall and doors. *If the shooter had a shotgun, we would've had two murders in a single day.*

He sighed, took a sip of Diet Dr. Pepper, and moved on to the photos of the sniper shooting. One by one, he clicked on each photo. He looked at the close-ups of Hamim and wondered: What was this guy involved in? Why would someone want him dead? Was Ruby Walker really murdered? If she was, what did Hamim have to do with it?

A few minutes later, Clark walked out the back door of the building, and Sa'diah watched him drive out of the parking lot. Sa'diah followed him south on Main Street, and Clark turned left into an alley, stopping at the back door of New Laundry Cleaners. The area was fairly secluded: Dumpsters, stacks of crushed boxes, barred doors, no foot traffic. Sa'diah thought that this could be his best opportunity.

Clark got out and entered the back of the business. He left his car door open, an indication to Sa'diah that he didn't have much time to act. Sa'diah parked two doors down and, as he got out of the car, had to adjust his .45, concealed in the small of his back. He carried a briefcase as a prop and walked towards the idling car.

Clark walked out the back door carrying some shirts, glanced at Sa'diah, and then heard someone call his name. Clark turned to the back door as a clerk met him there with some additional dry-cleaning. Quickly, Sa'diah altered his direction and headed the other way. Clark got in his car and drove out of the other side of the alley.

Sa'diah ran to his car, started it, and barreled out onto the street. He looked at the traffic light and barely caught a glimpse of the gray Chevrolet making a right turn. Sa'diah swerved around a garbage truck and made a sharp turn on red, causing a car from the opposing direction to slam on brakes to avoid a collision.

Sa'diah followed Clark's car for several blocks until it gave a signal for a left turn into a restaurant parking lot. Sa'diah decided to make his move, until he saw two other police cars parked there. "Damn!" he shouted, slamming his fist against the steering wheel.

Ten minutes later, Sa'diah returned to the house and he noticed Yasin's car was gone. He walked into the den and crouched at the edge of the area rug. He peeled back the corner of the rug and removed a piece of block floor tile that concealed a compartment. He removed a cell phone, sat down in a chair, and made a call.

"Hello."

"It's me. I've only got a second."

"What's the matter?"

"These Stuartsboro detectives are all over us. If we don't do something quick, everything will be in jeopardy." He then made a proposal of what he'd like to do.

"Are you sure it's necessary?" the voice on the other end asked. "It's extremely risky. What you suggest may spoil everything. How much in the way can these locals be?"

"Look, I'm telling you, they're getting too close to us. Today, they sent one of their detectives here to the house posing as a tax appraiser."

"How do you know he was a cop?"

"I saw him at The Meadows. Remember? The shooting."

"How many of them are there?"

"I don't know, five, maybe six. With your approval, I could resolve this quickly, before it blows up in our faces. Send them all some kind of message."

"I don't have the authority to give you the go ahead on that. But, if you could get to their supervisor, wouldn't that be sufficient?"

"I doubt it. The others probably know what he knows. Besides, he's hard to get to. Either he's in his office or he's out in the field with people all around him. I had him isolated a few minutes ago, but I was interrupted."

"You're a trained professional. Can't you handle this?"

"What do you want me to do? Walk into the police station and demand to see him?"

"You can have help, if you need it."

"Yes, I know."

"Where have you followed him on your surveillance?"

"Several places. A lady's home in town, a local gym, his house."

"Well, catch him at home and take care of the matter. But it sounds as though you don't have a lot of time. Don't botch this."

Sa'diah turned off his cell phone, stood up, and, just as he did, he heard a voice behind him.

"Stop! Don't turn around and don't move." It was Yasin. "Slowly, put the cell phone on the table beside you and take one step forward."

Sa'diah obeyed and Yasin limped cautiously up behind him, placing the cold metal of the semi-automatic silencer against the nape of his neck. Yasin leaned over, picked up the phone, and pressed the redial button. It rang several times, then a woman answered and Yasin hung up.

Yasin continued. "I worried about you so I followed you into town. It appears to me that you knew this taxman and who he really was, knew where he was going. There have been questions about you, concerns, and now I think I know...."

Suddenly, Sa'diah turned and struck Yasin on the arm, knocking him off balance. Sa'diah dropped to the floor and spun around, reaching to his back for his gun. Yasin regained his balance and fired two shots...*pift, pift*...into Sa'diah's chest, knocking him across a table and to the floor. Sa'diah was dead.

When Yasin pressed the redial button a moment earlier, the woman who answered said, "Good afternoon, F.B.I., Charlotte office." Sa'diah's real name was Tony Ricardo. He was a federal agent who had infiltrated this group, and he had been working undercover in the assignment for the last fourteen months.

* * *

Clark's cell phone buzzed, while Detectives Whitaker and Esposito were playfully arguing over ownership of the last chicken wing.

"Look at your plate, man," Esposito barked. "You've already had five…see…count 'em; I've only had four. This one's mine."

A couple of patrons at the next table turned around to check on the commotion. For Stuartsboro's finest, chicken wings at Dragon Garden were the best in town; more officers threatened to go to fisticuffs over rights to the last one than any other dish.

"Hey guys, we're attracting a crowd here," Clark said, leaning over the table, whispering his warning. "The manager's going to start making us check our guns at the door. Keep it down a little."

The other officers at the table chuckled at the reprimand.

Clark answered his phone. "Hello."

"Hey, it's Sarge. Y'all still at lunch?"

"Yeah, we're about to finish up. Just as soon as Steve and Price go to blows."

"Chicken wings?"

"You got it. What's up?"

"Got a call from GPD. They had a bank robbery this morning at the First National on Nimmons Road. Some of the stuff with their case sounds like ours."

"Such as?"

"Three-man job, for one. They used semi-autos, like our perps. Real aggressive, too."

"Tell me there's more."

"A little something else. One of the robbers fired a few rounds at the door, like our shooter."

"Anybody get hit?" When Clark asked that, everybody at the table got quiet.

"Nah. A customer was about to enter the bank and saw the robbery from the breezeway, so he ran."

"Did they recover any bullets?"

"Only one out of four or five. It lodged in the aluminum casing of one of the doors. The others penetrated the glass. Nine-millimeter, like ours."

"Anything else?"

"They wore gloves, masks, like ours did. Race unknown. That's about it."

"Well, maybe we can get a match on the bullet or the casings."

"Uh, that's everything, I believe. Has Steve had a chance to check into the owner of the house on Regal Road yet?"

"Some. The owner is Curt Thompson, older guy in his sixties. Steve got his contact info from the Tax Department. Thompson lives out near the Courthouse, on Gillie Road. Steve called the number and spoke with his wife. Thompson's out of town on a fishing trip. Should be back today, tomorrow, she's not exactly sure when."

"What reason did Steve give her for needing to contact him?"

"Next of kin notice. He thought that was safe since Hamilton was an alias anyway. Our guys make some pretty good liars, don't they?" Clark asked, then his pager buzzed. He looked at it then continued. "Turns out this Thompson guy owns several houses out in that area. We need to get in touch with him ASAP. Right now, that house is the only lead in a big case—how big we don't even know yet."

"Maybe the County can check by there periodically for us. We can tell them that it's a death notice call, too."

"Yeah. I gotta run; the Chief just paged me. I'll see you at the office."

"Yeah, I need to run, too. Marilyn said that a big school group is coming for a tour in a few minutes and I'll be tied up with that. Patrol's working short today and I got stuck with it."

"See you later."

About twenty minutes later, Marilyn called Sgt. Cunningham and informed him the tour group had arrived from City Hall. He straightened his necktie and walked out to the lobby. It took a minute to establish quiet in the rowdy group, which consisted of sixty middle school students, several teachers, and about ten parent volunteers.

"Good afternoon, I'm Sergeant David Cunningham," he said in a loud, cheery voice. "Welcome to your Police Department." The students looked bored, but Cunningham was enthusiastic, partly due to a couple of fairly attractive teachers and moms in the group.

Marilyn buzzed Cunningham through the secured door to the employee area, as the long train of kids followed. There were other adults who came in at the back of the group: A vendor, an attorney, and several community service workers.

Cunningham led the group down to the patrol division, located on the basement level, and showed them several points of interest: The arrestee bullpen and processing room, the equipment storage area, and the sally port. Then he escorted them back upstairs to the administrative offices, and introduced the group to Chief Brinks, who spoke briefly to them.

Cunningham took the group down the hallway to the area where the detective offices were located.

"These are the offices where the narcotics and criminal detectives work," he said. "This is my office and next door here is the juvenile detective's office; you can see by the nameplate on the wall that the detective is Price Whitaker. Do any of you know him? He used to be the school resource officer at your school."

Several students, from front to back, raised their hands.

"And here is Lt. Dixon's office. He is the person in charge of all of us who investigate crimes."

The large group moved slowly by the offices. They peeked into each one, while Cunningham discussed the kind of cases that each detective specialized in. The students didn't seem too impressed with who did what or where the office of each detective was located. But most of the adults appeared to be interested, especially the one in the back who walked with the limp.

CHAPTER THIRTY-EIGHT

Abbas Al Farran examined the label on the box of frozen lasagna as if he were trying to memorize it.

Amid Ismail bumped him lightly from behind with the grocery cart and said, "Let's not stay in here all afternoon, we have work to do."

Al Farran scanned the frozen foods section for potential eavesdroppers. "I'm trying to act the part of suburban shopper searching for best value," he said. They laughed and continued down the aisle. "How do you think everything looks?"

Ismail placed a large bag of frozen French fries in the cart and pretended to mark off an item on the list in his hand. "The alarm system is the same as the...."

Just as Ismail spoke, a shopper wheeled around into the aisle and headed toward them.

Ismail continued in Arabic. "*...the same as the ones in Charlotte and Atlanta. This store appears to do much business. Very good for us; it will make our mission worth while.*"

Al Farran placed some more items in the cart, listening carefully, while Ismail continued in a low, deliberate tone.

"*The manager will leave at approximately the same time as last night, I would think.*"

Al Farran nodded.

The shopper, an overweight woman with bleached blonde hair, wearing tight-fitting white knit slacks, strolled by as they eyed her.

Ismail reverted to English. "These Americans are fat and lazy. Our work has been so easy. I will certainly miss taking money from these infidels. They have no idea how to defend themselves."

"And they are as spoiled as they are helpless," Al Farran said, reaching in a freezer for a box of nutty buddies. "Hey, these are the kind I have been looking for."

"What are they?"

"They have the chocolate in the bottom of the cone," Al Farran said in a pleased tone. They worked their way to the next aisle. He continued to drop items in the cart and Ismail made some observation notes.

The aisle was crowded, so Al Farran continued in his native language. "*I have checked the surrounding area,*" he said, reaching for a case of bottled water, "*and I have a good place to drop you and the others and park. A place where I can blend among other vehicles.*"

Ismail followed. "*This will be our last project away from our base. I have been proud of you for the work that you have done. You are all fine, dedicated soldiers; I would go into battle anywhere with you.*"

"Thank you, Amid. It is because of your leadership and the guidance of Kasim that we have been successful. Allah has protected us, and we will be victorious."

As they continued shopping, they studied various security points: Doors to offices and service areas, exits, overall layout. They also tried to identify all the managers on the floor. Ismail always planned for an interruption or a foul-up, but so far every operation had been smooth and successful.

He and Al Farran worked their way to the last aisle and saw the manager walking into the office. Ismail was about to make his move, but Al Farran grabbed him by the arm and said, "Wait a moment, Amid. Wait until he is on the phone or someone approaches him. It will give you more time."

A couple minutes later, another employee walked over to the office, propped himself against the doorway, and chatted with the manager.

Careful not to be seen and using Al Farran as a shield, Ismail opened a large carton of orange juice and poured it on the floor. "Tsk, a shame, what a mess someone has made, Abbas," Ismail said, snickering. "Meet you at the front."

Al Farran nodded and rolled the grocery cart to the checkout line. Ismail walked over to the office door and stood behind the employee, hoping to thoroughly survey the office before he was noticed. He recognized the manager, who was seated at the desk, as the one who closed the store the previous night. Ismail looked at his watch and figured that with it being this late in the day, this manager would probably close again tonight. Ismail knew the manager's routine, even down to where he parked his car in the lot.

Ismail eyed the large safe when the manager opened it, removed a cash tray, and handed it to the employee. The safe door was left ajar and Ismail could see that the shelves were full of money trays with bundles of cash. The layout of the office was the same as those of the other Food World stores that

BLOODY NOVEMBER

they had robbed. He knew where the hold-up button was concealed at the desk. Ismail commented to himself that this manager will never have a chance to use it.

The employee turned to walk away and almost bumped into Ismail. The manager, returned to his desk, looked up and asked, "Hey, can I help you?"

"*Yes, I wish to report*...uh, excuse me, I want to tell you that someone has spilled a large container of juice on aisle number eighteen. I am afraid that someone will get hurt if this is not cleaned right away."

"Aisle eighteen?"

"Yes, that is right."

"Thanks for the heads up. We sure wouldn't want anyone to get hurt."

"Yes sir, that is right. That would be very bad," Ismail said, smiling. He walked away and muttered in his language, "*But that will depend on you.*"

* * *

Kasim Al Sabah, the cell leader, worked tirelessly at his laptop, responding to a screen full of messages from the other teams. There had been a flurry of activity in the last couple of weeks, so communications had been held to a minimum. This was one of the largest projects Al Qaeda had ever attempted on foreign soil, and Al Sabah was the mastermind responsible for its coordination. He had served as an officer in the Saudi Army, where he developed a thorough understanding of operations planning and a respect for logistics.

He received replies from three of the teams, and was pleased to read that none had sustained any casualties thus far. His calculations showed that before today, the combined efforts of the seven teams led to sixty-two successful sorties. As he prepared to send a tactical message to the team in Savannah, he heard Shahin shout from the bedroom. "What is it?" Al Sabah asked from the kitchen table.

"Another good day for our people!" Shahin yelled, and then he walked into the main room. "They have shown on the news where we attack two police stations and a training center in Baghdad today, and kill seventeen of their police force."

"Another good day, indeed," Al Sabah replied cheerily, and gave his colleague a high five.

Shahin returned to the bedroom and finished his dumbbell workout with four sets of chest presses. Afterwards, he went to the kitchen and wiped his hands and forehead with a towel. Shahin was large, about six feet, two, and weighed 230 pounds. Powerfully built, like a professional boxer, he had massive hands to match the physique. He was the group's enforcer, the one who was called upon when a task required brute strength and had to be done quietly and effectively. "How are things looking?" Shahin asked, taking a big gulp of milk and peering over his leader's shoulder.

"We are on schedule, my friend. So far…" Al Sabah said, but stopped in mid-sentence to receive a message from Atlanta. "So far, it appears that each team is on track to complete its work in time for the next phase."

Shahin took a seat at the table with a box of cleaning supplies and began to wipe down his Uzi. He stroked the barrel with a wire brush and asked, "What about money? Are we to make our goal?"

"Wait a moment. Let me see." Al Sabah took figures from the computer screen and began to press some numbers on his calculator. He continued figuring, when Al Farran and Ismail came in the door with several bags of groceries.

"Shahin, there are more things outside, can you help us?" Al Farran asked.

"Yes, right after this," he replied, waiting for the bottom line answer from Al Sabah. Al Farran and Ismail tuned in to the business at hand, placed their bags on the kitchen counter, and stood attentively at the table.

Al Sabah erased a figure and then penciled a tally at the bottom of the piece of paper. "This is the best news; we are on target to meet our goal," he said, clapping his hands together. "To this date, we have, excluding expenses, the amount of $2,147,000.00." Then he said slowly for effect, "and some change."

Everyone broke out in laughter, except Nimr Atef. He sat studiously on the couch, listening to music on his headphones, and writing. Shahin walked over to him and pulled the headphone away from his right ear. Atef looked up at him as Shahin leaned over and said in a loud voice, "Did you hear that, Nimr? We are meeting our goal!"

Atef was caught off guard, embarrassed that he was the center of attention. He smiled, and then continued with his writing. Ismail looked at Al Sabah and asked, "What is he doing with all his concentration?"

"A crossword puzzle. Nimr is consumed with them. He has become so excited and, how do you say it, uh, academically challenged with them since he completed his first one last week. He thinks he is now a professional, you know."

Al Farran opened a box of pastries and passed them around the table.

Atef looked up from the couch and said in a loud voice, "A word that means a loan; an advance of money...five letters, starts with 'p-r' and ends with 't'."

Everyone turned to Al Sabah.

"How many letters did you say?" Al Sabah asked loudly.

"Five."

Al Sabah thought for a moment. "Try prest."

Atef nodded.

A few minutes later, they gathered around the kitchen table and ate deli sandwiches with French fries. Ismail began the briefing by covering major details of the layout of the store and its security, and information about adjoining stores and their operating hours. The men had heard this drill, over and over, a number of times in the last few months, but each time they listened carefully for any nuances. This was the fourth Food World that they were going to hit, and the one here in Springdale, South Carolina, on the outskirts of Columbia, was like all the others in its security measures and practices.

Next, Ismail gave them a description of the manager who was on-duty and would most likely be closing tonight. They asked questions about such things as the time of closing, where the manager's car was parked, and where the drop-off point would be. Using a hand-drawn map, Al Farran showed them the roads in the area and the proposed get-away route. He briefed them on how often the police patrols drove through last night on his reconnaissance.

They finished dinner and decided to take a drive by the store for one last look over. As Al Sabah stood at the table, the group became quiet. He told them about the incident that forced them to move the Food World assignment up to tonight, and that generated quite a bit of discussion.

At the end of the meeting, Al Sabah raised his glass. "This is our last mission before we travel back to our base. There, we will wait for the call that will start a chain of events that will bring this Great Satan to its knees. To Allah, be the glory."

His soldiers chanted, "To Allah!" as they raised their glasses in unison.

CHAPTER THIRTY-NINE

Clark walked to his car in a light rain, and heard the distant rumble of thunder. On the drive to Lana's, he reviewed what his squad had accomplished today. He believed that some major cases were finally beginning to take shape, and he would be getting definitive answers in the next couple of days from the S.B.I. lab. The house on Regal Road was the big question mark now, and he hoped that its owner could help them fill in the blanks about Hamim's associates. Esposito's undercover assignment proved to be fairly successful; he was able to get inside the house and that would be an advantage later, if a search warrant was forthcoming.

The rain began to pick up, and Clark's thoughts shifted to the Ruby Walker investigation. He turned on his wipers and, as they whipped back and forth, it reminded him of the alternating opinion of Ruby Walker's death: Natural causes-suspicious-natural causes-suspicious. Perhaps now there would be a resolution to her case. The investigation into her death seemed to spark quite a few events.

Clark hoped the media had gotten its fill of Stuartsboro and would move on to some other city. The last thing Clark wanted, and most dreaded, was too much media exposure. That might prompt the chief to buckle under to politics and meddle in their investigation. Clark could feel that he and his men were close to breaking some cases open. Real close. Just a little more time and a little bit of luck. That's all they needed. Time and luck—two precious commodities in the trade.

Clark pulled into Lana's driveway and, under a steady downpour, he dashed to the porch. Lana opened the door, and greeted him with a smile. "Hey there, your timing is perfect," she said.

Clark wiped the water from his face. "Why, I don't think I've ever been greeted at the door with that kind of compliment before. Thanks." To Clark's surprise, she reached over and kissed him on the cheek. He loved the fragrance of her perfume—for an instant, it took him back to last Thursday morning. The kisses.

"Come on in," she said. "Need a towel?"

"No, I'm okay, thanks."

She turned and gave him a second look. "Hey, you've changed clothes."

"Now how would you know that?"

"I just saw your interview on Channel Nine and, may I say, you looked very dapper. Navy coat, white shirt, red tie. Classic, traditional look. I would guess gray slacks."

"Sounds like I may have a stalker on my hands here."

She laughed. "You wish."

"No, it's true. We celebrities face that kind of predicament on a daily basis. You know, fanatical fans. Hero worship they call it."

"Again, you wish. On a good day."

He looked at his clothes. "Yeah, I confess. I ran home and changed. Nothing like blue jeans and a pull-over, after a tie and dress shoes all day." He followed her to the kitchen, and noticed she was wearing jeans, too. Hers looked a lot better than his. Jeans and an olive silk blouse.

"Looks like every camera in North Carolina was at City Hall today," she said, pouring him a steaming cup of coffee.

"Thanks," he said, and then took a sip. "Chalk it up to what was most likely a slow news day with the media. With them, it's all about supply and demand. Whatever you have in the way of news depends on what's going on everywhere else. Your story is only good if less is going on in other places."

"Sounds like you've got it all figured out, this media thing."

"After all this time, I should. By the way, I served up an official 'no comment' today in honor of you. Did you catch it?"

She put her cup down, paused, clutched her hands and sighed dramatically. "Oh yes, Clark! You stole my heart away—first the jelly doughnuts and now this."

Clark laughed.

They drank coffee and caught up on news from the weekend. The smell of fried chicken filled the kitchen with an enticing scent, and Clark suddenly realized he was starving. Every so often, Lana got up and turned the chicken.

"You don't know how good that smells," Clark said.

"So do you like gravy with your mashed potatoes?"

"Do I like gravy? Oh, yeah. It's been ages since I've had it. That sounds great."

She sat across from him. "I have that, peas, and fresh homemade rolls for dinner. How does that sound?"

"Like the best thing I've heard all day."

"I didn't fix dessert. I hope that's all right."

"What, no jelly doughnuts?"

Lana smiled. "No, no jelly doughnuts." Then she reached over and placed her hand on his. "But I do have some marshmallows we could toast."

"Marshmallows? And where did you get those?"

"On the top of a very inviting pile of leaves," she said, her eyes beaming.

"That was a sweet thing to do. Thank you, Clark."

"I wanted to surprise you. Hope it brought back a pleasant memory."

"Like nothing else could have."

They ate dinner by candlelight, and Clark enjoyed everything. The chicken was tender and juicy, and the thick gravy, slightly salty, was a delicious complement to the mashed potatoes. Clark reached for seconds, trying hard to slow down. He told her that fried chicken was one of his favorite dishes and this was the best he had eaten in a long time.

He sipped his coffee, and listened as she talked about going back to work. *She looks very lovely tonight.* It was as though she looked more beautiful every time he saw her. Clark noticed her silk blouse was open down to the third button. He tried to train his eyes on her face and focus on the conversation. A difficult task. As they talked, he could hear the roar of thunder in the distance, and it was getting closer.

* * *

Al Farran circled the block two more times. He continued to monitor the flow of traffic, while Ismail, Atef, and Shahin changed into their uniforms. Atef rechecked his sub-gun and fed the magazine back into the receiver. He adjusted his earpiece and took a sip of bottled water.

Ismail called up to Al Farran, "Watch your speed, Abbas. We do not want to be stopped." Al Farran nodded. Ismail looked at his watch, then he called back to the motel room to Al Sabah and gave him an update.

Shahin snuffed out a cigarette and asked Atef to hand him a rag that lay beside him. Atef smiled, handed it to him, and Shahin wiped his rifle. "What are you smiling for, Nimr?" Shahin asked.

"I do not know exactly. Several things, I believe. This is our last mission and all this will soon be a pleasant memory. This means that we are one step closer to the finish of a battle inside of a war that we will win. That, and I completed my third crossword puzzle tonight, another successful mission."

Ismail laughed, and Shahin lit another cigarette.

Al Farran blurted out, "Shhh, quiet! There is a policeman behind us." Al Farran decided to pull into the parking lot of a convenience store, but the police car turned in, as well. Al Farran reached back, closed the divider to the cargo area, and placed his .38 revolver under his right thigh.

* * *

"Lana, it was absolutely the best. If I were Colonel Sanders, I think I'd consider leaving town."

She smiled. "I'm so glad you liked it, but don't leave yet. Remember, we still have dessert."

He was having such a wonderful time, and he dreaded telling her about his improved situation with Sam.

They carried coffee into the study and Lana started a fire. The cool room made the idea of a fire very appealing. Lana lit the starter log, and the scene reminded him of his first visit. Clark got up and helped her place a couple logs on the growing fire. Over the next few minutes, the increasing heat began to feel good. As the flames grew, the rain picked up. Clark could hear it beating rhythmically against the side of the house.

"That's a nice song. Is it Sinatra?" Clark asked.

"Tony Bennett. But he does sound a little like Sinatra there. I love Bennett's music, and I remembered that you said you liked him, too."

"I could listen to him all day. I bought a CD of his greatest hits about six months ago. I've just about played it non-stop over the last few weeks: 'I Left My Heart in San Francisco', 'Rags to Riches', 'The Shadow of Your Smile'."

"'Boulevard of Broken Dreams'."

"Oh, yeah. Love that one." Clark sat on the sofa drinking his coffee, enjoying the growing fire, but enjoying the view of Lana more.

She tossed a couple of pillows on the floor and sat on one of them, at the hearth, and invited Clark to join her.

Watch yourself, Clark.

"Now, this brings back some happy times," she said, a look of contentment on her face. She handed Clark a coat hanger; he unwound the handle and straightened the wire. She opened the bag of marshmallows and handed him one to spear.

The fire was blazing and it didn't take Clark long to toast one.

"Whew, this cooks fast," he said. The marshmallow caught fire and he blew it out. He gingerly bit into it and it was tasty, just like he remembered from childhood days. "Are we eating the whole bag tonight, Lana? I need to know how to pace myself here."

"We'll see. Depends on how much jumping we plan on doing in that pile of leaves you raked up."

* * *

The officer parked his car at the sidewalk of the store, got out, and went inside. Al Farran drove out of the other side of the lot. About ten minutes later, after checking the area thoroughly, Al Farran pulled behind a building that adjoined the property of the Food World store. They synchronized their watches, inspected communications equipment, and pulled masks over their faces. Ismail, point man on the robberies, adjusted the squelch and volume on his walkie-talkie.

One last time, they went over the contingency plan. On command, Ismail, Atef, and Shahin rolled out of the back of the van and disappeared into an area of brush and woods.

In single formation, they jogged about seventy-five yards to behind the Food World store. They watched a couple of employees walk out of the back door and throw several boxes and bags of trash into one of the dumpsters. Then the employees got in their cars and drove away.

Al Farran radioed to them that the manager had just let two employees out of one of the front doors, then three more, and it appeared that he did not relock it. Ismail looked at his watch and, as their research revealed, several lights in the parking lot automatically turned off. This gave them the cover they needed, and they darted in and out of the shadows along the south wall.

Al Farran continued to circle the block and he hadn't seen a police car in the last couple of rounds. He timed his return to the store with their arrival near the front of it, and he radioed to them that the area was clear.

As the manager walked to the door to open it, Ismail forced it open, caught the manager by surprise and Shahin punched him in the face with the butt of his rifle.

* * *

The fire was roaring so Lana and Clark moved back a little from the hearth. Over the next few minutes of conversation, Clark discovered that they shared more common interests: Eating at the Pavilion Restaurant in

Greensboro, watching old movies, weightlifting. They toasted another marshmallow, and Clark's pager buzzed. "Great," Clark said in a disappointed tone, "the Police Department. Can I use your phone?"

"Sure. The one in the hall is the closest."

"Sorry. Be right back." Clark called the PD, and the telecommunicator answered. The storm, rare for this time of year, was moving closer and Clark's conversation was broken up several times with static and crackling sounds. After the call, he headed back to the study.

"Everything okay?" Lana asked from across the room.

"Yeah. Rallingview had a robbery earlier tonight and...." Clark cringed when he was interrupted by a loud boom of thunder that sounded like it was coming from upstairs. "Now that's getting close...anyway, Rallingview thought we would be interested, but it doesn't sound like our guys."

"I didn't realize there was so much crime in this area, until I met you."

"Thanks a lot. Guess that's why most people shy away from cops—always the bearers of bad news. But believe me, it's not just Stuartsboro, it's the time of year for this sort of thing."

"Really?"

"Between Thanksgiving and Christmas, we have all that we can handle with larcenies and robberies. Half of what's reported over the course of the year happens this season. But it's the same everywhere."

"Speaking of the holidays, have you made plans for Christmas, yet?"

Clark saw the opening and took a deep breath. He'd better go ahead and level with her about Sam. The longer he waited, the more difficult it was becoming. "Lana, I've really enjoyed getting to know you. You're a very special woman, and you make me feel important, every time I'm around you." Then he paused. Hesitated.

"And?"

"Well, there's something that I need to tell you, about me and my ex."

"What is it?"

"Sam and I have kind of made a step toward getting back together."

"A step?"

"A small step. We, uh, got together over the holiday, unexpectedly you might say." He paused again. "I just want to be up front with you about everything."

She gave him a long, appraising look. "Thanks for your honesty, Clark. Now I'm going to be honest with you. I think you're a kind, considerate man. You have a nice, soft way about you. Trusting eyes. I feel safe when I'm with you. I haven't felt safe in a long time, and I want to thank you for that."

"That's sweet of you to say."

"It's true. You said you and she, Sam is it, have made a step toward reconciliation?"

Clark nodded.

"I think you and I have taken a step or two, as well. Don't you?"

"Yes, I do, but I didn't want you to…."

Clark was cut-off in mid-sentence when Lana laughed and crammed a marshmallow in his mouth. "Clark, sometimes you talk too much, you know that?"

* * *

Atef and Ismail stormed in behind Shahin. They dragged the manager, bleeding profusely from his nose and mouth, to the office. They ordered him to open the door and turn off the alarm. The manager was stunned from the blow and fumbled frantically for the key on the ring. They knew they only had about thirty seconds on the delay, so Shahin drew a knife from his waist and held it, from behind, against the manager's throat to persuade him to hurry.

The manager found the key and opened the door. They rushed in and Ismail shouted, "Turn off the alarm! Quick!" The manager pressed some numbers on the panel and several red lights went out. Ismail noticed the panel now looked the same as it did when he was in the office earlier.

"The safe!" Ismail shouted. "Open it!" The manager crouched, and shook his head in an effort to regain his composure. Blood dripped on his jacket sleeve as he turned the combination on the safe. Ismail and Shahin looked at their watches. They had two and one-half minutes.

Shahin turned to Atef and said, "Go check for anyone else."

Atef nodded and left the office. He enjoyed this part, the hunt. It excited him. He stayed away from view at the front windows. He worked his way to the back of the store, hungry to find someone there.

* * *

Clark returned the favor, and they enjoyed playfully feeding each other. After a couple more exchanges, the treats were offered a little slower. A little messier, a little stickier. When it was Lana's turn, she reached for the marshmallow, and gently pulled and twisted it from the tip of the wire. He noticed the melted marshmallow on her red fingernails as she tugged at it.

"Are you still hungry?" Lana asked.

Without answering, Clark slid over beside her. The fire had died a little, and now the periodic, fierce lightning lit the room. She placed the marshmallow against his lips, and rubbed the sticky film on the corners of his mouth. Clark took a bite, and then another, working his way to her fingers. He looked in her eyes, took the last bite, and stopped.

Lana whispered, "You're not finished yet."

Clark felt an intense heat stirring and driving him. His heart pounded as he licked the syrup. She tenderly stroked his lips with her fingers, until he slowly guided them into his mouth, devouring the last taste of marshmallow. Lana moved over, pressing against him, and placed her warm mouth over his. Her tongue swirled around his lips, capturing the leftover sweetness—blurring into the taste of him.

* * *

Ismail reached into the safe and Shahin held the nylon bag for him. The manager sat like a helpless child, watching from the corner. He wiped the blood from his nose and the corners of his mouth, trying not to glance at the picture of his wife and two daughters on the desk.

They cleaned out the safe, and Atef returned to the office and told them, "All is clear."

Shahin turned to him and asked, "Are you sure?"

"Yes."

Ismail looked at Shahin as he emptied the last tray of cash into the bag. "How much time is left?"

Shahin twisted his wrist to check his watch. "About one minute. We make good time."

Shahin pushed the manager against the wall and bound his hands behind his back with duct tape. He wrapped them tightly, and then spun him around and wrapped his mouth. The manager was fearful, but he hoped that this was a sign that he was not going to be killed.

* * *

Thunder cracked overhead as they wrapped around each other. He quickly removed her blouse, felt her soft skin, and smelled that intoxicating fragrance. Her body was incredibly toned and shapely, and he caressed her in the flickering light of the fire. The claps of thunder matched the throbbing in his soul.

The lovemaking was slow and delicate. She took off his shirt and massaged and kissed his chest. Each kiss was more exciting than the one before, and she overwhelmed him with her touches. The sight of her was driving him to the edge. He could feel her writhe in ecstasy, as the kisses grew hotter, wetter. Deeper.

Finally, he looked into her eyes, which seemed to say, "Timing is everything and this is our moment." The last few seconds were fiery, spiraling out of control, and the shouts of their passion were barely covered by the explosion of thunder.

* * *

Al Farran radioed to Ismail that a police car was weaving in and out of parking lots on security patrol and working its way toward them. Quickly, they collected their equipment and headed for the office door. The manager was balled up in the corner, panting for breath. He felt an enormous relief when they left the office and closed the door. He rolled over and, after a couple of attempts, got to his feet and steadied himself.

Suddenly the door burst open. Atef charged over to him, smiled, slowly placed the end of the sub-gun barrel against his chest, and fired a shot. The impact of the bullet knocked the manager against the wall and to the floor, and he lay there writhing in pain. Atef walked over to his crumpled body and, for good measure, fired another shot into his chest at point blank range.

CHAPTER FORTY

Clark was tempted to hit the snooze button a third time, but decided against it. Slowly, he rolled out of bed, stumbled over to the window, and leaned against the sill. He looked out at the front yard and saw the ruin of last night's storm: Broken tree limbs strewn about the yard and the last of the leaves blown from the trees. *That was some storm. Here and on Gordon Street.*

He went in the bathroom, gazed in the mirror, and toyed with the idea of not shaving, but he knew he better. With the media prowling around, it wouldn't do to be caught on camera with a five o'clock shadow first thing in the morning. As Clark shaved, images of the heated moments with Lana flashed in his mind—snapshots as bright as the lightning that sliced the sky.

He walked into the closet and decided to skip the shirt and tie. He dressed in a beige turtleneck, khaki slacks, and brown and rust tweed sports coat. By the time he got downstairs, Alex was pulling out of the driveway heading to class; he hated that he didn't get to see her. Giving her a kiss and getting to chat with her, albeit briefly, was the highlight of his mornings. He poured his coffee and thought about how much Alex would despise him seeing another woman. Despise it.

She had left him a couple slices of bacon and a blueberry muffin on the counter. Beside the snack, she left a note from Mrs. Bergen, who had called last night asking to show the house on Wednesday. Clark hated the idea of selling, but his finances weren't in good shape, and they were getting worse.

Clark called headquarters on his police radio, announced he was in service, and headed to work. The debris he passed on the drive to the PD reminded him of the mess his personal life was in. Just three weeks ago he was so alone and now, as suddenly as a storm, he was sharing his heart with two women.

Sam and Lana. In some sort of peculiar analogy, he viewed his life and happiness as if they were one of his own investigations, and Sam and Lana were the prime leads. Sam had proven to be the reliable lead for a very long time. A sure bet, almost as irrefutable as a DNA or fingerprint match. But over the last few years, the lead turned into a dead-end, largely because of poor commitment and other priorities and, before you knew it, the case was shelved. Recently though, this lead resurfaced, as Clark took a fresh, new look at it, and seemed to be back on track. And right out of the blue, in a fortuitous encounter, Lana, a new lead, developed. There were a number of compelling reasons to think that she could be a better lead. In fact, the more this new lead was investigated and pursued, the more promising it became.

Two convincing leads, but which one was the right one? Clark pulled in the back of the PD, thinking about the comparison. He couldn't help but find a touch of humor in his predicament, comparing his personal life to his work. He had forgotten what love tasted like and having these unexpected feasts rekindled his spirit and gave him a renewed vision. *Two beautiful women. Wish all my investigations could be this exciting.*

When Clark walked in the squad room, he met Capt. Blackburn. "Morning, Richard."

"Good morning, Clark. How's it going?"

"Fair." Clark walked over to the shelf, placed his satchel on the counter, and began to sort through the police and arrest reports, and citations from the previous day.

"What's the matter?"

"What do you mean?"

"I don't know. Guess you're looking a little slow, a little down this morning."

"Didn't get much sleep last night," Clark said, browsing through the reports.

"The storm?"

"You could say that." When Clark responded, there was a blast of traffic on the radio. "What's that all about?"

"Haven't you heard?"

"Heard what?"

"Oh, that's right. The storm knocked out all our pagers last night. We got another B&E at Nick's All-Seasons. They found it near shift change this morning. Lt. Balsley is calling for a K-9 to track."

"Thank God we found it. How bad?"

"They're still doing inventory. Sounds like another big hit, though. Night shift called Cunningham. He just got there."

"Terrific," Clark said sarcastically. "Wonder if their new alarm system got hit by lightning?"

"Maybe. Alarms went off everywhere last night. No way our guys could check 'em all."

"I'm already short with Sloan on vacation until tomorrow. Now another big case. I don't know if I can stomach old man Evans again. Not today."

Clark went up to his office, read over the reports, and made assignments. As he was about to finish up, his phone rang. "Lieutenant Dixon, may I help you?"

"Clark, it's Greg."

"Hey, how's it going?"

"Not bad for a Tuesday. Did you survive the storm last night?"

"That remains to be seen."

"Huh?"

"Nothing. So did y'all get a lot of wind and rain?"

"Yeah, we were hit pretty bad. A lot of power outages in the area. Our paging system and cell phones are still down this morning. Tell you the truth, I kind of like the sudden lack of communications."

"Our stuff is still down, too, but that didn't stop crime here overnight. We're out at our John Deere dealership and it looks like they got hit again."

"Another one?"

"Yeah."

Greg grunted. "You guys need some sort of break. Ever consider posting signs that read 'Closed to Crooks' at the city limits for a while?"

"Wouldn't do any good."

"Why not?"

"Most of our thugs can't read."

Greg laughed. "I have your ballistics results on the bullets you brought over Monday. Rosalie bumped the case up, and got to it last night. She's trying to atone for past sins."

"Tell me you got a match on Harris Teeter with one of the guns from the Charlotte bust."

There was a pause, one that was too long for Clark.

"You got a match, Clark, but the Harris Teeter bullets didn't match anything that Charlotte had."

"Knew it was too good to be true. So did we get a match on the bullets with the bank robbery?"

As he asked that, Marilyn appeared in the doorway and motioned him to call her.

"Strike two," Greg said. "Brace yourself. The gun that shot your kid at the grocery store is the same gun that killed Marcellus, or Hamim, or whatever you call him."

Clark was silent.

Greg carried on. "The question that you need to answer now, assuming the bullet was meant for him, is how did Hamim fit in with this gang. Hate to break it to you, Clark, but your backyard may have been the home office, at least for a short while, for a group that's terrorized the Southeast."

"Why here, though?"

"Isn't that what we all ask when the shit hits the fan?"

"So this guy Hamim, who was on an F.B.I. watch list, gets offed by one of these robbers…the same one who shot our kid?"

"That's the way it's stacking up. They hit Stuartsboro on a robbery, and a few days later, they nail this Hamim dude; makes them sound local, don't you think?"

"Have you made any headway on why your boss was keeping secrets over there?"

"Honestly, I've been so busy the last few days, but he's at a conference later this week. If I get the chance, maybe I can snoop around a little, check his e-mail."

"Whoever wanted Hamim didn't mind a whole lot if he clipped a cop in the process. We got to do whatever we can to get these guys."

"Didn't you say it was a sniper shot on Hamim?"

"Just about had to be. Figure it was about a 100-, 125-yard shot. At least."

"I'm impressed. You got a skilled shooter on your hands."

"We need to move on this thing and find out why somebody wanted Hamim dead."

"Unless, of course, it was a miss."

"Nah, I don't think so."

"What have you found out about that house in the county?"

When Clark began to answer, Marilyn reappeared at the door, and seemed more pressed for him. He acknowledged her and answered Greg, "Not much yet. We've been slowed a little in our efforts. The owner is out of town, and his wife isn't sure when he's coming back. She said in the next day or so."

"Do you have enough for a search warrant?"

"Probably. But do we want to show our hand and let them know we're on to them? We made undercover contact yesterday with a guy who's probably one of these robbers." Clark then filled Greg in on the spy work that Esposito did; he also told Greg about the need to track down the license plate number on the Altima. "Looks like everything is finally coming together. Far as I know, we still have the element of surprise."

"Whether you go in now or later is a tough call, and it's yours to make. But if you do go in, you better have all the firepower you need. These guys are dangerous and they have nothing to lose."

"Do you have any connections at D.M.V.?"

"Yeah."

"Can you get us the registration info on the Altima tag?"

"I'll try. Give it to me."

Clark gave him the plate number. "Thanks. I better get down to the chief's office and break your news to him. If and when we get ready to execute the search warrant, could you help us since it's in the county? We could use that shiny state-wide badge of yours."

"When do you think you might do it?"

"Haven't decided yet. If we do it, today, maybe tomorrow."

"Today's bad for me. We're helping the Secret Service with the background work on the President's visit on Friday. I'm leading an investigative team on running down some local threats. Then we have to conduct security assessments of the area around the site where the President will be speaking. What about tomorrow or Thursday?"

"Sounds good. Thanks for the info."

"Talk to you later."

Clark called Marilyn. "Good morning."

"Good morning, Lieutenant. Sorry to keep bothering you, but the chief wants to see you in his office right away. He's called for you twice."

"Any idea why?"

"No, sorry. He sounds charged up, though."

"Thanks."

Clark walked in and stood at Brinks' desk while he filled out a personnel form.

"Have a seat, Lieutenant," he said, without looking up.

Clark sat down and wondered if the chief had already gotten a call from the manager at Nick's. Brinks continued with his writing, while Clark continued with his sitting.

Finally, the chief looked up with hard eyes and spoke coolly. "Good morning."

"Good morning, Chief."

"How do the reports look today?"

"Not too bad, until this morning. Nick's All-Seasons got hit again last night, and we're out over there now."

"I've heard. Any of your people on it?"

"Yes sir, Cunningham. Too early to tell what's been taken, but at least we found it this time."

"I hope it's not as bad as the last hit."

"That makes two of us. Wonder what happened with their new alarm?"

"I don't know. What's your staffing level like the next couple of days?"

"Whitaker and Wilkens are off at the end of the week, and Jerry is off through today." Clark shook his head. "We have so much going on right now. Like being on a merry-go-round running about sixty miles per hour."

"Jerry's off more than today."

"Excuse me?"

"I just got off the phone a few minutes ago with a woman who's filed a complaint against him."

"Against Jerry? What kind of complaint?"

"Sexual assault."

"What?"

"A sexual assault. She claims he raped her."

"Who is she? What did she say happened?"

"She's afraid to give her name. She said that Sloan stopped her car last Friday, let her go, and followed her to her motel room. He told her he needed to speak further with her about the traffic stop. She said she made the mistake of allowing him into the room, and when she did, he raped her."

"You know that's absurd, Chief. Whoever she is, she's crazy. That's not Jerry. Not him at all."

"Oh, it's not?" the Chief asked in a raised voice. "I've told you more than once that you need to keep a close eye on him. Haven't I? That boy flies by the seat of his pants, and it looks like his cowboy behavior and antics have finally gotten the best of him. I'm thinking about calling the Bureau in to do the criminal investigation."

"Hold on a second," Clark said, raising his hand in objection. "There's no way Jerry would do something like that. You said the woman wouldn't give her name?"

"That's right. She said she's afraid."

"Afraid? Of what? Jerry would certainly know who she is from the traffic stop or from the motel registration. You *are* going to look into this further before you put him on leave, aren't you?"

"Are you questioning me, Lieutenant?"

Clark opted to avoid the obvious answer. "You know how covered up we are right now. Why not try to corroborate this woman's complaint before you bench and brand a good officer?"

"Clark, I don't have to tell you that right now we're under the watchful eye of the City Council, not to mention every camera in the area." Brinks took an uncharacteristic pause, and then continued in a lower voice. "She threatened to go to the media if we didn't take immediate action on it."

"So now we're being strong-armed by an anonymous caller?"

"Say what you want. You're responsible for your division, but that nameplate sitting there in front of you says I'm responsible for the entire Department. True, she may be embellishing, or even lying. But I receive a lot of complaints over the phone, and she spoke intelligently and convincingly. She said she was traveling through this area on business. She spoke with a slight accent, British I would say. Does that sound like your typical bogus complaint?"

"What do you say we split the difference? What if I put him in the office on second shift? Keep him out of the public eye until we can corroborate some of this."

"I can't take that chance."

Clark had his fill of the chief. His pretenses and lack of empathy. Clark caught himself leaning forward in his chair, squeezing the armrests with his hands. Before he realized it, he sprang from his seat, leaned over the chief's desk, and shouted, "For once, why don't you try standing up for the officers and taking a little heat? I really need him, and so does this Department!"

"Watch it, Lieutenant! You don't know what you're saying."

"What I do know is that we're getting all these cases rammed down our throats, and I need every man I have to investigate them."

"Sit down."

"Now I get a call from Williams and he tells me that the same gun used to shoot the stock boy in the Harris Teeter robbery is the same one used to murder Hamim at The Meadows. And this is the same gun, by the way, that…"

"I said sit down!"

"…that has been used to commit violent robberies all over the Southeast! It appears that a well-organized violent gang may have been under our very noses for some time now, assuming Hamim was part of it. And on top of all this," Clark shouted, "we have no clue at the moment as to what awaits us on…"

"That's enough!"

"...REGAL ROAD! And you want to take away twenty percent of my manpower, and damage the reputation and morale of a dedicated officer? And all because of an anonymous telephone complaint from a woman with an accent who spoke intelligently?"

The Chief rose to his feet, shouting, "Get the hell out of my office before I fire you! Your last warning, Dixon."

Clark turned, kicked his chair against Brinks' desk, knocking his nameplate over, and stormed out.

* * *

An hour later, Cunningham returned to the office with his findings and the evidence from the All-Seasons break-in. He entered the conference room where Clark and Wilkens were discussing the probable cause for the search warrant for the Regal Road house.

Cunningham tossed some latent lift cards on the table. "What do ya think, Lieutenant? Got these off a piece of glass from the back door. Probably belong to old man Evans."

One by one, Clark picked through the cards, examining each. "This one's good," he said, and then tossed a couple to the side. "This one's good, and this one may go through A.F.I.S." Clark looked up at Cunningham, "How bad was it?"

"Not nearly as bad as the last one. Here's the damage."

Clark read over the inventory and, as he did, Esposito called into the conference room from the hall, "Lieutenant?"

"Yeah. In here."

"Good news," Esposito said, walking in.

"I wondered if anybody was going to say that to me today."

"I just got a call from the County. They went by this Curt Thompson's house a few minutes ago and his wife said he's on the way back from the coast. Should be getting back later today."

"Good," Clark said, "maybe he can give us something on Hamim that'll strengthen our P.C. for the warrant." When he said that, everyone's pager buzzed or beeped with the same message, a Raleigh phone number. "Be sure to have the County check there every chance they get."

"I'll give the supervisor a call."

Wilkens stepped over to the office planner and marked his upcoming days off.

Clark walked over to Cunningham and whispered, "When we finish in here, I need to tell you something about Jerry."

A minute later, Whitaker walked to the room and paused in the doorway, looking pastey and lost. Cunningham could tell something was wrong, so he turned back to Clark and gestured to Whitaker.

Clark spoke first. "Price, great news. We got a match on your Harris Teeter shooting." To Clark's surprise, Whitaker didn't respond, so he continued. "The lab got a match on your shooting with Hamim's murder. Same gun. Looks like your perps killed Hamim, so maybe they have ties to this area, after all."

"So you think that Hamim was connected to this gang in some way?" Whitaker asked, slowly and deliberately.

"Very well could have been. Why?"

"Didn't you guys just get the page?" Whitaker asked.

"Yeah."

"Who was it?"

"It was Raleigh," Whitaker answered. "They just received two reports this morning of stolen tags registered to Ford E-150 vans."

"Great news. Where were they stolen from?"

"One was from Holden Beach."

"Do you think you oughta give them a BOLO call?" Cunningham asked.

"I don't think that'll be necessary," Whitaker said.

"Why not?"

"Because the other report was taken an hour ago by one of our patrol officers at McGinty's Repair."

Wilkens and Cunningham turned to Clark, who walked over to the window and stared out at the side of the public library across the alley. After what seemed like a minute, he spoke. "This time we'll be ready."

* * *

At nearly the same moment that Clark made the statement, the telephone rang at the S.B.I. office in Greensboro.

"Good morning, State Bureau of Investigation. How may I route your call?"

"I would like to speak with someone about evidence that our Department submitted recently, please."

"Sir, that office is located on Pierce Road. Hold for transfer, please."

"Thank you."

"Evidence room, Agent Wright."

"Good morning, this is Lt. Dixon with the Stuartsboro Police Department."

"I'm sorry, sir, there's a bad connection. Could you repeat that?"

"Yes, is this better?"

"Yes, go ahead."

"This is Lt. Dixon with the Stuartsboro Police Department. Sorry, I'm in a bad location."

"That's all right, Lieutenant. What can I help you with?"

"We brought a lap top computer to your Department in the last several days to be analyzed. One of my younger officers needs to bring over some attachments that go with it, and he doesn't know the way. Could you advise me where the evidence is stored, so that I may give him proper directions?"

"Sure, Lieutenant. Our evidence control room is located directly behind the administrative building here on Pierce Road."

"If you would, please, give me the directions from the highway; it's been quite some time since I have been there myself."

The evidence technician gave him the directions.

"What time do you close today? He will be arriving at your facility late this afternoon."

"I'm sorry, Lieutenant, you faded again. What was that?"

"What time do you close today? My officer will be coming at the end of the day."

"We close at five, but we don't accept any evidence after 4:30."

"Thank you, Agent Wright, you have been most helpful. Good-bye."

CHAPTER FORTY-ONE

Al Farran circled the block one last time, scanning the area for any sign of police. As was the routine, Ismail discussed the contingency plan, while Atef and Shahin inspected their rifles and radio equipment.

Al Farran called to Ismail in the cargo area. "Everything appears to be okay, Amid. We will be at the drop-off point in about five minutes."

Ismail nodded and asked his colleagues, "Ready?"

Atef nodded.

"Ready," Shahin said. He noticed that Ismail looked deep in thought. "What is the matter?"

"Nothing," Ismail said. After a moment of reflection, he continued. "It is strange that the Best-Deals closed earlier than the posted hours. I wonder why. This is a very busy time for them."

"What are you thinking?"

"I am not sure. Perhaps since our last strike here, some of the stores have taken new security measure by closing earlier."

"So instead of this, we should go to Best-Deals, anyway."

"No, no. That would be useless for us, without the ability to get into the store's safe."

"Ismail, we have explosives. I am sure we could take care of that."

"But money that is destroyed will not do us any good."

Al Farran drove slowly by the Harris Teeter. The parking lot was nearly empty, and he could see the manager letting employees out of the front doors. "Three or four are walking out now," Al Farran announced. "There are only two cars remaining in the lot. One of them appears to be the manager's car; it was here the last time we hit them. That, I remember."

"Is it parked in the same place?" Shahin asked.

"I believe that it is."

Atef smirked. "What is it that these infidels say about thunder not striking twice in the same place?"

"Lightning, Nimr, lightning," Ismail said. His cell phone rang; he spoke briefly in a low voice, and then hung up. "That was Al Sabah. Faraj, Mahmud, and Raboud have arrived here safely from Atlanta. They will be joining us for a few days."

"I served with Mahmud in the army," Atef said. "He is a fine soldier, dedicated and brave. It will be good to see him again."

"When did you serve together?" Shahin asked.

"We were assigned…."

Al Farran interrupted them. "We are at the drop-off point. Everyone ready?"

Ismail instructed them to synchronize their watches. "We have ten minutes."

As he said that, Al Farran stopped the van and they jumped out of the back doors and dashed for the wooded area adjacent to the store.

Over the next minute, they maneuvered their way around several construction dumpsters and moved to the front corner. Al Farran gave them radio updates from the street on activity at the front of the store. Several lights in the parking lot were cut off, and then the manager returned to the front door, unlocked it, and another employee walked out. Al Farran studied the scene with binoculars and radioed the information to Ismail. "It appears that the manager left the door unlocked when the employee left. The street is clear. Go!"

From the corner of the building, they ran to the entrance, crouched, and stealthily slid inside the front door. From the point, Ismail motioned for Atef and Shahin to stay low, concealed behind a magazine display. Ismail heard steps so he glanced over the counter and saw the manager, about seventy-five feet away, walking into the office.

Suddenly, there was a loud crash in the back of the store. Ismail glanced at his watch, concerned about the loss of time. He spoke in his mike in a low voice, "Atef, go see what that noise was in the back, quickly, and then meet us at the office."

Keeping low, Atef darted away through a checkout lane.

Ismail radioed to Shahin, "Ready?" Shahin nodded. "Let's go!"

They barged into the office with rifles drawn while the manager was reaching for a file cabinet drawer. Ismail shouted, "The safe, open it now!"

Startled, the manager turned, raised his hands and stammered, "Pl-please, don't shoot. I'll do wha-what you say. I have a family."

Ismail rammed his gun against the manager's chest. "Open the safe, fool!" he screamed.

Shahin turned and studied the eight video monitors over the desk. He focused on the only screen with motion, the one that showed Atef shuffling to the back of the store, his sub-gun at the ready.

The manager squatted and turned the combination to the safe, the barrel of Ismail's assault rifle pressed hard against his back. The manager, sweating profusely, wiped his forehead with his sleeve, and spun the dial left twice, and then right. After a final turn, he grabbed the handle and tried to open it, but failed. He tried again, re-setting the combination with two spins to the left. Ismail checked his watch and Shahin unzipped the nylon duffle bag. With their backs to the door, neither of them noticed a light sprinkle of dust that fell from the ceiling tile across the room.

All of a sudden, several lights went out in the store and it startled the robbers. Ismail grabbed the manager by the nape of the neck and shouted, "Who else is here?"

"No one."

"The lights, who turned them off?"

"They're on automatic timers. I swear nobody's here but me."

Right after the manager said that, there was another loud crashing sound in the back of the store. Shahin turned to the video monitors but Atef was not in view.

Ismail told Shahin to go help Atef. Shahin surveyed the scene from the doorway and then ran out of the office.

Ismail radioed to Atef that Shahin was on his way to the back to assist him. Then he turned back to the manager, who lifted the handle and opened the outer safe door. "Hurry, before I shoot!"

Moments earlier, when Atef heard the crashing sound, he crouched low and scanned with his rifle. He had made his way to the stockroom, peering between large boxes, but he had difficulty seeing. The stockroom was dimly lit and spanned the width of the store. It was divided into three areas, and shelves were stacked as high as twenty feet in some places.

Shahin jogged down the far left aisle of the store, searching for Atef at the back. Then he entered the stock room from the opposite end from where Atef had entered. He looked at his watch and knew they were running out of time. Only four minutes to go.

In the office, the manager reached in the safe with his left hand and pulled out a large tray loaded with several bundles of cash. With his right hand underneath the tray to support it, he fumbled for the compact Glock .45 that was taped to it. As Ismail hovered over him, shouting, the manager fingered his way to the trigger, spun around, and fired several shots at point blank range into Ismail's chest. The impact of the shots knocked Ismail over a chair, causing him to drop his rifle to the floor. Protected by his armored vest, but stunned, Ismail reached for his rifle and, when he did, the manager fired two shots into Ismail's head.

At that precise moment, several ceiling tiles in the office exploded, falling in pieces to the floor near Ismail's body, and two officers repelled from ropes. Esposito landed first and covered the door and Capt. Blackburn followed. He turned to the manager and said, "Great job, Sarge." Blackburn looked down at the body and then to Cunningham. "Bet you had no idea running a grocery store could be such a headache."

"Damn, that was close," Cunningham replied, shaking.

Esposito maintained watch at the door. He adjusted his headset and spoke in his hands-free mike, "One suspect down here, two suspects are in the back."

Blackburn studied the corpse for another moment. "Nice shooting, David. Mighty fine. You okay?"

"Yeah," Cunningham replied, walking over to the body. He knelt and pulled the mask up, examining the face through the smearing of blood. Then he turned to Blackburn. "You think what I'm thinking?"

Blackburn nodded.

Cunningham looked at Blackburn and Esposito and said, "Be careful. I'll stay here and cover the front door, in case you flush them this way."

Before leaving the office, they scanned the video monitors and saw no activity. Cautiously, they stepped out and headed down separate aisles, Benelli shotgun and AR-15 drawn. Cunnningham radioed to the back that Blackburn and Esposito were heading that way.

Clark tried to radio to the stakeout team at the other store for back-up, but he couldn't get through. He assumed that the construction of the building was preventing him from transmitting, but he hadn't heard anything from the other team, either.

Suddenly, Clark heard a noise on the other side of the stockroom. Quietly, he tried to position himself so he could see from his perch atop the shelf. He radioed to Wilkens and Whitaker, who were on the far side of the adjoining room, that he heard someone approaching between their two points.

Since the gunfire at the front of the store, Atef hadn't received any radio messages from Ismail. Atef knew that it was a bad sign; something had gone wrong. He decided to abort and work his way to one of the stockroom exit doors. He peered through shelves as he took slow, even steps, and when he saw an exit light, he decided to head for it.

Clark was growing impatient, and decided to move to another location. He surveyed all directions and, seeing no one, placed his Glock .45 in his belt and climbed down the stock ladder. When he reached the floor, he drew his gun and, as he turned to look around some shelves, he was grabbed by the throat, yanked backwards. His Glock was knocked from his hand.

The noose tightened, choking him. He struggled to grab the object, but he couldn't work his fingers under it. He tried to cough but kept gagging instead. Every time he tried to kick behind him, a powerful force jolted him side-to-side. Each successive kick was weaker, and he knew he was strangling.

Clark began to lose consciousness—the pain was relentless. His eyes bulged from the pressure, he heard himself making gurgling noises. His face was on fire. For a moment, he saw splotches of black. Then there was darkness.

Complete darkness.

Slowly, a scene came into view; he saw his children seated in the booth of a restaurant. First, he saw Brianna, and then Ian. Their faces were blurry, like an impressionist painting. Their lips were moving but there were no sounds. Beside Ian, Clark saw Alex. To his surprise, her face, in contrast, was clear and finely focused; she was looking across the table at him, crying uncontrollably. As he watched her, she clutched her throat, and then she gripped her necklace, the one that she never took off. With both hands, she ripped it from her neck.

The next moment, Clark saw the ceiling of the stockroom, spinning around, and he began to see splotches again. A warm, peaceful feeling, a numbness, overtook him and he wondered if he was dying. He lifted his left leg up near his right hand, but his weight shifted and he lost his balance.

On what he thought might be his last chance, he lifted his leg again, and this time he snatched the pant cuff. He reached down, unsnapped the ankle holster, and drew his .380. He raised it to his shoulder, pointed behind him, and fired several shots. Clark felt himself falling backward. Then he passed out.

CHAPTER FORTY-TWO

Clark began to see splotches of black mingled with light, and then things went dark again. He kept hearing a familiar voice that sounded like it was coming from far away. Slowly, Wilkens came into view, crouched over him.

In an echo, Wilkens said, "Take it easy, Lieutenant. Don't try to…yet…some really bad bruising around…."

Clark tried to cough, then passed out again.

A couple minutes later, he felt a tugging at his shoulder and he could hear the wailing of sirens in the distance. Wilkens was still kneeling at his side. Was this a dream?

Clark slowly regained his senses, recalling sketchy details of the events that occurred right before he passed out. He gazed up at Wilkens and then noticed Whitaker crouched behind him, his hand over his eyes. "What…happened?" Clark asked, coughing.

"Take it easy, boss. Relax. You had a close call."

"What happened, Brad?" Clark grimaced, trying to clear his throat. He felt a burning sensation in his throat, and nausea overtook him. He heaved twice, and then turned on his side and vomited.

"Easy now. One of them grabbed you from behind. He almost had you with a piece of wire. You got him, though," Wilkens said. "You got him good." He nodded in the direction of the robber's body, which lay in a small pool of blood a few feet from Clark.

On his back, Clark painfully turned to see. He coughed again and cleared his throat, massaging it with his hand. "Brad," Clark said in a weak voice.

"Yeah, Lieutenant?"

Clark motioned him to lean over and get closer, which he did.

"Yeah, Lieutenant?"

Clark whispered, "Don't ever take a piece of wire to a gun fight," then he slowly sat up.

Wilkens smiled and handed him his Sig and Glock.

"What's wrong with Price?" Clark asked.

Wilkens turned to Price, then back to Clark. "It's Steve, Lieutenant. One of the robbers surprised him at the back door. Unloaded on him. Steve took some rounds in the back."

"How is he?"

Silence for a few seconds.

"He didn't make it," Wilkens said.

"What about his vest?"

Wilkens lowered his head and shook it. "Price thinks he may have hit the guy with a round or two when he ran out the door, but there's no sign of blood outside."

"What about the van?"

"Got away."

"Why didn't one of our cars stop them?"

"Something's wrong with our radios. Nobody can transmit, headquarters can't copy anything and we can't hear them, either. Everybody's having to use their cells."

Clark wiped some blood dripping from his nose. "We need to get a BOLO out on the van ASAP. Far as we know, they still don't know that we've I.D.'ed it."

"Already taken care of."

Wilkens helped Clark to his feet and he steadied himself.

"Where's Steve?" Clark asked.

"Over by the backdoor."

Clark stumbled around. "Where's Sarge?"

"He's up at the office with the other body."

"Everybody else okay?"

"Yes, sir."

"Thank God."

They could hear the sirens out front, as a caravan of units was pulling into the parking lot.

Clark slowly shuffled over to where the body lay face down. He knelt beside Esposito, placing a hand on the back of his head. Clark swallowed hard, looking in disbelief. Tears began to swell in his eyes, and then he stopped. *Revenge will be better.* He looked up at Wilkens and Whitaker. "We're going to finish this for him." Whitaker found a large black tarp and covered the body.

At the front office, Cunningham and Clark discussed the chain of events, while E.M.S. techs, officers from the other stakeout, and patrol officers filed into the grocery store.

"We've got enough to do here with scene processing to last us the rest of the night," Cunningham said. "I've called the chief. I reckon he'll have to call the Bureau to come in and do the shooting investigation."

Clark walked over to the body of the robber that lay in the office, and examined it. "Looks Middle-Eastern," he said. "Mine, too."

"What the hell is going on?"

"They've hit all over this area. And that's just what we know of. All that money is going somewhere."

"Terrorists? Here?"

"We need to get the Feds ASAP."

A few minutes later, the Chief and Capt. Simmons arrived on the scene and Clark filled them in on the details. After the briefing, everyone sat in a heavy silence, mourning the death of their colleague.

The Chief spoke first, in a subdued manner. "As far as I know, he's the first line-of-duty death in the Department's history. Captain, will you help me with the visit to his house?" Capt. Simmons nodded. "We need to do it right away." Simmons nodded again.

"What about the shooting investigation, Chief?" Cunningham asked.

"I'll call the S.B.I., and the D.A.," he answered. "Clark, what's our next move?"

"We've got a BOLO, extreme danger, out for the van. Other than that, we can watch the house on Regal Road for the night. See if this van shows up there. Maybe it will. We know that one of these robbers gunned down Hamim. We just don't know how they're connected to Hamim and the house."

During their discussion, Clark's pager buzzed with a 911 message from the PD. He called the office and the dispatcher informed him that a County car had just made contact with Curt Thompson. He jotted down the phone number and made the call. Clark motioned to the group to listen in on his conversation.

"Hello."

"Mr. Thompson?"

"Yes, speaking."

"This is Lt. Dixon with the Stuartsboro PD."

"Yes, what can I help you with? My wife said you've stopped by the house a few times today. Something about a death?"

"Uh, yes, Mr. Thompson. We need to get word to one of your tenants, Harris Hamilton, about a death in his family."

"Hamilton? Oh yeah, the black fella, handicapped."

"That's right. We're having trouble getting in touch with him and we were hoping you may be able to help us."

"You say he's not at home?"

"No sir. We've been by there a number of times, but no luck."

"Wish I could tell ya where he might be. Truth is, I rarely see him, Officer."

"Is that right?"

"He's one of my better renters. I've got twenty-four rental houses and guys like him are mighty good to deal with. Never a problem or a word outta him, you see. Always pays his rent on time, pays in cash. Never have to call him for nothin', and he never calls me for nothin', neither."

"Do you ever go by and collect? Does he bring it to you?"

"He always mails it to me, 'cept once when he rode over here in the van and paid me. Other than that, all I have to do is walk down to the mailbox first of each month and there it is. Don't really know much else 'bout him. Wish I could be more help."

Clark could feel the dead-end coming. "Yeah, the black van. We've been on the lookout for it. So far, no luck. Listen, Mr. Thompson, thanks for the help. We really appreciate it. Have a good...."

"Naw," Thompson said, interrupting, "not black."

"Excuse me?"

"It ain't black, the van I was talkin' about."

"What color was it?"

"Green."

"A green van?" Everyone made a step toward Clark when he asked the question.

"That's right. A Rodriguez fella that I rent to brought him up here on rent day, oh, I'd say 'bout four months ago. Rodriguez don't speak no English so Hamilton interprets for him, takes care of his business from what I understand. Harris is the one that asked me to rent to Rodriguez. Tell ya the truth, that was the first time I'd even seen the guy. Always dealt with Hamilton."

"This Rodriguez man, would he be a plumber?"

"Yeah. Must be a purdy darned good one, too. Got a good business."

"What makes you say that?"

"'Cause the day he brung Hamilton here to make his payment, I seen the van and asked Hamilton to ask Rodriguez if he was interested in doing some plumbing work on my rentals. But Hamilton said Rodriguez was already way too busy."

"How does Rodriguez pay his rent?"

"I'll tell ya how. On time, that's how. Hamilton takes care of that, too. Lot of times he mails me both payments. Cash on the barrel. Never a word out of 'em."

"You ever go by Rodriguez' house for anything?"

"Let me think a second." A pause. "Yeah, one time that I can remember. I needed him to sign a paper. Pretty dark-haired girl come to the door. I figured she's his wife or girlfriend. She couldn't speak English, neither. They seem like private folks, right decent. Take good care of things."

"Maybe they can help me locate Hamilton. Can you give me directions to their house?"

"Sure. He don't live far from Hamilton. But 'less you got somebody that speaks Mexican, you're wastin' your time."

"Oh, I think they'll understand what we have to say." Clark wrote down the directions and repeated them to Thompson, while the others listened in. "Thanks, Mr. Thompson. Please keep this information confidential. It's very important. Okay?"

"Sure thing. Good luck."

Clark hung up, turned to Brinks, and filled him in while the others listened. "Hope Thompson doesn't leak any of this. That could be bad for us."

"What now, Clark?" Brinks asked.

Clark paused for a minute, all eyes on him, etching the mental outline of a plan. Then he asked Brinks, "Can Simmons supervise this until the Bureau arrives?"

"Yes. I'll get somebody from patrol to go with me to Steve's house."

"I've got an idea," Clark said, "but we're gonna have to move fast to make it work."

"Don't you think we better get the County and Bureau to help us?" Brinks asked.

"There's not enough time. It'd take the County at least an hour or two for their S.R.T. to respond, the Bureau even longer."

"What's your plan?"

"I need three things."

"Name them."

"I need Blackburn and one of his S.R.T. squads."

"All right. What else?"

"I need a couple of unmarked units. How about your jeep and the narc's Mustang?"

"They're yours. What else?"

"I need Sloan."

Brinks was caught off-guard, cornered, so he paused to consider his options. He looked around at the others for a reaction, and turned back to Clark. After a moment, he nodded.

Clark went over the details of his plan. They made a couple of adjustments, after which their pagers buzzed and beeped with a 911 message from the PD. Clark called the office, and the others got quiet. When he hung up, he shook his head, looking in disbelief. Then he turned to the Chief. "The S.B.I. won't be helping us tonight."

"Why not?"

"What's going on?"

"There's been an explosion," Clark announced. "About an hour ago, the Bureau's tactical and special ops building out on Pierce Road blew up. Three agents were killed and several were injured. They're still looking for bodies."

CHAPTER FORTY-THREE

"Hello."

"Good evenin', this is Curt Thompson. Could I speak to Mr. Rodriguez?"

A pause. "Who?"

"Mr. Rodriguez. Can I speak to him, please?"

Another pause, followed by some background conversation. "Hold on."

A few seconds later, "Hello."

"Mr. Rodriguez?"

"He is not here."

"Who am I speakin' to?"

"This is Juan, his cousin. Who is this?"

"I'm Curt Thompson, Mr. Rodriguez' landlord. Sorry to call at such a late hour, but I wanted to tell Mr. Rodriguez that the police just came here lookin' for Harris Hamilton. You see, I rent to Mr. Hamilton, too, and I know that Hamilton and Rodriguez are friends. Maybe he'd know where Hamilton's at. There's been a death in Hamilton's family and the Stuartsboro Police Department is trying to locate him to pass on the news."

Silence on the other end of the line.

Thompson continued. "Anyways, the police told me they've been lookin' all over for Hamilton, and can't find him. Since Rodriguez and he's good friends, maybe Rodriguez will know where he might be. The police are on the way to your place to speak to Rodriguez."

"How do you know that they are friends?" When Al Sabah asked the question, he snapped his finger and all activity in the den froze.

"Well, I know that Hamilton takes care of payin' Rodriguez' rent. And I remember a time a few months ago when Rodriguez drove Hamilton over here to make a payment. The police seemed to know right much about the two of 'em."

"Is that right?"

"Yes, sir. Again, sorry to be disturbin' y'all at such a late hour, but I think most folks like to know ahead of time when a bunch of cops are comin' to knock on their door late at night."

"What is this you mean by 'a bunch'?"

"Two squad cars of 'em stopped by here. They must be workin' on something mighty big, though, in addition to huntin' for Hamilton."

A short pause. "We were getting ready for bed, Mr. Thompson. How long do you think it will take for them to arrive here?"

"Well, let's see. They just pulled out of my drive 'bout a minute ago…so I'd say 'bout fifteen minutes. Yeah, fifteen. I imagine they'll be right out there. They seemed real anxious to get in touch with Rodriguez."

"How many officers did you say there were?"

"'Bout seven or eight. Nobody got outta the second car, they just waited in the…."

Click. The phone went dead.

"Hello? Hello?" Thompson placed the phone back on the receiver and turned around. "He hung up on me."

Lt. Festerman smiled, gave Thompson a nod, and put the other phone down. "That went really well, Mr. Thompson. Sounds like their English improved quite a bit too, don't you think?" Festerman made a quick call on his cell phone. Then he turned to Thompson and said, "You did real fine. We're very appreciative of how you helped us here tonight."

"You're welcome, Lieutenant. Ain't exactly sure what I done, though. But from the looks of it, I'd say I come home from one fishing trip and just went out on another'n."

Festerman laughed. "I suppose that's one way of putting it. Now, let's just hope they take the bait."

* * *

Al Sabah hung up and barked the order. Everyone scrambled, emptying drawers and closets, loading suitcases and bags with precision and order, as if they'd practiced the drill a thousand times. They placed everything at the front door, and Al Farran and Mahmud loaded the car and SUV. Yasin limped over to the door and placed two metal boxes of ammunition on the floor. He asked Al Sabah, "Have you notified the other teams, yet?"

"We will have time to do that when we are on the road. If we don't get out of here, everything will be compromised. Everything."

"Shouldn't you at least send out a message, Kasim?"

Al Sabah looked at him and snapped, "We have to get away from here! Now move!" Al Sabah went in the bedroom and, momentarily, returned with two small packages and handed them to Al Farran. "When we leave, place these at the two doors. I have already set the sensing mechanisms on them. All you have to do is press this button to activate each one."

Suddenly, the walkie-talkie blared on the living room table. "A police car is coming! Police coming!" Faraj shouted. He was the lookout down at the road.

Atef grabbed his MP-5 and tossed AK-47s to Mahmud and Raboud. After a few seconds of radio silence, Al Sabah called to Faraj, "What do you see now? Tell me."

"The car has driven slowly past us, on down the road. They are looking for us."

"Hurry, everyone! We do not have much time," Al Sabah yelled. "Only take the things that you must have."

In ten minutes, the two vehicles were loaded. "Where do we put the electrical equipment?" Raboud asked Al Sabah.

"In the trunk of the car, with my computer. It will be safer there, in case...."

"In case, what?"

"In case we do not get away."

As Al Sabah said that, Faraj called back on the radio. "The police car turned around and drove past us again. Now it is driving away, back in the direction of the main road."

"Good," Al Sabah said. "Move quickly everyone, they will find this house very soon."

Raboud got behind the wheel of the SUV. Mahmud loaded supplies in the back and then hopped in the passenger's seat.

Atef loaded the remaining rifles and tossed extra magazines on the seats of the vehicles. Yasin checked through the rooms one last time, being careful not to leave any clues behind. He hobbled out the door and made his way to the car; Atef noticed it, leaned over the front seat, and whispered to Al Sabah, "His limp has become worse, Kasim."

Al Sabah turned to Atef, "Shhh." Then he shouted to Al Farran, who was crouched at the front door, "Hurry!"

Carefully, Al Farran edged the bomb just inside the door. He made a minor adjustment to the sensor, and slowly closed the door; he walked with soft steps across the front porch. Then he got in the driver's seat of the car, joining Al Sabah, Atef, and Yasin, and backed out of the driveway, the SUV in tow.

At that moment, Clark's cell phone rang. "Dixon."

"This is Frazier. They just pulled out. We got two vehicles—light-colored Chevrolet sedan, four-door, and an SUV, looked gold in color, behind it. The SUV stopped at the end of the driveway for a second, and now it's following the sedan."

"Looks like they may be on the run," Clark said. "The landlord's call flushed them out. Could you tell if they loaded up the vehicles with anything?"

"Nah, the house is set too far back off the road. Couldn't see nothin' but about seventy-five feet of driveway. Barely see a light or two at the house. I mean that's it. Tell ya, Lieutenant, I've lived in this town all my life and I never knew this place was here."

"Hold on a second, Allen. Let me pass your info to Sloan; they're heading his way."

"I'm holdin'."

Clark called Sloan, "7 to 35, Sheriff's tactical channel."

"35."

"Two suspect vehicles on the go—light-colored Chevrolet four-door and an SUV, probably gold."

"Occupants?" Sloan asked. He turned to Cunningham and quickly gave him the descriptions.

"Unable to advise. They should be surfacing onto the main road, coming at you, in about a minute."

"10-4. If they split up, who do I run with?"

"Go with the Chevrolet. It could be the same one that was in the driveway at the other house, where Esposito did the undercover." When Clark said "Esposito", that sick feeling came back. Only worse. Like waking up from a nightmare, then falling back asleep and returning to it. Things were unfolding so quickly that they didn't have time to mourn Esposito's death.... *"rats on a tread wheel...running as fast as they can, but never getting anywhere...."* One fell off the wheel and couldn't finish the race, and nobody had time to stop for him. His death really hadn't sunk in, yet.

When Sloan heard "Esposito", he gripped the wheel with white knuckles. *Somebody's gonna pay on this trip.* "10-4 on the Chevrolet, 7," Sloan responded.

"Let us know as fast as you can which way you're going. We got four cars relying on you to get us the info fast." Clark had staged two cars in the area, but a couple were coming from the PD and would have to catch up. The S.R.T. had to dress and load their equipment in the truck. They had just pulled out from the station.

"10-4," Sloan answered. He looked at Cunningham, who was plugging his cell phone charger in the cigarette lighter. "You ready, Sarge?"

"Ready as ever, Jerry. You think this Ford of yours can keep up with them?"

"It'll be a cold day in hell before I let a Chevy outrun me."

Cunningham gave a thin smile, turned the other way, and wiped his eyes. Clark returned to the phone. "Allen, could you tell how many occupants?"

"Couldn't see anything."

"No green van, huh?"

"Not yet. You want me to try to get a closer look at the house?"

"Better not. Don't want you walking into a hornet's nest by yourself."

"How far are y'all gonna be able to go outside the city and still transmit on the Sheriff's channel?"

"Don't know. If we get out of range, we may have to do some of this by cell phone, and pray we get a signal. Everything hinges on which way they go."

"Is SHP gonna be able to help us?"

"Headquarters is trying to get in touch with the First Sergeant, but so far no word."

"What do you want me to do now?"

"Wait a few more minutes, and if no more traffic comes out of there, then try to join…."

Their conversation was interrupted.

"19 to all units, 19 to all units," Cunningham radioed. "We've got some headlights coming out of Sudbury Lane. This may be them."

Clark finished with Frazier. "Try to join us when you clear from there, okay?"

"10-4."

Then Clark radioed Sloan and told him they couldn't determine number of occupants.

Wilkens cranked the Honda Accord, as Clark looked over at him and said, "This is it, Brad, pray that it works."

In the backseat, Lt. Hoffman loaded his magazine and fed it into the AR-15. Then he dropped the magazine to his Glock, checked the ammo, and reloaded.

"You think these are the robbers, Lieutenant?" Hoffman asked.

"I don't know. I'd feel better if we were following a green van. That way we'd be sure. But we'd be fools to assume that these aren't the guys we're looking for."

CHAPTER FORTY-FOUR

"19 to all units, confirmed—suspect vehicles spotted." Cunningham gave the make, model, and color of each vehicle and the direction of travel. "They're making a left onto Cedar, staying together."

Over the next five minutes, Cunningham radioed updates as the suspects made several turns, the SUV following the Chevrolet.

Clark called headquarters on the phone and confirmed that his radio traffic on the Sheriff's Department's channel could be picked up through the PD console. So far, so good. But he was more concerned about traveling out-of-town, away from the County's antenna towers. That could render their radios useless. Then he called Capt. Blackburn on his cell.

"Blackburn."

Clark was interrupted by radio traffic.

"19 to all units, they're turning onto the Southern Connector, heading east."

Then Clark continued. "Hey, it's me. Which way do you think they're going?"

"Hard to say, but we ought to know something shortly," Blackburn said.

"What's the status on the Sheriff's Department helping us?"

"Bad news there. I talked to Staff Duty and they said the shift commander said he can't afford to cut anybody loose."

"You're joking, right?"

"Wish I was, Clark."

"Just for the record, we're following what could be considered the most violent, and I might add successful, robbery gang in the region. And they can't afford to loan us a couple of deputies?"

"He said he'd be glad to activate their S.R.T., but he couldn't justify sending us any cars, unless we had warrants in-hand."

"That's bullshit! It'd take too long to get their S.R.T. up and running; I can't believe he wouldn't give us anybody."

"I cussed him out. Guess Brinks will be hearing about it tomorrow."

A minute later. "19 to all units, suspect vehicles still together. Both are turning south on Reid School Road."

"Sounds like they're heading either east or southeast," Blackburn told Clark.

"Let me call you back," Clark said. "I want to see where the Mustang is." Then he radioed Officer Rodney Coleman, "7 to 32."

"32, I'm on Barnes Street, approaching the Connector."

"10-4, 32. Checking to see if you're in position."

"10-4. I'll be there shortly."

Clark was relieved to hear that Coleman had almost caught up with the suspects. "Man, he's hauling ass in that Mustang," he said to Wilkens and Hoffman. Clark knew the success of the mission depended on whether Coleman and Officer Kent Travis, his passenger, could pull off their part of the plan.

"Lieutenant, if we cross over to another county, any chance SHP in that county will help us?" Hoffman asked. Wilkens, interested in the response, made a left turn, and glanced at Clark.

"Don't know," Clark said. "One thing's for certain. If we head east, you can forget Guilford County lending us a hand."

"Why?" Wilkens asked.

"Guilford's in a free-for-all. Since the explosion, every available officer in the city, local, state, federal, is being activated. They're racing to protect some of their potential targets: The airport, oil farm, water supplies. They're calling in bomb-sniffing dogs from as far away as Charlotte. They've even...."

Clark was interrupted again.

"19 to all units. Suspect vehicles are heading east on Freeway Drive...repeat, east on Freeway Drive."

Clark tried to call Blackburn back, but he lost contact twice. He was successful on the third attempt. "You copy that? They're going east."

"Betcha they're heading toward Burlington or Greensboro...."

The phone went dead.

Then Blackburn turned to Officer Hunt, his driver. "I figure we're about a mile behind. Pick it up, Walt. We gotta catch up with them." Then he yelled to the back of the S.R.T. truck and instructed Lt. Johnson to make sure he, Canine Officer Edwards, and Officer Holden were prepared. "Be ready for a sudden stop."

"19 to all units. Suspect vehicles are turning east on Business 29, repeat, east on Business 29."

"32 to 19," Coleman called Cunningham.

"19."

"I'm 10-23 your location, heading east." Coleman had caught up with Sloan's truck.

"10-4, I see you back there."

Two vehicles were now tailing the suspects.

Clark radioed to Blackburn and Officer Boyd Ross, who was behind Clark in a Jeep Grand Cherokee. "7 to 3 and 40, Sheriff's channel."

"3."

"40."

"It appears that they're heading to Greensboro."

The officers acknowledged.

Clark had planned on the suspects leaving the city and they did. Then he hoped they would head north or west, but they didn't. Those routes were usually less traveled. But at least the pursuit was taking them outside the city to open highway. Clark radioed Blackburn and asked for his location, "3, 10-20?"

"We're turning onto Freeway now from Scales. We'll catch up with you shortly."

Over the next couple of minutes, Wilkens picked up his speed and made some ground. Then he saw what looked like Mustang taillights. Wilkens called Coleman, "24 to 32."

"That's him, Brad," Clark said.

"32," Coleman answered.

"I think I see you. Did you just pass Parks' Motors?"

"10-4."

"Hit your left turn signal, then your right." Wilkens saw the signal lights. "10-4, we're behind you. Ross is behind me in the Grand Cherokee."

Just then, a pick-up truck pulled out of a driveway onto the road in front of Wilkens, and he hit the brakes. After on-coming traffic cleared, Wilkens and Ross passed the truck and were back in the game.

Four vehicles now tailing the suspects.

"19 to all units. Suspect vehicles continuing east on Business 29. We'll be approaching the four-lane to Greensboro in about five minutes."

All units acknowledged.

"7 to 35," Clark radioed to Sloan.

"35."

"Let 32 take the lead, so you don't get burned." As Clark requested, Coleman then passed Sloan's truck.

"7 to 3, 10-20?" Clark asked Blackburn for his location.

"We'll be pulling onto Business 29 in about thirty seconds."

"Hustle it up. Everybody else is in line."

"10-4."

In a couple minutes, the S.R.T. truck caught up with the pack.

Now, all the police vehicles were in pursuit.

The Chevrolet and SUV turned right down the access road, and then merged onto Highway 29, heading east. In forty-five seconds, all the police vehicles had rolled onto the divided four-lane road, as well. Traffic was light.

Clark called the Sheriff's Department on their channel and gave an update on the convoy's location and direction of travel. "Contact SHP fast and see what their status is. We're getting near the county line."

"10-4, Stuartsboro 7," the Sheriff's dispatcher answered.

"7 to 32," Clark called Coleman.

"32."

"Everybody's in tandem now, 32," Clark said. "Time for you to take off."

"10-4, 7." Coleman put the Mustang's 4.6-liter engine to work. Travis readied his M-1 rifle in the back seat, just in case, keeping it low and aimed to the right. Coleman sped up to eighty-five miles per hour and passed the SUV, then the Chevrolet. He had to get a big lead on the suspects.

Clark radioed Sloan and told him to pass the suspects and stay just in front of them. Next, he called Ross who was behind him. "Pass me and take the lead behind the suspects. Then pull out into the passing lane, and keep pace with them so they can't get around you—but don't make it obvious." That left Wilkens' car and the S.R.T. truck in the back of the pack.

Sloan pulled out and, as he passed the SUV, they approached a red light. He slowed to a stop, drew his Glock, and placed it between his legs. Cunningham racked a round in the pistol-grip shotgun, keeping it below window level.

Eyes ahead, Cunningham spoke, "Be ready, Jerry."

They slowed to a stop beside the Chevrolet under bright fluorescent streetlights.

Yasin glanced to the left, flicking his cigarette out the window, and saw the passenger in the truck. The light turned green, and all the vehicles slowly accelerated through the intersection. "The passenger in that truck," Yasin said, "he looks familiar...I have seen him somewhere."

Al Sabah looked at the truck and then turned to the backseat. "Where?"

"Where have I seen him?" Yasin asked himself aloud. He thought for a moment. "Abbas, try to pull up beside the truck."

Al Farran accelerated, but by the time he caught up with the truck, they were too far from the well-lit intersection to get a good look at his face. Yasin tried to place the man's face, while they continued east on the highway.

Coleman was now about a half-mile ahead of the caravan, and he radioed his position back to Clark. Ross and Sloan steadied their speed as they ran blockade formation on the suspects, making it difficult for them to pass.

The Sheriff's Department called Clark, "Sheriff's Office to Stuartsboro 7."

"Go ahead, County."

"SHP advised they are not in position to respond."

"10-4, County." Clark tried to get Blackburn on his cell, but once again he lost his signal. He reached him on the second try.

"Blackburn."

"Phones aren't working too well out here, must be in a low service area. Guess you heard the County."

Some static with the call.

"Yep, win or lose, this one's ours. I've been monitoring GPD and Guilford on the scanner. They're swarming like bees over there. They've confirmed that the explosion wasn't an accident. Now, every crackpot in the city is calling in bomb threats. Utter chaos. Hey, speaking of Greensboro, is your buddy Greg okay?"

"Yeah. Narcs were in the building when it exploded. They just picked the wrong night to be working late."

More static, crackling noises.

"This is it, Richard. I think these are the robbers."

"Me too, I...."

Too much interference to hear the end of the message. More static.

"Hey, you're breaking up. What was that last part?"

"I said I think these are the guys, too. The call to the house put them on the run."

"Hope we're right," Clark said. "Better to bring this to a head under our terms. Can you hear me okay?"

"Fair."

"God, if these phones go out, we may be sunk."

"Not as long as we got bullets."

"Or cops to shoot them. If these guys we're following are heading to another score, then there's no telling what they've got in their vehicles."

"What do you say we do Dragon Garden tomorrow, my treat?"

"You're on. But before we make this stop, sure you don't want to go ahead and pull your pin? Take the next exit up the road here? Retire four months early?"

"That's three months, two weeks. Wouldn't miss taking these bastards down for nothing."

"Me, neither." Clark called all units, told them to get ready, and hold all radio traffic. In four or five minutes, they would hit a fairly isolated stretch of the highway, about ten miles from Greensboro. So far, everything had gone smoothly with the plan.

That's what bothered Clark the most.

CHAPTER FORTY-FIVE

Coleman maintained a speed of 100 miles per hour and picked up a mile-and-a-half lead on the caravan. He pulled off the road nearly losing control on the gravel shoulder. After he stopped, he turned on his flashers and raised the hood. Travis hurried to the trunk and pulled out the nine-foot stop-strip, pricking his finger on one of the sharp spikes.

Sloan and Ross drove at a steady speed and kept the suspect vehicles in check, as they approached the area where Coleman waited. Sloan radioed their location to Coleman, and the other units tried to keep pace.

When Sloan reached the top of the next long, sloping hill, he saw the Mustang's flashers. He signaled Coleman with his lights, then everybody braced for the stop. The Chevrolet tried to pass Sloan's truck but Ross kept it boxed in. Sloan sped up, hoping the suspects would stay in the right lane. It worked.

Wilkens and Hunt tried to keep traffic behind them, and it was backing up, even at this late hour. A tractor-trailer was tailgating them, switching back and forth, trying to pass. The driver continuously flashed his bright lights, in an effort to get them to pull to the right.

"Remind me to write that imbecile a ticket when this is over," Wilkens said to Clark.

Clark smiled nervously, reaching down and grabbing the mike.

Sloan radioed that he was approaching Coleman's location, and about to make the shift to the left lane.

Clark took a deep breath. *Here we go.* He pressed the mike button. "Stuartsboro 7 to County and all units. Hold all radio traffic, repeat, hold all traffic."

Sloan quickly shifted to the passing lane, and Ross and Wilkens sped up directly behind him, forcing the suspects to stay in the right lane. With the suspects' vehicles only about a quarter of a mile away, Travis tossed the stop-strip out across the road. He pulled it back over to cover the right lane, then stepped away.

In a few seconds, the Chevrolet ran over the stop-strip spikes, and a couple seconds later the SUV followed. Air began pouring through the spikes embedded in the tires of the vehicles.

"What was that?" Al Sabah asked, feeling the bump.

"I do not know," Al Farran answered. "Perhaps uneven road or a piece of tire tread." Al Sabah returned to his phone conversation with Mahmud.

"We just ran over something," Mahmud said. "Is that what you were speaking of?"

"A bump in the road," Al Sabah answered. "Nothing."

"When do we reach the Richmond turn-off?"

Al Sabah gave Mahmud the route, and then he noticed the car was beginning to vibrate. After a few seconds, they heard a rumbling sound that grew louder, as the vibration worsened. Al Sabah told Mahmud that they were going to pull off the road and check it out.

When the call ended, Mahmud and his group began to experience the same trouble with the SUV.

Atef spoke up from the backseat, "What's going on?"

Al Farran tightened his grip on the steering wheel as the vibration increased. "Flat tire!" he shouted over the thunderous noise. "I am pulling off the road up here!"

"Right here, turn here," Al Sabah said, pointing to a road sign that indicated a service road turn ahead.

Al Farran made a right turn and Raboud followed. The rumbling noise changed quickly to loud, constant metallic clattering and grinding.

"Sounds like you are dragging something under the car!" Al Sabah shouted to Al Farran.

Yasin and Atef turned around and saw the SUV following them, bright sparks shooting from its wheels.

"We both ran over something back there!" Yasin yelled in an agitated tone.

The police cars slammed on brakes to make the unexpected turn with the suspects, but all the drivers, except Wilkens and Hunt, overran it.

Sloan cut sharply and drove across the narrow grass median between the highway and the service road; he hit uneven terrain, almost flipping over. He recovered then swerved his truck onto the service road, heading back toward the convoy.

Clark shouted in the mike, "Lights out! Cut off headlights!"

Al Farran took a left off the access road, his car screeching and roaring down a dark, narrow two-lane stretch that led into the side parking lot of a high school. He decided to pull under a streetlight between a school activity bus and walkway shelter.

Al Sabah turned to check on the SUV and, when he did, he saw the convoy converging on them. "Everyone get out! Get out! Behind us, they're coming at us!"

Al Sabah and the others jumped out of the car with weapons drawn, shouting and pointing to the parking lot entrance behind them.

Faraj turned around and saw several vehicles moving in a line toward them, blocking them in.

"Cover! Cover!" Faraj yelled, as Raboud abruptly stopped the SUV behind the Chevrolet.

Mahmud and Raboud grabbed rifles, bailed out of the SUV, and sprinted for a wall on the side of the school. Faraj stayed in the backseat, crouching low and chambering a round.

They found cover quickly and opened fire on the police. The officers ducked, bullets and glass raining into their cars; they drove to within twenty yards of the suspect vehicles, forming an arc behind them.

Atef sprayed their windshields with his Uzi, while Al Sabah and Yasin ran to the school and hid behind a dumpster and low brick wall.

Before he could park, Coleman was shot in the head and his car rammed into the back of Raboud's SUV, activating the Mustang's airbags. Travis, who had moved to the front seat, was pinned behind his bag and couldn't maneuver his M-1 rifle to return fire. He tried desperately to free himself.

Atef saw the officer and ran over to his window, as Travis looked helplessly at him. Travis then closed his eyes, lowered his head, and muttered some words. Atef fired several rounds, bullets blasting through the window and striking Travis in the face.

The back doors of the S.R.T. truck popped open and the officers jumped down to the pavement. Lt. Johnson's helmet fell off and when he scooped it up, he took two rounds in the leg and went down hard on the pavement.

Clark saw Holden inching his way over to rescue Johnson and shouted to him, "On three, take off! I gotcha!"

Holden nodded and watched Clark count.

On three, Clark stood up and fired at the building, while Holden crouched low and shuffled over to Johnson. Nine-millimeter bullets whistled above his head, ripping a line of holes through the side of the S.R.T. truck. He dragged Johnson behind the truck, and Edwards fired his Colt-SMG at the brick wall on the side of the school, covering for them.

Blackburn ran over to Sloan and Cunningham behind the pick-up to strengthen the left flank. Wilkens, Clark, and Hoffman ran to the right, taking cover, dropping behind an embankment.

Ross worked his way up to the wrecked Mustang to check on Coleman and Travis; he couldn't even recognize their battered faces, slumped against the air bags. Then he kept low and skirted along the left side of the SUV, which was about twenty-five yards from the suspects' positions near the school. Slowly, Ross rose to peer through the windows of the SUV, trying to get a better fix on the suspects' locations. He tried to focus through the darkened windows and, when he did, he saw a dark figure rise in the backseat. Faraj shot through the side glass, shattering it, and hitting Ross with several rounds in the shoulder and neck.

Wilkens heard the blast, turned, and saw Faraj; Wilkens carefully aimed his laser sights at him, squeezed the trigger, and fired. Faraj fell out of view. A moment later, Faraj's arm dangled out of the right rear door.

Atef saw the exchange and engaged in a volley of fire with Wilkens.

Clark had never heard such a barrage of gunfire, not even in his younger days of S.R.T. drills. The unrelenting noise created from the immense volume of fire was deafening. He looked up at the streetlights and saw that the gun smoke created a canopy of gray haze over the scene that seemed eerily stationary. Over the *k-boom* sounds of the .223 rounds of the assault rifles, Clark shouted to his officers to begin to work their way toward the school where the suspects were positioned.

Al Sabah knew his men's ammunition was running low. They had two options: Get back to the car for more rounds or retreat through the school buildings to the other side of the campus. He squatted, reloaded, and told Yasin, "We have to move—we're outnumbered, Ali. We will have to run for the woods behind us." He looked down at Yasin's leg, but he didn't say anything.

Yasin nodded, then he raised, fired several rounds, and ducked again. "Give the word, Kasim. Then I will draw their attention. It will give you more time."

At the truck, Blackburn told Cunningham and Sloan, "We have to make it to the corner of the building over there." The two men nodded. The building was thirty yards ahead of them, and to the left of the suspects. He yelled to Sloan, "Give us cover!"

Sloan slid around them to the front corner of the truck, just as its windows shattered. He stood and fired several shots at the school wall.

A shard of glass struck Cunningham in the back of the neck, stunning him. He and Blackburn kept low and shuffled across the lot.

At the precise moment they ran for it, Yasin got up from his cover and hobbled out into the open fifteen yards in front of them. Clark saw Yasin and shouted a warning to Blackburn, but he was too late. Yasin shot Blackburn and Cunningham at close range and they fell to the pavement.

Clark aimed his shotgun at Yasin and pulled the trigger. Click. He was out of rounds. He turned his head and closed his eyes. He felt like throwing up. Instant void.

Holden stepped out from behind the S.R.T. truck, ran to within fifteen yards of Yasin, and dropped to one knee. Yasin changed magazines in his gun as he limped toward the dumpster to take cover. Holden shot him in the back, knocking him to the ground. Then Holden made the mistake of getting a follow-up shot. He ran over to Yasin and fired a second shot at close range, but Holden was already in Raboud's sights. Holden took several hits and dropped to the pavement. He got up on his knees and Raboud shot him again.

Clark and Wilkens crawled up to a brick planter. They were twenty yards to the right of the wall where some of the shooters were positioned. Patiently, Clark waited for one of the gunmen to rise and shoot over the wall, as Wilkens raced to the corner of it. Mahmud, running to his left, was surprised by Wilkens' advance. Clark was ready, and so was Wilkens. Clark pumped three rounds from his shotgun into Mahmud, just as Wilkens reflexed and fired his .45; red splotches burst from Mahmud's chest as he dropped, and his body draped over the wall.

Atef and Al Sabah backed up and retreated between two buildings, making a run for it.

From his crouched spot, Sloan saw them, ran to the back of his truck, and grabbed a camouflaged nylon bag. He shuffled over to check on Blackburn and Cunningham; both were too bloodied for Sloan to tell where their wounds were. He checked Cunningham for a pulse, but couldn't find one. Then, Sloan got up and sprinted to the left, around to the front of the school, in hopes of cutting off the fleeing suspects. When he made it to the front corner, he saw two of them dart across the parking lot on the far side of the school and disappear into the woods.

When Sloan hit the tree line, he estimated he was about seventy-five to one hundred yards from the suspects. He knelt and reloaded his shotgun, pausing for a moment. Then he got up, and thrashed through a thick gauntlet of pine trees. Every few seconds, he stopped and listened, and then resumed his pursuit. He paused again and all he could hear was the gunfire on the other side of the buildings. He ran another ten to fifteen yards, stopped again, closed his eyes and listened. Sloan was in his element.

At the school, Al Farran maneuvered his way to the edge of a wall and riddled the police cars with fire; Raboud ran to the front of the activity bus, trying to make it to the car for more ammunition.

Edwards saw him working his way to the car and prepared his canine, Kobey, for an attack.

Al Farran reloaded and picked up with another round of fire, then Raboud dashed for the Chevrolet.

Edwards gave the order and Kobey raced to the suspect. Raboud jumped into the front seat from the right, as Kobey leapt in from the left and lunged for Raboud's throat. When Edwards heard the scream, he and Hunt ran to the car. Raboud wrestled with the dog and managed to push it back. Raboud stumbled back out of the door, and was met by a hail of gunfire from Hunt.

The last two minutes, to Clark, felt like two years. Over the next few seconds, his mind raced while he peered around a wall to see if Blackburn or Cunningham showed any sign of movement. What other types of weapons did the suspects have at their disposal? How many suspects were there? Were they circling around to ambush the officers?

Clark knew that he had to get to his car and call for help. He shouted at Hoffman to give him cover. On signal, Hoffman stepped slightly from behind the bus, and fired several rounds at the wall, the bullets chipping away at the brick. Clark zigzagged his way back to the car and tried to get the Sheriff's Department on the radio. He called twice but couldn't even hear the squelch. He looked down to adjust the radio, and saw it was destroyed. He reached for the cell phone on the seat and tried to make a call. No signal.

At the edge of the woods, Atef was nursing a wound to his shoulder. Al Sabah saw some lights in the distance that he thought might be coming from a house. "Stay here and get your breath," he said. "I will go check and see how it looks."

Atef nodded, still too winded to respond.

Sloan watched him in the darkness. Without a sound, he laid the nylon bag on the ground and opened it. He pulled the graphite bow and razorback broadhead from the bag, while never taking his eye off Atef, thirty yards away. Sloan knocked the arrow, but his heart was racing so he took a deep breath to regain his composure and control his breathing. Then, he slowly, methodically raised the bow and drew it back to his anchor point. He glanced to his left and noticed a better opening in the trees a few feet away. He shuffled over, took a deep breath, and redrew the bow.

Sloan held his sight firmly. He zeroed in on the back of his target for about twenty seconds and steadied his arms. He stood as motionless as a statue. Then he sighted his target one last time, released the string, and the bow snapped crisply. The arrow went rocketing through the trees, striking his target in the back in a quarter of a second.

Atef was paralyzed by the shot and couldn't get his breath. He gasped, tried to yell to Al Sabah, but only whimpered. He dropped his MP-5 to the ground, fell to his knees, and then on his side.

Sloan drew his shotgun to low ready and jogged to his prey. He carefully approached, and knelt behind Atef. While scanning for others, Sloan examined the entry wound made by the arrow, still embedded in Atef's back. He flashed his mini-lite on the wound and saw that the blood was dark red and most likely coming from his liver. Blood gushed from the arrow point, which protruded several inches from his abdomen. Sloan estimated that the man didn't have but a few minutes to live.

Atef squirmed a bit, struggling for some relief, as blood began to seep from his mouth. He spoke in a gurgling, low voice, "I am…hurt. I demand…that…you get me medical…."

Sloan didn't speak, continued his lookout, shotgun balanced atop his thigh. Finger lightly pressed against the side of the trigger.

"I know my…rights. You…I…have rights…I have…."

Sloan studied his adversary. "You want your rights?" Sloan asked in a whisper. He reached behind him and pulled his hunting knife from under the protective vest. He placed the razor sharp point of the knife against Atef's throat…. *"Steve, you put it right here in the middle of the deer's neck, right where the windpipe is…."*

Then, Sloan bent to within inches of Atef's face. "This is for my partner."

Atef gasped and gurgled in horror as Sloan slowly and carefully sliced a deep, clean line across his throat.

"You have the right to remain silent, you sonofabitch."

CHAPTER FORTY-SIX

E.M.S. units that were scrambled into service after the bombing of the S.B.I. building arrived at the school within ten minutes. Several minutes later, Guilford County Deputies and Highway Patrolmen, coming from the Greensboro area, raced into the parking lot in a steady flow.

Sheriff Voss Speaks assigned Major Cecil Huskey as incident commander of the crime scene. Huskey was a tall, slender man in his late fifties with short silver hair and a smooth distinguished look. Huskey had retired from the S.B.I. as an Assistant SAC in the Coastal District; he was handpicked by Speaks after his last election to overhaul and upgrade his CID. Huskey was faced with the arduous tasks of searching for any fleeing suspects, securing and protecting the massive crime scene, and dealing with the media onslaught. No veteran officer at the scene could ever recall a deadly force incident of this magnitude in the state, or nation for that matter.

A helicopter from the Highway Patrol scoured the area, panning with its searchlight, while police canines from four agencies sniffed for suspects in the hilly woods and community around Western Guilford High School. Officers searched door to door, and checked on the safety of the residents.

Several agents from the S.B.I. cleared from the bombsite and raced over to assist with the scene; they were eager to see if the shoot-out was connected to the bombing. Their preliminary suspicion that it was would be quickly validated.

Capt. Blackburn was rushed over to an E.M.S. truck and Clark and Wilkins lifted him into the back. Clark jumped in beside Blackburn, who opened his eyes briefly, staring blankly at the ceiling. Clark grabbed his arm, leaned over him, and spoke in his ear. "Some guys will do anything to get out of paying for lunch."

Blackburn's eyes closed.

"Hang in there, Richard, you're gonna be okay." Clark hopped out and seconds later the truck sped out of the parking lot, its siren bellowing, following the other E.M.S. units.

Major Huskey walked over to Clark and asked, "How're your other men, Lieutenant?"

Clark swallowed, trying to keep his composure. "Uh, let's see. Holden? It's a miracle that he's alive. Hanging on, just like Blackburn. Their vests may have saved them. Johnson's going be all right; he took a couple rounds in the leg. Both shots were through and through."

The bodies of Cunningham and Ross and the windows of the Mustang were covered with blankets. Clark walked Major Huskey and Agent Denny Jones, supervisor of the S.B.I. shooting team, carefully through the outer perimeter of the crime scene, weaving inward, briefing them on the chain of events.

A deputy approached Huskey from the building and yelled to him, "Major!"

"Yeah?"

"Just got word from the development across the creek," the deputy said, pointing in the direction. "We got somethin'. Report of a beige Subaru stolen from a garage. The owner thinks it was secure around eleven last night. Sounds like it could be our guys."

"Anybody hurt?"

"No, sir. Owner left the keys in the car."

"For once, I'm glad to hear that. Thank God. Get a BOLO out ASAP: 'Possibly Extremely Dangerous'."

The deputy nodded and got on his cell phone.

"Hey, Skip," the Major called back to him.

"Yes sir?"

"Make sure we knock on every single door and confirm that everyone is accounted for and okay."

Again, the deputy nodded and returned to his conversation.

Agent Jones wiped his brow with a handkerchief and glanced at Clark. "This is terrible, Lieutenant. I'm very sorry for the loss of your officers."

Clark didn't answer. He turned to look at the covered body of his sergeant, tried to speak, wanted to speak. Nothing he wanted to say seemed to make sense.

A large U.P.S. delivery truck pulled into the parking lot from the main entrance. And, for whatever reason, the officer serving as gatekeeper didn't stop it from entering under the crime scene tape; the truck moved at a deliberate pace in the direction of the officers.

Huskey saw it and was furious. He radioed to his officer, "Eddie, why in the hell did you let that vehicle in? Stop all other traffic from coming in!"

Then he looked apologetically at Clark and Jones. "Damn, sorry 'bout that. Rookie."

The truck turned and drove slowly at them, and Clark gave Jones a look of confusion that shifted suddenly to one of concern. "So what's a UPS truck doing over here this early?" Clark asked. He drew his gun and held it down at his side.

Jones did the same.

The officer radioed back to the Major that the driver had shown a badge. A little puzzled, they walked over to the truck as it parked near them.

The driver and front seat passenger, wearing black tactical uniforms, got out first. The back doors opened and six or seven more men in the same sharp military uniform, carrying large black nylon bags, jumped down to the pavement and joined them. They walked over to Clark's group as one of the men emerged to the front.

"I'm Special Agent Garcia, F.B.I. Charlotte office. Who's in charge?"

"I am. Major Cecil Huskey, Sheriff's Office." Then he made the introductions.

After everyone shook hands, Garcia and his assistant huddled with Huskey and Clark, walking a few steps away from the group. Garcia spoke first, offering Clark condolences for the deaths of his officers.

"Thanks," Clark said. After a pause, he asked, "How'd you get here so quickly?"

"We were heading this way in response to the bombing at the Bureau office. We picked up your traffic on the...."

"You're the Anti-Terrorism Task Force, aren't you?" Clark asked.

"That's right."

"So the bombing was an act of terrorism?"

"Fairly certain it was."

"Damn," Clark said. He and Huskey sighed. "And this?"

"My guess is the two are connected, but there's more that needs to be investigated. Lieutenant, we're somewhat aware of what you were working on. Agent Pegram contacted us a few days ago and told us about your development of Hamim. He's been under investigation for some time now."

"By 'some time' do you mean recently?"

"Yes."

"But Pegram said Hamim hadn't been of interest to the Bureau in the last few months."

Garcia paused for a moment, then motioned for them to walk farther from the group. Then he continued. "That's what Pegram thought, anyhow. What

I'm telling you now is highly confidential, highly. This may sound kind of corny, but it's true if it ever was—national security is at stake." He waited for a gesture of understanding from both officers.

Then Garcia continued. "For a while now, we've been investigating Hamim and the group you ran into tonight. It all started about a year ago when we learned about a gang of extremists in a federal prison in Ohio that had strong ties to radical Islamic groups in Detroit and Chicago. We placed one of our agents deep under in the prison to investigate them, see what they were up to. Eventually, they recruited Hamim and some of his cronies, and began to develop some serious plots, so we decided we better keep tabs on them. When a couple of them were released from prison, our agent stayed with them and gradually worked his way into their organization."

"So Pegram didn't know about this?" Clark asked.

"Not all of it. He knew about Hamim and his group, but he didn't know about our undercover operation. This project's top secret, straight out of Washington."

"How secret?"

"Our Director, his Assistants, the S.B.I. SAC for this district, the F.B.I. SAC in Charlotte, me and my team. And now, you two. We knew you guys were getting hot on the suspects' trail, but we didn't anticipate everything unfolding this quickly."

"How did you know we were getting close?"

"First, your investigation of Hamim, coupled with the hits with I.B.I.S. on the bullets from your robbery. Then we were informed on Monday that you showed up at the house where a couple of the cell members and our undercover were staying. You sent a detective in, posing as some sort of inspector or something."

"So that was your guy at the house?" Clark asked.

Garcia nodded.

Clark paused a moment, trying to absorb everything; it all overwhelmed him and he had to take a seat at the curb. "Where's your undercover now?"

"Afraid we don't know. We lost contact with him a couple days ago, so we sent a team down to search for him. The house was abandoned and we didn't know where the other cell members were hiding out. We've tried to monitor their activity through your channels, but we've had trouble picking up your radio traffic. We haven't heard from our man since mid-day Monday. Not a good sign."

"So this cell offed Hamim? One of their own?"

"Yeah. He was attracting too much attention from you guys. Became expendable. He and a few of his prison pals were recruited by Al Qaeda primarily to serve as their conduit here in the states. Hamim was only a puppet."

"That much we figured."

"Mostly, the cells use them to conduct their public chores, pay the rent, purchase their vehicles, acquire their documents, things such as that. Do anything for them to keep them from being exposed to the public. Anything to facilitate keeping their operations going."

"What do you know about their operations?"

"Al Qaeda's been pulling off a large number of armed robberies, high-gain, low-risk, to finance their operations both here and in the Middle East. They've set up small cells in key locations in the South, from Virginia to Florida, to Tennessee to the west. They've hit large retail stores, just like yours, with regularity and success...that is, until you guys finally caught them. Anyway, their M.O. is simple. They hide out in rural areas near large cities where there are plenty of soft targets. They rent houses in secluded areas, no condos, apartment complexes where they would stand out. So they need non-Arabs to do their surface work for them."

"And we just got lucky that they picked our town?" Clark asked, rhetorically, in a discouraged tone.

"Lieutenant, I know you probably may not feel this way right now. You may not completely understand things; you've lost some men who meant a great deal to you. But to put this in a national text, you and your guys are heroes...honest-to-God American heroes. You don't know the magnitude of what you may've disrupted here this morning. You see, not only is it Al Qaeda's purpose to fund their plots with these robberies, but we think they're using their experiences to develop and cultivate intel on a number of vulnerable targets in the South."

"For what?"

"For what we think is, or we hope *was*, a widespread terrorist act or series of acts intended to devastate the entire region."

"Like what?"

"My guess: Agri-terrorism. Informants have told us that the terrorists were already in the planning stages of hitting the next region, probably the Northwest."

"Obliterating one region at a time," Huskey concluded.

"Until America comes tumbling to her knees...their ultimate vision," Clark said.

"Like I said, Lieutenant," Garcia added, "without blowing smoke, your Department's saved the day."

"But if your man was on the inside, why didn't you move in and take them down?" Clark asked.

"Because we knew of the existence of other groups, but not enough to locate and capture them. As they often do, these cells worked autonomously, independent of each other, one not knowing the identities or locations of the others. Take this cell, for example. Our agent's been deep here for a few months and didn't even know the other cell was right up the road from him. Extremely disciplined. Most likely, only a captain or two knew of the whole enterprise. They're the only ones who can put this entire scheme together. And I'm afraid that's what we need…some kind of something to identify and tie these cells together. Some kind of glue. What we need is the glue."

"Any idea who or where this captain is?"

"We don't know, not yet anyway. That's why we were trying to gain intel before we made our move. We're thinking the leader may be in this group, but who knows. If he's not lying on the ground over there, then he's probably long gone. I'm sure the other cells are heading for the borders as we speak."

"Why would you think the leader is in this cell?"

"Our undercover believed that one of the shooters most active was affiliated with the Stuartsboro cell. When the lab tech in Greensboro matched your bullets with the others, it confirmed his suspicions. We've charted his shootings chronologically from Florida to here. So we figured that a group like this that hit early and was so mobile would have some brains in it."

"So the S.B.I. SAC here in Greensboro knew about this operation?"

"Yes, and he was ordered to keep it under wraps."

"You know, if you guys had informed us of all this a little earlier, what we were up against, I might, just might know a few fine officers who would be going home this morning."

"You're right," Garcia confessed, "absolutely right. But the Director called all the shots on this one. Like I said, we were close, so close to moving in. But let's face it, Lieutenant. Really, what do you and I count for when it comes to national security? A handful of men die and millions are saved. It's what we're paid to do. Right?"

"So your Director is going to take the heat for any of this?"

"Not just him."

"Who else?"

"The President."

They talked some more about the case as they rejoined Agent Jones for the walkthrough. Already, all the major news networks were arriving on the scene, some opting to by-pass the bombing site to get there quicker. Two television networks had helicopters in the area in the next few minutes. One of the helicopters got a little too low for the officers' comfort and was warned by the Patrol helicopter to back away, or else.

Clark and the others continued their inspection of the parking lot. They carefully sidestepped the graveyard of shell casings, broken glass, blood puddles, and fluids that had trickled in little streams from the vehicles. They made notes of the casings and tried to recreate officer movements by piecing together the story of which officer fired which weapon from which spot. After they gave the police cars a cursory look-over, they moved inside the perimeter and approached the suspects' vehicles.

When they walked over to the Chevrolet, Clark reached in and cut off the engine. He removed the keys from the ignition, and joined the others at the back of the car. Carefully, he opened the trunk and they looked down at the weapons, ordnance, and supplies that were packed in it.

Something on the top of the stack caught Clark's eye, though, a small, black leather case. Clark examined it for a moment, and then reached in and unzipped it. Then he looked at Garcia.

It was Al Sabah's laptop computer. The computer. The glue.

CHAPTER FORTY-SEVEN

When Clark woke up, he couldn't remember where he was. Something white caught his eye in the dimly lit room. He lay there trying to figure out what it was and, as he studied the object, it slowly began to take shape. *A sink?* Beside the sink, he saw two vending machines. A computer on a desk. A large conference table and chairs. At first, he thought he was in the break room at the PD. Then it came to him: A teachers' lounge at the school where the shoot-out occurred.

He had slept hard, but needed the nap after the grueling debriefing with the F.B.I. He stretched and yawned, trying to remember the last time he felt this exhausted and drained—seventeen years ago when Samantha had Brianna; he had worked a homicide all the night before and ran to the hospital to catch the labor, all thirty-six hours of it.

Clark slipped into his shoes, and re-wrapped his gun and holster on his ankle. He started to get up but, as an afterthought, slumped back against the couch and decided to sit in the darkness for a minute. After enjoying a brief moment of solitude, his mind raced to overload as it wandered through the events of the last twenty-four hours. More questions than answers: Was Blackburn still hanging on? Had the slain officers' families been notified? How had Esposito's wife taken the news? If some of the suspects escaped, had any of them been captured, yet? And the most difficult questions of all: *Why Stuartsboro? Why us?*

His reflection was interrupted by a loud humming noise above the building. In a few seconds, windows began to rattle. Clark recognized it as another helicopter landing at the school. He massaged his throat, got up and stretched again, walked out into the hall, and looked out the window. The front parking lot of the school looked more like a military base than a place where school buses, sports cars, and pick-ups parked.

As he watched the activity, his attention was drawn to the main entrance where he saw two white SUV's pulling into the parking lot. Law enforcement officials, agents, and tech support crews had been shuttled in from Regional Airport in Greensboro in a steady flow throughout the afternoon.

Clark trudged up the main hall to the administrative offices and library where the two Bureaus had set up their operations. Agents and police officers, some in plain clothes, others in tactical uniforms, criss-crossed paths and scurried in every direction; thick black electrical cords, like giant pythons, had been laid about the commons area, visual cues of the technical gurus that Quantico and Washington had flown in.

In the midst of all the bustle and chatter, Clark heard a familiar voice. He picked Greg Williams out in a huddle at the library doors, and called to him. Clark walked over to him and they shook hands.

"Hey man, how're you doing?" Greg asked.

Clark sighed and yawned. "Wish I knew what to say." A pause. "We lost so much here this morning. It's hard to believe we saved the day when we lost so much." As Clark continued his assessment, Wilkens and Sloan walked up to join them. "Greg, sorry about your guys, too."

Greg looked down at his clipboard and then to Clark. His lip began to quiver, but he gained control. "Funny thing, Clark. You know, I actually entertained the idea of going out there last night to pick up some evidence, so I'd have it ready for court this morning. If I'd run out there like I planned, I would've been right there in the middle of it."

"What made you change your mind?"

"Liz and I had a fight about me always going back into work at night."

Clark shook his head.

"She saved my life."

Wilkens took another bite of his sandwich, then interjected, "Lieutenant, just got some good news."

"Blackburn?" Clark asked.

"Yes sir. We got word he came out of surgery okay. He's still critical, but he's stable."

"Thank God. How about Holden?"

"No word, yet."

A bit of commotion outside prompted them, and officers nearby, to look out the windows. Five or six black SUV's were being escorted into the front entrance by a long line of police cars and what looked like SWAT vehicles.

"Who in the world is that, the President?" Wilkens asked.

"Close," Greg answered. "Homeland Security Director, F.B.I. Director, all the Who's Who in the Washington justice community."

"What took 'em so long to get here?" Sloan quipped.

"They had to be convinced that everything here was totally secure," Greg replied.

"And is it?"

Greg chuckled a little. "Is it? You couldn't even get the Pope in here for mass. Major Huskey's evacuated the entire area. An hour ago, the Governor declared a state of emergency in the Piedmont. National Guard's here, SWATS from GPD, our West SRT. I'm telling you the media couldn't get within a mile of this place. Of course, most of the reporters are heading to your fair city at this very moment."

"Why?"

"Trying to find out everything about you guys that there is to know. Who your tenth grade English teachers were. Where your favorite restaurants are."

The guys laughed. Wilkens and Sloan looked at each other and, with a single nod of the heads, said in unison, "Dragon Garden."

"What exactly does the media know?" Clark asked, as he rubbed his face.

"At noon, the F.B.I. released a statement announcing *'Police and Serial Robbers Engage in Shoot-Out at Local School'*. But word's leaked out that there's more to it. Some dude with CNN or Fox has already gotten a little of the scoop on Marcellus and cameras have been seen at the apartment complex where he lived."

Clark turned to Wilkens and Sloan. "Oh brother, I bet the chief's having a field day with this. His dream: Perpetual news cameras."

Greg carried on. "It's just a matter of time, before all the news gets out; you know how this goes. All the networks, major cable stations, national newspapers are here, digging in deep."

"What's the Bureau waiting on?"

"They're trying to buy a little more time. Their assault teams have been activated and have already taken down cells in Richmond and Charleston. The Bureau's running phone records, checking transmissions, financial records, all that stuff. And they've identified two other cells to go after."

"God, they move fast, don't they? Rich in resources."

"It's all in the element of surprise…thanks to you guys. These cells operated late at night, so most of the targets were at home when we rang the bell. Their M.O. of laying low in rural areas proved to be their undoing, too."

"How so?"

"The isolation made the takedowns easier and safer."

"How did the Bureau uncover the cell locations so quickly?"

"Follow me around the corner here, I want to show you something," Greg said.

They followed him to a window on an adjoining hall.

"See that Winnebago out there?" Greg asked.

Clark and his men looked beyond the rooftops of several police cars parked next to an entrance; they saw the upper portion of the large white vehicle, several antennae and small dishes perched on its roof.

"Yeah?"

"What is it?"

"That's the Bureau's pride and joy," Greg said. "They've nicknamed it the 'Gates-Mobile'."

"Gates for...?"

"They claim it's got the most advanced, sophisticated computer analysis equipment in the world. Word is, with contents, worth over fifty million...excluding scientists' salaries. They drove it down from Quantico, and their computer forensics team went straight to work. They've processed the perps' cell phones and pagers, but the ace in the hole was the laptop computer that you found. Evidently, and lucky for us, the guy that used the laptop had a lot of data in it that connected the cells. Most likely some sort of leader in this operation."

"Everything's falling into place, then?"

"My guess is that the President and the Homeland Security Director will call a press conference, probably in the...."

"Lieutenant Dixon!" Garcia yelled and waved, walking toward them at a swift pace. Garcia was a few steps ahead of a group of expensive suits that was following him.

Clark and his men walked over to him.

"Lieutenant Dixon," Garcia said, nodding to the entourage behind him, "Homeland Security Director Matthews and F.B.I. Director Wade would like to meet you and your officers."

"Why?"

"As soon as they arrived, they said that before they got to the first order of business, they wanted to meet the heroes that made all this possible."

"Right now?"

"Yes sir, now."

* * *

Within the next few hours, the F.B.I., in an unprecedented effort, marshaled the vast resources at its disposal and destroyed two more terrorist cells in Miami and Nashville. With the assistance of state and local agencies, fourteen terrorists were either captured or killed, and members of two other cells were identified; federal warrants were issued for their arrests.

EPILOGUE

The snow was beautiful. Clark sipped his coffee as the steam from it rolled onto the window in front of him. He watched the lazy flakes fall on two large spruces on the front lawn, then walked back to the refreshment table and added a little more creamer. As he stirred, he heard Sloan and Blackburn chatting in a light tone, but the only word Clark could make out was "Ruby". After a little more conversation, they burst into laughter. "Okay, okay, what's so funny over there?" he asked.

Blackburn looked up from his wheelchair and cracked, "Inside joke, partner."

His response spurred Sloan and Wilkens to chuckle even louder. Chief Brinks and Mayor Donovan heard the babble and walked over.

"Fine," Clark said, "consider me an insider."

"We were talking about this whole ordeal," Blackburn explained. "Start to finish…Marcellus, the sniper, the terror cell. Discovery of their plan. Everything. All this came about as a result of the investigation into Ruby Walker's death."

"Don't you mean Ruby Walker's glasses?" Clark asked. "Remember, it was just about a file 13 until we noticed that her glasses were missing."

"Go figure," Wilkens blurted, "those glasses. The clue that ended up saving the South from ruin. What's that, about fifteen million people per lens?" Wilkens turned to Clark. "So the autopsy was inconclusive?"

"That's the word. The M.E. said there was a 'modest indicator' of strangulation. Also said that she may have choked on something. Signs of petechial hemorrhaging. That's the best that he could do. Truth is, we'll never know for sure. One thing's…." Clark was interrupted.

Sloan raised his cup in toast, and spoke loudly, "Hey, everybody, here's to Ruby Walker, the woman who saved the day!"

"Ruby Walker!" everyone cheered.

Then Clark continued. "Autopsy or no autopsy, one thing's for sure, in my book anyway."

"What's that?" Brinks asked.

"She was murdered and Marcellus, Hamim, had something to do with it. Things were too coincidental. She visits him and he just happens to be about the last person that we know of to speak with her. Then he notices that she's having some sort of health problem. Too much." Clark paused to think, taking another sip of coffee. "You know, Chief, we ought to create some kind of Community Watch Award in her memory. Call it 'The Nosey Neighbor Award'. Bless her heart. Ruby, we love you."

Brinks added, "If she was murdered, we'll never know why."

Clark nodded.

The door at the back of the room opened, and a nurse rolled in Officer Holden, in a wheelchair. Everyone applauded and Holden raised his hand in acknowledgement. A couple of the officers walked over to shake his hand and speak with him, and Clark walked back over to the window to enjoy the view. Agent Garcia, who had entered the room behind Holden, walked over, poured a cup of coffee, and joined Clark.

"Nice view, isn't it?" Garcia asked.

"Prettiest one I've seen in some time. Big flakes. 'Course, they're all pretty if you don't have to work in them." In the three weeks since the school shoot-out, Clark and Frank Garcia had developed a friendship. Clark found him to be a straight shooter, and there were a number of differences between them and their backgrounds, enough to make their acquaintance an interesting one.

As Clark and Garcia conversed, a dark-skinned man in a suit downstairs worked his way around the unmanned security desk and metal detector. Then he started up the stairs, heading for their room.

"Clark, take a little time to think over the offer. Give it a couple of weeks if you need to; let me know something after Christmas. Just promise you'll call me back, will you?"

"Thanks, I will. It's an attractive offer. I'll think it over." Clark never took his eyes off the snow while they spoke. "This terrorism thing, it's changed everything, hasn't it?"

"Everything. Forever."

There was a roar of laughter on the other side of the room, as Clark spun around to see. Sloan appeared to be giving the attractive nurse his autograph, signing a magazine.

"Well," Clark conceded, "almost everything."

Garcia smiled as if to say that he understood the remark.

"What's the biggest lesson from all this?" Garcia asked.

The man stood outside the door and listened for a moment; then he pulled a compact walkie-talkie from his coat and spoke in a low voice.

Clark contemplated. "One thing that I've learned, for certain. A crisis like this may never come, not in thirty years. But if it does come, you better be ready."

"You guys were ready."

"But you know, Frank, even if that big test never does come, you're still every bit the good cop. You're out there every day, serving the public. Sometimes it really isn't what you do that counts, it's what you're willing to do." Clark was amused at his own philosophy spin.

Garcia raised his cup to Clark. "Here's to the brave and bold."

Suddenly, the door on the east side of the room opened and the man entered. Barely noticed, he walked to the center of the room and surveyed the group. He reached in his coat, and spoke over the noise, "Which of you is Lt. Dixon?"

Clark turned from the window, looked in the direction of the man and then to Garcia.

The man recognized Clark, before he could answer, and stepped over to him. Then he pulled a black object from his coat and asked, "Are you Lt. Clark Dixon?"

"Yes, that's me."

The man handed Clark his itinerary and shook his hand. "I'm Agent Hines, Secret Service. It's a privilege to meet you, Lieutenant. The President would like very much to meet you and your officers now." The agent radioed to a colleague that he was en route with the guests.

Clark took a deep breath and addressed the group. "Okay, everybody, it's time. This is for the ones that couldn't be here."

After a moment of silence, they headed for the door.

On the walk to the Oval Office, Clark reflected on the previous month and all that had happened. Certainly, an unforgettable November. The last few years of his career had seemed so lackluster, uninspiring, and so did everything else in his life. Then, out of nowhere, the Ruby Walker mystery popped up. That investigation set in motion a series of events that ultimately led to the takedown of Al Qaeda terrorist cells and destruction of its deadly plot. Good police officers died an honorable death defending far more than their city. It was an unforgettable November. *Bloody November.*

As Clark rounded a corner that led into a larger hallway, he thought about his family. His kids meant even more to him now, if that were possible, after this life-changing experience. And the passionate night he shared with Sam seemed to put them back on some kind of course.

Then Lana. He had felt so alone until he met her. She had made him feel alive again. Rescued his soul.

For sure, his personal life was still unresolved. But it drove home the point that life's mysteries sometimes were a little more complex, a little more difficult to solve than investigations at work.

As the agent escorted the Stuartsboro brigade to the door of the Oval Office, Clark hung back to allow his guys to enter first. He and his team did their job and did it right. He beamed and felt a wave of satisfaction wash over him.

Clark had made some tough calls and the mission was successful. *Yeah, everything worked out pretty well doing it my way.* The words of Frank Sinatra's big hit echoed in his mind. A lot of similarities there, a lot of truth. He entertained the idea of singing a line or two, but decided against it.

Then he smiled.

—THE END—

AUTHOR'S NOTE

On my map, the imaginary town of Stuartsboro is located a few miles west of Reidsville. I thought that I would place the town a little closer to the mountains, in the western Piedmont, nestling it in the perfect spot. I named the town for my favorite novelist, Stuart Woods. Throughout this novel, you may notice characters, streets, and other places bearing the first or last name of many of Reidsville's Finest, past and present. They have made Reidsville a safer and more orderly place in which to live, and it is for them that I have dedicated this novel. I've included the names of a number of businesses in Stuartsboro that actually exist in my town. Every day in these places, I encounter fine folks— symbols of the many kind and appreciative people that police officers serve. Besides, I couldn't imagine any town, fictional or otherwise, without a Dragon Garden Restaurant.

Printed in the United States
64550LVS00002B/304-426